WHEN TWO TRIBES GO TO WAR

Paddy Kelly

WHEN TWO TRIBES GO TO WAR

DOUBLE DRAGON

ISBN 987 1 78695 790 0

This Edition Published 2022 by
Double Dragon
an imprint of
Fiction4All
https://fiction4all.com

Cover Art and Graphics by: Pedro Sperandio

Edited by
Katherine Mary Kennedy

Paddy Kelly

"Everyone's your friend 'till the rent comes due!"
- Satchel Paige

When Two Tribes Go To War

Dedicated to:

Geoff & Mel Meade

Two reliable friends who were there when the rent came due.

Paddy Kelly

INTRODUCTION

The evolution of the terrorist phenomenon is not a 20th Century anomaly. However, claims that the Zealots of the First Century were some of the first recorded terrorists as written about in *The History of Terrorism* by Chaliand and Blin I believe is false. Terrorism by definition is armed violence against unarmed or civilian targets to achieve a political goal. The Zealots, for example, attacked primarily Roman soldiers and their supporters they considered opposed to their beliefs, not just any civilians. It was considered dishonorable to attack an unarmed individual.

It was however, when the Zealot leaders, circa 63 A.D., decided to extend their covert stabbings and assassinations to civilian 'officials and their supporters that the emperor sent in the troops to erase the territories of Canaan ending in the fall of Masada and the annihilation of Jerusalem about eight years later.

Politics, like religion, is by its very nature controversial because, like religion it is largely composed of opinion. Some even argue that politics is a religion and vice versa. Even the most steadfast researchers and factologists disagree on what certain, 'well documented' events mean. Toss in a healthy measure of skepticism followed by a heaping tablespoon of home-grown paranoia flavored with a sprinkle of bias and the end result is at best arguable.

When Two Tribes Go To War

When Two Tribes Go to War is a work of fiction framed by historical events and deals with the rise of the terrorist group calling themselves Hezbollah, 'The Party of God'. They were formed in the early Eighties evolved from a small coalition of jihadists who came to believe the forces fighting to expel the Westerners were not radical or violent enough and had not killed enough of these 'infidels'. The fact that these French, Italian, British and Americans were genuinely trying to help bring about peace and rebuild Lebanon was summarily ignored.

In conjunction with Hamas, both largely funded by Iran in the east and left wing liberals in the west, they have grown to be the dominant threat to peace in the Middle East.

Following the Carter years, which were unquestioningly marked by weak even flaccid foreign policy, the overt aggressive nature which had won Reagan the election, seemed to amplify with each successive speech and each new proposed foreign policy shift, particularly in the military arena. By September 1983 and the events of The '83 Nuclear War scare chronicled in *Children of the Nuclear Gods,*, Reagan's distain for the Soviet leadership had swelled to the point that Andropov's *Operation RyAn* was instituted.

RyAn was undoubtedly a panic response on the part of the Politburo to Reagan's aggressive approach towards foreign policy. Inclusive in his foreign policy plans was his covert approval of the overt PSYOPS intrusions into Russian territory and the so called 'Star Wars' system which was later exposed as a scam, as at that point in time the required technology was not only non-existent but decades away.

The fact that the most massive and audacious PSYOPS operations were launched in the first quarter of his first presidency is indicative of the mentality he entered into public office with. From all contemporary indications Yuri Andropov had no illusions about which way the foreign policy winds would shift once Reagan got in and so initiated his own covert Intel measures.

Some Americans have argued Andropov was 'backed into' his moves by Reagan's aggression. The historical record doesn't support this. Yuri Andropov's predecessors had long sought conquest by overt force for example their activities in the Pacific basin, Africa and invading Afghanistan less than two years before Reagan was elected.

It was no coincidence that almost immediately after Ronald Reagan took office the American hostages, after 444 days as political prisoners of the far left Iranians, were released.

By way of example the year-long pointless negotiations with the Iranian terrorists pretending to be students showed no signs of resolution during Carter's tenure but the day after, when Reagan got the keys to 1600 Pennsylvania Avenue, Tehran magically offered a solution.

On the other hand, the shoot down of the passenger liner KAL flight 007 on August 31st, 1983 which may or not have actually been a passive probe to agitate Soviet defenses over one of their most sensitive installations, Petropavlovsk Naval Air Base near Vladstok, and was certainly one of their most vulnerable, was the bitter icing on the cake for Andropov and the Politburo.

There is no shortage of proof that Moscow was advising the hostage takers in Iran, (atheist communists advising radical Muslims? There's a black Sit Com waiting to be written!), but it was just one more step inching us closer to the inevitable confrontations of 1984, the story you are about to read featuring much of the same characters albeit in much different situations.

How is this relevant to today?

Given that both Reagan and Andropov were victims of distorted views of the other's intentions and as such were acting on mis or incomplete information, one need only to peruse the latest headlines to read the rampant distortion of events by today's major news networks a.k.a. the Mainstream or 'Legacy' media.

Facing frigid relations with Canada on the northern border after shutting down the Keystone pipeline while endorsing the Russian oil pipeline to Germany, Chinese expansionism in the Pacific with this morning's crowing coming from Beijing of potential nuclear war with America, invasion and chaos on the southern border and damaged relations with the E.U. to the east, all aggravated by Russian cyber-attacks, the present administration is showing the limitations of yet another flaccid leader.

However, to the detriment of America, this one is surrounded by economic illiterates, left wing radicals and overt racists pointing the finger at anyone who disagrees with them while labeling those accusers racists, sexists and white supremacists.

Under the current democratic leadership, with inexorable financial ties to China and Russia where they have, on multiple occasions, demonstrated that they can be bought and sold to the highest bidders and that those now in power will do anything to stay in power, the people of the United States are today faced with a decision. A decision they have faced before. A decision, it appears, most will cower from.

That decision is first to recognize the new threat from the Chinese communist leadership and whether or not to once again confront those that advocate peace at all costs, even if it means war, or to allow the country to be plunged into a socialist system and then face war with itself.

This will of course require Americans to remember what their country is and what it was founded on. It seems that in the din of the race hustlers and victimologists and their sorry, largely fabricated and phony cries of oppression, many have forgotten this.

This book is a work set several months just after *Children of the Nuclear Gods* and is of historical fiction, however the names, dates and places of the terrorist attacks and military responses are factual. The TFR, though a fictional anti-terrorist group are composed of real men I served with during my 13 years in U.S. Special Operations.

When Two Tribes Go To War

The U.S./U.S.S.R. military and political events which transpired through the month of January of 1984 occurred pretty much as written and followed the events of the 1983 Nuclear War Scare chronicled in *Children of the Nuclear Gods.*

As with all my novels I write books dealing with events which have never been novelized before and this book is a work of Roman a Clef fiction founded on real world experiences but it is not a documentary, not a history book. It is a work of fiction.

Thank you for taking the time and I hope you enjoy the read.

****

14

PROLOGUE

In September of 1972 at the Olympic games in Munich a small band of disturbed, Palestinian fanatics declared war on the West. It was only years later that they were associated with the PLO.

Their cowardly actions against unarmed civilian athletes forever cemented the word 'terrorist' into the Western consciousness.

A short three years later, backed with money and weapons from Iranians posing as holy men, offshoots of these terrorists saw further opportunities to kill perceived enemies, almost always unarmed civilians, and attack those with a different god then their own. They are directly responsible for dozens of kidnappings, bombings and assassinations.

In addition, their actions helped to accelerate a deadly civil war in Lebanon which would last fifteen years, produce over 120,000 known casualties and displace over a million people.

Fortunately, they have now been mostly eradicated, and although other religious fanatics have taken their place, since the 1972 Munich massacre the United States is not alone in contributing brave men and women from all over the world who have also arisen to fight this scourge of civilization who kill in the name of a mythical pedophile who rode a white, winged horse to heaven while swinging a flaming sword.

One such group of those fighting terrorism is a group of men who call themselves TFR . . .

When Two Tribes Go To War

Task Force Romeo.

****

"If he is terrorizing the terrorists, if he is terrorizing America the terrorist [...] I am with him. Every Muslim should be a terrorist."

— Zakir Naik

"Is killing a known terrorist wrong? I ask this, did the terrorist allow any of his victims quarter? No, then allow him no quarter and hoist the black flag."

— T. R. Wallace

"The reality is that **any** peacekeeping force sent to Beirut was put in a position which made it virtually impossible to be seen as neutral by **any** of the warring factions."

— The Long Commission, 20 December, 1983

CHAPTER ONE

Bruce McCandless half stood half floated just above the deck, staring upwards as the long cargo bay doors slowly lumbered open and the lifeless, inky black of the most hostile environment known to man stared back, challenging him.

"Via con dios partner!" Crackled in his ear.

"I'll tell ya Vance, it might have been a small step for Neil . . . but it's one helluv'a big leap for me!"

"We got ya back, brother!"

After mustering the required seven million pounds of thrust shuttle Discovery had reached and maintained its orbital velocity and now, on their fourth day in space, the crew prepared to execute their next mission.

The crew of STS 51-A, space shuttle Discovery, included Vance D. Brand, mission commander, pilot Robert L. Gibson, and mission specialists Robert L. Stewart.

Now suited out in the MMU, Manned Maneuvering Unit and preparing to exit the aircraft, which was traveling at 17,500 miles per hour, to execute the first untethered spacewalk, was the youngest crew member Bruce McCandless, a member if NASA's Group 5. Group 5 composed a select group of 19 astronauts chosen in the late Sixties to lead the way to achieve the moon landing and beyond. A fourth crewman, McNair stood by to assist McCandless.

When Two Tribes Go To War

Liquid nitrogen hissed from his back tanks and astronaut McCandless was, for the first time ever, gently propelled from the cargo bay of STS 51-A to float out into space without benefit of any restraint.

Now in its fourth day it was earlier in the mission that the crew had deployed two communications satellites but neither reached geosynchronous orbit after booster rockets on both satellites unexpectedly shut off after only about 20 seconds, putting additional pressure on McCandless' Extra Vehicular Activity, or EVA, as well as ratcheting up crew tension. Nobody wanted to return home with a failed mission on their score card.

Following literally thousands of simulations in rehearsal of the planned EVA, the Boston born, third generation naval officer, McCandless was chosen to be the first person to attempt the unfettered spacewalk.

Only an hour ago McCandless had completed his final pre-check of the Manned Maneuvering Unit or MMU, essentially a space-age jet pack-suit with twin liquid nitrogen tanks powered by a NiCad battery.

To avoid the point where orbital mechanics would take over and they would dangerously separate at an exponential rate, distance management was critical. The back-up plan, in the event McCandless could not safely return to Discovery , was to maneuver the shuttle to intercept the runaway astronaut, open the cargo bay doors forming a giant catcher's mit and essentially play a life and death game of catch with McCandless as the baseball.

Following literally thousands of simulations in rehearsal of the planned EVA, it was via what must have been the first helmet cam that the images of McCandless floating through space on his own were being transmitted to the shuttle as he also hurtled through space at 17,500 mph.

It was a well-publicized mission, one that would produce one of the most iconic photos of the NASA program.

Wow, if I don't mess these pictures up, I'm going to get the cover of Aviation Week. He quietly mused to himself.

"Getting a little far out there partner. Better pull her back a touch. Something happens to you I don't wanna be the one to have to face your wife when we get back!" Commander Brand radioed.

"Can't say as I blame you Vance." McCandless returned as he activated his retro unit and started a 180.

McCandless continued pulling the trigger on his arm rest but as he completed a partial rotation the retros on the MMU stopped responding. He tried several times pulling the trigger on his arm unit but still there was no response.

"Bruce you plan on taking the long way round back to the ship?" Commander Vance radioed. There was no response and through the port side cockpit window McCandless seemed to now be drifting further away at an obtuse angle relative to the ship.

"Bruce, can you read me buddy? I think we're at the furthest edge of the excursion. Time to reel it in."

"Ahh, think I've got a little problem here skipper. The retros aren't responding."

"None of them?"

"Ahh that's a negative. I don't seem to have any directional control."

"Stand by one." Vance turned to Bob Stewart who sat next to him in the co-pilot's seat. Bob how long to get the second MMU unit up?"

"It's up."

"Have we got Gibson on standby?"

"Already ahead of you!" Stewart shot back as he pushed from his seat in the cockpit and quickly floated back down to the cargo bay.

"Bruce, keep playing with it, we're gonna send Gibsy out there to give you a hand."

Ahhh, Houston here. Do we detect a problem up there?

"Ahh negative Houston. We think we have a small problem with Mac's MMU. We're working on it. Under control at this time. Will keep you advised, Discovery out." Brand then retransmitted to the crew. "Guys Houston just gave us a call. We're two and O, top of the ninth."

As Houston control essentially sits on pins and needles from the moments before each lift-off to final touch down and so has a tendency to cancel experiments or even entire lift-offs at the slightest provocation, crews on a mission are reluctant to give ground control an excuse to cancel anything.

Prior to lift off each astronaut team agree on a word or phrase to switch off coms with Houston and turn to a predesignated channel as a signal to each other to speak freely. Whoever remained at the control panel in the cockpit would still have multi-channel control and so would still be able to intercept coms from ground control in the cockpit.

Discovery's crew agreed on the code 'two and O', a baseball term.

Down in the cargo bay Gibson, already suited up and having launched off for his EVA was also immediately in trouble. His Snoopy cap strap had popped open as he yawned to decompress and was now, in the weightless environment, working its way up his head. With his entire head set including mic, sitting over the cloth cap he was now partially deaf and dumb in terms of ability to communicate. His chin strap and mic floated in front of his face significantly blocking his vision.

"How we looking Bruce?" Vance asked.

"Been better." Now more than 120 meters out in space all were getting genuinely worried.

"Still no luck Skipper." McCandless radioed back.

"We just sent the cavalry out there to give you hand. So hold on."

Gibson was cautious as he drifted out into the void because he had to maintain a steady speed as he maneuvered himself towards McCandless. Able to discharge only short bursts he had to judge each release just right or risk overshooting his colleague, worse yet possibly mis-vectoring the intercept and then having to try to correct.

Once reaching McCandless it was near impossible, with their bulky stiff space suits to reach for each other much less grab on due to the rigid arm rests which house the controls of the MMU's. This required Gibson to do all the maneuvering to get behind Mac then work his way around in front of him, a task made nearly impossible due to his Snoopy cap and headset now nearly blinding him altogether compounded by the sweat caused by his cooling system which was now blocked by ice in the narrow hose system.

"Bruce we got us a little situation here." Gibson calmly confessed.

"Why do you sound so faint? Your comms okay?" Bruce asked.

"My damn Snoopy cap's come loose, slid down and I can't see." Gibson yelled at this mic set. "I'm gonna need you to guide us in back to the ship."

"Roger that buddy! We're looking to be about 150-180 yards out from the port side of the ship which is now off our three o'clock and drifting fast."

"Keep holding on, turn me in the right direction as best you can and tell me when to fire off!"

Bruce, now sweating as well due to the extra exertion, struggled as he pushed against the nothingness of open space only barley managing to point them in the general direction of the ship.

"Fire one. Give it one to two second blast."

Gibson obliged and they were on their way.

"Skipper do you read?"

"I copy Mac."

"Skipper open the cargo bay doors all the way, we're coming straight in and have Rob standing by to anchor us, once we're aboard." McCandless requested.

"Will do Mac!"

Ten minutes later, employing their improvised, buddy-tandem method they were back in the cargo bay.

Discovery, Ground here. How're we looking?

"Discovery to Houston. We read you Houston. Bruce had a slight problem with his retros, but we're looking good now. Discovery out."

An hour later, the cargo bay doors were closed over, the ship re-pressurized and the crew were back on track.

"Things your master's degree doesn't prepare you for, huh?" McCandless commented to no one in particular as he climbed out of his MMU rig.

"Had us worried there for a minute partner!" Stewart patted him on the back.

"That's why we get Hazardous Duty pay." McCandless quipped.

****

Meanwhile more than 400 kilometers below, in the Bakaa Valley just east of the Litany River outside Beirut . . .

A single olive tree on the hillside deep in the valley just below the Temple of Jupiter, afforded a young boy enough shade to garner at least partial relief from the afternoon sun.

23

Malmut consulted his prized Micky Mouse watch, a 9th birthday present from his uncle in Chicago, then gazed up noting the sun's position as his father had taught him.

Micky's cover crystal was cracked and the hands had long ago stopped moving which didn't detract one iota from the sartorial pleasure he derived by sporting a fashion accessory none of his classmates could boast. He didn't need Mickey's hands, as all the valley's inhabitants knew how to use Allah's original clock.

He gazed out across the river transfixed as a collection of maybe 30 or 40 men down in the valley floor worked away.

He didn't recognize their uniforms but had seen one or two of them in the village on and off in the last two months.

Who they were no one knew. No one spoke to them and they spoke to no one. But over the last week they had worked feverously day and night to build a small collection of buildings of some sort. Strangely there were no roofs and the men didn't occupy the structures, they slept in tents and on the ground.

Now however they did the strangest thing of all. They repeatedly drove two white vans from outside the fake compound stopped then drove away again. They repeated this over and over as two men timed them with stopwatches.

Very strange the young boy thought.

But now it was time to bring the sheep in. Malmut rose, gathered the small flock and headed on up the hill back to the village on the other side of the ancient temple.

Two days later, a car bomb at the U.S. Embassy in Beirut left sixty-three dead including seventeen Americans.

****

According to the *Amarna Letters* from the New Kingdom of Egypt, written around the Sixteenth Dynasty or 15th Century B.C., the Triangular peninsula midway along the Lebanese coastline of the Levant, Beirut, had become the location of early settlements due to its sea front availability and relatively flat terrain features. Backed by a spine of the Lebanese Mountains the area is a prime location to have established a permanent civilization.

A keystone land of the Levant in the Eastern Mediterranean, Lebanon, a one-time luxurious and prosperous holiday destination featuring one of the most diverse cultural and religious communities in the mid-East, had in just a few short years, metamorphosed into a war-torn, unproductive wasteland. The former "Jewel of the Med" had become the "Malediction of the Mid-East".

Route 30, running south from the main seaport for about seven kilometres before veering east, continued on into Syrian territory.

Located directly west of the eastward bend in Route 30 is the main airport, Beirut International.

Due to strategic military decisions concerning resupply, reinforcement availability and medevac access it was here, in and around the public parking lot that the bulk of the U.N. Peace Keeping forces, French, Italian and American, were currently situated, to include the barracks housing the 1st Battalion, 8th Marines 2nd Marine Division which had been sent as part of the multi-national peace keeping force.

This step was taken when the relentless brutality of the war teasingly slowed to the point that some leaders of the international community were lulled into believing now was a good time to once again play their individual political 'Peace in the Middle East' cards. Cards first played by the Romans in the late First Century when they had to suppress the Zealots.

After eight long years of bloody, no-holds-barred fighting the U.N. was finally able to achieve its primary function – a ceasefire in Lebanon. It was deemed that the ceasefire, achieved at prolonged haggling, thousands dead and wounded with even more dozens hindering the process with political manipulation, a peacekeeping force had been assembled.

As was almost always the case at the time the U.S was called on to finance and equip the bulk of the force. They, along with the French and Italians supplied hundreds of troops and equipment to establish a 'Neutral Zone in the city of Beirut, center of the fighting. This came to be known as the 'Green Line'.

The U.S. embassy bombing just six months ago, killing more than sixty people, was still relatively fresh in the news cycle as local merchantman Jamal lie next to his wife and two children on the floor of the cramped lunch bar he had set up just outside the old airport administration building now home and headquarters of the 1st Battalion U.S. Marine Expeditionary Force in Lebanon.

By convention Friday is the Islamic day for rest and prayer while the Jewish Sabbath is Saturday. Sunday the 23rd was the day of the Christian observance of Western religious ceremonies and so the barracks, in reality a long since abandoned aviation administration building previously used as an Israeli army building, was quiet.

That morning at 06:22 in the barracks they were on stand down mode and so, with the exception of a few tending to morning hygiene, most slept. Outside, save for a few lightly armed Marines, there was a flimsy vehicle gate and some five foot high barbed wire.

Despite the fact that sporadic bombardment had been falling around the compound for days, the Marines had been ordered to not guard or patrol with loaded weapons.

Unannounced a 19 ton, Yellow Mercedes, stake bed truck pulled into and circled the parking lot several times. Then suddenly and without warning veered left and crashed through the two guard posts coming to rest beneath the ground floor of the building.

As the truck sped through the flimsy barriers the driver's intent became clear.

Sargent Russell, the Sergeant-of-the-Guard quickly tried to load his M-16 but there was no time. He sprang from the sandbagged position and ran through the building's open lobby shouting.

"HIT THE DECK! HIT THE DECK!"

Seconds later hundreds of Marines disappeared in a blinding flash and a lingering cloud of dirty white smoke.

Two hundred and forty-one U.S. Marines and six civilians, including Jamal, his wife and children were dead.

Minutes later about a mile away, as the wreckage still settled and the giant dust cloud lingered, the nine-story tall Drakkar building housing the French 1st Parachute Chasseur Regiment and elements of the 9th Reg. suffered the same fate.

Originating from a similar truck, stopped 15 yards away from the building, the blast was strong enough to produce another 55 KIA, 15 WIA along with 25 civilians including the janitor his wife and four children living in a small kiosk.

Later, in retaliation, U.S. ships shelled Hezbollah barracks in Baalbek in the Bakaa Valley.

The mock-up of the U.S. Embassy Annex across the Litany River in the Bakaa Valley, built by the Iranian Revolutionary Guard of the Sheikh Abdullah barracks in Baalbek, was later found by CIA satellite.

Among the carnage was a small arm with a Mickey Mouse watch around its wrist.

Thus, the global war on terror moved into its next phase.

****

When Two Tribes Go To War

---

4 months later . . .

CHAPTER TWO

Naval Regional Medical Center
Rockville Pyke
Bethesda, Maryland
6 February 1984

"What'a ya think?" The twenty-something civilian receptionist seated behind the glass pane queried as she lifted slightly from her seat and nodded out to the near empty waiting area. She continued to peer out as she spoke.

"Whenever, wherever and however he wants!" Came the immediate response from the Lt. JG standing next to her.

"Miss Condon, may I remind you that you are talking about a lieutenant in the United States Navy!" The older nurse officer rooting through the four-drawer filing cabinet behind her snapped back. But not before sneaking a peek for herself. "But I definitely would!" The senior nurse quietly declared.

"You're married!" Miss Condon fired back.

"I still would! You know what they say; 'The best fashion accessory a woman can have on her is a good looking guy!"

The subject of their mildly lurid but benign remarks bore an uncanny resemblance to a young Richard Gere.

The dark haired lieutenant sat patiently in the waiting area, his white combination cap siting on his lap on top of his unusually thick medical chart, his

O.D. green bag on the deck next to him. He was absorbed watching the broadcast coming from the wall mounted TV in the upper corner.

Lieutenant Dave Harden was being released back into the world from Bethesda Naval Regional Medical Center following four surgical operations, six weeks of physical therapy and an eight week hospital stay all to remove and repair the Soviet bullets he brought back with him from his first foray into the field.

As the *Officer and a Gentlemen* look-alike was being ogled over by female members of the staff, his attention was on the small TV tuned to NBC News. Reagan was addressing the Congress.

No where do we so effectively demonstrate our technological leadership and ability to make life better on earth. The Space Age is barley a quarter century old but we've pushed civilization forward with our . . .

With an over-sized American flag on the wall behind him and a small cluster of microphones in front of him it was from the congressional podium that President Reagan spoke to the assembled Congress announcing his establishment of an international space station.

Harden sat mesmerized while watching the president's proclamation.

As I speak, we have already achieved a collection of successful shuttle launches, a half dozen deep space probes, satellites and the first untethered space walk from STS Challenge.

Tonight, I am directing NASA to establish a space station and to do it within a decade!

"Lieutenant Harden? Come to the window please." Dave grabbed his cover, med chart and overnight bag, tore himself away from the TV and walked over to the window.

"If you'll sign here and take the pink copy for your records you can be on your way!"

"Thank you –"

"Tammy! Tammy Condon! And if you need anything in the future don't hesitate!" Tammy offered.

"Thank you, Tammy, I'll keep that in mind." Harden reciprocated.

"And remember Lieutenant, no strenuous exercise for the next two weeks!" She called after him as he pushed through the swinging glass doors.

"I promise to do my best." He called back.

Tammy sat and casually peeled back the page on Harden's record where his contact details were listed.

"Don't you even think about it!" The senior nurse scolded. "Give me that!"

Tammy slammed the medical record shut and passed it to the officer for filing.

Promptly, that afternoon Lieutenant Hardin, in jungle boots and UDT shorts, could be found taking a five mile run through the back woods of Maryland.

****

East Beirut, Lebanon
Friday, 16 March, 1984

A pair of emaciated hands brushed aside the flimsy linen curtains to reveal paned French doors which in turn were pushed open into the misty morning daylight. The old man shuffled out onto the third-floor balcony, water can in hand to tend to his tiny, roof-top garden. It would not be light for another half hour when the sun climbed over the mountains so best to water the plants before the sun rose.

Already nearly 26 degrees it would only get hotter as the day wore on. At least this close to the sea the humidity was somewhat stayed by the occasional off shore breeze.

Out of habit the old man glanced across the narrow street from his third floor apartment to observe that his neighbor hadn't yet risen. Artillery sporadically boomed in the near distance.

"Huh, they are up early this morning." He mumbled.

The old man froze and listened. The next rumble was further away. "Ah, good." He mumbled to himself as he made the sign of the cross.

Gloomy inside the one-bedroom concrete apartment across the way the neighbor was up and

34

about but out of habit kept the front room lights off until after sunrise.

The old man, mostly out of lack of companionship, took his time puttering around the balcony hoping to see his younger neighbor and give his cursory nod and wave.

One had to ration the occasional opportunities of normality these days, even if they were on pretext.

The old man was not alone watching for his American neighbor.

There was a second party standing a block away up the cul-de-sac. A pugnacious looking bearded Arab. But he was not looking at the concrete building down the road, he was surveilling it.

The one-bedroom flat at the end of the cul-de-sac lie on the east side of what was called the 'Green Line.'

Being such a close quarters battle space in the Lebanese Civil War, now in its ninth year, there was no definitive geographic physical features to form a DMZ, a 'No Man's Land' as it were and certainly no border to guard. The only geographic feature to mark the boundary was the burnt-out husk of the tallest building in the city, an ill-fated Holiday Inn.

An ironic fact given that the building was American as efforts to stay the bloodshed would come largely from an American peacekeeping force.

Thirty minutes later, inside the dark apartment across the street the old man's younger neighbor tied his tie, finished his coffee, grabbed his jacket and double locked the steel door to his flat then with brief case and newspaper in hand negotiated the narrow staircase amongst a cacophony of radio announcements and crying babies emanating from the surrendering apartments.

Car horns, machinegun fire highlighted by the occasional sonic boom of an over-head jet fighter could be heard as he made his way out to his car parked on the litter-strewn street. A street not littered with coke cans and discarded fast food bags as in 'normal' cities but littered with discarded items like web belts and damaged rifle magazines all sprinkled with hundreds of spent shell casings of various calibers.

The distant boom of an artillery salvo again echoed in the distance as he climbed into his '83 grey Renault Turbo.

He had no sooner reached the main street and pulled into traffic when he was overtaken by a black Mercedes which swerved and cut him off from the front. A second identical car immediately came up from behind and corralled him in.

Watching from his balcony the old man's neighbor realized instantly what was happening.

It was clearly a well-rehearsed routine as a squad of like-dressed Arabs clothed in field jackets, black balaclavas and brandishing well-maintained AK-47's piled out of the two Mercs, surrounded the barricaded Renault and dragged the driver out into the street.

From his balcony the old man watched in horror as his neighbor was crammed into the rear Merc.

Crouched in terror behind anything they could find, the few passers-by watched as the two Mercs screeched off into the distance the grey Renault, engine still running, driver's door open to the street, sat abandoned.

The old man scurried to his phone and dialed the U.S. embassy.

It was 07:15 when the Marine sentry patched the call through to the security officer's desk.

Jeremy Zeikel, State Department Deputy regional security officer listened intently as the old man related what he had seen.

Less than two minutes after leaving for work that Friday morning William Buckley, CIA Station Chief in Beirut had been abducted.

Having been good friends with Buckley, Zeikel, without a word, slowly replaced the receiver, leaned forward, and hung his head.

****

CHAPTER THREE

Potomac River Running Path
Washington D. C.
Sunday, March 18th
05:45 EDT

The light blanket of snow which had coated the ground overnight still lingered adding to the pristine white of the Lincoln Memorial and the other monuments. The dull, rhythmic thud of boots hitting the ground gradually grew louder.

Dressed in O.D. Green T-shit, Navy issue UDT shorts and jungle boots a lone figure turned the corner of the riverside path.

Lieutenant Dave Harden, like the sun struggling to peek out from around the white granite of the Washington Monument, appeared to be struggling a bit himself.

The silky-smooth sounds of Glenn Miller faded away into the staticy crackle of the end tape allowing the 'clomp, clomp' of his jungle boots to intrude on his mental meanderings. He reached to his hip, ejected the cassette in his Sony Walkman and flipped the tape.

Seconds later the satisfying rhythms of *Drum Boogie* flooding his ears gave him an added boost forcing him to pick up the pace of his run.

Introduced to Big Band music as a kid by his parents Lieutenant Harden, like few of his era, appreciated the generation which had gone before. He grew to accept and allow himself to be instilled with, what were by now considered old world values, much to the occasional consternation and criticisms of some of his peers. His beliefs in the values, fair play, loyalty and honesty, of his parents' generation were unshakeable. Heroism wasn't just an adjective named for an ancient Greek god.

Of course, there were those who didn't completely agree with Dave's particular code of behaviour. People like the ninth-grade bully Harden decked in St. Anne's schoolyard during a lunchtime fight. When Dave allowed him to recover refusing to kick him when he was down for the third time, the bully recovered, attacked from behind and broke Harden's nose.

Just south of the Teddy Roosevelt along route 84 he turned left onto the Arlington Memorial Bridge and headed east where he slowed his pace and became mesmerized by the beauty of the partially frozen-over river.

Like mini-tectonic plates, six-inch-thick slabs of ice gently pushed into and over one another. He noted the vastness of the Potomac compared to the Des Moines river back home.

The fact of the matter was Harden didn't really give a shit one way or the other about the size of the two rivers. He was just happy as hell to be alive, out of the hospital and well on his way to a full recovery. Oh yeah, and the fact that CIA Director William J. Casey himself finally got Dave the orders he had been chasing since first joining the navy five years ago served as no small boost as well. Orders to Coronado Island and Basic Underwater Demolition School/Scuba, BUDS/S a.k.a. SEAL training.

A mere two and a half months after being seriously wounded during the *Operation Ryan* mission, following twelve hours of surgery and being discharged from an eight week stay in hospital, Lieutenant David Harden had been granted the standard thirty days convalescent leave. Thirty days he intended to exploit in climbing back to peak physical fitness prior to reporting aboard at Coronado Island, San Diego.

Harden set off again but slowed his pace when he was startled by a black limo pulling over just up ahead as he crossed the halfway point of the bridge.

A door opened, there was an uncomfortable pause and he watched as what appeared to be a senior naval officer climbed out of the curb-side door, donned his combination cap and stood waiting for him to catch up. He looked closer and was able to discern the scrambled eggs on the bill of the officer's cap identifying him as a field grade officer.

Harden picked up pace and pushed hard the last fifty yards stopping, out of breath just in front of the full captain.

"Sir, my sister?" He panted.

"I'm sure she's fine and ready for the new semester back in Iowa Lieutenant Harden."

"My family?!"

"I'm sure they're all fine too Lieutenant. This is not about family business. You're wanted over at Langley."

Not the first time that Harden was confronted with the 'drop what you're doing and report to such-and-such' scenario, he knew better than to ask any questions, all except one.

"Do I have time to shower and clean up, sir?"

****

Less than an hour later Dave Harden, now garbed in his service dress blues, was dropped off at the back entrance to the main building of The Campus and escorted by a J.G. up through the marble corridor to a small office he had never been privy to in his seven years of service in Naval Intel.

The Junior Grade opened the door and Harden stood transfixed.

"Sorry to interrupt your run Lieutenant."

"Director Casey?!"

Seated alone at the end of an eight-chair conference table was President Ronald Reagan's CIA Director William J. Casey. Having been backed and supported by Casey all through last year's Nuclear War Scare crises Lieutenant Harden relaxed somewhat harboring the feeling that whatever it was he was called in for was not as serious as he initially feared. However, as it wasn't normal protocol for a junior intel analyst to be summoned for by the most powerful Spook in the western world, suspicion remained.

His initial fears were not about to be allayed.

"Have a seat son, let's talk."

"Sir." He affirmed as he set his combination cap on the table and took a seat to the right of Casey.

"Glad to see you're healing up alright!"

"It'll take more than a couple of AK-47 rounds to stop me sir."

"My report says you took three rounds Lieutenant."

"Only two sir. One to the chest, one to the neck. But the neck shot was a through-and-through so wasn't as much of a problem."

Bill Casey, endlessly amazed at how men of Harden's calibre could speak of life-threatening wounds with such routine detachment, smiled and shook his head.

"Well thank God for our superb medical corps."

"And poor Russian marksmanship." Harden added. "How can I assist sir?"

"We need your intel skills along with your newfound field experience but most of all I need someone in The Company whose judgement I can trust to be without bias or, more importantly who doesn't have a personal agenda to satisfy."

"I see."

"Let me bring you up to speed on events while you were on vacation in the hospital flirting with pretty nurses. The refugee situation after the Jews won the Six Day War has been worsening and increasingly exploited by Arafat and his PLO gang. Following the Coastal Road Massacre, numerous bombings, and cross border raids by the PLO into Israel, the IDF had had enough and invaded then established a 40 km buffer zone north of Israel into Lebanon. The operation was dubbed, 'Peace in Galilee'.

"I read about it. What's Arafat's end game?"

"We strongly suspect he wants to take over Palestine, Lebanon or both and he figures, with backing from Syria and the Russians his arm of the PLO is his ticket in."

"And he is using the PLO as terrorists?"

"No! That's the problem. They have committed terrorist acts before and will no doubt use them again. But we have a close eye on Yasser and his playmates. Arafat's got his hands full keeping an eye out for traitors and would-be usurpers. There's already been multiple attempts on his life by insiders. We think these latest attacks are coming from some new kids on the block. Possibly someone he had a spat with and now wants to establish their own circus."

"Makes sense."

"Bob McFarland and I are at polar opposites about exactly what to do in Lebanon. Get more involved or just pack up and get out in which case I believe this fundamentalism cancer will metastasise across the region."

"I see."

"I think we need to nip this in the bud, but we need more intel, especially first-hand humint."

"Well, I've got two full months before I report to Coronado and besides Director, I owe you my career for what you've done for me."

Casey's slight dip of the head was misconstrued by Harden as a gesture of modesty and thanks. In fact, it was the lead-in to some hard news he was about to deliver.

"I'm afraid we've had to temporarily bump your orders to Coronado, Lieutenant Commander Harden."

As trained Dave fought back the anger rising in him which clearly showed on his face as he fell back in his seat but only stared in shock.

"Sir, with all due respect you gave me your word that if I gave you the key to the Ryan code –"

"I realize that **Lieutenant Commander**." Casey reiterated.

Harden apparently didn't catch it the first time, so Casey emphasised it the second time by using Harden's new rank.

Harden looked up to make eye contact with Casey.

"You've had my promotion accelerated?"

"Seemed the least I, we could do. Besides we already gave you a medal. Two actually." Casey chided as he nodded to the Purple Heart and Silver Star ribbons on Harden's chest.

"I'm still not clear on what you need from me sir?"

"Well, you certainly recall the events in the operational theatre leading up to the barracks bombing?"

"Clearly sir, I was transferred to the Mid-East desk just after the massacre of refugees by the Phalangists. The president sent in the Marines to escort the PLO out of Lebanon. Arafat and the PLO left so the marines left. The PLO, who saw Lebanon as ripe fruit to be picked from the cedar tree for their own use, had no sense of humor about being kicked out like a bunch of disruptive drunks in a night club and so started their covert bombing campaign."

"Exactly." Casey affirmed. "That's when we sent in the *USS New Jersey* to join the *Kennedy* & the *Independence* to launch airstrikes against Syrian targets while the New Jersey did some landscaping in the Bakaa valley."

"Hiding place of Islamic Jihad Organization, the IJO who I believe is fronting for Hezbollah."

"Impressive!"

"I watched the news reports from my hospital bed."

"No doubt wanting to be part of the action?"

"I won't lie to you, it was frustrating just lying there Director."

"Well Lieutenant Commander, now's your chance. I'm offering you the opportunity to join the show."

"Naturally I'm extremely grateful Director but –"

"Why delay you from going to Coronado?" Casey beat him to the punch.

"Because we're pretty certain this one's gonna take some time, time and effort. It's messy."

"How messy sir?"

"The Reader's Digest version is we're faced with the Druze and Shia Muslims being backed by the Syrians against the Christian Phalangists. The Druze and Shias are divided amongst themselves, as are the

Christians. The Israeli pull-out from southern Lebanon is leaving a gap in those sectors that the Lebanese army probably can't fill. Compounded by the fact that nobody wants us there which is all backed by 2,000 years of vehement, universal hatred and bloodshed for each other. Any questions?"

"So nothing's changed. It's the usual Middle East love fest!" Harden quipped.

"Precisely. Additionally we, meaning I, don't want someone at the helm who's not gonna be able to see this thing through. Who's gonna have to hand it off to someone else who'll have to take time to be brought up to speed and who is not likely to share your enthusiasm for neutralizing the radical Islamic threat."

"I understand. What would be my brief?"

"Step one, compile a portfolio solely focused on the PLO's potential involvement with, links to or support of any person or group other than the PLO with terrorist proclivities who is active in the region."

"And number two?"

"Two, assemble a recommended plan of action to counter them from an intel perspective and three detail the best resources required to institute said counter measures."

"What's my time frame?"

"Take all the time you need. As long as it's no more than a week."

"Well sir, that's a lot of work for one man. I'll have to think about it." Harden stood. "Okay, I'm in."

"Well at least you gave it some thought." Casey commented. Harden offered his hand as the Director offered his. "The head of Anti-terror will get you a full sit-rep in the morning. I've set you up in the same Pentagon office you used for the Ryan operation. As usual anything you need order, any snags get me an inter-office memo."

"Any chance of a hint of exactly what it's about sir?"

"Like I said it's messy. The long and short of it is that there appears to be some new players on the board and we don't know the who, the what or the why of them."

"Black hats or white?"

"Definitely black."

"So, they've popped their heads above ground?"

"Two days ago. A string of unexplained terrorist attacks are being perpetrated by unknown assailants. Further, this came in late Friday evening." Casey passed a teletype message to Harden."

FLASH MESSAGE: EYES ONLY!

LOCAL: Beirut, Lebanon

TIME: 08:35:16 MAR 84

SUBJECT: CIA Station Chief in Beirut kidnapped. No further details at this time.

Dave's jaw dropped. Casey spoke first.

"I knew him. Bill Buckley, career soldier, former Green Beret, good man." Hardin re-read the message. "He was sent in to re-establish a network after nearly our entire intelligence contingent was wiped out in last April's Annex bombing. We've already lost touch with all his assets."

"THE ENTIRE NETWORK?!"

"One turned up at the southern border last night. The Israelis are holding him for us until we can vet him and bring him in"

"Where have they got him?"

"Mossad H.Q."

"Do we know how he knew to run so soon?"

"Not yet, but we'll find out. God damned place has more leaks in it then Capitol Hill!"

"The kidnapping, no details? Witnesses, demands from the other side?"

"An anonymous phone call from a neighbor, it was done in broad daylight so there are about a dozen witnesses, but you'd sooner get an eyewitness to a gang murder in Spanish Harlem before you'd get a passer-by in Beirut to come forward." He emphasized. "We've assembled a special task force with Agency-wide authority."

"So you want me on agent Buckley's case?"

"No, something just as important. Your record says your mother was a reporter stationed in Beirut as a correspondent for the *New York Times*?"

"No sir, my mother's a Republican. She reported for the *New York Tribune* and lectured there part time

48

in journalism. I attended my last year of high school at the American University there."

"I need you, using everything we uncover about Buckley's kidnapping as a starting point, what we already know about the bombings etc. to compile a comprehensive file on Hezbollah. I want specific information on who the likely honchos are and recommendations on -"

"How best to take them off the board?"

"That's why I pulled you for this job."

As from 1947 through the following years of the Cold War there was an unwritten rule between the Russians and Americans, to include their puppets; 'you don't kill one of ours and we won't kill one of yours'.

Military are considered fair game, true combatants but, with some exceptions, KGB and CIA were more or less considered off-limits. This also applied to snatches. A snatch could be considered worse as it was understood the victim would be tortured for information. Bad enough between Westerners, but with Arabs doing the kidnapping the racial hatred thing entered into it.

"Has Hostage Location been activated?" Harden enquired.

"As soon as we verified the report. The whole Bureau's in on it 24-7."

"Off the top of my head sounds like maybe the PLO has brought in their second string and decided to kick it up a notch."

"It's not anyone from Arafat's side, we know that."

"How can we be sure sir?"

"We've got a pretty good eye on Arafat and all his top people. Besides, the Israelis have a man inside the PLO."

Dave made no attempt to hide his surprise.

"Impressive! It's been over forty-eight hours. No message or contact of any kind?"

"Nothing, which leads us to believe they're gonna sit on him for a time before they start getting rough."

"So, no window for us to get in on?"

"No indications of any."

"In that case I better get to work! Sir, can you have the duty officer notify the Pentagon I'll be there in half an hour? And is it possible-"

"The J.G. that escorted you in is waiting outside with a vehicle to take you over." Casey cut him off.

"Director I'm glad were on the same team!"

"So am I Harden. I'll be in most of the week. Keep me close in the loop. I want updates twice daily."

"Roger that sir!"

"Director Casey before I get too deep into this, any advice on Admiral Watkins?" Harden cautiously probed.

Admiral James D. Watkins who had become the Chief of Naval Operations in 1982, had no sense of humor regarding the Secretary of State commandeering one of his analysts. Even less of a sense of humor regarding Casey over riding his objections to the formation of special Task Force Romeo, so Harden's primary tactic concerning Watkins had been, up to now, avoidance. The admiral would have by now certainly been briefed about the TFR and would want to know more at some stage. A briefing Harden would strive to avoid.

"You're briefing the Admiral on Tuesday morning at 09:45 sharp in his office."

So much for plan 'B'.

"But sir-"

"The Admiral has been informed that there was an idea floated around about a Task Force Romeo project, but it was just a concept and was ultimately rejected as too risky. Any questions he may ask you should respond along those lines."

"So he doesn't know anything about us and the Ryan op?"

"He just found out about it last week. I've decided to hold off briefing him fully. For now. If he gets too inquisitive just plead complete ignorance. And remember the Intel Service motto: 'Deny everything, admit nothing and make counter accusations!" He rose to leave. "Message me when you get settled in."

"Will do Director." Throughout the brief with Harden Director Casey skillfully neglected to mention that in accordance with new Navy regulations, O-4's and above were no longer eligible to receive orders to Coronado.

O-4, or Lieutenant Commander, was Dave Hardin's new rank.

****

Beirut, Lebanon
Settlement of Tannoura

Though few houses outside Beirut had basements, in the ancient settlement of Tannoura 30 kilometers south-east of Beirut, there was a small collection of wadis where one structure featured a man-made basement. A structure that lies on the western slope of Mount Hermon situated west of the Bakaa Valley a territory that was in the control of the Muslim factions including Arafat's PLO and Hezbollah.

Though not 'officially' joined as a unit the PLO and the so-called Party of God, Hezbollah, often worked in unison with varying levels of cooperation. The Hezbollah allowed Arafat plausible deniability when the killing of innocent and unarmed civilians was deemed necessary to intimidate or retaliate while in turn Arafat shared some of the hundreds of thousands of American and U.N. dollars, he surreptitiously received from Iran supplemented by a fund set up by the misguided Arab influenced U.N.

However, ties went much deeper.

Unbeknownst to western intelligence, Ali Akbar Aminpur was a multi-tasker also acting as Iran's ambassador to Syria. While pretending to be a diplomat he worked as the chief strategist and target selector for Hezbollah and likely moonlighted his advice out to other less prominent terrorist groups.

To add to his many black talents Ali Akbar employed his close ally and schoolmate, Hajj Radwan a.k.a. Imad Mughiyah, who was responsible for taking or the assisting in the taking of over 100 hostages at various times. Imad in turn employed his cousin and brother-in-law, Mustafa Badreddine, to build the bombs to help the infidels he butchered to see the error of their ways.

The family that slays together stays together.

It was Aminpur's trademark technique of using compressed butane gas cylinders, sometimes decorated with nails, scrap metal or ball bearings to act as shrapnel, along with C4 to ensure a greater kill ratio when perpetrating attacks, inevitably on a 'soft' target, i.e., unarmed civilians.

This cuddly little group were the founders of Hezbollah.

The paid invoice for forty, 47kg cylinders of propane gas   attested to the intended fruits of their currently continuing evil.

****

It was a mere two days ago that Raheeb ran until he could run no more. He walked and ran until he was clear of the city limits south of the residential areas of the Bir Hasan district in Beirut.

Along the way he had been careful to appear as inauspicious as possible and so pilfered an undershirt shirt, a shirt, some pants, and socks from a laundry line in route south and, after disassembly, discarded his AK-47 rifle, bandolier and uniform. Anything that could associate him with the military especially Arafat's people.

After two full days of travel by foot he reached the southern border of Lebanon and crossed over into

Israel where he turned himself in to the IDF border guard.

It turns out that the PLO defector was actually a former member of Bill Buckley's fledgling Beirut network.

So far he was able to only reveal a handful of details and information regarding the tenuous foothold Buckley had established before his disappearance.

Unfortunately, he was the only member of Buckley's network ever heard from again.

****

CHAPTER FOUR

South Eastern Territory, Canada
85 miles north of Ottawa
Wednesday, March 21st

Following the Operation Ryan mission Doc McKeowen, in addition to receiving a medal and an extra stripe, had been given the opportunity to request another school to add to his repertoire at the end of his Force Recon course. To anyone who knew him it was no surprise he chose cold weather training.

Now on a thirty-day Temporary Assigned Duty to Régiment aéroporté canadien in the northern sector of Quebec province for cold weather long range patrol, the shit as it inevitably did, found Doc.

The eight-man team he had been attached to was nearing the end of the first day of a three-day cross-country ski exercise when the radioman skied up and approached the C.O., Lieutenant Rochet with a message.

After a brief pow wow with his radioman and a coded confirmation the L.T. halted the column and signaled the team to circle up.

"Good news lads! Real world mission just came in! They need us in Ottawa."

"What's up L.T.?"

"Some camel jockeys have decided to invite themselves into the home of the Lebanese ambassador. We've been ordered back into the city to assist the RCMP, evaluate and advise as needed."

"What exactly are we supposed to do with training rounds?" A young team member asked the sergeant standing next to him as he brandished a magazine loaded with blanks. The seasoned sergeant pointed back at the L.T.

"H.Q. have got a CH-47 coming in with shields, gas, ammo and demo. The bird's due in bound in ten to fifteen minutes. Jocko, you and the Yank stand-by out in that field with yellow smoke. Rest of you take cover in the tree line, stand-by and listen for the chopper."

Doc and Jocko headed out into the field.

"Shields? What are we, superheroes?" Doc quipped as they leisurely skied.

"Bullet proof shields, don't you Americans us them in hostage situations?" Doc's Canadian counterpart asked as they moved down the slope and away from the densely packed pines.

"Nah! We just grab the nearest civilian and use them." The sergeant stared. "Well only if they're the right size of course." Doc shrugged.

Minutes later the Chinook touched down, they boarded and the nine-man team along with Doc McKeowen were air lifted back into Ottawa.

Just over fifty minutes later the chopper set down in Patterson Creek Park in the city two blocks away from the ambassador's residence.

As they disembarked after being briefed by the pilot as to where to find the RCMP command center,

Doc was temporarily distracted by the picture book residential street which could have been anywhere in the U.S.

Tree lined streets were graced by upper-middle class homes boasting well-manicured lawns some with pristine two door sedans standing sentry in their driveways.

The command center, a converted sixty pack, double decker tour bus parked two blocks away from the target house served as the mobile command center.

As Doc entered the lieutenant was already being briefed by a tall, portly RCMP captain.

"Three that we know of." The gray-haired commander informed Lieutenant Rochet.

"Any hostages?"

"Five that we know of. An administrator his wife, a secretary and a civilian couple who came in to renew their passports."

"Only five, that's not too bad."

"Probably all they could fit in that small building!" Doc whispered.

"Is anybody talking to the hostage takers?"

"I've had a hostage negotiator out there for the last three hours. Except for their demands for a tape recorder and a blank hour-long tape there's been absolutely no progress. That's why I requested the MOD bring you lads in. If I'm being honest, I don't have a good feeling about this one."

"Do we have any names?" Rochet pushed.

"Ambassador Boudreaux, his wife a Miss Clairmount, the secretary and the unknown couple.

One terrorist named Amin and another calling himself Mohammed, no name on terrorist number three."

"Can't have a terrorist situation without a Mohammed, can we?" McKeowen quipped to himself. "Just wouldn't be right."

"Demands?" The lieutenant pushed.

"The usual. Free all our political prisoners or we kill the hostages and blow up the building. "

"What prisoners?"

"Phalangists. Whatever the hell that is! What is a Phalangist?"

"No bloody idea Captain." The lieutenant shot back.

"Part of the Christian faction in Lebanon." Doc interjected. "They're tangled up in that circus of a civil war going on over in Lebanon just now." Doc informed. "That's probably why they attacked this particular ambassador's house."

The commander and the L.T. exchanged glances.

"This is Petty Officer McKeowen on loan to us from the U.S. Marine Force Recon unit down in North Carolina. He's a medic."

"Naval hospital corpsman sir." Doc corrected. "Medics are army black shoes."

After a minute or so of assessing the situation, Rochet immediately began to give orders.

"Captain do you have all the adjacent streets blocked off?"

"Of course! And we've cleared all the houses in a two-block radius." He added. "Lieutenant Rochet, be aware I expect the bloody news choppers to start buzzing around here any minute." The captain added.

"Bon! Then please pull all your men back to your nearest green line."

"Will do."

"And I need your negotiator please."

Rochet stepped back outside to address the men.

"LeMay, you and Caro cover the rear. Pepe, prep me two breaching charges. Jimmy, sneak around the side of that three story across the street and set up an over watch position."

"Consider it done Lieutenant!"

"L.T., I'm going to set up the triage and treatment station behind that tree." McKeowen indicated the thick elm tree off to the side 50 meters down the road. "In the event we take casualties I'll have to get to them quickly and I want to avoid this open area. If this turns out to be a prolonged gunfight scenario any wounded will need C&C."

"Do it! And tell the paramedics to reposition the ambulances closer in to your triage area but still keep them out of sight."

A short middle-aged man approached and introduced himself.

"Matri Marceau, RCMP hostage negotiator."

"Lieutenant Gérard Rochet, Régiment aéroporté canadien, good to meet you. In the event we need to breach the house I need you to distract them for three to four minutes."

"Shouldn't be a problem. If it helps the one called Mohammed seems to be in charge. They appear to have one guarding the back door and one guard on the hostages."

"Do we know where they have the hostages?"

"No, they could be anywhere in the house. In most cases the terrorists spread the hostages out to confuse any rescue effort."

"Merci Matri, if you think of anything else please let me know. Take this radio, go up to the red line and wait for my signal."

Marceau was handed a bullhorn and under cover of two RCMP walked the two blocks and approached the house.

In the interim Rochet gathered the remaining five men and laid out a hurried plan as they quickly moved up the two blocks to take up positions as designated.

Once outside the two story house, from behind a parked car, as the team moved up, Marceau raised his bullhorn.

"Amin, Mohammed this is monsieur Marceau." There was no response. "We have contacted the Lebanese authorities in Beirut as requested –"

His update was interrupted by a spray of gunfire through the front windows.

"That's our cue!" Rochet, approaching from just down the road said and they began running.

The two RCMP returned fire with a few shots purposely aimed to miss the windows completely but to force the terrorists to keep their heads down while they safely evacuated Marceau.

Paddy Kelly

"YOU LIE! THERE IS NO AUTHORITY IN BEIRUT! WHY DO YOU THINK WE COME HERE?!" One of them shouted out from the house punctuating his accusation with another shorter burst.

Without speaking the Canadian team disbursed, two veered off to the yard just before the house bursting through the tall hedge row. Rochet exposed himself by taking up position out on the street, down on one knee with a bead dead on center of the front of the house, while the remaining two ran around behind him, to the left laneway and prepared to assault through the side door. By virtue of their proximity in the back LeMay and Caro were, on Rochet's whistle, the first ones in the house.

Stepping over the dead terrorist LeMay led as Caro backed him up to clear room by room standing by to direct the other team members as they burst through the side door and swept upstairs.

The entire assault was over in seconds.

"Caro, disarm the bodies, LeMay cover the back door look for an over watch. Everyone else casualty check. "Pepe, hostages?" He called upstairs.

"All present and accounted for sir!"

One of the terrorists, still alive after being sniped through the shot-out windows in front took a chest hit and Rochet ordered he be carried out to McKeowen.

"Lieutenant, found a tape recorder." Caro passed the back plastic machine to the LT. who played the tape. They heard only static of the ambient air.

61

"Looks like the entire one hour tape has been run out, but there's nothing on it." He observed.

"I'm not surprised." Rochet answered pointing at the machine.

"Why is that sir?"

"Stupid bastard didn't press record."

Outside, as he was treating the wounded terrorist the grateful man pulled Doc in and spoke to him in a choked but hushed tone.

"Doctor . . . there is a . . . bomb in kitchen . . . under sink. Will . . . go off in . . . seven minutes."

Doc immediately alerted the sergeant.

"It's a trick!" the Sergeant snapped back.

"Why don't you check just to be safe?" Doc suggested.

A minute later the sergeant came running back through the house screaming for everyone to get out, there's a bomb in the kitchen.

Doc checked his watch, stepped down off the ambulance and jogged into the house. When he reached the kitchen, he carefully scanned the sink area but saw nothing. Gingerly opening the cabinet underneath, he peered between the pipes and spotted the military issue three block pack of C4 wired to the large wristwatch. Detecting no secondary wires, he gently removed the blasting cap from the end of each of the blocks of plastic explosive, placing the wired watch and caps in the sink. With C4 in hand McKeowen stood behind the kitchen door as the lieutenant entered from down the hallway. Doc blocked him from entering the kitchen.

"McKeowen what the hell-"

The L.T.'s interrogative was interrupted by a low-level but sharp crack like that of a large cherry bomb as the wrist watch ran out and the single blasting cap detonated in the sink. Rochet took in the scenario and put together what had happened.

"Well done Yank!"

"Thank you, sir. Glad I could be of service." Doc answered as he handed Rochet the inert blocks of C4 and walked away.

"And to think, just over a year ago I was getting drunk with a fat broad in a Pittsburgh dive!" Doc added as he stepped through the front door.

**

That night found Doc and the Canadians celebrating their victory downtown on York Street at the *Chateau Lafayette* a landmark saloon-style eatery and bar founded back during the gold rush days and popular with the college crowd.

Gathered at a cluster of back tables three of the Canadians were occupied chatting up a table full of college girls while Doc, Caro and LeMay had three other cuties sitting with them.

About forty minutes into the reverie the place quieted somewhat as two tall, uniformed RCMP accompanied by a plainclothesman entered, scanned the room and made their way to the back tables and approached the soldiers.

In French the plainclothesman demanded to know who Doctor McKeowen was. In equally demanding

French Sergeant LeMay informed them that there was no doctor at the table.

Hearing his name ping-ponged back and forth Doc jumped in.

"I'm McKeowen, what's the problem?"

The plainclothesman, dressed in a full-length, black leather overcoat, responded in rapid-fire French.

Doc answered in an exaggerated French accent.

"Pupu, croissant, soufflés, soufflés, balloon. Balloon, silly balloon! May we?" The desired effect was achieved, and the very pissed-off cop now spoke English.

"We have been sent from the Ministry of Defense. You are to accompany with us."

"Am I under arrest?"

"No."

"Then how about a little context Depardieu?!"

"It has been requested you return to your facility in . . . Amerika!"

"You have some kind of paperwork to verify this?"

The undiplomatic cop produced an official USN message requesting Petty officer McKeowen be found and instructed to return to the U.S. forthwith. But the puzzling part was the footnote instructing him to stop in Washington, D.C. where a car would meet him at Dulles International.

"Washington huh?" He declared out loud.

Doc pocketed the message, lifted his last shot and addressed his new comrades.

"This message from President Reagan looks pretty urgent guys, so I hate to drink and run, but . . . vive la Canadien!" He threw back the shot and said his goodbyes.

On the way out he addressed the cop.

"I got a book you should read, *How to Win Friends and Influence People*. You'll love it!"

The state official pretended not to understand.

"But I am looking forward to your appearance in the sequel to *Raiders of the Lost Ark* though."

An hour and a half later, after packing and collecting his passport at the hotel, Doc was on an Air Canada flight with a stop-over in New York City.

*

CHAPTER FIVE

Washington Naval Yard
O Street SE
Washington, DC

Razed to the ground by the British during the War of 1812 the Washington Naval Yard is the oldest shore installation in the U.S. Navy.

The country's first industrial steam engine was built and installed in its lumber mill, *the U.S.S. Constitution*, the world's oldest ship still on active duty, saw refit and repair there as did the *U.S.S. Monitor* after her famous shoot out with the *U.S.S. Virginia* following the historic Battle of the Ironclads.

Many scientific developments were produced there to include the manufacture of the colossal gears for the Panama Canal, the first shipboard catapult and, above the complaints of Thomas Jefferson, the first White House toilet bowl which Jefferson thought too unsanitary to have indoors.

Although the installation's primary functions have remained science, research and R&D based, the numerous spaces over the years have been converted into offices and it was here that Lt. Cmdr. Harden decided he should set up shop.

He chose the O Street location in lieu of the Pentagon primarily to maintain a lower profile but secondarily to avoid unannounced and unwanted 'drop-ins' from superior officers. It was in a back corner of the Naval Sea Systems Command building that Dave found a new, albeit a likely temporary, home for his unofficial Task Force Romeo spec ops team.

The duty driver dropped him off in the parking lot of the two centuries old red brick, recently converted two story structure.

Inside the timber frame skeleton provided a wide-open floor plan which joined with the vaulted industrial ceiling to lend an antiquated yet simultaneously modern feel to the place.

Hundred and fifty-year-old bits of industrial milling machinery had been shoved aside to create a ten foot wide aisle leading to the rear of the two hundred foot long building.

As he reached the back where the space had been divvied up into several ten foot by ten foot square work areas he heard something banging around in the corner office space.

He poked his head in through the door where he was confronted with an older woman wrestling with a vintage steel framed desk but not making much progress. She looked up and stared back.

"Well don't just stand there gawking at me! Get over here and help."

"Yes Ma'am. Right away Ma'am. At your service!" Harden mocked as he set his brief case aside and made his way over to her.

"What exactly are we doing?" He asked.

"The desk always has to face the door."

"Makes sense." He conceded.

Once in place to her satisfaction introductions were made.

"I assume your Mrs. Gaffney?"

Janean Gaffney was an . . . older woman who had served in government service her entire adult life and who was two years from mandatory retirement. At five foot four, with a full head of grey hair and of slight build despite her age still only needed glasses for reading the fine print on documents.

"Do you have family?" Dave inquired.

"Married fifty-one years. Two children. Daughter retired professor of economics Notre Dame. One son retired military."

"Oh! Navy?" Harden enthusiastically asked.

"NO! Damn fool! Army. Tanks. What an idiot!" She grumbled.

"I take it you don't approve?"

"No! Tanks?! Spam-in-a-can. His father was a naval aviator, damn good man. One of the first ones to fly off the *Kittyhawk*. Burns my chaff my son took the family name down a notch!"

"And your husband?"

"Dead!"

"I see. You have my condolences."

"Thank you but no need. Not gonna bring him back." She quipped. "Bring that chair over and put it behind the desk." She instructed before she led him across the back of the massive warehouse and to an identical office space next door.

"Can't argue with that." Dave mumbled.

"If you have no objections I'll set up in here." She informed her new boss. "We can have a two-by-two slide open window installed in this wall to communicate better of you like." She suggested.

"Whatever you say Mrs. Gaffney. I'm only the supervisor. Feel free to put in a request to base maintenance."

"Anything else?" She asked.

"May I ask about your experience in the area of research?" Harden reluctantly ventured.

"I was a corporate research librarian, back in the days when there was such a thing." She sighed. "Started off with Con Ed, moved to General Electric then worked for the president."

"You worked for the President of G.E.?"

"No, damn it! Harry Truman! You might of heard of him?" She made no effort to hide her sarcasm.

"Yes, I've heard of him. I assume you have a secret clearance level?"

"Secret but upgradeable with a request from yourself."

"Typing? Although I don't anticipate they'll be much typing involved." Harden added.

"One hundred and ten words a minute and I also take shorthand. Pittman, Greg and I'm semi-proficient in International Phonetic, although nobody really uses that much anymore."

"Well, impressive! And very pleased to meet you but I have some errands to run. In the meantime, get yourself set up, make us a list of supplies you think we'll need, take lunch then type yourself up a clearance upgrade request and I will be back around three. Sound good?"

"Sounds good. What exactly do we do here?"

"For the present just research. We have a dossier we have to get to State as soon as it's finished. I'll fill you in as soon as."

"As soon as what?"

"As soon as I know." He called back as he made his way up the aisle, "And see about getting us some phone lines please." He added.

"Already done. They'll be here tomorrow." She yelled back.

"Think I'm gonna like that old broad!" Harden mumbled to himself as he left.

****

Realizing that the current political unrest in and around Lebanon was, as is all culturally based political conflict, masterminded by politicians setting people one against the other and that such a universally applied tactic relies on propaganda and the resultant fulmination it garners is based on culture not color, Harden therefore concluded that an in-depth cultural analysis would be required.

To that end the first order of business, after getting settled in, was to contact the Mid-East desk at The Agency and schedule a briefing from their 'resident historian' a fellow named Dr. Anwar Buchardi a consultant professor of Arab Studies at Georgetown University.

The compilation of Harden's assigned dossier which he tentatively christened 'Project Waldo' after the Hanford children's puzzle books *Where's Waldo?* was foremost on his mind as he rode over to his next meet.

Although Harden was tasked with solving the puzzle of an unknown and hidden terrorist leader, it was anything but a game.

In the interest of openness and honesty Harden lied and told the Professor he was writing a book for after retirement.

They met at a café on the university campus and took a window seat looking out onto the ebb and flow of student traffic crossing the well-groomed quad.

"Well, most Lebanese speak English albeit with heavy French influence. Armenians are usually quardra-lingual however, there are no accurate census data since 1932 and even that was a little questionable."

"Did not know that." Harden conceded.

"Before the present war, even before Beirut earned the short-lived title of 'Paris of the East,' there was Byblos believed by some to be the oldest city in the world, established about 7000 years ago, along with Ur, Baalbek and Jericho which all lay claim to being the oldest city in the world. However, that argument is largely academic. What's important is all these places began and established what would evolve into what we now call 'civilization'.

Then came the Canaanites, the Phoenicians, the Carthaginians followed by the Romans then the various Arab nations.

"Please go on."

"As you know sir –" Buchardi started.

"Call me Dave." Harden interjected.

"Dave, as you may know the Coastal Road Massacre, where the PLO killed a bus load of civilian workers after taking them hostage, back in March of 1978, was the impetus to invade southern Lebanon & oust the PLO in the first place. That is what started this current round of tit-for-tat."

"Yes, I've been reading up on the whole situation and have a grasp on the basic outline, I just needed an expert to help line it all up, so-to-speak."

"The people in Lebanon operate very loosely on what remains of a government called a Confessional Democracy. The actual problem is there is no consensus on what Lebanese actually is. That is, what it means to be 'Lebanese'."

"Everyone has differing ideas of Lebanese nationalism. That's fairly obvious, but I get your meaning."

"A good place to start for the present troubles is in 1966 when Yousef Beidas' Intra Bank collapsed in turn collapsing the capital's economic infrastructure.

While the war in Syria raged on it was in 1967 that a second wave of Palestinians invaded as a result of the Six Day War prompting Arafat to use an unstable Lebanon as a base of operations for his PLO to continue attacks on Israel." Harden took the occasional note.

"By 1973 the factional leaders in and around Beirut, aided by Arafat and others decided it was a good idea to pit the three major communities against each other using financial inequality as an excuse, much like the American democrats use the blacks against the whites on a financial equity basis.

With no money coming out of the Beirut financial sector anymore, waves of refugees streaming over the border and no real indigenous military force to speak of to fight off the PLO, in 1975 the inevitable happens. Civil war erupts."

"I see."

"You recall the Sixth of June *Peace for Galilee* operation?" Buchardi asked.

"Yes sir, back in '82. Mossad were tracking the PLO's movements; found they had infiltrated southern Lebanon and launched the invasion. As I understand it, Prime Minister Sharon's intention was to push them back north at least twenty-five miles to form a buffer and stop them raiding and bombing the north of Israel. Then came the November car bomb incident." Harden added.

"Yes but now with Arafat's loss of control of the PLO and the formation of Hezbollah -"

"The Militant Shia Islamists?" Dave pretended to reaffirm.

"Yes. Factional fighting continues and by February of 1984 the Lebanese Army Forces, or the LAF, in nominal control of West Beirut since the Israelis withdrew, are easily ousted by the Anal Party allied with the Druze Progressive Socialist Party. What followed was a spate of kidnappings and murders, like something right out of a Mafia playbook, all were erroneously blamed on the Islamic Jihad Organization which turned out to be a Hezbollah front."

Dave now took detailed notes.

"Except to my knowledge the Mafia were careful to never intentionally murder or kidnap innocent civilians like Hezbollah." Harden qualified.

It is believed by those who study the Middle East that the concept of Hezbollah was germinated by a small group of radicals studying at the *Imam Ali Mosque* in Najaf in central Iraq and who were dissatisfied with any diplomatic efforts with the west."

"What's our time frame here?"

"As close as we can tell late 1980 early 1981 although they would have been becoming radicalized long before that, over an extended period of time."

"This Mosque in Najaf, pretty important place, is it?" Harden probed,

"The Ayatollah Khomeini taught there, it houses the graves of many of the prominent imams and is believed to be the place Allah will come to raise the dead-on judgement day. Apart from Mecca and Medina it is the most sacred place in the world, for the Shia Muslims that is."

"They've had some suspected activity in London also, no?"

"Sharon bombed their terrorist installations in Lebanon in retaliation for the botched assassination attempt on the Israeli ambassador to London, yes."

The professor added. "The irony is the assassins were from a splinter group actually hostile to the PLO and are suspected of having had orders to also kill Nabil Ramlawi, the PLO's representative in London. This yet another plot to oust Arafat."

"No wonder it's rumoured he sleeps in a different place every night."

"It's no rumor my friend."

Harden flagged a waitress and ordered two coffees.

"Professor, not to minimize the military and political tactics, but I need to know about the cultural mind-set of these people if I'm going to represent them accurately in my book."

"Well, I think the military tactics teach us a lot about their mind-set."

"How so?"

"Virtually all the leading Western strategic analysts agree on one thing. Arabs lose wars primarily due to lack of unit cohesion."

"Go on." Harden started jotting down more notes.

"This originates from the top, their leaders. All the major Arab world leaders maintain authority from the same play book: use of competing organizations, duplicate agencies, and cohesive techniques. This in turn makes military leadership difficult if not impossible."

"So it's essentially a trust issue?"

"Exactly. But a trust issue aggravated by poor leadership and poor collection, dissemination, and weak use of information. Specifically, the hoarding of information."

"What about the marrying your cousin thing?"

"You're talking about consanguinity."

"Yes, consanguinity, inter-marriage between cousins?"

"This also stems from ancient traditions of trusting only family members, and selected family members at that."

"Is there any scientific evidence to support that?"

"According to several medical studies and journals such as *Reproductive Health* there's strong evidence that consanguinity leads to congenital disorders, among them lower intelligence levels.

Upwards of 40% in a study released this year put consanguinity levels in Lebanon at 42% of the population, regardless of religion."

"So, sort of Arkansas hillbillies except they're Arabs?"

"Arab hillbillies? I'm not sure I would put it in exactly those terms but . . . yes, I suppose so." Buchardi conceded. "Something like that."

They stopped talking while a waitress brought their coffees.

"I'm an Arab but I have no dog in this social quarrel."

The Professor continued "The fact that Israel continually ranks in the top 20% for overall I.Q., Nobel prizes, literary and academic awards while the Arabic countries are usually not even rated is a recorded fact. Anyone can check the literature. It's not because they are stupid, it has to do with their poor educational systems stifled by antiquated

76

religious ideals which prevents them from being able to problem solve. The over emphasis on rote memorization stemming from their religious teaching techniques impedes growth of thought. This is unquestionably a primary contributory factor in the narrow range of thought these terrorists base their life's philosophy on."

"Fascinating."

"It goes further. This also leads some to believe that democracy is today, simply beyond the Arab nations."

"Do you concur? You think this is accurate?"

"Look at the 1947 land grant to the millions of displaced Jews by the U.N. Security Council following WWII. Result? All the Arabs declared War. The 1967 War, the 1972 War and the 1978 War. Today we have the Lebanese Civil War, simply the next chapter in the unending tome of the Middle East. All with no change of government in the Arab nations and no real democratic elections as a result."

"Who do think, here in the mid-East, it currently poses the biggest threat to the West?"

"At present? The PLO, but only temporarily. Arafat has drawn too much attention to himself pretending to be a world leader. But in the near future, if they are allowed to grow and propagate, then certainly Hezbollah."

Harden was slowly being convinced he had found his starting point.

"Doctor Buchardi, political history aside, do you think there will ever be peace in the Middle East?"

"In our lifetimes, no."

"Why not?"

"Neither the Arabs or the Jews think like us. You and I think in terms of yesterday, today and tomorrow. Days, weeks and months. They think in centuries, millennia, and eons. Remember, they all play by God's original play book and the Arabs, Jews, Phalangists and Druze all have a copy of that book. The problem is that even though all the books are still in circulation the publication dates are centuries off from each other."

Dave sat silent as the magnitude of what Buchardi was saying soaked in.

"The Palestinian Arabs never have and likely in our lifetimes, possibly eons, probably never will concede that the tiny little strip of 300 mile by 85 mile desert belongs to the Israelis. They won't even acknowledge that Jews have a right to exist. In my opinion this is wrong."

"Other than that, how did you like the play Mrs. Lincoln?" Harden quipped.

"What do you mean?"

"Sorry Professor, bad joke. Is there anything else you think I should know?"

"Not at the moment but if you need more information feel free to call me."

They shook hands and parted company.

"Professor!" Harden called back as Buchardi reached the front door. Dave moved in closer. "Who would be, in your opinion, the ultimate experts on these Hez-o-llahs?" In order to hide his real purpose for their meet Harden's mispronunciation was intentional. "Aside from academics I mean."

"Hezbollah! It's pronounced Hezbollah! It means the Army of God."

"Yes, of course! Hezbollah."

"Well . . . aside from academics, actual members and the American CIA of course, there would only be Nahum Admoni, Director of Mossad. But there is little chance you will get to see him."

"Thanks again for your time Professor."

"My pleasure." He turned as he stepped through the exit. "By the way, what is the title of your novel?" Buchardi called back.

"It's only a working title but, *Quaere Hominem in Tunica Nudata*."

"*Search For the Man in the Striped Shirt*? Interesting title. Best of luck with it."

"Thank you."

*

CHAPTER SIX

The Oval Office
1600 Pennsylvania Avenue?
Washington D.C.
Friday, 10 April

The "Foggy Bottom" is colloquial for the Secretary of State Building which is actually named for the D.C. neighborhood district on which it is located rather than the common assumption that it is part of the Washington 'Swamp'.

In one of the oldest D.C. districts the Harry S. Truman Building is its dedication name and came about as the bastard child of the War Department in 1940 when that federal branch outgrew its accommodations while dealing with a world-wide outbreak of crazies who wanted to rule the world.

Lacking the Corinthian columns or acanthus leaf carvings of most of the traditional structures the dull grey, utilitarian architecture is more reminiscent of a prison then a building so critical to the functioning of the largest and most influential government on the planet.

In contrast to its simplicity the building houses the government department with arguably the most complicated job in the federal system: that is to maintain peace and continuity with the rest of the world by applying a succinct mandate; promote foreign policy.

Given that foreign policy in the United States is like the weather in that it changes daily, this is no mean feat.

It had now been a year since the embassy bombing in April of '83, over six months since the Marine Barracks bombing in October of last year, six months since the not so popular invasion of Grenada only days later and the Soviets were still in Afghanistan, as they had been for the last three years and appeared to be on it for the long run.

In short there was plenty of news to keep the newsprint and radio gossip jockeys busy. All the news that fit to spin.

Unfortunately for the Reagan administration at the moment, the news was all bad.

As the president is the Commander-in-Chief it is U.S. military transport is used for international travel while Secret Service operated civilian transport is utilized for domestic travel.

At the moment in the back seat of Cadillac One, President Reagan was being briefed by his current, acting Press Secretary, Larry Speakes. They were in route back to the White House coming from a lunch meeting at the downtown Hilton with members of the Rotary Club.

The important meeting was originally scheduled to meet in the Harry S. Truman Building but the president had two follow-on meetings in the Oval Office and so, for convenience relocated this meeting.

In the car, once the motorcade was assembled and given the green light by the shift commander, Larry Speakes had already started the mid-day brief.

"Do we need to send FEMA?" Reagan asked.

"No sir but there were a couple of tornadoes in Wisconsin late yesterday afternoon. One in Barneveld injured dozens, killed nine and left millions in damage."

"Contact governor, . . .?"

"Earl, Anthony Earl."

"Governor Earl, Democrat or Republican?"

"Democrat sir."

"Screw him!" Reagan snapped. Speakes was shocked. "I'm joking damn it! Call him, tell him we can have FEMA reps out this afternoon! And have somebody call FEMA and set it up. You need to lighten up Larry!"

"Yes sir."

Larry Speakes, acting Press Secretary serving as a locum for James Brady who had been severely wounded and crippled by a crazed gunman three years ago in the first few months of his job, never really adjusted to the President's sense of humor, a habitual hold over from Reagan's days in Hollywood.

"And then we have the Lebanon report." Reagan pursed his lips as his jovial air evaporated. "Shall I read it to you sir?"

"No need. I'll get the latest assessment from Weinberger and Schultz."

No less than the Romans' misunderstanding of the Levant when they invaded Canaan in the First

Century, Reagan and his advisor's basic inability to grasp the depth of the cultural riffs in the Lebanese territories had entangled his administration into the feuds of the multitude of petty warlords inhabiting the geography of the Central Levant.

Two thousand years later the ancient tribes of the same territories of the Judeo and Lebanese lands were divided by irreconcilable belief systems difficult or impossible for educated people anywhere to fathom.

As the latest eruption of fighting in the Lebanese Civil War raged on into its ninth year the current meeting at the White House concerned a request from the United Nations.

Every president, indeed, every good world leader, has a squad of advisors. Some have a platoon. Reagan had an army. The downside of this was the inevitable infighting which any given leader had to contend with.

Already assembled in the Oval Office were George Schultz, Casper Weinberger and Robert 'Bud' McFarlane.

"Morning Casper. How's Janey doing?" Entering the Oval Office, the President went straight to his desk.

"Doing very well sir, thank you for asking."

"George, Bob." He nodded as he took a seat.

"Okay let's get the ball rolling. First on the list?"

"Lebanon." Bob McFarlane spurted out. Reagan cringed.

"The barracks attack and the follow-on bombings are really giving us a black eye." Weinberger reminded.

"Okay, so Vessey was right!" Reagan snapped. "Has the CIA got any good news?"

"We are following several promising leads sir." William Casey quickly answered.

William 'Bill' Casey, a native New Yorker, was Director of the Central Intelligence Agency, Bronze Star recipient from his time in the OSS and a lawyer who virtually invented the tax shelter during the convoluted New Deal's continuous flood of regulations. Additionally, he was one of the lawyers who helped draw up the *Point Four Program* to help rebuild 3rd World nations after the War.

"How promising Bill?" Reagan pushed.

"Now that we know they are headquartered in the Bakaa Valley and are receiving significant support from Iran, we're in a position to send in Marine recon units and call-in naval gunfire into the valley area. On your okay, of course." He added.

"Are there civilians in that valley?"

"Yes sir, a few, but yes, it's populated." Casey answered.

"I'm gonna meet with General Vessey right after this. Hold up and I'll get back to you. Keep everything on standby."

"Will do."

"We need a win damn it! Especially now that the Reds have Salyut and Mir floating around up there!" Reagan bitched.

"The *Space Station Freedom* project appears to be on track sir." McFarlane tossed out.

Robert 'Bud' McFarlane, at forty-seven years of age, served as Special Advisor to the president and Deputy National Security Advisor. Born in D.C. he was also a former Marine Corps officer and like Schultz served as an artillery officer. Through his career McFarland sought and received postings and earned credentials associated with strategies and planning primarily from the civilian side of the house.

"Well, that's something! NASA still on their launch schedule for the parts assembly?"

"Schedule not only unchanged but according to Dr. Syvertson who I spoke to this morning, they've moved the final shuttle launch up to November 8th instead of January." He gladly reported.

"The ESA respond to our invitation to join the project?" The President asked.

"The European Space Agency voted yesterday."

"And?"

"Yes. Tentatively . . . yes." He added.

"Tentatively?! Damn Europeans! Probably the French holding up the works!"

"They need to coordinate final estimates with their committees. Also, they're asking for at least two trips to be launched from their station in French Guiana."

"Coordinate them with the right people over at NASA, let them decide. Tell them that I'm behind it if it'll reduce costs to us."

"Yes sir."

"What about the Japanese?" Reagan followed on.

"They're interested. But asked for a meeting with NASA to firm up some technical details."

"Have Dr. Mark's people arrange it. How much are the details gonna cost us?" Reagan probed.

McFarlane shuffled through his notes before answering.

"The latest estimate from the Director for the estimated ten to twelve assembly flights will total $14.5 to $15 billion."

"Billion with a B?!" Reagan repeated.

"Yes sir."

"They'll never go for it!" Reagan fell back in his chair.

"But on the upside sir, we're only paying 97% of the costs with an in-kind claim to all resources later harvested going to NASA with 3% to the CSA for their contribution. Later to be joined by ESA and the Japanese."

"We're only paying 97%? Well, that's a relief!" Reagan sarcastically quipped. McFarlane appeared to be the only one to have not been amused.

"What else?"

"There's a request from the U.N. General Secretary."

The request sent by classified courier, asked that the United States send a significant force to add to what they already had partial commitment to send from France, Italy, Great Britain and others were sending to Beirut. This 'force', to be anointed the Multi-National Force or MNF by the popular press, was envisioned to be a collection of western military might led by, if they joined, the United States. If not, the U.N.'s concept of an MNF would, like the majority of their past peace efforts, wind up a footnote in the archives.

"What's your impression George?" Reagan asked Schultz.

"The current consensus is that, as of Israel's withdrawal from the Green Zone in southern Lebanon back across the border, all our intelligence indicates Iran now sees Lebanon as a ripe fruit for the picking. However, our main concern is whether the people of Lebanon become another radical, fundamentalist state or a potential Soviet satellite."

"The greater of two evils!" Reagan snapped.

Although Ronald Reagan had unrestrained trust in Schultz, The President not only fervently believed the Soviet economic approach, i.e., communism, to be wrong but potentially disastrous and was one of the first to see that economic and military industrial pressures to wear the commies down was the west's best road to victory.

"How in God's name would the Soviets manage a satellite country in the Levant?!" Reagan challenged.

"With a proxy. Most likely through Iran." Casey explained. "Pending who comes out on top after the dust settles in Iraq!"

"They can barely manage the Baltic states as it is!"

"Yes sir, but . . . let's don't forget about the oil."

"Point taken Bill." Schultz added.

"The Russians have all the oil they need!" McFarlane countered.

"They wouldn't necessarily want it for domestic use, besides access to a major Med port from the Black Sea?! Could have unlimited uses." Casey pointed out.

"Plus, they really stirred up a hornet's nest with Afghanistan."

"Compounded by a slew of other mistakes like the 007 Korean airliner incident and inability to keep pace with modern technology, rather than stealing technology from other countries." McFarlane added.

"That's the Chinese you're thinking of!" Schultz quipped.

"Communism is dead it just doesn't know enough yet to lie down!" Casey commented.

"We send more troops over there and it would be our second biggest mistake after sending those first troops to Beirut! It was like sending guppies to a tank of piranhas!"

"No not like a tank of piranhas. Worse! Like an ocean of big-assed sharks!" McFarlane added.

"I think the President has heard enough about losses." Observing The President's dejected countenance Casey terminated the debate.

"It's a rookie mistake to rely on centrally planned industrial expansion for economic growth, there are too many variables, especially in a country which occupies ten time zones for Christ's sake!" Reagan added.

"Eleven sir!"

"What?

"Eleven time zones."

"ELEVEN! Jesus, hope we never have to go to war with those people!" Reagan threw out.

"What you don't think we could win?!" McFarlane asked.

"Hell yes we'd win! I'm just worried about where we'd bury all those bodies!"

George Schultz, now sixty-four and also a New Yorker by birth, was named Secretary of State by the president two years ago. Also known as 'the Sphinx' by colleagues stemming from his balding head and what seemed to be a permanent poker face, Schultz was a Princeton and M.I,T, graduate, former Marine and economist by profession.

Singlehandedly revamping the Foreign Service by replacing all the key positions staffed by political appointees with those who had the most professional requirements for the job, not only improved the service but helped earn him no shortage of enemies on The Hill.

To his lasting credit Shultz was a key figure in the reduction of U.S.-U.S.S.R. tensions in November of '83 when animosity on both sides nearly culminated in a nuclear war.

Casper 'Cap' Weinberger, a Harvard educated lawyer now at sixty-seven years old, was by contrast to the east coasties a west coast elite. He served in the Army and now was employed as Secretary of Defense and was constantly at odds with State. Perhaps, some speculated, because he wanted the Sec State desk in lieu of serving as the Sec Def.

Though diversified in politics, economics and life philosophies all of these men shared a common attitude towards duty. They were, in a time of increasing world conflict, patriots.

With that Reagan signalled the end of the meeting by dishing out assignments.

"Bud, have your people get a message to Jeane Fitzpatrick, have them tell her we want to convene the Security Council sometime next week."

"Topic?"

"Lebanon solution. Stamp yourself as the P.O.C/ I'll have a bullet point list drawn up for you by the week's end."

"Will do Chief."

"George find out all you can on these Hezbollah clowns. I have a strong feeling we're gonna hear more from them before this is over."

"Yes sir."

Just then The President's intercom buzzed.

Mr. President, General Vessey is here with the Granada report.

"Thank you, Mrs. Osborne. Five minutes please."

Yes sir, I'll tell him.

"Thank you, Kathleen. Bud, keep me informed on the Discovery mission progress will ya?" Reagan requested.

"Yes sir, will do."

"An actual space station!" Reagan mused with glee. "To think the Wright brothers only flew for the first time three years before I was born, and now we're in space!" He stood to shake hands. "Thanks fellas, if nobody has anything else that'll be all."

There were no takers and the meeting disbursed.

After the meeting broke up and with Schultz hanging back to talk with the president, it was out in the hall that Bob McFarlane pulled Cap Weinberger aside.

"He really seems to be excited about this space thing." McFarlane opened with.

"He sees it as some sort of a personal project. As a kid he used to watch the first crop dusting flights file over his house in Tampico back in Illinois." McFarlane explained.

"Cap, I wanna run something by ya."

"Sure."

"One of the military guys approached me about an idea some of them had."

"What is it?"

"It's about Iran and the Contras down in Nicaragua."

"This note you scribbled on my latest directive." He passed the annotated directive containing Weinberger's handwritten note across the bottom which read: *'This is almost too absurd to comment on'*. Casey thinks it's not such a bad idea!" McFarlane defended.

"Have you run this past State?" McFarlane asked.

"No why? What'a you think the Big Guy'll say?"

"Well, given that we've only just a few months ago declared Iran a state supporter of international terrorism and we have an arms embargo on them that

The President's trying to get the rest of the free world to sign on too, what'a I think he'll say?! I'll tell ya what he'll say, he'll not just say no about selling weapons to the enemy! He'll say hell no!"

Weinberger silently wondered if McFarlane had been influenced by others to have at least partially accepted such a crazy scheme.

"But Cap, word has come down the pipe line that the Iranians are willing to have American hostages released if the U.S is willing to sell arms ammo and parts to the Ayatollah."

"Come down from who?"

"Peres."

"Simon Peres?! I don't believe it he's not got the moxy to risk the scandal!"

"Well from Simon Peres through a diplomat." McFarlane fumbled. Weinberger gave him a blank stare. "Well, through a diplomat from a friend . . . a consultant." He quickly added.

"A consultant named Ledeen?" Weinberger challenged.

"We could ship the arms through Israel, they'd get them to Tehran. Money would come in through one of our black accounts or Tel Aviv would be paid then pay us. Or we could just replace the weapons Israel traded plus a little interest as incentive."

"To what end?!" Weinberger was struggling to hold back.

"Ollie North thinks it's a good idea. He thinks it could work."

"Of course he |thinks it would work, he's a hawk!" Weinberger balked.

"It could work!" McFarlane insisted.

"And if it doesn't? The fact that it's completely illegal aside, what if it doesn't? Do you have any idea the political destruction such a move would cause? You're talking about international embarrassment, retaliations and possible Congressional investigations as the other side dog piles on and brings the whole thing down and us along with it! You can't negotiate with those religious fanatics! They've already proven time and time again they can't be trusted to abide by their agreements. They feel no obligation to be trusted by people of western cultures."

"But –"

"You want to ignore the *Boland Amendment* forbidding arms to the Contra rebels **and** violate an active arms embargo against Khomeini and the Iranians?! Just one of those things could get you sacked and five to twenty in Leavenworth!"

"But don't you see that by keeping the Iranians and the Iraqis at each other the rest of the Mid-East, especially our closest ally Israel, can focus on their own countries!"

Weinberger stared angrily making direct eye contact.

"Bud, we don't set policy! The President does!"

"Cap. if we don't supply them against Saddam Hussein the Soviets will!"

Weinberger took in a breath and again made eye contact as he lowered his tone and spoke slowly and distinctly.

"A self-governing democracy can only survive if people participate. If not, it is subject to usurpation by less honorable individuals." He clarified. "I won't back it!" Weinberger walked away as he mentally debated whether or not to let that be the end of it.

****

CHAPTER SEVEN

The Oval Office
The White House

If you passed him on the street, dressed in civilian clothes you'd mistake him for the friendly guy down the road who you see every Sunday on his way to buy the newspaper, or maybe think he was the local school teacher. The reality was very different.

At sixty-one years of age, a ramrod posture and sporting a greying head of close-cropped hair, General John William Vessey, Jr. was not only the last WWII combat veteran still serving on active duty as well as the longest serving member of the U.S. Army, but he was also the tenth Chairman of the Joint Chiefs Staff.

A Minnesota man, as opposed to all the New Yorkers in the cabinet, Vessey began his long and distinguished career as an enlisted man working his way from private all the way up through the enlisted ranks and receiving a battlefield commission during the slaughter of the landings at Anzio, Italy in January of 1944.

Later, during the Korean War, he served in various infantry divisions while earning his bachelor's and master's degrees in Political Science.

While serving in Viet Nam, at a firebase behind enemy lines, he and his small force were decorated for having fought off thousands of Viet Cong in a frontal assault, killing over four hundred of them and wounding hundreds more. Prior to the Marines deployment to Beirut, as part of an international peacekeeping force, Vessey had warned the administration not to send Marines to Lebanon as part of the police keeping force. The Marines were sent and just weeks later, 241 Marines were killed when a truck bomb was driven into the headquarters building.

The president recalled the Marines.

More recently, the magnitude of the Grenada situation was brought home when Reagan not only received near world-wide condemnation for the incursion, seen largely as an action to offset the damage America suffered by the bombing of the Marine barracks in Beirut, but Ted Weiss, a Democrat, on an act of pure political theater, introduced a bill to impeach the President for the controversial invasion.

Throughout the shit storm that ensued, General Vessey maintained a firm and decisive hold on the reins of military leadership. In short, John Vessey was by no means a short sighted, desk jockey of a 'paper general'.

Ever since the onset of The Cold War in 1947, East-West political relations had fallen into an irregular cycle of relative calm punctuated by one-up-brinksmanship where a nuclear confrontation seemed inevitable, or at least, right around the corner.

Back in September Reagan felt compelled to cut his three-week working trip out at Rancho del Cielo short after the shooting down of the KAL 007 civilian airliner over Sakhalin Island in the northern Pacific.

Now that things on the world stage were heating up again, Ronnie as well as most of the big dogs on The Hill, were more than happy to have someone of Vessey's proven caliber at the helm of the military.

That morning The President had requested that General Vessey consult with Bill Casey and Lt. General L.D. Faurer USAF, Director of the NSA, on what they believed may be the Soviet's next target.

To address what was being played up as the Soviet's latest incursion, having backed Cuban communists in the failed overthrow of the Grenadian government just last October, and after successfully invading and taking over Afghanistan a few years earlier, a string of international human rights violations were being leveled against the Kremlin by the U.S. and many other world leaders.

"Morning John!" Reagan greeted as he stood and extended his hand to Vessey.

"Morning sir."

Reagan came around from behind his desk and took a seat across from the couch where the General had taken a seat.

"Good to see you John. How's the family?"

"Fine sir, just fine. Wife sends her love."

"Can I get you a coffee or something?"

"No thank yu Mr. President. Had a big breakfast. Avis won't let me leave the house unless I eat half my body weight in ham and eggs!"

"You've got a good woman there John!"

"Thank you, sir and don't I know it."

"How'd you get on with Casey and Faurer?"

"Good sir, good. If it's alright by you sir, Director Casey asked me to bring you up to date a bit on the Grenada situation."

"Okay."

"A bit of trouble sir."

"Another coup attempt?"

"Yes sir. Apparently, Bishop was making moves to usurp the upcoming elections. The people put him under house arrest until he agreed to compromise with Deputy P.M. Coard. Bishop refused and when his people came to free him, Coard's people intercepted hem and a fire fight broke out."

"P.M.? Bishop?"

"Dead along with 18 or 20 others."

"Bloody bunch of street gangs! You'd think those idiots would have seized the chance we were offering them!"

"Limited vision backed by greed sir."

"The New Jewel Movement! The People's Revolutionary Government! Where do these people get these names?!"

"The names Democrats and Republicans were already taken I guess." Vessey quipped.

Reagan stared at him blankly then eventually smiled.

"Damned third world mentalities! And they wonder why they can't grow and prosper! They've nearly got the world's nutmeg market cornered for crying out loud! Why don't they build on it God damn it!" Reagan cursed. "As long as we got all those damn Cuban Commies outta there I guess!"

"We may have gotten rid of all the outside agitators sir but they still seemed plagued by their own internal power struggles."

"Factions within factions into factions all divided by fractions of factions. All wanting a piece of the pie until there's nothing left but crumbs." Reagan shook his head. "Maurice Bishop! Only an idiot would try to establish a communist government in a predominantly Christian nation!" The president opined. "What clown is running the show now?"

"No idea sir but Langley is working on it. We should know in a day or so."

"Did we pick the wrong guy to head the interim government, John?"

"We picked the best candidate available at the time Mr. President. We couldn't really predict his behavior after we put him in."

"Please tell me we're not gonna have to send more troops back down there?"

"Langley assures us that we won't and now it's up to the people. If the U.N. keeps their word to send observers to monitor the elections, we've obtained our goal."

"Onto more pressing matters." Reagan pushed. "General, what, in your opinion is the current potential terrorist threat to the U.S. and our allies of this new breed of madmen?"

"If you're referring to the Levant situation, we're pretty confident the Soviets have sent people down into Lebanon from Syria to test the waters. But, given the recent kidnapping and rescue of most of their embassy staff from the hands of the IJO terrorists, and how the KGB handled it . . . it's highly unlikely they're looking to ally with anyone in Lebanon now beyond the border groups aligned to Arafat whose PLO appear to be dug in where they are at the moment. Unless the PLO get a major injection of arms and cash, I don't think they're in a position to make any drastic moves anytime soon." Vessey explained.

"Okay, that's your conventional tactical assessment. I realize terrorism is not your wheelhouse but, give me your gut feeling on it."

"Mr. President, cards on the table, about the Russians. History has shown that the Soviets never quit. They just find a new avenue of approach."

"Meaning?"

"Meaning if the PLO, who we know are being used to distribute the money the Iranians, the Soviets and the U.N. give them to the other terrorist factional groups, are cut off by the Russians, they'll have to depend more on the drug trade. But the Turkish, Paki and Afghani drug production is not enough to sustain their so-called Jihad on the scale they want, especially now that Syria and Lebanon have flared up."

"I see those poly-sci degrees haven't gone to waste."

"Thank you, sir. My point is, terrorism offers them another potential stream of income."

"How do you see them using it?"

"By 'proving' themselves, their worthiness so to speak, with ever increasing attacks and especially death tolls, each faction can legitimately claim they are entitled to a larger piece of the illegitimate black money which fuels the radical Islamist movement world-wide."

"Are you hinting at what I think you're hinting at, General?"

"Mr. President, Director Casey and General Faurer are in a much better position to analyze the direct and indirect intel implications. But from a strategic military standpoint, if I were a bunch if disaffected terrorists and I needed funding, I'd plan and execute something that would make the Iranians and Soviets come to me and ask, 'How much money do you need?'"

"Plan and execute something that would make a big splash?"

"Big like the Cretaceous meteor hitting the Gulf of Mexico in the Yucatan peninsula big!"

Reagan got contemplative.

"I think we need a full Intel staff meeting, and soon!" He declared.

"Along those lines sir, just a suggestion, strategy-wise, we do as the Soviets are doing and keep our response small, contained. At least until we have more intel on exactly which proxies we're dealing with."

"You have my backing. Make it happen."

"Yes sir."

******

CHAPTER EIGHT

CIA Headquarters
Langley, Virginia

Established through a series of events before, during and after WWII, the United States' premier spy agency, the CIA, 'evolved' more than was actually intentionally 'founded'.

What came from the Office of Strategic Services, or the O.S.S. the American mother of deception which birthed the CIA in the early Fifties, could hardly have been founded by a more appropriate individual, to wit a successful New York City lawyer.

William 'Wild Bill' Donovan pointed out the two things that were sure to lead to the defeat of America if not corrected; the military infighting visa vie intelligence agencies competing with one another and the lack of a central agency or clearing house to act as a pool where each agency could reference anything known about any given foreign army, unit, government or individual.

The Department of State, the FBI and all the armed services all ran their own intel offices and were loath to share information with one another, even after being ordered by the President to do so.

The infamous "heavy water story" from WWII is the quintessential example.

Early in the war both sides realized that the first nation with an atomic bomb would win. The German supply of heavy water known as tritium, an essential ingredient to build an effective reactor and which was expensive and time consuming to manufacture, became the priority. So when the French Underground relayed that a Vichy ship loaded with heavy water was anchored in Marseilles, a secret mission was approved.

The Office of Strategic Services sent two teams to infiltrate the harbor, plant limpet mines on the ship and sink it.

A short time later the commando teams slipped into the harbor, were making final preparations and climbed into their rubber boats to go and mine the ship when it exploded, burned and sank right before their eyes.

In the sullen moonlight and the aftermath of the burning ship, the O.S.S. operatives sat dumbfounded as they watched three canoes paddling away from the burning hulk.

But not just any canoes, Klepper canoes, the hallmark vessels of the British Special Operations Executive or S. O. E. forerunners of the S.B.U. and the S.A.S.

The O.S.S. lads packed up their gear and went home.

In July of 1941 FDR gave his blessing to the OoCoI, or the Office of Coordinator of Information headed by Donovan.

Due to their overwhelming success in helping to organize covert efforts the O.S.S was refunded and in 1945 were reorganized and became the S.S.U. or Strategic Services Unit which in turn evolved into the Central Intelligence Group or C.I.G. which in July of 1947, under *The National Security Act* bill signed by Truman, formally established what is now called the Central Intelligence Agency.

In addition to being the material which has fed dozens of films and hundreds of books the daring duo days of spies parachuting into enemy territory to pilfer secrets, rescue key personnel or blow up bridges is still responsible for many a young person looking to join the Agency or go into MI6.

*

"I've advised the Sec Def to alert the Tenth Group SF people to prepare to brief several ODA teams on a possible clandestine infil with the Amal militia through the airport." Bill Casey said to Lt. Commander Harden as he entered the room even before he had taken a seat at the table. Harden took a minute to digest the information before responding.

"I think that's a bad idea sir. Knowing that's our primary ingress and egress point the PLO and their buddies have eyes on the entire port area 24/7. Besides there's no way to infill 12 Americans without it leaking out into the general population. Beirut is a city but it's a small city everybody knows everybody, who belongs and who doesn't. That town has more leaks then the White House and the Congress combined!"

"Do I correctly deduce Lt. Commander you have given the matter some thought?"

"As you know sir my mother lived in Beirut when she worked for the AP."

"Yes, worked in Beirut back when it was civilized. I read your jacket."

"I suspected as much. She reported locally through the *al Nahār* newspaper where she was by lined by several American dailies as well. The *Nahār* went out to the half million ex-pat Lebanese all over the western countries."

"I'm listening."

"She had a good friend, a Mrs. Isra Shaheen a journalist friend. I met her a few times the year I was there in the American high school."

"What are the chances she's still in country?"

"She'd be a bit older now, but I know for a fact Isra's a staunch patriot. She believed in the country 100% come what may."

"So what are you suggesting? You wanna go in and find her?"

"Yes. Given the fact that we have no humint assets since the loss of Bill Buckley and the last bombing if anyone can get us info on the state of play in the capital she could. Being a journalist and all."

"She's hardly likely to still be a reporter, given the state of the place." Casey challenged.

"Agreed but, I'm sure she's still plugged in."

"You think you have a chance of finding her?"

"I feel pretty strongly that even though after the murder of Chancellor Malcolm Kerr when my mom left, Isra Shaheen will still be there, somewhere."

"Somewhere? No ideas on any leads?"

"I can probably get her last address from my mom, but even if I had an address for her it's highly unlikely she still lives in the same place."

"Harden, don't forget this is the same area a dozen westerners including the engineer Dr. Regier was kidnapped from. You go in, you're on your own. They'll be no overt rescue attempts. At this point plausible deniability is the name of the game!"

"I understand sir."

"Get her last known address from your mom, then contact Langley, get them her details and description see if they can track her down. If that place is as leaky as you say it is, caution them not to contact the newspaper. Then get the most up-to-date intel on that area. Based on that we'll make a final decision."

"Roger that sir, will do."

****

Beirut Head Desk
Briefing Room
Langley, Va.

"John David Nobleman of *The Pittsburgh Sun Telegraph*." Dave Harden read aloud as the young, bespecled tech handed him his false I.D. then passed him a document.

"This letter is your official U.N. Palestinian Aid Council permission to be in Beirut for no longer than 48 hours and remember, although this letter of transit allows you to be in the city, provisions of the International Press Treaty stipulate you are forbidden from contacting any of the guerilla or party leaders without their expressed, independently verified permission."

He then slid a small handful of paraphernalia across the counter. Harden picked through the items as the documents guy spoke.

"The military liaison on the ground will compel you to surrender most of these things before leaving the perimeter. But if you didn't have them on your person, he might very well order you arrested. They're strictly to maintain cover."

Harden selected and smiled at one particular item. A taxi receipt for a ride from *The Sun Gazette* address downtown to the Greater Pittsburgh International airport, dated tomorrow.

"Double Cross Section and Ian Fleming would be proud! Thank you Q!"

"Who is Double Cross Section and please don't call me Q, Commander!"

****

Beirut, Lebanon
Wednesday, 15 April

Using the U.S. sixth fleet as cover the commander, posing as a U.N. sanctioned reporter, was given orders to be flown via Navy transport and report aboard the USS Kennedy currently docked on station, just out of artillery range, in the Eastern Med.

From there he was ferried ashore in a supply boat of humanitarian aid to the U.S. military outpost at the former airport. Although the Beirut airport had been sporadically open it was deemed too risky to chance landing a CIA operative in an active war zone.

As a precaution, for his own safety Casey forbade him carrying a weapon.

Having earlier sent a coded message through the CIA source Shaheen's current address was confirmed and verified with the one Harden's mother had given him.

After landing on the carrier *U.S.S. Kennedy* by helicopter Harden became what's known as a 'ghost', no uniform, no rank and no conversation with any of the crew save for the skipper the only member of the ship's compliment that knew that Lt. Commander Harden was in fact active-duty Navy.

Once ashore and after pretending to supervise some unloading, Harden quietly slipped away and made his way along the southern outskirts of the city northeast of the Green Line towards the university area and to his goal only about two klicks from downtown up the Paris Road to a house on the outskirts of town in northwest Beirut.

"Bon jour. Madam Isra Shaheen?" He inquired of the late middle-aged woman who answered the front door.

"Oui? Qui demande?" She challenged then momentarily stared. "AHHH, My God, David!" After peering up and down the street she carefully opened the door wider and allowed Harden to enter.

Paddy Kelly

Once inside he held his false I.D at eye level for
her to see. She read it and nodded in comprehension
to him before he pocketed it.

She urged him into the doorway and closed it over
before administering a deep, heartfelt hug. "My God
you have grown into a fine tall man!" She quietly
exclaimed. "Come in, come in. I've made tea." She
urged him in. "How is your mother? Well, I hope?"
Isra inquired as they walked back to the kitchen.

Artillery sporadically boomed in the distance.

"She is fine and still writing."

She led him down a dimly lit narrow hallway into
the kitchen where he stopped dead in his tracks
shocked at the three heavily armed men that greeted
him.

He turned to Shaheen and stared blankly.

In return she smiled back.

"I'm sorry! This is Monsieur Hinz, Monsieur Hinz
this is the friend I told you about, from the U.N.'s
Palestinian Aid Council." They shook hands. "John's
mother is an old journalist friend of mine. She wrote
for the *New York Tribune* here when I worked for the
al Nahār newspaper." She introduced.

Harden was immediately struck by Shaheen's
field craft using caution with only first names and
being careful not to volunteer any extra information
about the two.

"After the murder of Chancellor Kerr John's mom
was recalled from Beirut." She explained.

"I recall the unfortunate incident." Hinz affirmed.
"Please call me Mamoud."

The lady of the house busied herself with setting the tea as the two pulled up chairs at the small kitchen table. The two armed guards remained standing and noticeably alert.

"I understand you seek some information?" Mamoud started.

"I've been tasked to comprise a report to submit to the General Council in order to more efficiently allocate humanitarian aid to the Lebanese people."

"I see. Go on."

"What can you tell me about the various factions?"

"There are too many!"

"Most of the world seem to agree with you." Harden affirmed. "I understand there are The Christians, the Muslims and the Jews?" Harden continued.

"In broad strokes yes, along with the Iranians and Syrians with each group divided into multiple sub-factions. But the faction igniting the whole thing, back when there was at least an uneasy peace in 1975, are the PLO. As a result, of all the factions battling for control of the country it is the Arabs who have the most support, have relied on terrorist attacks and strategies and who have become the most ruthless. It is my belief they see Lebanon as their new potential 'homeland', another Arab country modelled no doubt on the Iranian fundamentalist caliphate."

"According to news reports it seems they have stepped up their terror attacks aimed primarily at western foreigners?" Harden probed.

"Yes they see a future in ransoms from rich western governments, have taken to being assassins for hire and are lately acting as a militia for the Iranians and Syrians."

"Et les drogues aussi!" The smaller of the two large guards interjected.

"Oui!" Hinz nodded. "And they have taken to transporting and trading heroin from the Turks throughout their regions of control. They trade mostly for weapons."

"I read they recently kidnapped four Russian diplomats?"

"To their credit they are chameleons, constantly changing ploys. Late last year with the bombings of the American embassy and marines they shifted rhetoric to decrying all foreigners in Lebanon. A new slant on the old Soviet 'Yankee go Home' slogan."

"Something works you stay with it I suppose." Harden reaffirmed. "Have you noticed any new kids on the block, new faces in the last year or so?"

By the nature of his questions Mamoud quickly came to the realization that Harden was anything but a U.N. aid worker. Likewise, by his bodyguards, his Armalite and his semi-formal dress, Harden knew that Mamoud was more than just another Lebanese freedom fighter.

"There is rumor of a well-financed group calling themselves Hezbollah, the "Party of God'." Mamoud threw out, as much as to test Harden as inform him.

"I haven't read about them." Harden lied.

"Not surprising. As the PLO have learned from the Soviets so Hezbollah have in turn learned from

Arafat and the PLO and so are constantly inventing new ways to hide their treachery."

"Such as?"

"Primarily through false fronts, artificial names of fictitious terror groups in order to confuse Israeli and American intelligence efforts and mislead the press."

"That's not too difficult. Do you think that it's working?"

"Do you know of the IJO? The Islamic Jihad Organization?"

"Of course! They are responsible for the Marine barracks bombing."

"In fact they not. They're a front. Hezbollah don't care about taking credit when it's not strategically important. They are only interested in the end result of their attacks."

"A sophisticated strategy!"

"These are not your average terrorists. These fellows have very grand ambitions. They don't see this as simply a war. They see it as steppingstone to one day controlling the entire Middle East."

"Sounds like a couple of crazies in Germany back in the thirties!"

"Yes, only much more dangerous. The Nazis only wanted to kill Jews, gypsies and artists! These fanatics want to eliminate all non-Muslims in the world!"

Harden began to realize Director Casey's personal interest in this 'dirty little war' now moving into its second decade while at the same time beginning to doubt that he knew as much as he thought he did about the situation here.

"Last year they started producing rudimentary, almost juvenile rockets." Mamoud continued.

"Rockets! With the blockades where would they get the components? The fuel?" The Commander pushed.

"Converted sewer pipes powered mostly by molten sugar."

"That's why they keep importing more sugar!" Harden realized aloud. "What about the explosives? You can't fabricate very sophisticated demolitions from household cleaning products."

"The mullahs of Iran supply them. To produce rockets, Iranian chemists and engineers teach them how to mix propellant from fertilizer, oxidizer and other ingredients in makeshift factories in and around Tehran or in Gaza."

Harden became laser focused on this, particularly the suggested locations of manufacturing sites. "Even after Egypt shut down most of the tunnels into Israel their key contraband is still being smuggled into Gaza via a handful of tunnels that remain, then over the border into Lebanon to be tested here in the war zones. Arafat has publicly praised Iran for its assistance, blueprints, engineering know-how, motor tests and other technical expertise. The U.S. State Department itself says that Iran provides $100 million a year to Palestinian armed groups.

"That's amazing!" Dave feigned shock.

"For now, these projectiles reach barely a few kilometers, fly wildly and caused little damage landing mostly inside Gaza or friendly neighborhoods.

Shortly after the outbreak of hostilities here they assembled a secret supply line from long time patrons in Iran and Syria, according to IDF reports. Longer-range rockets, powerful explosives, metal, and machinery will be flooding Gaza's southern border with Egypt to Sudan, then be trucked across Egypt's desert and smuggled in what they need through a warren of narrow tunnels beneath the Sinai Peninsula. According to the Israelis smuggling not only continued but gained momentum when Iran began to help logistically and financially."

"Mamoud, you paint quite a graphic picture."

"There is more my friend. They are quickly graduating from mere drugs, killings and kidnappings to more advanced ambitions."

"How so?"

"With help coming from Russia through Iran we have reason to believe they have begun to train naval commandos."

"For what purpose?"

"Suicide bombers of course! Instead of cars they intend to use small boats."

"Also with the help of the Red Chinese through the Pakis they are planning to install missile batteries all along the Gaza border." Mamoud stood and nodded at his bodyguards signalling the meet was over. On the way out he stopped at the door and spoke.

"I hope that was helpful."

"I appreciate your assessment. My report to the Secretary General will reflect that!" Harden informed.

"For the present, although they want the destruction of Israel, these groups aren't necessarily aiming for the military destruction of Israel as the final endpoint. The Russian communists have taught them well, taught them to bide their time, think bigger. Ultimately, these rocket, terrorist and other attacks are meant to build leverage and rewrite the rules of the game," Mamoud said. "It's psychological."

"How so?"

"Ultimately, Arabs cannot be trusted with democracy. They simply are not ready for such responsibility." Mamoud imparted as he stood to leave. One of the guards moved to the front door ahead of everyone else. "God be with you sir!"

"You as well Mamoud."

Mamoud moved down the hall and left leaving Isra to close the door over behind them before she returned to the kitchen.

"Your friend is very well informed Isra."

"He comes by his knowledge honestly. He is Doctor Mamoud Hinz, professor of Middle East political science. Before the terrorists took control and ousted the legitimate government and started this whole fiasco, he was a professor of political science at Al Azhar University over in Gaza."

"Well then, I guess he knows of what he speaks!" Harden acknowledged.

****

CHAPTER NINE

Doc McKeowen's two hour flight from Montreal touched down at Dulles International at 12:30 in the afternoon. Being Friday, traffic on The Beltway was moderate going into the city. As was customary most of the Swamp had headed home after lunch.

The taxi dropped him off at the O Street entrance of the Washington Naval Yard where he made his way to the Naval Sea Systems Command building.

"HM1 McKeowen. I work with Commander Harden." Doc introduced himself after making his way to the back of the open warehouse where he encountered . . .

"Mrs. Gaffney, Lt. Commander Harden's personal secretary."

"Pleasure to meet you. I didn't realize anybody had secretaries anymore. I thought they were all called Personal Assistants."

"Only the ones that can't make the grade as secretaries!" She quipped in return.

"I'm looking for the Lt. Commander."

"Take a number! He left here on Monday, said he'd be back by Wednesday. That was two days ago! I hope this isn't the kind of job where nobody knows where anybody is or what in blazes is going on all the time! Exactly why I left the Pentagon!" Gaffney vented. As she spoke she moved some chairs to the other side of the room. "I've been trudging around

116

this place the last two days looking for things to do!"
She disappeared back into her office mumbling to
herself. "Might as well transfer back to Personnel for
all the good I'm doing here!"

Curiosity slowly turned to suspicion as Doc
realized Harden wasn't the type of individual to
suddenly vanish for days at a time without leaving
prior notice.

Doc drifted into her office doorway.

"Mrs. Gaffney, do you know where Commander
Harden was headed when last you spoke to him on
Monday?" Gaffney looked up from her busywork.

"Said he was going over to Langley for a
meeting."

"Do you know with whom?"

She stood upright before replying.

"Hospitalman McKeowen, Lt. Commander
Harden's relationship with me has not yet reached the
level where we sleep together, share our meals or
even to the point that he keeps me informed of his
every movement." She calmly informed. "May I
suggest you check with somebody at Langley?"

McKeowen glanced around at the wooden framed
office spaces along the back wall.

"These spaces all spoken for?"

"Not so far. The one next door is the
Commander's, this one's mine. Far as I know all the
others are open."

Doc made his way to the largest of the remaining
five spaces, grounded his ruck and travel bag, dug in
his Lowe and produced a thick black marker then
printed the words 'SICK BAY' across the overhead

door timber followed by 'BY APPONTMENT ONLY!'. He then set his ruck and bag inside before turning to leave.

"What exactly are you doing young man?"

"Marking my territory Mrs. Gaffney." He explained before heading out. "Nice meeting you Mrs. Gaffney."

"Likewise Petty Officer McKeowen." She called after him as he headed up the open space between the old machinery. "If you find your errant commander, please tell him to check in!"

"Will do Mrs. Gaffney."

Twenty-five minutes later McKeowen was over at Langley waiting outside Director Casey' office.

Mrs. Pembroke, send him in please, and hold my calls. Casey's voice came through over the intercom on the secretary's desk.

"Yes Director." She nodded at Doc who went in.

"I've been expecting one of you guys to show up!" Casey snapped.

Not a good start! Doc's internal dialogue whispered.

"Here's what we know. He was sent over there-"

"Sorry Director, over where exactly?"

"Beirut boy! Have you not been briefed at all?!"

"Sir I'm just off the plane. I've been in Canada on an operation."

"Oh! That reminds me." He depressed a button on his desk intercom. "Mrs. Pembroke.

Yes sir?

"On his way out give Petty Officer McKeowen that citation arrived for him yesterday please."

Will do sir. His secretary replied.

Doc looked surprised but suppressed the urge to enquire about it.

"It came yesterday. Well done, good job, expect nothing less, et cetera, et cetera, et cetera."

"Thank you sir."

"Harden was supposed to check in Wednesday morning at ten hundred."

"Director Casey, what was his mission?"

"He tried to convince me to let your team, the RTF, go -"

"TFR sir. Task Force Romeo."

"The TFR to infil in through Beirut to sniff out these new Hezbollah crazies given we have no reliable humint in that sector."

"His mother worked over there years ago." McKeowen interjected.

"Yes, as a journalist. He thought if he contacted an old friend of hers he might be able to ferret out a lead." Casey continued.

"Yes, Mrs. Shaheen. We've talked about her before. What's the plan then sir?"

"The immediate plan is for you to stand down so as not to complicate matters. I've got a meet with Secretary Schultz and the head of the NSA in about an hour to hash out a plan and decide our next move. Meanwhile should you hear from our misplaced Lt. Commander you will report to me immediately! Me and no one else! Clear?"

"Yes sir, clear. Meanwhile I'll get the team into the –"

"Petty Officer McKeowen, you will stand down and stand by! The last thing we need is an international incident."

"No disrespect intended Director but, if Commander Harden is in the shit and has fallen into the wrong hands . . . they'll be a helluv'a lot more than a scandal to deal with!"

"Don't you think I know that son?!"

"Yes sir."

"And I don't need to remind you this whole thing is classified!" Casey commanded. "At least until we know more about these pajama garbed clowns who like setting off bombs in crowded areas!"

"I understand Director." Doc rose to take his leave but hesitated at the doorway. "Director, you will let us know as soon as you hear something?"

"You have my word Petty Officer McKeowen."

"Thank you sir."

"By the way, there was a handwritten note from a Lieutenant Laroche attached to your Canadian citation. Apparently somebody in the Canadian government thinks you did better than a 'two four' up there, whatever the hell that means." Casey informed.

"It's a twenty-four pack of beer Director."

"Well, I guess that's a good thing. Eh?" Casey affected a mock Canadian dialect.

"They really don't like when we do that sir." Doc informed as he left.

****

"Mac it's Doc."

It was inside an hour after leaving that Doc was back in his new sick bay and on the phone requesting an outside line. He adjusted the empty crate he was sitting on while dialing the phone which in turn sat atop an empty barrel also pilfered from the warehouse floor to act as temporary office furniture.

"DOC! How the fuck are ya buddy?! How's my third favorite corpsmen? What's -"

"Mac how soon can you be in D.C.?"

Petty Officer First Class Ray MacDonald was a specialist in demolitions both NATO, Soviet Block standard & improvised. Along with Petty Officer Ricky 'Boom Boom' Matson, formally of Seal Team Three who worked in weapons and tactics along with Staff Sergeant Danial 'Danno' Byrd of the 10th Special Forces, a communications and electronic surveillance specialist were, in addition to Hospitalman First Class 'Doc' McKeowen trained in medical, demolitions and linguistics, the members of the newly formed Task Force Romeo.

On stand down since helping to crack the secret Ryan code, the TFR team was formed and led by Lt. Commander David Harden an Intel officer and the team's leader, who was now unofficially officially MIA.

"Doc, I'm on leave! My girl just had our baby!" Mac protested.

"Congrats! You sure it's yours?" Doc asked,

"Well yeah . . . ahhh . . . I mean pretty sure it's mine. I didn't find a dew rag or any size twelve Converses under the bed or nothing. You think I should bring him in so you can give him a blood test?"

"Has he got a small dick?"

"Yeah."

"No need. He's yours."

"Wow, thank God that was close!"

"Ray, this is a serious call! How soon can you be back in D.C.?"

"What's going on? We been alerted?"

"Something like that." Doc gave a slight pause. "Need you here yesterday, Mac!"

"Okay Doc if you say so. How's the L.T.?" Ray asked.

"Need you here yesterday, Mac!"

MacDonald was silent for a full half minute before Doc broke back in.

"Come to the Washington Naval Yard, the O Street gate. The L.T. has our new home set up over here in an old warehouse."

"I can leave Norfolk in an hour, be there by fifteen, sixteen hundred the latest. Gear?"

"Bring everything you'll want in the team room. There's a shit load of lockers here already. And be ready to pack a bug-out bag, I'll fill you in once you're here."

"Will do Doc. Be there nagay lap tuc! Mac out!"

McKeowen's next call was to Danno Byrd their commo man and then to Ricky Matson their weapons guru telling them to report to the O Street team room as soon as possible.

Meanwhile Doc set to work on a plan starting with a way to finagle transport over to Beirut.

*** * ***

It was just after 1700 when Mac showed up at the team house having driven up from Virginia.

After giving MacDonald the Reader's Digest version of Dave Harden's situ, Mac immediately agreed they were required to launch a rescue effort. The caveat was Mac and Doc were the sole military assets at present.

"The only fifteen hour direct flight at present is via Air Egypt but Beirut international is a no go area for all commercial air." Doc explained.

"Where's the next closest airfield?"

"The next closest open airport is Haifa in northern Israel. A two-hour drive from the southern Beirut border."

"So we fly into Haifa. Do we need visas?"

"I had Mrs. Gaffney ring the embassy. I told her my older brother wanted to visit the eastern Med."

"You don't have an older brother!"

"So?" Doc defended. Mac sat back and stared.

"So you lied to a sweet, little old lady?"

"Well, she is little and she is old. But yes I lied."

"You're going to hell!" Mac declared.

"Good, I'll be with all my friends. The embassy said no visas required at this time."

"You alert Ricky and Danno?"

"Yes. Danno's coming down from Boston, be here tomorrow and Ricky's coming in from the Dakotas. Be here late tomorrow."

"North or South Dakota?"

"Does it matter?"

"Just askin' Mr. Vaguery! That means the team won't be wheels up until sometime Friday! Which means the bad guys will have had almost a week's head start on us!"

"Allow me to correct you my waterlogged friend! They won't because when Danno and Ricky arrive on station you and I will already be in Indian County finding our missing team member!"

"Did anybody okay this split team concept we're about to undertake?"

"Higher-up was unable to comment because they couldn't be reached." Doc explained.

"So you didn't tell anyone? Director Casey, SOCOM the DOJ folks, nobody?"

"We can respectfully request permission to cross over the border into Lebanon once we're in Haifa. Sometimes it's better to beg forgiveness then ask permission."

"Oh, we're going to Haifa! Good to know. Your balls have definitely grown bigger since we last worked together!"

"Why thank you Ma'am, that's the nicest thing anyone's ever said to me!" McKeowen answered with an exaggerated southern drawl.

"Better reserve an extra seat on that airplane for that nutsack you're haulin' around there Doc!" Mac quipped as, a half an hour later they climbed into the taxi.

**

Their flight departed Dulles in D.C. at 19:30 and was due to arrive in Tel Aviv for a thirty minute passenger exchange then take off again and arrive in Haifa at 05:15 Saturday morning.

"Bernard 'Bernie' Horowitz has a cousin in Tel Aviv." Doc explained on the plane.

"The Jewish drone guy from last year, on board the carrier Lex? On loan from NASA?!" Mac realized aloud.

"Back in September, yes. I tracked him down back in D.C. while I was waiting for you. His cousin Avi is an intel officer in the IDF, he's gonna meet us in Haifa."

Although it was a fifteen-hour flight the seven hours difference, with Israel being seven hours ahead of D.C. put their touch down time in Tel Aviv at 03:30 local. It was just after five when they stepped out of the connecting aircraft onto the Haifa airfield and headed across the tarmac and into the terminal.

"How will we know this guy?" MacDonald asked.

"To tell the truth I don't know. He just said we'll know him when we see —"

Suddenly Mac back-handed Doc on the arm.

"I think I found him!" Mac nodded down the small line if people to a short dumpy guy in jeans, sweatshirt and Ray Bans. He was holding a sign. 'Swartz Limo Service for 'Dr. McKeowen and nurse'.

Doc smiled. Mac didn't.

Greetings were exchanged and the guys were led out to a dark blue, compact Lexus.

Tossing their bags into the back seat, Avi produced a small black device, hung it from the mirror and switched it on.

A tiny, red LED indicated it was operational and Avi started the car.

"Avi, what's with the good luck charm?" Mac asked.

"Anti-spoofer device. Sporadically emits micro-burst signals to block any homing devices that may be tracking us."

"Okay, what the hell's a spoofer?" Doc pushed.

Avi laughed a bit before answering.

"Forgot you Yanks aren't in the loop yet. Since the KAL 007 shoot down your president Reagan has okay'ed GPS for civilian use. But it has to be modified."

"You mean downgraded?" Doc clarified.

"Yes. As a result, the Russians are right on top of it trying to steal whatever they can from western scientists. The reason it's taking some time to down grade the system for civilian distribution is due to having to install security measures to prevent military access." Avi explained.

"Commies stealing technology! Imagine that!" Mac interjected from the back seat.

"So have they gotten anything yet?" Doc asked.

"Apparently not much. Our guys in Moscow have recently discovered they've started to try and establish their own system. The trouble they're running into is a lack of satellites."

"So back to my original question, what the hell's a spoofer?!" Mac pushed.

"Spoofers are able to counter act and confuse any GPS system by detecting a GPS signal, tracing it to its source and then retransmitting it to another location." Avi detailed.

"Like a false echo location device. The way some moths have learned to confuse bats!" McKeowen compared.

"Exactly!"

"So even after the Russians get their own system, you guys'll be able to defeat it?" Mac deduced.

"It's the eternal story of warfare my friends. He who has the technology . . ."

"Where exactly we going?" Mac asked as they pulled into a small hotel parking lot on Na Amat Street.

"I reserved a room so we can set a plan for going into Lebanon, mounting our search and most importantly getting back out!"

"Good thinking Batman!" Mac blurted out.

"Why Batman?" Avi asked.

"Batman! As in Batman and Robin?!"

Avi stared and shrugged.

"Never mind, bad joke." Mac apologized.

"Also I thought you might like to clean up and have a quick meal before we head north." Avi suggested.

Over some sandwiches and coffee their guide quizzed them on details about Lt. Commander

Harden while Doc and Mac in turn probed Avi about the territory ahead as well as the latest intel from Beirut city where they hoped Harden was still being held.

Over a road map laid out on the table Avi filled them in.

"Because of the current negotiations with the Lebanese and the Syrian government for an Israeli forces withdrawal, there is a temporary truce. But it's not likely to hold. So there is one border crossing open into Beirut from here and that is open to day light crossings only. But passage is not free." Their guide explained.

"We are aware of the payola system." Doc informed.

"You have travelled in such territories before? Where you have to pay bandits to obtain passage?"

"Yeah. On vacation in Mexico." MacDonald replied.

"Barring any trouble, how long's the drive?" McKeowen inquired.

"Naharryya is less than an hour north along the coast road. Then its 35 kilometers to Tyre." He pointed out on the map. "From there the Beirut leg is only another forty-five kilometers. But because the Marines are long gone and I have no up-to-date intel on any of the factions, this will be the most dangerous stretch."

Avi slid the car keys across the table to Mac.

"What's this?"

"Keys to the Lexus! You'll have to do the driving from here to Beirut."

"But . . . I've never driven in a foreign country before, much less a hundred kilometers up and back through hostile territory! Well except for that one time I was lost in Korea Town in L A. But –" Avi held his hand up and shrugged.

"I have a TS clearance and so would make a very juicy target for any one of the militia. As a consequence I'm forbidden to travel north of the Israeli border."

"I see."

"However, after you find your commander and if you get in trouble I have arranged for a Shaytet 13 unit to rendezvous with you . . . just here." He pointed on the map. "As a primary exfil point or here about 500 meters away, just north on the other side if the airport." Doc and Mac both noted the locales.

"A couple of last things; there's a tool kit in the boot along with a pair of old Lebanese license plates. Pull over somewhere and change them out before you reach the border. The rental papers have been adjusted to those reg plates as well."

"Anything else?" Doc asked.

"Once you are north of Tyre it's not likely you'll come across any shops still open so, I'd pack some food if I were you."

Forty-five minutes after arriving in the room, just as the sun rose over the Med, Doc and Mac were back on the road.

*****＊*****

CHAPTER TEN

The Naharryya check point was still controlled by the IDF so there was no problem getting through and the Tyre checkpoint, for some reason, appeared to be abandoned but once they were within a few kilometers of the city things picked up quite quickly.

Military traffic began to appear at regular intervals then tapered off. However, they attracted more and more attention the further north they travelled until just short of a kilometer outside the city limits an Israeli command car heading back south slowed down, perused their car and then manned his radio as they passed Doc and Mac observed.

"I think they made us!" Doc observed.

"I agree. We're close enough. I vote we pull over, ditch the car and hoof it into the city!" Mac suggested.

"I second that motion. Grab your bag and let's go."

They pulled well off the road took their civilian rucksacks, locked the car up and started walking gradually drifting off the shoulder and deeper into the suburb of Ghobeiry.

"Fortunately we only have to get within about two klicks of the downtown in an area called the Ghabi. She lives on the outskirts of town in eastern sector." Doc explained.

The hike in to their destination was uneventful as nearly abandoned suburbs gradually gave way to city streets. Out across the Mediterranean the sun was now high on the horizon when Doc knocked on the front door of Mrs. Isra Shaheen's house.

McKeowen politely introduced themselves and briefly explained they were there looking for a friend.

Shaheen wasn't expecting them but, recognizing they were Americans, quickly invited them in off the street and offered tea as they entered the kitchen and took seats at the table.

"Mrs. Shaheen –"

"Call me Isra." She offered as she set the kettle.

"Isra, we believe Dave Harden is –"

"Here in Beirut. Yes, I know." Mac and Doc exchanged surprised glances. "Word on the street has it that a foreigner, probably British or American, is in the city. But there is, as of yet, only speculation why."

"Has he been here?"

"Yes of course he wanted information about the Hezbollah."

"Who?"

"The Hezbollah. A new group of fighters, as if we need another bunch of animals with guns running around the city!" She sat and rolled then lit another cigarette as she spoke. "They hire out their services for money, weapons or services in kind. Mercenaries. Muslims, who hate anyone not Shi'ite."

"He only arrived just over forty-eight hours or so ago so there's a good chance he'll still be in the Beirut area." Doc reasoned.

"Providing he was not kidnapped by another radical Muslim group!" Isra qualified.

"Why do you say that?" Mac asked.

"In that case they would have whisked him away over the mountains and into the Bakaa" Isra opined. "His only chance is for you to find him before they do!"

"We're banking on the fact that due to his rank they will not have killed him yet. He's much more valuable as a hostage."

"The fact that there has been no contact by any group, ransom demands, no public announcements for P.R. exploitation et cetera, could mean he's still anonymous to his kidnappers." Mac suggested.

"Which is a good thing!" Shaheen added.

She related the meet with Monsieur Hinz and his associates which took place earlier.

"Is it possible to re-contact this Mr. Hinz?"

"It would be much faster if I took you to them." She suggested as she rose to take the kettle off the stove.

Doc leaned in and whispered across the table to Mac. "How much money you got on you?"

"A couple of hundred, why?" Mac whispered back. "What for?!" Mac demanded.

Doc nodded over to Shaheen replacing the small bottle of milk in her near empty fridge. Mac complied and passed him the money which Doc folded over and stashed under the sugar bowl on the table.

"Well, I guess we're all set! We'd better skip the tea for now." Doc suggested.

"Very well. I'll get my coat." Shaheen announced.

"Isra, I'd feel a lot better if you stayed here and just rang them. Tell them we're coming. Give us some kind of a pass word or something." Doc signaled MacDonald with raised eyebrows.

"Yes! Yes, me too! I'd feel better about that too, Mrs. Isra." Mac smiled, lifted his rucksack from the floor, dug through it and produced a pair of 9mm's laying them on the table. "Of course, I'd feel a hell-of-a-lot better if we had some 9mm ammo!"

"How in the hell'd you get those past airport security?!" Doc questioned.

"You said, 'bring everything you need'!" He passed a weapon to Doc.

"Plastic Glock 19's!" McKeowen noted checking the action on the one he now held.

"The Austrians gave them to our SEAL team about a year ago to field test. Only the barrel slide and the recoil spring are made of metal. There's a couple of other small springs but we found out they're too small to set off the metal detectors."

"I don't even wanna know where you hid the bullets!" Doc quipped.

"Bullets? We dun need no stinking bullets! It's fucking Beirut Baby! This place makes South Central look like the Hamptons! We'll find ammo!" Mac confidently assured.

Without a word Shaheen reached up into the cupboard then returned to the table to set a large, teddy bear cookie jar between them.

Both men looked up to her and she nodded at the colorful jar.

Doc lifted the lid, reached in and his hand returned with a full box of 9mm Parabellum.

"Told ya we'd find ammo!" Mac boasted.

"Dave told me you were a qualified teacher and journalist!" Doc blurted out.

"I am a qualified teacher. In the old Beirut!" She shot back, the half smoked cigarette dangling from her lower lip.

"Well, looks like you're also qualified to teach in South Central L.A.!" Doc commented. Mac nodded.

"And in Compton and in Detroit and in the South Bronx!" Mac added as he opened the box and started to load the magazines.

Mrs. Shaheen moved to the wall phone, rang up a number and spoke a mixture of French and Arabic for less than a minute. From what Doc could discern she introduced herself to party or parties known to her, asked a few questions then terminated the business-like call.

"I've arranged an escort for you."

"Where exactly are we going?" Doc asked.

"To the headquarters of the Assistant Deputy of the Christian Militia. If your friend is still here he will know who has him."

"Thank you Isra!" Doc offered.

"Don't thank me yet. Finding your friend's whereabouts guarantees nothing. You still have to get him, along with yourselves, out of here. We have over two dozen factions fighting here now and once he is discovered missing all parties on both sides will be hunting you like hounds to the fox!"

"We have a car stashed just south of here in Ghobeiry."

"I assume you left it there more than an hour ago?" She conjectured.

"Yes, why?"

"That car is long gone and is likely being dismantled as we speak."

"Geez! Feels like home already!" Mac quipped.

"There's at least a small chance it hasn't yet been discovered, no?" Doc asked.

"Either that or they haven't had enough time to finish rigging it to detonate when you open the door."

"I hate when that happen!" Mac punned.

Minutes later there was a knock at the door.

Two armed men stood either side of a young boy Doc and Mac both judged to be no more than 15 or so. But as they were shown into the kitchen it was he who initiated the conversation which quickly turned negotiation.

"These are two of my best men. Both have been in this fight since before the '75 offensive. We will escort you to the place we think you may find your friend." The teen dictated more than advised.

"This is Mohammad." Mrs. Shaheen introduced.

"Of course it is!" MacDonald scoffed under his breath.

"We are grateful for your help Mohammad." Doc nodded over to the young man who nodded back.

The boy, decked out like a Sandinistian guerrilla complete with a WWII era Mauser rifle and a cross-shoulder bandolier, led the way out and down the street.

Skirting the Green Line, an arbitrarily agreed upon demarcation which ran north to south through the city center separating the predominantly Christian sector in the east from the predominantly Muslim dominated districts in the west, they continued south through the unimaginable devastation that now replaced the once rivaled glamor of Paris or Berlin.

With one of Mohammad's men on point and the other covering their six, they tactically turned and moved up a narrow street to an area where the American was last reported to have been seen.

They tactically made their way through the streets for over thirty minutes not passing or even seeing anyone else but knowing all the while they were being watched.

"Feel like we're in a fucking Stephan King novel!" Mac commented.

"More like H.G. Wells!" Doc whispered back.

Fully conscious that nightfall was a few hours away, the militia leader fell back and let McKeowen catch up.

"Doctor, I must tell you, if we have not found your friend by dark we must to take cover until —"

Just then a disturbance was heard coming from the second story of one of the windowless, what-appeared-to-be a bombed-out apartment building.

Everyone quickly took cover and drew a bead on the general area the noise came from.

Doc and Mac were back-to-back, pistols pointed a high 45 degrees to each other.

Seconds later more bits of rubble again tumbled down from the adjoining blown out window, everyone adjusted their aim but quickly stood down as Dave Harden's soiled face suddenly popped out from behind the empty window frame.

The patrol swiftly moved into the ground floor of the former hotel building to meet him.

"About time some of you assholes showed up!" Harden snapped as he descended the partially destroyed staircase. "You got any food! I'm fucking starving. Dominoes doesn't deliver on this side of town!"

"Sorry we're late sir. Director Casey wouldn't give us permission to launch a rescue effort." McKeowen informed.

"Why the hell not, God damn it?!"

"Said since you were gone so long you were probably dead and no longer worth risking resources or good men for."

"That why he sent you two?" Harden said as he led the way out. "I need water." Harden bitched. Doc passed him a water bottle from the side of his pack.

Mohammad's men looked puzzled and one of them spoke to the leader in Arabic. The young guide answered in French. Doc translated to Mac.

"They want to know why our commander is angry not happy."

The two escorts looked to their boss for an explanation.

"Américains! Pa juste dans la tête!" Mohammad commented as he stepped over some rubble.

"What'd he say Doc?" Mac asked as they followed on out of the building.

"Americans! Not right in the head."

With Mohammad again in the lead, they headed further south into the Sabtuyeh District and one of the most contested areas of the city at the time.

With one of Mohammad's men again on point and the other taking up the rear, Mac eased up to the young fighter.

"Mohammad, this place is the size of Manhattan, but all the buildings are reduced to rubble. There's no street signs left. Even most of the roads are gone. How can you know where we are, especially in the dark?" Mac pushed.

"Artillery explosions always come from east, near Bakaa. Sound of jets, American, always come from west, from big, flat ship. Artillery on right mean you go north. Artillery on left mean you are heading south."

"What happens if you want to go east?"

"Walk until somebody shoot at you. Then you know you in West Beirut. Turn around and go back."

Using the giant grain towers as a reference point to mentally track their route as they went the Americans noted they were now cautiously heading north, north-west for about forty minutes until they were within sight of the sea then turned back north keeping the sea to their left.

With their local escorts displaying well trained C&C techniques the six of them hunkered down behind an abandoned gas station where Mac took the time to show Mohammad the rendezvous spot they needed to reach on the fighter's own map.

They were now about twenty minutes away from their intended rendezvous near the airport.

Within the next twenty minutes they had made their way across the southern zone of the western sector and to just south of the airfield where the intended exfil point was approximately 300 meters south of the runways.

Across from the two-lane black top which they recognized as Route 51, a man-made jetty served as their reference point.

It was in a small, abandoned and partially destroyed beach resort between the roadway and the sea which served as a temporary rally point for the patrol.

As Mohammad's point man made it across the 100-meter open stretch of road the others double-timed behind.

Several shots rang out when the last man across, the rear guard, cried out and fell to the ground grasping his leg just in the middle of the roadway.

All headed for the small berm on the other side, hit the prone position and carefully scanned from flank to flank.

The wounded militiaman in the middle of the black top road started crawling but was clearly not going to make it across.

The firing came from the lone two-story warehouse back across the road.

"TROIS HEURES! PREMIERE ÉTAGE!" Mohammad yelled out.

"THREE O'CLOCK, FIRST FLOOR!" Doc echoed. "CORRECTION! SECOND FLOOR!" McKeowen repeated by way of translation.

"PICK A FLOOR DOC!" Mac yelled back just as several more shots rang out from the window and bit into the sand around them.

"THAT FLOOR!" Doc yelled over.

Knowing he was well out of range but relying on the muzzle flash in the still shadow light to draw fire and open the target up for the militiamen's rifles to have a better chance of tagging one of the two snipers, Doc aimed high and squeezed off two rounds then dashed out into the open to retrieve the wounded militiaman.

"MAC, GOING OUT!" Doc yelled.

"GO!"

Realizing what was happening the Lebanese adjusted fire and as the rifle rounds pumped at the windows by Mohammad and his troops combined with the twenty seconds it took McKeowen to run to the casualty and drag him back across the road got the casualty out of immediate danger. Once over the berm he passed the casualty's weapon to MacDonald along with a couple of magazines from his LBE and attended to his patient.

Mac did a quick functions check then joined the fire fight.

140

Doc's casualty was hit in both legs above the knees with the right leg a through-and-through and the left leg an entry wound in the median aspect of the left calf only. However, he assessed there were no broken bones.

"You're lucky Bro! Now you will have lots of girls!" Doc declared as he dressed the wounds and administered a shot of morphine from his med kit,

"Je ne comprehends!"

"Maintenant tu vas avoir plein de . . . de filles!"

"Huh?!"

"Beaucoup chatte!" Doc encouraged.

"Ahh Oui!"

Mac reloaded a magazine and joined the other two in defense.

After dressing his wounds and as he was drawing a red 'M' on the fighter's forehead it was without warning, that dozens of chunks of brick work were spit out of the factory façade as the roar of a fifty-caliber resonated over the beach from behind.

Everyone ceased fire and looked around.

A second burst of .50 cal raked across the three factory windows from the west. A splat remained where one of the snipers used to be while, seconds later his fair-weather friend was spotted hang-dropping from a side window and running off back across the field minus his weapon.

Doc signaled to Harden by pointing out to the sea where a pair of Sayetet 13 swift boats were closing in at 45-degree angles from about 300 meters out. Their twin .50's were ripping chunks out of the masonry across the entire row of second story windows as they rooster tailed across the harbor firing intermediate bursts as they closed in on the shore.

The sniper fire was halted but by now, having heard the gunshots, several Muslim fighters had filtered through the surrounding streets and were scurrying to the scene while firing random shots from a distance at the boats.

One of the swift boats launched a twin engine Zodiac over the side as the other covered the maneuver. The half dozen arriving Muslims were clearly organizing while trying to regain and secure the high ground inside the warehouse.

"L.T.! CASUALTY STABILIZED. WE'RE GOING FOR EXFIL!" McKeowen yelled out.

"DO IT!" Came Harden's response.

Several AK's now bristled from the windows across the road. But only briefly.

A Bell AH-1 Cobra hovered at wave top level three hundred meters offshore for less than a minute before firing one Hellfire missile to transform the warehouse into a rubble strewn parking lot.

Minutes later everyone was loaded aboard two Zodiacs and zipping out to the furthest swift boat to be safely transported five miles offshore to the *U.S.S. Kennedy*.

"We have no money but take these." In route Mac offered the two plastic Glocks to the militia leader. "They take standard 9mm but treat then nice! You won't be able to find spare parts for another couple of years!"

142

The young rebel leader smiled and tanked him.

******

Aboard the Kennedy Harden, McKeowen and the militiamen were met by the Officer of the Deck, who had a medical team standing by to transport the casualty to surgery and the Assistant Ops Boss who was sent down from Command and Control to verify everyone's identity.

"Sir, this intel officer has been MIA for nearly three days behind enemy lines without food or water." Doc informed.

"And who are you exactly?"

"I'm Special Ops Medic McKeowen and this is Petty Officer First Class Ray MacDonald of SEAL Team Three. We were sent in to find the Lieutenant Commander and get him to safety. I'm sure the debrief we have for you can wait until he's properly fed and cleaned up."

The Assistant Ops Boss, a greying Lieutenant with a well-trimmed beard, noted Harden's ragged appearance, thought for a moment then glanced at the OOD and decided it was alright.

"Call up to the C&C . . ." The Asst, Ops Boss instructed. ". . . and relay to the Skipper we're on the way up. Then send a runner down to the galley and have them send up three –"

"Cough, cough!" Harden interrupted as he held up five fingers.

"And have them send up **five** meals!" He amended.

Upstairs in the C&C the guys were greeted by the C.O. and surprised by the order to hold all conversation until they retired in privacy to the officer's mess.

But before they could begin their story the C.O. pulled a telex from his top pocket and brandished it about.

"Apparently you fellas are quite popular at the moment back in D.C. Please tell me your being here isn't about to get me in the shit!"

The trio exchanged glances before Harden answered.

"Sir, I volunteered to do a recon of the Beirut area and infilled three days ago."

"I remember, you're the ghost we had on board for a couple of hours last Wednesday." The captain recalled.

"Yes sir. My mission was to contact a potential asset, obtain some information and return. But it got complicated."

"Were you able to contact your asset?"

"With all due respect sir, I can't really discuss any aspect of the operation to personnel not directly involved."

"I understand. Well then, I am ordered to pass on to you that I received word from D.C. that you are to contact the Pentagon as soon as anyone heard from you Lt. Commander."

"Anyone sir?"

Several orderlies arrived with the five food trays and two pitchers of fruit juice.

The four settled onto a nearby table and Harden assaulted his three plates of bacon and eggs by dumping all three onto one plate, smothering the pile in ketchup and black pepper then, ignoring the other three staring at him, attacked what looked like a mangled pile of the West German flag. The captain continued.

"Apparently they sent out a Med-wide telex from Admiral Train of Atlantic Fleet Command Stamped Sec Nav from the DoD. Doesn't get much higher than that." The skipper studied Harden's face for a reaction. Save for chewing and swallowing there was none. "I gather your mission has quite a high priority?"

"To say . . . the least . . . Captain." He replied in between chewing. "In that event . . . can I request you send back the code word Waldo Located?"

"'Waldo Located', I'll order it done as soon as soon as we're done here."

"Thank you, sir."

"Additionally, I am ordered to inform you that you have one hour to clean yourself up and report to the aft flight deck."

"Alone sir?"

"Negative. Any 'stray' elements," He nodded over to Doc and Mac, ". . . you may have collected along the way are to accompany you."

"Am I at liberty to ask our destination sir?" Dave inquired.

"You can ask Lt. Commander, but I can't tell you. All they told us is south into Israel."

Harden sat back eyeing Mac's food tray.

When Two Tribes Go To War

"You gonna eat that bacon?" He asked.

"No, it's cold." Mac replied. A minute later Harden swallowed the last bit of bacon.

****

CHAPTER ELEVEN

Mosque of the Shrine of
Imam ali Bin abi Talib
Najaf Governorate
Central Iran

A t 175 kilometers directly south of Bagdad across the desert and one kilometer west of the Euphrates River the ornate Shrine of the Imams is believed to be the place where Allah will come to raise the dead on judgement day.

The Ayatollah Khomeini once taught there, it houses the graves of many of the prominent imams and apart from Mecca and Medina, it is considered the most sacred holy place in the world, for the Shia Muslims.

With the territory surrounding the shrine inundated with at least two dozen other mosques the area is seen by some as the Vatican of the Muslim world.

By those who study the Middle East, it is believed to be the place where the concept of 'Hezbollah' was hatched by a small group of radicals studying at the Mosque of the Imam Ali Mosque in Najaf who were dissatisfied with any diplomatic efforts with the west and who favoured increased violence to force capitulation from the west.

After arriving outside the brightly lit holy grounds by Mercedes limousine early that evening from the airfield two kilometers away Ali Akbar Aminpur, now flanked by Hajj Radwan, who was directly responsible for taking of over 100 hostages and his brother-in-law Mustafa Badreddine, master bomb maker, they strode across the open courtyard toward the tile encrusted main building of the mosque shrine.

Dressed in their black thawb tunics these men were just three of the reasons the most high-profile terrorist of the time, Yasser Arafat, slept in a different place every night.

Israeli Defence Minister Ariel Sharon having recently bombed their terrorist installations in Lebanon in retaliation for the botched assassination attempt on his ambassador to London gave more fuel to their hatred and so added impetus to their current 'mission'.

The golden yellow, inverted Umayyad teardrop dome glistened brightly as they entered the grounds but was offset by the garish blue, red and green neon lights lending a circus-like aura to the holy shrine.

Despite the evening hour a plethora of tourists milled about the neon lit courtyard as the three passed by the towering, herring bone-tiled minaret and entered an iwan to the right and followed it down to a hallway on the left where a descending staircase took them to a below ground warren of hallways. They headed straight to an office they obviously knew well.

As above in the mosque area, the below ground narrow hallways were punctuated with Arabic calligraphy along the tiled walls, floor and ceiling which contrasted with the plushly carpeted floors.

At the end of one of the hallways they came to a young man at a small desk who greeted them warmly.

"A salam a laikum." Akbar greeted.

"A laikum salaam." The young man returned. "The Imam is expecting you." He waved the men in as he opened the door.

No one paid any mind to the janitor sweeping and mopping down the tiled floor at the other end of the long, narrow hallway.

"Brother Akbar! God's greetings to you!" The elderly imam offered as they entered the room.

"And to you most holy man!" He shook hands vigorously with the Imam then placed the holy man's hand to his own fore head. "I hope you are well."

"I am well but not as well as you have been Mr. Akbar Aminpur! Some of the villagers are already singing songs about you and your victories against the American infidels!"

"Thank you, holiness."

"Why so down my brother?" Imam enquired.

"You have no doubt heard of the retaliation by the Russians?" Akbar asked.

"Yes, unfortunate business! We should stay away from their people in future. They have a different mentality than the Anglos! The Russians are animals!"

"Worse yet they have extended their retributions." Akbar added.

"How so?" He asked as they all took seats on the cushion festooned floor.

"The offer of missiles they agreed to sell us which we planned to arm Gaza and the southern Lebanese territories with has been withdrawn."

"I see! When did you find out?" He asked with obvious concern.

"The day before yesterday. Our Washington/American contact overheard a diplomat at a party speaking with a Ukrainian."

"Have you verified this information?"

"Yes, indirectly. We sent a message to our Russian cutout a week ago and have received no word back."

"Did you send them the usual 'it was a splinter group' cover story?"

"Yes. And they have yet to answer. They have never taken more than one or two days to respond."

"Perhaps they are getting used to that excuse or actually know who committed the kidnapping of their diplomats."

"They sent only this." Akbar passed a folded over note across the table.

The Imam immediately recognized and read the Qu'ran passage aloud.

"'Verse 40:19'. Allah does not guide the plan of betrayers!'" He nodded. "They know." He added.

"Yes. Given this development we have other but less effective targets we are considering." Akbar pushed. The Imam thought for a moment.

"I'm sorry we have failed imam."

"You have not failed! And not to demean your accomplishments! You have done very well! The

150

cowardly president Reagan wasted no time in calling his marines home after you hit them a blow, they will not recover from any time soon!"

"I fear we have put you in a difficult position Imam."

"Not necessarily. But I have to tell you that the bulk of the U.N. humanitarian aid has been ear marked to buy ammunition and uniforms for the Republican Guard." The Imam informed. "However, if you are willing to do some work for the Chinese . . ."

"Of course! They too have Katyushas!" Akbar realized.

"I'll contact their embassy in Tehran and request a meeting. Meanwhile have you drawn up the list of feasible targets the Council has asked for?"

Akbar reached into his shoulder bag, produced a handwritten list of several one or two-word items and passed it to the Imam who perused it.

"Ambitious I must say! You think you can actually hit one of their desalination plants?"

"Actually, we already did but the charges were discovered and disarmed by the Jewish SAPIR's before they could detonate."

"A car bomb in front of the Immigration Bureau building? Why, strategically speaking I mean?" The Imam questioned.

"With the aim of further disrupting the Lebanese infrastructure to undermine their attempts at stabilizing their government and to show the world that we are in control of what happens in Beirut."

"And this petro-chemical plant? Is it not located a bit close to Gaza? There might be contamination spread?"

"It is a bit close to the two schools and the hospital, but we have a plan to notify them to evacuate in time plus *al Manar* and our source at the BBC will run the story that hints at faulty Israeli workmanship in the generator room."

"I'm not sure about the potential casualties in the Gaza." Imam challenged.

Akbar's immediate impulse was to argue his true feelings, to wit; any Arabs who died due to a chemical leak in Israel would be worth the sacrifice on two counts. First, they would die for the cause and secondly their deaths, if blamed on the Jews, would increase hatred for them and possibly even bring new recruits to the PLO, Hamas or even to Hezbollah. However he refrained from expressing his rebuttal.

"Several of our members have raised that same concern Imam. But it's still in debate."

"Well, you and your men have certainly proven yourselves these last months. But if I am to approach the Grand Council for more money and to ask them to allow me to contact the Chinese, I'm certain they will want some input on target selection and acquisition. You know the other holy men, myself included, are not comfortable working with communists of all people."

"Actually, we are nearly set to execute a major operation before the end of the year. We are currently in the final stages of planning."

"You have my ear."

"I am sworn to absolute secrecy until we have all the elements assembled, but I can tell you that what we have in mind will make a big splash on the international stage!"

"How big, exactly?"

"Bigger than the Munich Operation!"

Outside the room the janitor quickly moved his ear away from the door, grabbed his mop and bucket and scurried up the stairs before they exited.

*** * ***

"A CH-53 Sea Stallion has a max distance of 540 nautical miles with a cruising speed of 150 knots." Mac shouted over the roar of the rotor blades. "I've been watching our flight time since we left the carrier."

Doc and Harden, now in clean clothes garnered from the *U.S.S. Kennedy's* unclaimed laundry, listened intently. "All we have to do is note how long our in-flight time is, times it by the average in-flight speed, about ninety miles per hour, and we can know where we are!" He proudly deduced.

Doc leaned into Mac who sat closest to the pilots and wore the only spare headset.

"Why not just ask the pilot? Just a wild guess but, he probably knows where we're headed." Doc suggested.

Mac sat back, stared and drew a blank face but eventually leaned in and asked the co-pilot before calling back to Doc.

"Some guy named Ben Green's place." Mac called back to the other two.

"It's Ben Gurion Einstein! It's in Tel Aviv." McKeowen corrected.

After lifting off from the ship it was just over two hours later that they touched down in Tel Aviv where they were met by Bernard 'Bernie' Horowitz in an unmarked IDF sedan and driven to Mossad headquarters where they were signed in, given I.D. badges and escorted down to the Political Action & Liaison Branch.

As opposed to the spacious, modern briefing rooms at Langley this room was little more than a spacious but low ceilinged, concrete bunker with steel tables and chairs.

"It's like a dungeon down here!" Mac quietly declared as they stepped off the elevator into the moderately lit space.

"If you were hit with missile attacks ten or fifteen times a month, you'd want your critical infra structures in concrete as well!" Harden shot back.

"Point taken sir." MacDonald conceded.

They were escorted into a smaller, sound proofed conference room and seated at an eight-place table. A five-foot-wide screen of some description hung at the front of the room which also featured a podium with a flexi-microphone off to one side and an overhead projector.

"We are waiting for Director-General Admoni's representative to join us for your debrief Lt. Commander." Their escort informed.

"My debrief?"

"Yes sir. No one told you?" He asked.

"Yes, you did. Just now!" Doc and Mac fought back smirks.

"Director Admoni sent a request to Director Casey yesterday and he decided rather than delay with two separate briefs on your mission it would be better if-"

"Yeah, yeah, I get it." Harden quickly snapped as he shot the other two a quick glance. They both immediately engaged in fake busy work adjusting their packs on the floor and removing their jackets.

"So who's this Colonel?" Harden asked.

"Deputy Head Colonel Naheem. The Colonel will be able to answer any questions you may have sir."

"Anything else we should know Mr. Horowitz?"

"No sir. I'll leave you gentlemen to it. I've been temporarily transferred too *Operation Harpoon*."

"What's that?" Mac asked.

"It's a new initiative to intercept and destroy terrorist money making operations." Bernie Horowitz explained.

"Tell your boss to talk to the folks in Congress! They know how to disrupt billions per year!" Doc quipped.

"Gentlemen your teleconference is due to start in ten minutes. Best of luck" As Bernie began to leave two others entered the room.

A tall, statuesque, dusky blond woman in uniform came in accompanied by an enlisted soldier. She sat a thick folder on the table. Whether out of common courtesy or to get a better look, the men stood. Most likely to get a better look.

Bernie moved back into the room.

"Lieutenant Commander Harden meet Colonel Kristina Naheem of Israeli Intelligence, Deputy Head of Political Action & Liaison Branch." Bernie introduced.

"Pleased to meet you Lieutenant Commander." She offered her hand and they shook. "This Rabat is Corporal Grier, my very efficient aid."

At five foot nine her dusky blond hair rolled into a tight bun on the back of her head and piercing green eyes the Americans were compelled to stare longer than etiquette dictated.

Her light green beret was folded over and stuck under the left epaulette of her light blue blouse contrasting against her dark blue skirt. But no one noticed her uniform.

Just then a high pitched, telephone-like tone sounded several times in succession filling the room and signaling the tele-conference was about to start.

Naheem nodded to Horowitz who acknowledged her.

"Yes Colonel." He answered and left closing the sound proofed door over behind him.

The others retook their seats as Naheem moved to the podium, manned a remote and answered the call.

Mac quickly went to work scribbling out a note and passing it to Doc.

Somebody took Michelle Pfeiffer's head and put it on Lynda Carter's body!

Only hotter! Doc scribbled back.

At first the date and time flashed on in the upper left-hand corner of the large screen: *11:00 TelAv-*

156

18:00 D.C. followed by a pixelated, black and white picture which began to blossom across the wall screen then slowly saturated with color.

"Colonel, Director Casey here. Did my men make contact?"

"Yes Director. Lt. Commander Harden, Doctor McKeowen and Mr. MacDonald have just arrived."

"Ahhh, Colonel, I'm not actually a doctor." Doc quietly inserted which garnered a nod from Naheem.

"And I'm a navy SEAL!" Mac added. He was ignored.

"Lt. Commander, how you holding up son?" Casey asked. Harden looked around for a microphone.

"Just speak to the screen Commander." The colonel instructed.

"Quite well Director, thank you for asking. I think I have some useful information for you."

Under pressure and heavily influenced by a strong suspicion that a terrorist attack of some description was imminent which he was loath to reveal without proof, Lt. Commander Dave Harden opened his debriefing with the requisite formality but no introduction.

In attendance over in D.C. that morning were William Casey for the CIA, George Schultz representing the State Department and General Lincoln D. Faurer of the NSA all accompanied by their first tier aides.

Casey took the time to inform the group that the president was due to attend but was out of town on a fund raiser and would be briefed later by Casey and Schultz.

Harden dove right in.

"Sirs, for all intents and purposes the city we knew as Beirut no longer exists. Those who could have gotten out already did and those that remain are subsisting on a day-to-day basis. Hand-to-mouth at best."

"They're getting millions in international aid!" General Faurer countered.

"With all due respect general, the warring factions are getting millions in aid. Conservative estimates are that the residents who are trapped there are lucky if they see a tenth of what is sent in aid." The consternation in the room was palatable. "The family of four that hid me the first night I was there had half a dozen cans of vegetables in their cupboard, hadn't seen a loaf of bread in over a month and had no regular access to clean water. The night before I arrived they lost their oldest son. He was shot stealing food from a sparsely stocked local store. The only one in the neighborhood not yet bombed out."

"Lt. Commander Harden," General Faurer interrupted. "We all sympathize with the residents of Beirut and the sons they've lost. May I remind you the allies have lost upwards of three hundred soldiers, sailors and marines trying to bring peace to that area?"

Harden rested both hands on the table and hung his head.

158

"Sirs, permission to speak freely." He softly requested.

"Permission granted." Schultz blurted out.

"Mr. Secretary, Director, General, gentlemen . . . I apologise for my diversion from the subject at hand. We are all painfully aware of the fact that there will be never, ever be peace in the Middle East. EVER! If we are not, we should be."

"Are you saying give it all up?" General Faurer again challenged.

"No, I'm not saying that. Not saying that at all."

"What then?"

"It is my considered opinion, after being involved on the intel level for several years, and now having talked with locales on the ground first-hand, that we should focus our energies on containing the terrorist elements to their respective territories. Whatever that cost."

"Harden what are you trying to tell us son?" Casey pushed. "That all that we accomplished by losing those marines is to embolden the terrorists?! In essence by showing them that, what in their minds is a paper tiger, can be defeated?"

"Negative sir. All I'm saying is hit them hard or get out!"

"You telling us you think we made them stronger?" Faurer challenged.

"When a new kid enters the school yard, he's gonna get picked on."

"You can hardly argue we're new to the Mid-East!" Schultz added.

"Not us sir. This new terror group, the Hezbollah."

"Hez-bo-laa?" Faurer repeated.

"Yes sir. Additionally, through our guys in operations as well as various field sources we know they get increases in funding the more westerners they kill and the more property they destroy. Kind of a reward-incentive system ergo I believe we should expect an attack on America directly."

"When?"

"Soon."

"Where?"

"As of now sir we have no clue. However, I believe we've discovered the main terrorist group, who form, use and dissolve front groups like the Islamic Jihad Organization, much like the tactic the Allies used during the Second War by falsely labelling units with higher numbers like the 101st Division when in reality there were only about 90, 91 divisions in total."

"Are we talking the same IJO that took out the Marine barracks?" Faurer asked.

"With all due respect general, there is no Islamic Jihad Organization. The IJO is Hezbollah. The IJO are a lose bunch of thugs, guns-for-hire akin to the Mafia's Murder Inc. back in the day, only not as professional. As I said earlier, they are the same thugs that the GSG9 took out during the Turkish airlines stand-off a few years back."

"Any clue where they're headquartered?"

160

"From what I could gather and the satellite images the Agency has them centered in the Bakaa Valley in the eastern border of Lebanon. My point is they will strike again as long as they have an excuse,"

"What kind of excuse do you mean Commander?"

"A perceived reproach or insult. Any trace of foreign troops in or around the Valley, or in Lebanon for that matter. There's little doubt in my mind they intend to conquer Lebanon and make it their own no matter what it takes. They have no intention of following any rules we've played by before. They really believe they're fighting and dying for a super god!"

"Go on." Casey pushed.

"Our intel confirms everything the Commander has reported so far Director." Naheem concurred.

"As near as I can figure Director," Harden continued without notes. "Hezbollah emerged during the opening chaos of Lebanon's civil war somewhere in the mid to late Seventies. As the Lebanese factions, Palestinians, Syrians, and various proxy powers destroyed the country, the ground was fertile for Iran's post-1979 revolutionary leaders to demonstrate that their example could be replicated elsewhere in the Arab world."

"Nothing succeeds like success!" Faurer interjected.

Colonel Naheem picked up the narrative.

"Exactly general! By a few individuals exploiting the long-standing grievances of Lebanon's Shiite Muslim underclass they were able to establish a solid base of cult followers who felt the PLO and other

161

terrorist groups were not going far enough in their subversive activities."

"How in hell did it get to be so messy?!" Faurer asked.

"In the complicated balance of the so-called 'confessional system', sir. As you no doubt know, it was a system adopted in 1943 after Lebanon's independence. Government positions were allocated according to religious sect." She continued. "These were apportioned by the demographic weight of each group as reflected in a now wildly and completely outdated 1932 census that, given the political implications for Lebanon's shrinking Christian population, has never been updated."

"Okay, major political screw up! But where did these Hezbollah guys come from exactly?" Schultz pushed.

"They were essentially founded by three . . . three radical student clerics is best how I can describe them. An Imad Mughniyeh, Mohammad Hussein & and one Ali Akbar Aminpur, probably the ringleader. We think he may be a failed cleric as a way into the upper echelons of Muslim society. Sorry there are no photos as of yet available. He's pretty careful about avoiding photos."

"Let me guess, hairy, fat with beards all of 'em!" Faurer quipped.

As Naheem spoke she reached for her folder, leafed through it and pulled a thin stack of black and white surveillance photos. She slid them over to Harden.

"Bill, see about getting with Lt. Commander's Mossad asset and see what they can furnish us!" Schultz instructed.

"Will do George." Casey responded.

"Already done Mr. Secretary." Harden informed. "The good Colonel has just furnished us a set of surveillance photos. Quite impressive photos actually!" He commented as he shuffled through them.

"I'll have them sent over to you Director Casey." Naheem said.

"Much obliged Colonel."

"We should have a classified dossier there by diplomatic pouch before noon tomorrow." She assured.

"How'd you come by your information Mr. Harden?"

"Two of my TFR team, McKeowen and MacDonald liaised with a Mossad contact, a Bernard 'Bernie' Horowitz. They then followed up after my exfil. I've sent a memo request up through channels to list Horowitz as a cleared contact."

"I'll see that it's approved." Casey informed.

"Thank you Director. The other two," Harden continued, ". . . are Mohammad Hussein & Ali Akbar Aminpur. Unfortunately, at this early-stage information is very limited on any of them and it's highly likely they are travelling under aliases. But this guy Imad Mughniyeh, I'll get the research people over at Langley working on him as soon as I get back. Looks like he could be the intel and information guy of the gang."

"Tell us what you do know then." Schultz urged.

"These people are beyond fanatical! You think the Japs on the Pacific islands were bad during the Second War? You think the fact that their soldiers were witnessed tossing Chinese babies in the air and catching them on their bayonets was an atrocity? These people we are facing would make baby tossing an Olympic sport! I'm convinced they are infected with a super strain of sadism. It actually gives them pleasure to kill anyone they see as an 'infidel'."

"Anything else we should know Commander?" A slightly disgusted Faurer pushed.

"Other than that, they condone female circumcision, honor killing women accused of pre-marital sex and pedicide? No that's about it." Harden concluded.

"Sounds like they hate everything and everybody that doesn't conform to their mentality." Casey observed.

"They are our worst nightmare. Seventh Century killer mentalities armed and equipped with modern technology." Faurer added.

"Exactly General." Harden reinforced.

"These guys sound like they make the three hundred years of the Spanish Inquisition look like a day at the beach!" Director Casey blurted out.

"Aside from my recommendation of containment I suggest we consider focusing some resources on scanning the horizon for any suspicious activity, particularly anything that might indicate a domestic attack."

"Sort of a head-them-off-at-the-pass type of strategy?" Schultz paraphrased.

"Well sir, it's certainly not my place to set policy but yes, exactly Mr. Secretary!"

"Like what for instance?" Secretary Schultz queried.

"Like a task force, for instance. One dedicated to hunting these people and their supporters down." Harden shrugged.

"A task force?!" Secretary Schultz, who was by now fully aware of Harden's TFR team, mockingly declared. "Good idea Commander Harden! When can you start?"

"Well . . . I . . . ah . . ."

"Excellent! I knew you were the right man for the job! I'll expect the rough outline of a plan on my desk by day after tomorrow." Schultz said as he stood to leave his aid trailing behind. Good-byes were exchanged with the others.

As he passed by Casey leaned into the screen to address Harden who had flopped back into his chair in exasperation.

"You walked right into that one son!" The Director whispered.

"Question Director?"

"Shoot!"

"The rest of my team sir? Byrd and Matson?"

"They're wheels up as we speak with an ETA of 0200 local. You'll join up and set up a temp op room at the Rabin military base there in Tel Aviv. All the details have been provided by your Mossad liaison."

"Who would that be sir?"

"Colonel Naheem I believe." Naheem and Harden nodded and traded smiles. "I'm sure we'll get along just fine. I'll do my best Director Casey."

"Harden, this work is critical. You did a good job last year on the RYAN thing but that was an international effort. You had lots of back-up. This one's all on you! My guys are tied up trying not to lose any more agents in other theaters of operation, Faurer's people are babysitting the Reds and the FBI . . . well, let's not talk about the FBI."

"I understand sir."

"And Harden, I want you to work closely with the colonel!"

"I'm sure there's a lot we can learn from one another sir." He glanced over at Naheem as she was flipping through her folder and replacing the photos.

"Colonel Naheem, thank you for sending us that info."

"My pleasure sir. I'm sure we'll talk again Director, Shalom."

"Harden, message me when you have something. Casey out."

"Will do sir. Harden out."

The wall screen went dark and Naheem manned the table top phone and dialled the switchboard.

"Operator? This is Colonel Naheem at the P n' A Liaison Branch. Can you ring the motor pool for me please? I need a vehicle to transport two service members to the officers' barracks at Mahaneh Rabin. Yes, I'll have them upstairs waiting." She went to the door and summoned Corporal Grier. "Rabat, there's

166

a jeep coming over from the motor pool. Escort these two soldiers to the officers' quarters over at the Mahaneh Rabin and get them three-"

"Colonel." Dave interjected as he held up five fingers.

"Make that five billets and chow passes."

"Ken, gvirt'ee." He replied.

"Catch up to you guys later." Harden bade them as he and Naheem left together.

"Meet us at the chow hall at 1800!" She instructed.

"Yes ma'am!" MacDonald shot back as they left.

Corporal Grier saluted Mac and Doc as they stepped out of the room.

"You don't have to salute us, we're enlisted." Doc said.

"Leave the kid alone!" Mac elbowed Doc. "We're in his country, we do it his way!" As he returned the salute.

****

Kristina Naheem invited Harden to take a tour of the facility but he suggested they get a late lunch somewhere nearby first. She agreed and took them to a place called *New York Pizzeria* just off Dizengoff Street.

As it was late afternoon they easily found an isolated booth in the back where they could talk.

Ten minutes later Harden cut into and took the first bite of his plate-sized pizza Margarita. He immediately spit it back out onto his plate then looked down at his plate of pizza and stared.

"I don't know what part of New York these guys learned to make pizza in, but . . ."

Naheem looked over and laughed.

"I'm sorry! I forgot to tell you. It comes with uncooked cheese. Most people in this district are strict orthodox."

She took his plate back up to the counter and in Hebrew explained he wasn't orthodox.

A few minutes later she returned with a properly cooked plate of pizza and sat down to her large tuna salad.

You think they'll take your advice? I mean regarding how to approach this new threat?" She asked partially out curiosity but mostly out of professional probing to enhance her after action report to her boss.

"No! Casey and Shultz might but the interim politicians will do whatever is best for their individual careers. Our government rarely displays the backbone required to do what's necessary to deal with a serious terrorist attack much less a mere threat. How do you suppose such bad guys get a foothold in the local populace?" He probed regarding the Hezbollah.

"Essentially . . ." She shrugged as she ate. "The same way the gangsters got a foothold in Chicago or New York in the last century. Luciano for example, when things were bad in the Thirties and after, especially during the Depression, he offered an alternative to the people."

"The Italian gangsters were hardly terrorists!" Harden argued.

"Terrorism is defined as taking political power by force and intimidation, is it not? Did these gangsters not assassinate people or set car bombs?"

"Good point." He responded.

"The Italian gangsters in America were born of the Sicilian gang wars. Capone personally applied very little force and intimidation himself but paid others to do it. Much as Akbar and his henchmen now pay the fake front of the IJO and others to kill who they are told to by the Imams of Iran. The imams, same as the capos of the Mafia, pay Akbar to kill the enemies of Iran. The only elements to distinguish them from the American gangsters are that their actions are on a much bigger scale, they are primarily using race as a motivating factor and therefor money is not their ultimate goal."

"What is then?"

"Conquest! Also, they kill without respite for women, children or the elderly. Most gangsters considered it dishonourable to kill women and children."

"Wow! You make history come alive!" Harden chuckled at his own joke. She didn't. "I'm sorry! That was out of line!" He apologised. "You know quite a bit about American history!" He complimented as penance.

"The IDF paid for my master's degree. I did graduate school in New York at City University, Long Island."

"Doc McKeowen our SF medic did time there."

"We are supposed to be trading notes on Hezbollah Lt. Commander!"

"Yes of course." He finished his coffee and adjusted his seat. "Okay, so, they're basically gangsters on steroids. I can see that. Please continue."

"In regard to your inquiry as to how such bad guys got a foothold in the locals? As opposed to the corruption and cronyism of traditional Lebanese leaders, Hezbollah cultivated an image of crisp efficiency and honesty. By the early 1980's, when Hezbollah's initial manifesto was made public calling for, among other things, the establishment of an Iran-style Islamic republic in Lebanon, the group was already notoriously known internationally for its methods of simultaneous suicide attacks."

"And for its hostage-taking all later copied by other terrorist groups!" He added.

"Exactly. Now starting to draw on an extensive expatriate Lebanese Shiite population in Latin America and Africa, Hezbollah is mastering the criminal links of smuggling, money-laundering, and drug trafficking."

"Wait, wait a minute! Your people have evidence of money-laundering, drug trafficking and operations in Latin America?!" He quietly challenged.

"Lt. Commander Harden, while your people argue about racial injustice, proper pronouns, if women should be in combat and whether or not the quality of toilet paper is best sold by dancing, singing cats or by a picture perfect housewife squeezing it, we Israelis are taught meritocracy from childhood. We have had women serving since the birth of our nation and can only hope that the latest Hamas, al Qaida or Hezbollah rocket attack hasn't destroyed the last of our essential food supplies!" She finished her salad and pushed the plate away. "Additionally we don't have to fight our way through a fresh brigade of politically correct politicians every few years who pay only lip service to combating terrorism."

"I take your point but . . . in America's defence, it was a woman who sewed our first flag! Sooooo . . . as far as women's rights, we have that going for us!"

At first angered at what she misinterpreted as flippancy, Naheem began to realize that Harden was only trying to lighten the mood and decided to reciprocate by becoming less tense.

"Most importantly for Iran," She continued. "Hezbollah-affiliated fighters, backed by Russian air power, have started to play an increasing roll, actually an essential part of Bashar al-Assad's survival in Syria."

"Casey will see that as very valuable information! Thank you. Do your people have fighter types or numbers assigned?"

"No, we have no satellite assets we can dedicate to the tasking."

"I'll run it by the guys at Langley, Bashar al-Assad's Order of Battle is something they're working on. They'll be interested to know more so I think they'll be glad to share some sat shots with your folks."

"Thank you that would go a long way to helping our ground troops. As I was saying, for Iran, Hezbollah is becoming a malevolent version of the Swiss Army knife, with special capabilities always at the ready for distinct tasks."

"So, Hezbollah has worked their way up the feeding chain to become a force multiplier for Iran and as such –"

"As such a significant threat to Israel, yes." She added.

An hour later they were back at her office rounding off a short tour of the unclassified spaces of the Mossad branch.

"I was told there was a defector who surrendered to you on the birder?"

"Yes. Would you like to interview him?"

"Hell yes!"

Naheem pressed her intercom and issued a request in Hebrew. Someone answered in the affirmative.

A short few minutes later, dressed in what appeared to be street clothes, the defector and former Bill Buckley asset was escorted into an interrogation room by an armed guard where the colonel and Harden were waiting.

Naheem nodded and the guard stepped outside.

Harden gave him the once over and noted he had not been physically abused and appeared well fed and rested.

"Does he speak English?" Harden asked Naheem.

"Yes, I know English, French and Farsi." The prisoner responded.

"English will do. You operated in Bill Buckley's cell, yes?"

"Yes. He was good man. It is bad we lose him."

"Can you tell me what happened?"

"Kidnapped from the street by Hezbollah. We tell him many times, 'Buckley it is very bad you walk always by yourself. You need be more careful! Maybe have some bodyguard or something. Beirut is not sunny California! Many enemies here! We say to him but, he don't listen."

"How did you escape Beirut?"

"I walk. Mostly in the night."

"He surrendered on the northern border. We're holding him pending vetting." The Naheem added.

"What can you tell me about Hezbollah?"

"Not so much. There is one man, he work in very important mosque near Bagdad, many imams. He is Arab Christian but they don't know this. He work as . . . as how do you say? Man who fix and clean things?"

"Janitor?"

"Yes, janitor. Hezbollah kill his father so he help us in fight. In March he send some information from meeting with three terrorists and one imam."

"Do you know what the meeting was about?"

"About targets." Harden's eyes widened as he glanced over at the colonel.

"Targets?!"

"Yes." He affirmed. "Was only general target list, bridge, government buildings, maybe airports."

"So they were there to ask the imams for money to hit a target?"

"Yes, more money. But I think Imams and Hezbollah leaders don't truly trust each other."

"Why do you say that?"

"Messenger say Hezbollah say to Imam, 'we have target in mind'. When Imam ask, 'which target?' Hezbollah leaders say, 'can't tell you yet'. Imam, he don't like this."

"Is it still possible to communicate with this messenger? You have a code name for him?"

"Don't know. Buckley always do messages."

Harden traded glances with Naheem.

"Is there anything else you can tell me?"

"Thank you for your help." Harden said by way of ending the interrogation. Naheem signalled the guard to collect the detainee and take him back. "I hope there can be peace in our lands someday." Harden imparted as he was led out.

"Peace in this place? Only way will be peace in this part of world will be when comes Armageddon!" He snapped as the guard escorted him out.

"He seemed cooperative." Harden casually commented.

"Yes, so far."

"What will happen to him?"

"That will be up to the director. Normally we keep prisoners indefinably until there's a truce exchange or some other development. But he wasn't a belligerent to Israel so I venture he will eventually be let go. Possibly under the classified relocation program."

****

CHAPTER TWELVE

Boris Solomatin's Office
Lubyanka Building
KGB Headquarters, Moscow

The residents at 1600 Pennsylvania Avenue were by no means the only folks in a major capital monitoring and involved in the now nine-year-old Lebanese civil war.

Virtually every government within 1000 miles of the Levant, the Kremlin included, had a vested interest in the war. After all it was the Soviets who invented Yasser Arafat and his PLO some of the prime instigators of the war. Although widely unrealized at the time Arafat had built his terrorist organization to appear to be seeking legitimacy while in reality viewing the broken country of Lebanon as a prize he and his minions could take over, move in to and set up house in.

Both D.C. and the Kremlin were fully aware of these intentions. The Kremlin through the KGB and collaboration and Washington through CIA intercepts, moles and the defection and rescue of Oleg Gordievsky just last year.

Now with the furor of the endless boycotts and embargos against Russia as retaliation for the KAL 007 shoot down appearing to subside somewhat, more attention could be paid to the Middle East.

Paddy Kelly

✱

Nagatino-Sadovniki District
Central Moscow

Since he accepted Director Chebrikov's offer of forming a new department of the KGB dedicated to monitoring U.S. activities in the European Theatre, particularly the Middle East, Boris Aleksandrovich Solomatin had hardly spent a night sleeping in his own, well-appointed Moscow flat. Instead, he was semi-permanently camped out in his new office at the Lubyanka building in Moscow.

Soviet troops had occupied Afghanistan, the Soviets were supporting the Syrian dictator Hafez al-Assad and perhaps most critically were seeking to block the West from tightening the noose around the U.S.S.R.'s south-western region by occupying those adjacent territories.

Already having a detailed knowledge of the NATO and Western nations' political hierarchy, particularly with regards to Britain and America, Boris was in a good position to launch into his Intel gathering phase straight away.

Coincidentally, not one week after Solomatin set up shop in Lubyanka, KGB field agents in the U.S. reported an interesting item which was not paid much attention to by the U.S. Press but appeared buried on page six or seven of the major dailies. There were to be about a half dozen key position replacements in the Reagan Administration.

Upon learning this Solomatin immediately went to work putting together a report then scheduled a meeting with KGB Chairman Chebrikov.

It was agreed when they set the meet and put together what would be the first official report Solomatin was to submit as head of the new department, that as a sign of mutual respect, Chebrikov would come to Boris' office.

Chebrikov showed up right on time and was pleased but not at all surprised to see Boris at his desk, head down, sleeves rolled up and an ashtray filled with cigarette butts. Taking his cue from this scenario, they got right down to business.

"I have something I think is of interest." Boris opened with.

"Tell me." Chebrikov instructed as he leaned forward to light Solomatin's cigarette, his fifth in the last half hour.

"There are some significant shifts in the lower and upper hierarchy in the Reagan administration coming up. Are you in a hurry or do we have time to go over this?"

"May I?" Chebrikov indicated the intercom box on Solomatin's desk.

"Of course!"

"Major Kirkof, cancel my appointments for the afternoon." Chebrikov ordered into the machine.

Yes, Comrade Colonel. The voice on the other end crackled through. Chebrikov shifted into a seat next to the desk.

"Where do we start?" Chebrikov queried.

"One of the major elements of which we are virtually certain is that if the Americans attack the initial attack will occur on a holiday weekend." Boris began.

In line with Andropov's firm belief that the Americans were still planning to attack the Soviet Union, the KGB had been ordered to focus on a potential defense after determining how the U.S. might initiate.

"If we assume the next holiday, we're talking about November 7th or only weeks away!"

"If not in October, then certainly the fourth or seventh of November, yes." Solomatin conceded as he took the thick folder offered him by Boris.

"Agreed, essentially the same time frame." Chebrikov added. Chebrikov perused the substantial folder and smirked at the title.

"*The Seven Dwarfs*, I like that!"

"They are listed more or less by rank, but it doesn't follow that the higher-ranking individuals are the most important changes."

Solomatin lit another cigarette.

"First up we have Reagan himself. Though not due to leave office any time soon he is included for the sake of thoroughness. A notable change in his strategy is worth mention." He took a long drag on his cigarette and gulped a half cup of cold coffee. "As things have escalated, so too have his opponents, particularly concerning his nuclear arms strategy. His somewhat skewed philosophy of mutual assured destruction is coming under increasing fire and we believe this is partly the reason, these changes are being instituted."

"Is there anything significant in his speeches these last two weeks?"

"Not that we've noticed. Just the usual Soviet bashing, exaggerated statistics and a somewhat stronger push for Star Wars support. But nothing new."

"Next is Bush." Chebrikov read from an identical folder he held.

"Though not seen as a hard-core hawk or a hard line conservative he does submit to Reagan on all military issues, strange as he's a war veteran, one would have thought him more independently minded, particularly on military issues. However, back in 1980 he was quoted in the press as being optimistic about coming out on top of the Soviet Union following a nuclear exchange."

"He said that?" Chebrikov asked. Solomatin rifled through a second folder and produced a single page from which he read.

"'You have a survivability of command and control, survivability of industrial potential, protection of a percentage of your citizens, and you have a capability that inflicts more damage on the opposition than it inflicts on you. That's the way you can have a winner.'" The article quoted Bush. "The fact that they think there can be a winner is only usurped by the fact that they think they can win!"

"We don't yet have a complete picture of the administration as a whole in terms of opposition, but

180

yes it does appear the majority of Reagan's people see America as being able to fight and win a nuclear confrontation."

"Remarkable!"

"But we think Bush may have an ulterior motive in his public views." Chebrikov sat up at this and was interested in what was to come next.

"Such as?"

"He regularly meets with industrialists, but not just random industrialists. Primarily those who have a strong history of political involvement."

"It's common knowledge that it is the industrialists who select the presidents in America, how is this different?"

"He apparently favors those with a history of backing presidents. Backing them with substantial financial support."

"Do we think he has his eye on the White House?"

"He's made no outward overtures, but I think it's worth following." Solomatin suggested.

"Interesting. Well done."

"Now, the Defence Secretary . . ."

"Weinberger, the hawk!"

"Yes. Considers the standoff between the U.S. and the Soviet Union akin to the situation between Britain and Nazi Germany in 1938, with himself playing the part of Winston Churchill. Worse yet he has clearly stated on several occasions that any attempt at arms control is nothing but appeasement."

"And regularly attends mass on Sundays!" Chebrikov sarcastically added. Boris continued.

"The newest member of our Hit Parade is the most outspoken opponent of arms control. Richard Perle who has recently been appointed as Assistant Secretary of Defence. He will now work hand-in-hand with a man he strongly agrees with, a man named Ikle who is an ardent anti-arms control man and who is responsible for peeling back the original SALT agreement we struck with the U.S."

"Yes, I remember he also wrote a speech last year advocating a 'five-year plan' of escalation leading to a situation whereby the U.S. would win a nuclear confrontation with us."

"Yes. Also worth noting is that Perle cut his teeth as the security advisor for Senator Henry Jackson, Reagan's chief arms control officer."

"Ah yes! 'Scoop' Jackson, a chief arms control officer who has made a career out of being an obstructionist!"

"Also dubbed 'the Prince of Darkness'." Solomatin added as he produced a New York Times article and read it aloud. "'The sense that we and the Russians could compose our differences, reduce them to treaty constraints and then rely on compliance to produce a safer world. I don't agree with any of that.'"

Chebrikov sat in silence as he scanned the documents. Solomatin offered an analysis.

"This taken in conjunction with the fact that National Security Adviser Clark categorically opposes all U.S.-Soviet contacts of any kind clearly signals to me that the hardliners have gained the upper hand."

Chebrikov flipped through the remaining few pages of the report.

"Reagan appointed Eugene Rostow to head the Arms Control and Disarmament Agency, the ACDA, who flatly opposes any sort of arms control or disarmament agreement with the Soviet Union. He also led the CPD fight against the SALT II agreement. 'Arms control thinking drives out sound thinking', he said." Boris explained.

"He also told the Senate that the U.S. could certainly survive a nuclear war citing Japan as an example saying, 'they not only survived but flourished after a nuclear attack.' The man's insane! And an attack of hundreds of nuclear warheads instead of two?"

"He told them that he estimated that between ten million and one hundred million might be lost but argued the human race is 'very resilient'. Victory is possible if the Americans are prepared to fight."

For the third time Chebrikov shifted in his seat.

"That can **only** be an obvious reference to supporting nuclear proliferation!"

"This one was confirmed day before yesterday. At the end of last week Reagan personally appointed Mr. Richard Burt to head the State Department's Bureau of Politico-Military Affairs, the State Department's primary liaison with the Defence Department."

"Yes."

"Burt is a former *New York Times* reporter and one of the few journalists sympathetic to the CPD. He called the SALT agreement 'a favor to the Russians.'"

"I see! So he is a strong proponent of peace in nuclear arms controls." To quell his rising fear of the picture Chebrikov continued to employ sarcasm.

"Last up is a quote from Pentagon official Thomas Jones who last month told a reporter from *Time Magazine* . . ." He brandished a clipping of the original article as he spoke. ". . . that the U.S. could easily survive a nuclear exchange and fully recover within two to four years, if the populace digs plenty of holes, covers them with wooden doors, and buries the structures under three feet of dirt.' And my favourite quote, 'If there are enough shovels to go around, everybody's going to make it.'"

Viktor Chebrikov now, reinforced by Solomatin's Intel report, was convinced more than ever he was on the right track, closed over the folder, sat back and stared blankly out the window.

"Apparently Reagan's 'Peace through power' argument is more dependent on power than peace."

Boris, observing Viktor's 1000-yard stare, suddenly realized this job wasn't just a favor to keep him around or give him something to fill in his time as he previously suspected. The overall situation was far more serious than he previously had known.

"Comrade Director, are you alright?" Viktor hesitated then answered in a mechanical voice without moving a muscle.

"Interesting picture we have here Boris. Excellent work by the way." He snapped back to reality. "What are you working on at the moment?"

"I was thinking to prepare a presentation for the Politburo."

"Let me give the information to Secretary Andropov first and I will enquire whether or not he wants a full-scale briefing after. If he does, I will let you do it."

"Thank you." Boris rose to leave. "Comrade Director?" Solomatin followed him to the door.

"Yes Boris?"

"If this thing happens . . . if a hostile exchange appears imminent . . . give me your word I will be returned to active service!"

Chebrikov, the reports tucked under his arm, smiled and patted Solomatin's shoulder."

"Incidentally, I have a meeting with Acting Premier Chernenko this afternoon. I'll be advising his office to issue an alert to all the Middle Eastern and European embassies to take extra precautions with their personnel."

"Do we have an intel alert from the field?"

"No but these animals calling themselves The Army of God don't seem very interested in choosing sides. They've murdered several citizens from a half dozen countries, kidnaped a half dozen more and seem to have a fondness for blowing things up."

"Sounds like a renegade gang from the inner city!"

"Agreed. Pass the word along to your people as well will you?" Chebrikov requested.

When Two Tribes Go To War

"Will do."

****

Professor Frank Regier never imagined in a hundred years he'd be sitting in a closet, dressed in orange and white pajamas, bound blindfolded and physically abused by a bunch of Arabs he had no earthly connection to when he left America last year to lecture at the American University in Beirut.

In the hours, days and weeks following that Saturday afternoon back in February, since he sat in torturously painful positions unable to find sleep, he had searched his mind for some kind of reproach, insult or injury he might have caused these people. Search as he might he couldn't find one.

He didn't need to.

In their blind racism fueled by religious hatred instilled in them from childhood, his kidnappers had found one for him; he had been born in America.

Despite warnings from his wife, before he left West Virginia, his friends and the State Department Regier travelled anyway.

Terrorism, like serious car accidents, was something that happened to other people. Something you saw on TV or in the movies. It didn't happen to you.

He was abducted while leaving the campus over two months ago. Regier knew the terrorists, about a week after his own abduction, had brought in another prisoner, presumably another hostage. Although one or two of them spoke English sometimes, it was from his closet prison that he could hear them speaking French with the new captive.

Fortunately, the terrorist cell of the IJO, Islamic Jihad Organization, a group employed by the Hezbollah as a front who in turn were being largely paid and supported by the Imams of the Iranian government, were a bit careless in underestimating the knock-on effects of kidnapping citizens of two of the most well-equipped, well-armed and, by virtue of their intel services working together, well-informed countries in the West.

At the same time the technologically ignorant thugs were gathered around an old kitchen table, arguing how much ransom to ask for, patting each other on the back and basking in their glory, units of the Amal Shia militiamen, a Moslem resistance group earlier informed by elements of the western intel services, were tactically surrounding the west Beirut house where the hostages were being held.

In a textbook operation, minutes after it had begun, all the terrorists had been killed or captured while Regier and the Frenchman Christian Joubert, also an engineer, dazed and confused by what had happened were being taken to a local hospital.

Hours later the few captured terrorists never imagined in a hundred years they'd be sitting in a closet-sized cell, bound blindfolded and physically abused by a bunch of Christian Arabs.

Karma can be a bitch.

****

The Lubyanka Building, now the KGB Headquarters, in central Moscow was said to be the tallest building in the world. Because you could see Siberia from the basement.

The mixed Neo-Baroque and Neo-Renaissance architecture was out of place in the open Lubyanka Square and perhaps that was intentional because the structure certainly jumped out at the public.

The young, army motorcycle courier looked up at the twenty foot tall statue of Felix Dzerzhinsky, founder of the Cheka, the secret police and forefathers, of the KGB, as he rounded the statue which stood sentinel outside. Compelled to circle twice he was hard pressed to find a suitable spot to park as the place was strewn with construction equipment and materials. A new wing was under construction.

Settling for a spot up against the building, he parked then shut down the little 125cc bike, took the steps to the entrance two at a time and bounded up to the reception desk.

"Chairman Chebrikov's office please. Message from the Presidium."

"Sign here. Second floor, last door on left. Be sure to write time, here." The clerk pointed to the last line on the right of the page.

"Thank you comrade! Long live The People's Republic."

"Yeah, yeah." With the wasted enthusiasm of youth he didn't wait for the lift but took the stairs, again two at a time.

Heading through the door he was confronted with a long counter shielding a rank of four desks only one of which was occupied.

A burly major pushed out from behind the second desk and came to the counter as the boy withdrew a small envelope from his messenger's pouch.

"For the Chairman. From the General Secretary."

"Sign here." He mimicked the ritual from downstairs.

"I will take it for him." The Major reached forward but the boy refused to hand it over.

"It is a message for the Chairman only."

"Really?!" The major's high speech tainted with a heavy Ukrainian dialect stood out as he leaned forward on the counter and stared at the boy. "I once had a message for the Chairman, Chairman Andropov, I ask him, 'When do I get promotion?!' Do you know his answer?" The boy shook his head. "I give you hint. I used to be general! HA HA HAA!" He roared as he pounded the counter top. The young messenger failed to see the joke. "Hey boy! You gonna stay in this army you better get a sense of humor! The Chairman is down in The Cellar give me message."

"Sorry major, I have strict instructions. My hand to Colonel Chebrikov's only!"

"Suit yourself. Have a seat." He gestured to the long wooden bench against the bulletin board festooned wall plastered with aging notices.

****

'The Cellar', Lubyankian for the dungeons, was actually located in the basement and that was where Chairman Chebrikov and his #2 man, Kryuchkov, were at the moment.

They had just taken delivery of a blanket chest sized crate delivered by a special unmarked vehicle. Chebrikov signed for the item and the two heavily armed guards who had placed the crate on an iron table against the wall were now closing up the small delivery van and preparing to leave.

Neither KGB man spoke until the van drove back up the ramp and disappeared around the curve to exit the rear of the building.

"Help me get it on the floor." Chebrikov instructed. They pried the lid open and peered down through the dim light into the open crate.

"I've never seen one." Kryuchkov commented. I always pictured them as being much bigger."

"Huh. I always imagined they were smaller. And black, not orange. An orange black box!" Chebrikov countered.

"Let's get it to a safe place. Give me a hand." They closed it over and carried it down the damp, stone passageway to a narrower hallway off on the right lined with what looked like medieval prison cells and entered the last cell on the left. Inside there was an open floor to ceiling steel vault with several shelves.

They wrestled the closed crate onto the bottom shelf, closed over the door, being careful to hear the combination lock engage before Chebrikov spun the dial several times in both directions.

The antique phone hanging on the wall in the corridor buzzed twice in succession. Kryuchkov went out to answer it.

"There's a messenger for you upstairs. He's from the Kremlin."

"You go. I'll be right up. I have to log this in." Chebrikov instructed.

Kryuchkov left as Chebrikov pulled the cord dangling from the single light bulb, closed the cell door over and locked it.

The critical message the young motorcycle troop had brought concerned orders as to what to do with the successful fruit of the month long massive search the U.S.S.R. and the U.S. Navy had been involved in the previous year immediately following the KAL 007 disaster.

Unbeknownst to the world the Soviets had won the race and now the top brass at the Presidium had decided to secretly stash said item in the dungeons of Lubyanka.

The KAL 007 black box was destined to sit unopened in a Russian dungeon until the fall of the Soviet Union years in the future.

*

The White House
Vestibule of the Oval Office

When Two Tribes Go To War

Early Evening

"I want to be absolutely clear on this!" The president spoke in a low voice and made direct eye contact with Howard Baker, the Senior Democratic Party Leader, whom he had cornered in the hall only seconds before. "I don't want any bi-partisan crap on this! You get together with Bob Byrd have dinner, get drunk, get him laid! I don't care, do whatever it takes! I want the SDI appropriations through both chambers by the end of November!"

"Mr. President, the reality of the situation is . . ."

"It's time Mr. President." Someone called over to him.

"Okay." Reagan answered then strode into the Oval Office, which once again was decked out with the full array of T.V. broadcast equipment, sound mics, lights and cameras.

"TWO MINUTES EVERYBODY! TWO MINUTES!" Somebody in the overcrowded room shouted. There was a last minute flurry of activity, Reagan took his seat behind his desk next to a tele-screen which sported video images of multiple missile trajectories and which was on pause.

A director stood in front of the center camera and began the countdown on his fingers as he spoke.

"Five, four, three, two . . ."

"My fellow Americans, thank you for sharing your time with me tonight. The subject I want to discuss with you, peace and national security, is both timely and important. Timely, because I've reached a decision which offers a new hope for our children in the 21st century, a decision I'll tell you about in a few minutes. And important because there's a very big decision that you must make for yourselves."

A pair of senior aides standing in the wings looked at each other in shock. The speech had not been written by the usual writers and most of the staff knew nothing about its contents or intended purpose.

"Deterrence means simply this: making sure any adversary who thinks about attacking the United States, or our allies or our vital interests, concludes that the risks to himself outweigh any potential gains he believes he might achieve. Once he understands that, he won't attack. We maintain the peace through our strength. Weakness only invites aggression."

Meanwhile, over at CIA Headquarters in Langley the CIA Deputy Director, John N. McMahon, had been having a coffee in the canteen but was now racing to the nearest house phone. He found one hanging on the wall in the corridor and hurriedly rang a four digit number.

"George, are you near a television?!"

"I'm watching. What the hell is he doing?!" Schultz asked.

"It would appear he's going public with the anti-missile laser beam nonsense!"

"Did he say anything to you about a press announcement?" Schultz queried.

"Jesus no! The last thing we discussed was extending funding for feasibility studies! Our grandkids won't have that level of technology fer cryin' out loud! Did he suggest anything to you?"

"Not a hint! We need a fallout meeting on this tomorrow." Schultz insisted.

"I'll set something up for ten." McMahon assured him. They hung up and the Deputy Director went back to the canteen's television to follow the rest of the broadcast.

This strategy of deterrence has not changed. It still works. But what it takes to maintain deterrence has changed. It took one kind of military force to deter an attack when we had far more nuclear weapons than any other power; it takes another kind now that the Soviets, for example, have enough accurate and powerful nuclear weapons to destroy virtually all of our missiles on the ground.

For 20 years the Soviet Union has been accumulating enormous military might. They didn't stop when their forces exceeded all requirements of a legitimate defensive capability. And they haven't stopped now. During the past decade and a half, the Soviets have built up a massive arsenal of new strategic nuclear weapons – weapons that can strike directly at the United States!"

The United States introduced its last new intercontinental ballistic missile, the Minute Man III, in 1969, and we're now dismantling our even older Titan missiles. But what has the Soviet Union done in these intervening years . . . ?

Two senators sat at a local Washington bar, staring at the corner television in astonishment at

Reagan's comments regarding no new missiles in the U.S. inventory since 1969 and his further demonizing of the Soviets.

Well, since 1969 the Soviet Union has built five new classes of ICBM's, and upgraded these eight times."

"What can he be thinking?! Is he trying to bluff the Russsians or spook them?" One asked.

"He didn't get the carte blanch approval he wanted on The Hill for his Star Wars nonsense so now he's trying to bypass us and take it to the people!" The other responded.

"The Senate are the people who have to decide the funding for such an undertaking and that in turn means you, the people who vote for them must decide."

"Christ! This just weeks after he calls them 'The Evil Empire'!"

"Three weeks. It was three weeks ago." The other one corrected.

"Oh! That makes all the difference!"

"Another round, make it a double!" One of the senators called over to the bartender.

. . . But with these considerations firmly in mind, I call upon the scientific community in our country, those who gave us nuclear weapons, to turn their great talents now to the cause of mankind and world

peace, to give us the means of rendering these nuclear weapons impotent and obsolete.

Tonight, consistent with our obligations of the ABM treaty and recognizing the need for closer consultation with our allies, I'm taking an important first step. I am directing a comprehensive and intensive effort to define a long-term research and development program to begin to achieve our ultimate goal of eliminating the threat posed by strategic nuclear missiles.

My fellow Americans, tonight we're launching an effort which holds the promise of changing the course of human history. There will be risks, and results take time. But I believe we can do it. As we cross this threshold, I ask for your prayers and your support for this great land which is the last hope of mankind. Thank you and God bless you.

Back in the White House, still standing off to the side was the V.P. and a senior aide who leaned over and whispered to Bush.

"Mr. Vice-President, if the Press finds out we don't have anywhere near the technology for that program they'll crucify him!"

"You mean **when** they find out they'll crucify all of us!" An astonished Bush mumbled.

*

**The Presidium
Moscow**

19:45 local

"The man has gone insane! Completely insane! All those cowboy movies he made have gone to his head!"

Konstantin Chernenko, now awaiting approval to replace a dying Andropov as the General Secretary, moved to the liquor cabinet and poured a large drink of Johnny Walker Red Label.

"He actually believes the man with the biggest gun has the right to rule!" He added after he downed the scotch.

Just as wandering medieval envoys brought sacrificial offerings to ancient rulers to curry favor modern travelling diplomats wishing to impress Politburo members routinely offered black market western products to score points as well. American scotch, blue jeans and jazz records were among the top prizes

Chernenko along with several members of the cabinet had just listened to Reagan's T.V. address concerning his appeal to the American public to petition their senators and representatives to lobby for the funds to build his Strategic Defense Initiative, the much touted SDI anti-missile system.

Though Reagan was known for his usually sound political judgment, neither the general public, the Congress nor the Soviets had any way to know that, aside from being cost prohibitive, the required technology was decades away.

However, the immediate affect was unforeseen. The Soviets panicked as their already peaked paranoia of what President Reagan might do next red lined their pressure gauge.

"Our ships have to find that black box before the Americans do!"

Andropov was the only one in the hierarchy who didn't panic about the black box. Telling no one, he knew a week after the shoot down that the Soviets had already found the much sought after orange black box.

****

198

CHAPTER THIRTEEN

Intelligence Building
13th Army Headquarters,
Office of Colonel Yermolayev
Kiev, Ukraine

The tall, muscular blond, thirty-something Dunaeva burst out through the barracks door and quick-timed down the company street. He continued through the laneway up onto and through the headquarters building. Taking the four flights of stairs two-at-a-time he was barely breathing hard when he stopped at the desk which sat in front of the office door labelled: *Chief of Intelligence.*

The duty sergeant at the desk stood to address him but by the time he opened his mouth Dunaeva had knocked once and stepped through the office door.

Unperturbed the older officer glanced up from his writing.

Captain Sergei Ilyavich Dunaeva's father, an aeronautical engineer before the war, was awarded the Order of Lenin twice, but was killed while serving with the 13th Army at the Central Front during the battle of Kursk. He was awarded once while still alive and once posthumously putting him in a unique group of only101 people of the 12,777 awarded the medal to have received the award two times. His mother, now retired, was a well-respected professor of physics.

"AHHH, Dunaeva! I was just about to send for you!" The unknown colonel looked up as he returned Dunaeva's salute. "Have a seat." He smiled. "Do you know who I am?"

"No comrade Colonel, I have never seen you in the area. I came to speak with . . . where is Colonel Yermolayev?"

"I am Lieutenant Colonel Kravtsov and I am Chief of Intelligence of the 13th Army."

Dunaeva stared quizzically.

"I have just come to ask why Colonel Yermolayev has taken away my company command?! Am I being charged with a crime? Am I under investigation?"

"No Captain, you are not under suspicion for anything. Should you be?"

"No! Colonel Yermola-?"

"Yermolayev thinks he is still Chief of Intelligence, but he's not. He has been relieved of his post and will be discharged without pension, although he does not know that yet either."

"May I ask why?"

"No, you may not, it is no concern of yours." Dunaeva suddenly felt the need to sit up straight. "You are not to repeat anything we discuss here today is that understood?"

"Yes, comrade colonel, understood."

"Don't concern yourself with Yermolayev's order to relieve you."

"Thank you, comrade colonel! My company?"

"Don't thank me yet. He is not relieving you, I am."

"I don't understand sir?"

"Yermolayev thought a company was too much for you. But after reading his report and then examining your record I concluded a company was too little for you." Dunaeva's mind raced to keep up with the pace of events. "I have a new job for you. Chief of Staff of the Division's Reconnaissance Battalion."

"But comrade colonel a battalion is normally the responsibility of a major at least!"

"Captain Sergei Ilyavich Dunaeva, you should know by now that in the Soviet army rank and position are flexible.
And we must be flexible in a fluid situation. I am only a lieutenant colonel, but I have been appointed head of 13th Army Intelligence. As such I have the authority to assemble my own staff of which you will be a part, if you think you can handle the job. If not, you are welcome to remain here tramping around in the mud with company level grunts for another ten to twelve years until you make lieutenant colonel. Maybe."

"Yes, of course I accept but, I don't want to seem ungrateful Comrade Colonel but, why me?" He asked.

Kravtsov put down his pen and sat back in the high-backed chair.

"Dunaeva, where is the 406th tactical fighter training wing of the United States Air Force located?"

"In Saragossa, Spain, of course." He shot back.

"What is the composition of the U.S. Fifth Army Corp?"

"The 3rd armoured division, the 8th Mechanized division and the 11th cavalry regiment, but the Corp commanders are considering a conversion of part of the 8th Mechanised supply to an additional tank battalion by next year."

"That's why I picked you, Captain."

"I see. Will there be a promotion?" Dunaeva tentatively asked. Kravtsov's eyes shot across his desk. "I don't ask out of ambition comrade Colonel, but out of concern for respect of the men below me."

"Good to see you are as clever as I gave you credit for. Yes, there will be promotion." He returned to his paperwork.

"My company? What shall I tell them?" Sergei rose to leave.

"Tell them there is a family emergency, your wife is ill in hospital."

"But I'm not married."

"Then your sister."

"They know I have no sibling." Kravtsov was losing patience as he continued to sign the small stack of forms in front of him.

"Dunaeva, if you are going to work in the upper levels of intelligence you will have to learn to be a better liar!"

"Yes sir!"

"You've got thirty minutes to get your things together. Our bus leaves for Rovno at 17:30. If you miss it it's a long walk."

Dunaeva saluted smartly and left.

*

He had begun to mentally adjust to his new role, smiled at his good fortune and folded his field jacket into a makeshift pillow then leaned into the bus window to try and get some sleep. As his mind wandered Dunaeva, on board the full military bus, looked out over the dark, near-featureless land scape and settled in for the four-to-five-hour ride. Next to him Kravtsov struggled to read his book in the dim light.

As a child Sergei once saw a dog, a blond and black German shepherd and favourite of the neighbourhood children, hit by a speeding delivery truck. The poor animal was mercifully killed instantly but was left in a terrible state split open from chest to belly.

The children froze in terror, little girls screamed and cried, boys turned away and ran to their mothers. But Sergei, barley nine at the time, was curiously drawn to the lifeless mutilated mess. Standing and staring at the viscera spilled across the road he was not attracted by some gruesome, morbid thrill as he stared into the lifeless eyes but rather by a sense of wonderment. Wonderment at how the god his grandmother taught him was all knowing and all loving could take such a beautiful, innocent animal and turn him into this mess. A beautiful creature that never attacked anyone but instead only brought joy to everyone, adults and children alike.

He stared for what seemed like hours, in reality minutes, until his mother scurried across the street and pulled him away. As she did, they passed the beautiful, dark-haired, green-eyed young woman whose dog 'Pulya' had been. The daughter of the local saloon owner, she was brought to her knees in hysterical convulsions, in yet another event Sergei had witnessed for the first time that day.

It was at that point in his young life, lying in bed that night, that Dunaeva came to the realization that his babushka, pious as she was, was wrong about her god. There was only nature. The reality of life was indifferent to people's feelings, emotions and petty loves and hates. The universe would carry on regardless. As much joy as the dog had brought to the people of the neighborhood, he was also capable of bringing pain. Neither of which was relevant to nature.

Balance was the secret. Balance is what Sergei decided was the order of the universe and balance is what he would accept as his life's mantra. Even when it came his time to be hit by a truck. He would accept that it was just the inevitable restoration of balance.

The bus was just over forty-five minutes into its journey when a black, four door Chaika limousine sped past on the outside, pulled off the road in front of the bus and two civilian men climbed out and signalled the bus to pull over.

One of the men boarded the bus and without explanation politely but firmly proceeded to issue orders.

"Apologies comrades for the delay. We assure you it will be brief. Everyone please get off the bus."

Outside in the cold evening air the thirty-two passengers were asked to line up and the second man who had not yet spoken but was also dressed in a black leather trench coat and fedora, perused the line-up with a flashlight.

"Captain Sergei Ilyavich Dunaeva?" He half asked, half stated to Sergei.

"Who's asking?" Sergei challenged.

"You are Captain Sergei Ilyavich Dunaeva born August 17th 1952, on the outskirts of Kiev and formally of Signal Company Number 3."

Sergei looked over at Kravtsov who stared back expressionless.

"Yes."

"We are from the 9th Directorate. You will come with us." One of them took an arm and forcefully escorted him back into the back of the black, Chaika.

After the others had re-boarded Kravtsov ordered the bus driver to drive on and watched through the door of the bus and nodded to Dunaeva with a smile as he was led away.

******

It was the 47-year-old Markus Slavinsky, the older of the four diplomats taken hostage just two days ago, who was roughly taken from the room dragged out to a car and crammed down into the trunk.

For what seemed forever he felt the car drive out of the yard of the two-story house on Beirut's north quarter and onto the open road.

Finally, he felt the car stop and without shutting down the trunk was opened and he was roughly dragged out.

By the stench and the screech of sea gulls Slavinsky realized they were in a garbage dump.

An hour later the local police were notified to send a unit to the remote garbage dump just west of the valley where Slavinsky's still bound and blindfolded dead body was discovered.

The Russian diplomat had been executed with a single shot to the back of the head.

****

In route to wherever he was being taken, Sergei Dunaeva had had a black sack pulled down over his head as he sat in the back seat of the Chaika, an unknown thug either side of him.

Counting each turn and keeping tally of lefts and rights, Sergei tried to discern and keep track of each of the road surfaces the vehicle was driving on. Unable to view his watch he counted out the minutes by tapping his thigh with a finger but into the second hour he began to lose track.

Finally, the car slowed, he heard the rattle of a chain linked gate, they turned, sped up then slowed again this time to a full stop and shut down.

Led from the car and once inside the building he was escorted down a long hall to a room on the right. After being seated at a table the hood was removed and the two thugs exited.

Minutes later an older well-groomed man smoking a cigarette entered, sat across from Dunaeva and snuffed out his cigarette on the sole of his shoe, removed a handkerchief from his breast pocket, spread it in front of him on the table and carefully crumbled the extinguished butt into it.

As he folded the hanky back up and pocketed it he finally addressed Dunaeva.

"Do you know where you are?"

"You abduct me from my new assignment, you whisk me away in the night in front of my men and keep me blindfolded while you drag me here -"

"Surely you can guess." The older man pushed playfully.

"Somewhere an hour and a half south of the capital. Probably a KGB detention center."

"Your training and three years with Spetsnaz continue to serve you well."

"Whatever the game I'll find out sooner or later."

"Well then, no sense keeping you in suspense." He produced another cigarette and lit it.

"By virtue of orders under the 7th Directorate you and four others of your status are being reactivated for a mission."

"What mission?" He challenged.

"Not like the Kabul operation on Tajbeg in '79. This one is small, contained and will only be executed by veterans of the Kabul palace operation."

Immediately realizing that the unknown man was referencing a five-man cell Dunaeva was alerted that it was a SPETSNAZ mission. His attitude immediately improved.

"You're activating a Spetsgruppe Alpha team? A Spetsgruppe Альфа?"

"Not I! I am just a lowly KGB General from the 9th Directorate. Director Chebrikov has ordered you activated. My people have only been tasked with collecting you misfits whose time in Spetsnaz has finished and who have moved on with their careers."

"Why?"

"Your team will be comprised of members all of which are original candidates commissioned back in 1974 under Zietsev when Andropov ordered the first A Teams organized."

"Good, then I will know them. But why all the trouble? You have active Alpha teams already on duty? Besides I have been out of the teams for nearly two years!"

"Ahhh true Captain but, Big Brother thinks of everything. My guess why they want you is so no one can trace you and therefore the Presidium can maintain plausible deniability. Just in case."

"Would this mission be in the Middle East?" There was no answer. "In the area of Lebanon?" Again, there was no answer.

The two exchanged glances.

"I don't understand. Lebanon is the West's problem, Israel and America's headache. We have no real interests there. What do they want?

"Apparently they want support for pro-Syrian fighters in Lebanon. But none of that is your concern." The general divulged. "You are to be flown to an isolated facility where you and your team will be briefed on the mission and be given 24 hours to plan while officials continue to feign negotiations."

"If there are terrorists holding Russians hostage, as reported in the Western press, how can we be sure we have 24 hours to plan?"

"Tomorrow's Friday. We are betting they will be too busy praying to their god to murder." He rose to leave. "Best of luck Sergei!" He tapped Dunaeva on the shoulder as he passed by. "Make us proud."

Sergei sat alone in the dimly lit room until someone came for him.

****

Two days later it was with a controlled sense of urgency that the black rental car pulled up in front of the old, abandoned house in the Bourj Hammoud suburb on the eastern outskirts of Beirut.

Four men, all dressed in black camo with black net covering their faces, hurriedly disembarked while a fifth drove the car around back out of sight. All of them carried AKMS model Kalashnikovs and a secondary weapon, a pistol or an Uzi.

Of the four two scurried to flank guard positions while the other two very roughly escorted a slightly overweight Arab in his underwear, blindfolded and gagged with his upper arms and wrists bound with zip ties behind his back, into the house and down into the basement.

In minutes the unfortunate Arab was tightly and inescapably bound hand and foot to a chair bolted to the floor which attested to the fact that the set-up was not only well-financed but had been prepared beforehand.

His blindfold and gag were removed and as he struggled to see more clearly through the harsh light glaring directly into his face, the first light he had obviously seen in quite some time. He observed the men in black setting up video equipment.

"Who are you?! What do you want with me?!" No one answered. "I demand you release me! Do you know who I am?! I have-"

"We know exactly who you are my gluttonous little friend. Who you are is exactly why you are here, Abbas." Sergei Dunaeva quietly informed through his black mesh face net.

"What are you going to do with me! I demand to know."

"We are going to film you while we to cut off your balls and send them to your brother who has unwisely decided to pick a fight with Mother Russia."

Abbas' flabby face drained of color as his eyes glassed over and he stared in disbelief.

"But . . . but I'm not a terrorist! I'm a merchant! I never hurt anyone, I don't approve of what my brother and his cohorts do! I'm not a member of their organization! Why torture me?!"

As Sergei and the Arab carried on the exchange two others worked setting up two cameras on tripods, lights and a microphone. A fourth stood guard at the top of the stairs as the driver entered through the back door of the house then also took up guard duty.

"What is the name of this organization?" Sergei probed. "Tell us and perhaps we will spare you."

"I don't know! I'm not involved! I swear I never talk with him about it, I don't know. I'm not a terrorist!"

"The diplomats your brother's gang are holding are not terrorists either. They also have never hurt anyone. Yet they decided to murder a father of two."

A second member of the team approached tapping the air out of a loaded syringe.

"WHAT IS THAT!? WHAT ARE YOU GOING TO DO WITH THAT?" As the reality of his predicament began to dawn on the Arab his desperation intensified.

"WAIT, WAIT! There is a safe house they use in Sabtreyeh district! A white two story! The number is 127!"

As he was being ignored, he again resorted to pleading.

"WHAT ARE YOU GOING TO DO WITH THAT?!"

"Something to put you under first. After all, we are not animals!" Sergei casually replied.

"NO WAIT! LET ME TALK TO HIM! LET ME TALK TO HIM! HE WILL LISTEN TO ME, HE WILL . . . AGGGHHH!" With one operative holding him firmly across the chest and peeling back his T-shirt sleeve the other injected the sedative into his left shoulder.

"Besides, we don't like the screaming." Dunaeva calmly explained.

The next day the 'package' was delivered along with the home addresses of two other relatives of the terrorists to the 'safe house' at 127.

A day later, in the afternoon edition of the *Jerusalem Post,* the following story was run:

Three remaining Russian diplomats, missing for over a week, were this morning dropped off outside the Russian embassy.

The *Post* article closed with a footnote:

Meanwhile six Americans, also suspected kidnap victims missing for the last two years, are yet to be heard from.

****

CHAPTER FOURTEEN

The events of last year surrounding *Operation Ryan* led everyone concerned to where they now found themselves.

Not wanting to make public the fact that the Soviet missile detection system was not only defective but had brought the world the closest it had ever come to nuclear annihilation, the Politburo had ordered the officer-in-charge, Stanislav Petrov, arrested.

Strongly suspecting there was a malfunction when the Soviet computer flashed red and signaled to retaliate, Petrov refused to push the button and fire on America thus avoiding the ignition of World War III.

Weeks later, after the malfunction in the system had been discovered, he was released from detention and discharged from service, but promised financial reward for his heroic action.

None ever came.

What did occur however, was that a double agent, Olaf Gordievsky was revealed to the Russians when he tried to warn both sides. This left him no choice but to defect.

Among the ancillary personnel held in involuntary detention by the Russians was anyone deemed an 'accomplice' to the knock-on events.

Assigned as Olaf Gordievsky's escort to the west, Major Natasha Feordorova Kavolchuck was also implicated and arrested.

When Two Tribes Go To War

Held in detention from October to mid-November following the September fiasco and following Stanislav Petrov's release and the fact that Gordievsky acted alone when he defected, Major Kavolchuck was finally released.

When events came to light in the public about the military computer mishap the Reagan administration declared Stanislav Petrov an international hero and newspapers dubbed him "The Man Who Saved The World", the Politburo decided it should award him a medal also.

Through a paper trail Kavolchuck was cleared when Gordievsky defected and eventually allowed to return to her post at Lubyanka, albeit with a lower clearance. She was put on the Assignments Desk with a 'No Field Work' stipulation attached to her file.

Her life in the last ten months had been little more than that of a glorified secretary typing, filing and writing or reviewing reports. In a word uneventful.

Until today.

It was a typical Tuesday morning as the staccato clicking of the clunky typewriters cluttered the air interrupted only by the occasional ringing of the black, Bakelite telephones when suddenly a messenger appeared in front of her desk.

"The First Deputy wishes to see you."

"What about?"

"Don't know but he used the word 'immediately'."

214

"Then I suppose I'd better go upstairs . . . immediately!" Kavolchuck nodded as she shut down her typewriter and stood.

Upstairs Kryochkov's secretary led her into his office and closed the door over behind her. Major Kavolchuck was not invited to sit. Not a good sign.

In lieu of any formal introductions the First Deputy simply launched into his inquiry.

"Major, you were assigned to accompany the traitor Gordievsky on a cross border mission into the west late last year, correct?" He probed from behind his desk.

"Yes Comrade Colonel."

"While on this mission, did you deviate whatsoever from your assigned task?"

"'Deviate' Comrade Colonel?"

"Participate in any unauthorized activity that might have endangered your mission? Revealed your true purpose for being in America?"

"Of course not Comrade Colonel! Anything and everything I or former Comrade Gordievsky did in our time abroad was dutifully reported to our Intel section during my detention. Everything from the time we arrived in Holland until the unauthorized abduction of former Comrade Gordievsky has been duly reported and recorded."

"Yes, that was a bit overzealous and now believed to have contributed to his defection."

"I'm sure someone thought it necessary at the time sir." The Major feigned empathy.

"This is why you are here." He slid an open letter across his desk. It was a letter she had written to Doc

McKeowen. "Chairman Chebrikov has asked me to pursue your possible relationship with this American."

"We've corresponded one or two times. After all Comrade Colonel we –"

"One or two times?" He cut her off as he opened and reached into his middle desk drawer and produced half a dozen more mimeographed copies of letters between the two written from the beginning of the year up until last month.

Although her heart silently skipped a beat as she stood there she took solace in the fact that he apparently only knew about less than half the correspondence McKeowen and Kavolchuck had exchanged over the last months.

"You have romantic feelings for this American, Kavolchuck?!"

"Of course not Comrade! I was merely developing him as a lead."

"A lead for what Major?"

"In the event I was returned to field operations. I thought he might prove useful."

Vladimir Kryuchkov sat back in his chair and perused the major. Following a long pause he returned the letters to their cover folder and the folder to the drawer.

"Sit." He curtly commanded. When next he spoke his demeanor was noticeably more cordial but not friendly. "What do you know about something called T.F.R.?"

"Nothing colonel. I've never heard the term before."

"Uh huh." He came around to sit on the front edge of his desk. "Chairman Chebrikov has authorized me to initiate an investigation. And due to your familiarity with this American you may be the most suitable person to use to start this . . . inquiry shall we say. It may require travel abroad."

"I'm on indefinite suspension from field duty." She reminded.

"Not if you take this assignment and agree to our terms."

"Anything for Mother Russia."

"Good. Your mission, along with an assistant, is to uncover the exact definition, composition, members if any, primary function etc. . . of whatever this Yankee operation T.F.R. is."

Kavolchuck, having been around more than a day, immediately recognized the word 'assistant' meant babysitter. This carefully chosen 'minder', in all likelihood already waiting in the wings, would have his own secret channel of communications with Kryuchkov to issue regular babysitting reports.

Further she knew she would have this baby sitter's number as soon as they met if he invoked the phrase, 'just getting started', 'just breaking into the business' or words to that effect.

"Your command of English will be the reason you will run the five day mission. I'll have mission parameters drawn up along with formal orders, an expense account number along with all the travel arrangements."

"Yes Comrade Colonel!"

"Finish up whatever paperwork you're currently working on by Friday and be prepared to leave by Monday morning."

"Yes Colonel! May I ask where I'm going?"

"Washington D.C. via Frankfurt am Mein and New York."

"What is my ultimate destination in D.C. Colonel?"

"You already know that, Major." He answered as he retook his seat behind his desk.

"Sir?" She questioned.

"To which address have you been writing to this doctor McKeowen?" he casually responded. "You are dismissed."

"I see." She turned to leave.

"I hope your old father is well?" He quietly inquired as she left.

"He's better now that he's over the loss of mother. Thank you for asking sir."

Natasha knew better than to take his inquiry at face value. She saw it for what it was – a warning and a reminder not to get any clever ideas while being allowed to run around in the west free of her leash.

*

Major Natasha Kavolchuck, accompanied by Arnt Sabrinsky, rank unknown, touched down in Dulles International that Monday evening around six and headed straight for their hotel to clean up and eat.

Surrounded by other travelers on the journey over Natasha and Sabrinsky never really had a chance to rehearse the bare minimum cover story given them by the Assignments Desk at Lubyanka so they agreed, this being a short 'in-and-out' mission they would discuss it in private over a late dinner.

As was basic operational S.O.P. the agents would stick as close to the basic facts as possible regarding their personal lives while still remaining nebulous about critical details.

"So you are from Minsk?" Kavolchuck kick started the conversation.

"Originally yes. But after the gymnasium at Poly Tech shipped off to Petersburg for university." Sabrinsky volunteered. "Then the army and finally volunteered for this. And yourself?"

"Moscow born and raised. Father was an Orthodox bishop now retired. Mother housewife. Passed away last year."

"My condolences."

"Thank you. She was sick for a while. It was actually a small relief when she passed. You? Military background?" She gently pushed.

"I actually volunteered for this. I was told I needed to get as much field time under my belt as possible."

"So you are new?"

"Yes. I was in Army Admin, two years. Incredibly tedious. Volunteered and made it through the Aquarium. Finished last year. Now, just breaking into the trade." She mentally registered that her initial suspicions were confirmed. "So what's our plan?" He pushed.

"I'm going to make first contact after dinner tonight. The mark doesn't know I'm here so he will no doubt invite me out this evening. I'll decline but set a meet at a public place for tomorrow mid-morning. I'll let you know where after I talk with him. You'll arrive early and observe."

"Okay. What's our objective?"

"You weren't briefed?" She knew full well he had been.

"Only that you were running the show and I was to take instructions from you Major."

"I'm to find out what I can about an operation we suspect our mark is currently involved in."

"And we only have five days to do that?"

"I thought you weren't briefed?"

"I was not! I was only told to expect to be gone about a week."

"Well, that makes sense." She lied. "They normally do that."

"How will I know this American if I am standing at a distance?"

"You'll know him when we greet. I'll kiss him American style, only on one cheek."

It had only been a couple of days since the T.F.R. team had returned from Los Angeles when Kavolchuck tracked Doc down, rang him at the team house and announced she was in on 'vacation'.

They spoke by phone and as predicted, he was excited to meet with her. But she had the little problem of her 9th Directorate blood hound she had to drag along so she explained she had some things to attend to and suggested they meet tomorrow evening at her hotel for dinner.

He didn't think it strange that she asked him not to come in uniform.

*** * ***

Capital Hilton
K Street, D.C.

Doc was seated but stood as he saw Natasha crossing the room to his corner table after checking her light jacket at the cloak room. She was eloquently but modestly dressed in a green evening dress and heels.

Sabrinsky had come in through the door a few feet behind her and asked for a seat at the bar where he could overlook most of the dining room. He took a stool and watched as she kissed Doc on the cheek.

"Is first time I ever see you in jacket and tie!" Natasha commented with a broad smile as she mentally adjusted to a language she hadn't used in over a year.

"You like?" Doc modeled his jacket and tie.

"I like very much." Natasha complimented.

"You're looking pretty spiffy yourself!"

"This is good, spiffy?"

"Better than good! Much better than I remember!"

"Your Lieutenant, he is doing better I hope?"

"All healed up and back to full duty. He asked about you."

"That's very pleasant of him."

A waiter arrived and they ordered drinks.

"So, what have you been making these last months?"

"Doing! What have you been **doing** these last months?"

"Sorry! 'Doing' these last months." She self-corrected.

"Don't apologize! Your English still beats hell outta my Russian!"

"Comrade Gordievsky told me your German is quite good though!"

"How is he these days?" Doc nonchalantly asked.

"Very clever!" She snapped.

"What?!"

"You are knowing what! You know how is Gordievsky better than me! You are just testing to see what I am knowing!"

"Why do you say that?" he feigned innocence.

"They know Gordievsky is here!" She authoritatively declared in a low voice. Doc sat back and stared at her. The last thing McKeowen needed was to get dragged into some KGB hunt-&-kill plot.

"Is that why you're really here? To locate Oleg Gordievsky and report back to the Kremlin?"

"Most definitely not! But if you can contact him tell him there are at least two separate death squads having left U.S.S.R searching for him."

"Well, I truly have no idea where he is but wherever they have him I'm sure he's safe." There was a long pause before Doc continued. "Was there trouble for you after November? Back in Russia I mean."

"Not really. They keep me in detention for few weeks. Lots of questions but when Oleg defected, they came to conclusion he acted alone. At least no help from me."

The waiter returned and they ordered dinner.

"How about your work now? Anything exciting?" She continued.

"After November I get a promotion and a new posting."

"You are happy with new job?"

"Yeah, I volunteered for it . . . sort of." He shrugged.

"Volunteered? Then it must be dangerous, no?" Kavolchuck probed.

"Not really." He lied. "But sometimes frustrating."

"Why is this?"

"They sent us out on a snipe hunt last week."

"What is snipe hunt?"

"A fool's errand, wild goose chase. A useless task."

"How was the result?"

"Let's just say it could have gone better. A lot better! We were sent out to meet someone who may not exist."

"You were sent to catch someone and they didn't show up?"

"Something like that." He grinned at her from across the table. "What'a you a mind reader or something?"

"No but this sometimes happens. Some of our guys were sent out last year to locate Chechen terrorist who ordered the bombing of primary school."

"Jesus, nice guy! They get him?"

"He wasn't where he was supposed to be. They never find him."

"Was the school bombed?!"

"Yes and no." She shrugged. "Bomb was detonated before getting to school. Three terrorists dead two wounded before capture."

"Mark one up for the good guys!"

As per her plan Natasha had arranged with Sabrinsky that if she were making progress with Doc, to whom she referred to as her 'mark', she would signal her colleague with a nod as she passed by the bar on her way to the rest room. This was to be interpreted as she would invite McKeowen up to her room for the night and meet Sabrinsky next morning at a prearranged rendezvous at around eleven.

Forty-five minutes later Doc and Natasha Kavolchuck were standing in front of the elevator waiting to head up to her room.

******

That morning after the team's run, Doc headed straight to Dave Harden's office and gently closed the door over behind him.

"Sir, we. . . I have a problem." He quietly began.

224

Harden, scratching out some paperwork didn't look up as he answered.

"You're a corpsman. Prescribe yourself something. I hear penicillin is the usual treatment."

"Sir I'm serious!"

"Sorry Doc!" He sat back and looked up. "What seems to be the issue?"

"As you know Natasha has been in town and we've been sort of –"

"Attached at the hip? Yes we've all noticed. You do realize she's highly likely KGB?"

"We know for a fact she's KGB ever since we met her in the Netherlands with Gordievsky!"

"She was only acting as an escort for cover. Since when do you know for sure she's a dedicated field operative?"

"Since she told me." Now Doc had his commander's genuine interest.

"When did she divulge this minor, not unimportant detail to you, petty officer McKeowen?"

"Last night when she also told me she wants to defect." Harden looked up and stared at Doc.

"She spilled her guts to you and confessed she wants to cross the fence?"

"Yes sir."

"When exactly did she do that?"

"During breakfast at my place."

"Where exactly in your place?"

"At the table, in my apartment." He shrugged. Harden raised his eyebrows and gestured for Doc to continue. "In my apartment. Okay, in the bedroom. Before breakfast." Harden continued to stare challengingly. "WHAT?!" McKeowen challenged back.

"Doc, how old are you?" Harden set his pen on his desk as he casually pressed on.

"What?! You trying to tell me you think I was being manipulated? Being used?"

"Doc think! She's been here now what? Three full days, 85% of that time with you. Yet she picks the night when you two are doing the Horizontal Bop to pop the question? Pardon the pun."

"So I **was** being used!" Doc emphasized as he stated down at the floor. "Well whatta-ya-know?!" Doc admitted. Harden took a breath as the truth dawned on his favorite corpsman. "I guess I **was** being used." Doc walked over, stepped through the opened office door then yelled out into the team room.

"HEY GUYS! GOOD NEWS! OLD DOC HERE HAS BEEN USED BY A BEAUTIFUL RUSSIAN GODDESS!" Mac and Danno gave a weak applause.

"Again?! What street corner you'd meet this one on?" Mac called back.

"Better get over to sick bay Doc and get a blood test!" Danno added.

As she heard the yelling Mrs. Gaffney appeared and popped her head through the office door.

"Lt. Commander, you allowing these boys to drink this early in the morning?" She asked.

All smiles Doc went back in to the office.

"So what's the verdict sir?" He pushed.

226

Paddy Kelly

"Well, if you're sure she's for real Doc, I'll run it up the flagpole. Hell, I'll take it straight to Casey! But I'm pretty sure he'll say she's gonna have to give us something!"

"Already approached her on that matter!" Doc boasted.

"That sounded a bit too easy!"

"She's on the level sir."

"Yeah? What'd she offer?"

"How about the entire OB of Lubyanka?"

The O.B. or Order of Battle is the hierarchy of any military structure. It typically includes the names of the ranking individuals, the formations and the equipment contained there-in.

Harden fell back in his seat.

"You shittin' me Doc?!"

"Hell Commander I wouldn't shit you, you're my favorite turd!"

"Never gets old Doc." He drolled. "I'm pretty sure I can sell that. Providing it's on the level!" He quietly nodded. "Only one way to find out I guess."

"There's one more tiny problem." Doc added.

"Of course there is." He fell back in his seat. "What, her family, she has a kid? Wants to bring her parents to America?"

"No, no kids no parents. Both deceased, mother last year father a day ago. That's what prompted her final decision."

"I see. What then?"

"Her KGB babysitter who was no doubt sent from the guys who act as internal affairs monitors -"

"The Ninth Directorate. They're the enforcers for the KGB mob."

"Well they sent one over with her. She's being watched pretty much 24/7 and her orders only authorize her to be here for another two days."

"Forty-eight hours huh? Piece of cake! Let's go!" Harden quipped as he came around from behind his desk then yelled into Mrs. Gaffney's office.

"Mrs. Gaffney, please ring Director Casey. Tell him we're on the way over. I need a quick word with him regarding our current mission."

"If he's not available, shall I leave a message?"

"He's in by now. Tell him it's about an old friend from last year. Just mention the word 'Ryan', he'll understand."

"Already dialing the phone Lt. Commander."

"Remind me to get you a bonus Mrs. Gaffney!" He called over as he and Doc headed up towards the front door.

A bonus?! As soon as hell freezes over! Mrs. Gaffney mumbled to herself as she finished dialing.

****

That evening Natasha met with Doc again as planned. They met around half eight at her hotel in full sight of Sabrinsky. They feigned another friendly dinner, a few drinks and when the time felt right, Doc gave her the plan.

"Here's what we need to do . . ."

"I'm worried!" Kavolchuck confided.

"Don't be! You're in my neighborhood now!" They were careful to avoid any stilted gestures or any other body language that might betray their actual conversation. "Now's when you have to dig deep and draw on your training." He assured as he lightly laughed as if one of them had just made a joke. Sabrinsky took note.

"My commander talked with a very high up individual who has authorized him to appoint a guide to bring you in. They'll meet you tomorrow at the Lincoln Memorial at eleven o'clock on the dot!"

"Then what?"

"I assume you have no photos of this Sabrinsky guy?"

"No, but I can get him to wear a colored cap or something."

"That'll work." He assured. "When you see him next tell him you have a meet with a Polish informer."

"Can I bring anything with me?"

"No! Just your handbag and I.D."

"Which one?"

"All of them."

"Of course! I leave all other things I bring with me in hotel room."

"We'll take you to the State Building on C Street."

"No! Not to U.S. State Building, no!" She insisted.

"Well there's no Russian State building here!"

"Not to U.S. State Building!" She reiterated.

"Why not?"

"They have people watching building 24/7." This came as no surprise to Doc. "Or not to your CIA at Langley also." She quickly added.

"Okay."

"Or to J. Edgar Hoover Building either!" She added.

"What about to Madam Tussard's or the zoo?!" He sarcastically quipped. "Just how many people do you guys have in Washington?"

"I don't know exactly but let us just say that before he die Andropov would relax to American jazz music and Johnny Walker scotch each night. All bought from duty free shops in Washington."

"Huh!" Doc grunted,

"Connections between east and west were never completely severed." Kavolchuck added.

"Son-of-a-bitch!" He chuckled.

"Why do you laugh?"

"I can't picture Reagan eating borscht, drinking Stoli's and relaxing to Tchaikovsky!"

"Is it forbidden here to play Tchaikovsky?!"

"No no, not at all! It's just that . . . never mind. The courier will escort you to a safe place and we'll take care of your babysitter."

"You do not mean 'take care of' as in *Godfather* movie 'take care of, yes?!"

"As long as he doesn't draw a gun and shoot, he should be okay. He'll likely be held, questioned and released to the care of the Russian embassy."

"Alright." She conceded.

"I have to also warn you they are going to keep you in isolation for a week or more and there'll be a thousand questions. Answer them honestly. Give them nothing to be suspicious about. Intel people are basically cops and cops are naturally suspicious of everyone! Including their own mothers!"

"I have had five weeks of practice at hands of KGB after last year!"

"Good! After they feel they can trust you, somewhat, they'll probably ask you to look at some Intel to verify it."

"I can do this."

"All this means we won't see each other for some time."

"How long sometime?"

"There's no way to know. Maybe days perhaps weeks. I won't lie, I have no way to know."

She reached across the table and took his hand.

"I trust you Doc!"

"And I trust you Natasha."

At that point he felt they had said all they needed to say about business and so moved to change the subject.

"That's a classy green dress you have on." He complimented her form-fitting evening dress.

"You are recognizing this dress?" She smiled.

"I'd have to be in the early stages of Alzheimer's if I didn't! It's the same dress you wore the last night we spent together in Long Beach!"

"You have good memory!"

"Sweetheart, there are somethings a man never forgets!"

"I go to WC now. I be right back." Natasha excused herself to go to the rest room.

Seated in a different location was Sabrinsky and, out of sight of Doc, she again nodded as she passed by. When she returned a short time later, she slipped a folded over note to the barmaid and asked her to give it to Arnt at the other end of the bar.

It read:

'Tomorrow 11:00 Lincoln Memorial.
Wear red baseball cap.'

*

Lincoln Memorial Circle NW
Sunday, 10:45

It was clear and cold that morning with a slight but steady breeze coming in off the Potomac when Arnt Sabrinsky, dressed in a grey overcoat and wearing a red and gold baseball cap approached the Memorial from the east along the Reflecting Pool to afford himself a 360-degree view of the layout as he casually wandered around as would any tourist.

Simultaneously Harden and Doc were driving south from O Street in a grey unmarked government sedan and headed for the 23rd Street turn off onto Memorial Circle where they could pull off onto the side, partially obscured by the tall bushes surrounding the memorial.

232

However, with the ninety-nine foot tall roof, supporting the forty-four foot tall Corinthian columns encompassing the more than 4.3 million cubic feet of marble structure the Lincoln Memorial was simply too massive to observe the entire monument all at once regardless of where one stood.

Due to the unpredictable outcome of the trap combined with the uncertainty of how Sabrinsky would react to losing control of his charge, Natasha had been picked up earlier by a Company agent dressed as a taxi driver and taken to a safe house outside the city.

Consequently it was decided that Doc, the only one with any chance to likely I.D. the agent based on Natasha's verbal description, should go inside.

Doc left Harden and the sedan at the junction of the Memorial Circle and 23rd Street and made his way across the grass to the monument and up inside.

The D.C. Police had been notified of the clandestine meet and requested to stay away from the area between half ten and half eleven to avoid any tip-offs or tells while Bill Casey requested the FBI lend him some agents to surround and apprehend Sabrinsky before he had time to escape and warn his embassy when Kavolchuck failed to show for their meet.

At a few minutes after the hour a D.C. police car drifted by and cruised around the circle then back out onto the main road.

From inside his vehicle Harden let out a quiet curse.

Having crossed the road at 23rd Street Sabrinsky was already mounting the stairs heading up into the monument proper. He noticed the patrol car but thought nothing of it. As Natasha had instructed, Doc was looking for a guy wearing a cheap red cap.

What they all had failed to take into account was that it was the weekend. A weekend in October which means football.

They were all soon reminded as four busloads of tourists pulled up around into the circle outside the monument's sprawling staircase to do a bit of sightseeing prior to the game.

The Sunday game was scheduled to kick-off in a few hours that afternoon between the Dallas Cowboys and the Washington Redskins. The Washington Redskins whose team colors were red and gold.

Without warning a couple of hundred Redskins fans, most wearing red and gold hats and similar shirts of some description, poured out of the buses and flooded up the stairs and into the monument.

Sabrinsky meanwhile drifted back towards the rear corner where he could see across most of the floor and scan the crowd but after a few minutes, he decided to drift out back to the staircase where he continued to peruse for Kavolchuck.

Ten minutes later when Natasha still hadn't shown Sabrinsky began to suspect something.

Soviet State Security protocol dictated that meets, if fifteen minutes late or more, were to be cancelled and rescheduled.

It was when the same D.C. Police cruiser with the same two uniforms inside passed by for a second time that Arnt's suspicions were aroused. But when he spotted Doc mounting the stairs on the other side of the entrance he instantly decided to abort.

Out in the sedan Harden observed several things at once as he struggled to peer through the crowd.

He observed a man scurrying down the left side of the large granite stairs ripping off his Redskins cap as he did so. He deduced the man wasn't a tourist when he watched as the man picked up pace and ducked through the aggregate nest of shrubbery adorning the side of the building.

Then he noticed Doc at the center top of the stairs.

Harden watched as best he could as he stepped halfway out of the car and honked across at Doc who, due to other traffic and the distance didn't hear him. He decided to speed around the circle and meet Doc at the monument. McKeown saw him coming and headed down the steps two at a time and met him at the curb.

"He's making a run for it!" Harden informed as Doc climbed in.

"You saw him?"

"Six-foot, muscular build, dark hair. Wearing a grey overcoat open at the waist."

"You should'a been a cop."

"Couldn't qualify. Too honest."

Sabrinsky at first appeared headed toward the Arlington Bridge but at the last minute veered left and scurried down the small knoll across Ohio Drive weaving in between the heavy traffic and down to the river.

"Please tell me this jamoke is not gonna make us go swimming in this weather!" Doc pleaded as Harden sped the car around the remainder of the circle to the main drive.

"What's this 'we' shit Doc?! You're the combat swimmer!"

"Ya know, I used to like you!"

As the sedan came around onto Ohio Drive, they watched as Sabrinsky vanished down behind the river's embankment.

Harden shot across the oncoming lane and drove up onto the footpath in time to see a small motorboat driven by a blond-haired man in khaki circling about and heading back north up the Potomac and under the Arlington Memorial Bridge.

His passenger was Sabrinsky.

"Where the hell are the Feds?! I thought we were supposed to have FBI back up?" Harden cursed as he pulled back out onto the road and headed south.

"This is gonna look great on my report to Casey!" Harden cursed.

"How were you supposed to know they'd assign you as her handler?"

"I should have guessed!" Harden shot back.

"Why?"

"If this all goes south, despite the fact that we may have brought them one of the most valued assets of the year, they'll need a scapegoat!"

"For what?"

"For the press!" Dave answered.

"Oh yeah, the press!" Doc shook his head. "The U.S. Government where no good deed goes unpunished!" Doc added. "The boat's heading north, why we going south?"

"We have to go south to get back on Ohio Drive north or over to 23rd Street to follow the river north!"

"Where the hell's he think he's going? It's not like we're in a limitless mega-metropolis!" McKeowen questioned aloud.

"SHIT!" Harden suddenly declared as he slapped the wheel.

"WHAT?!"

"I know where he's going! If we had a radio we could get back-up to intercept!" Harden observed. Doc quickly searched the under dash and glove box.

"How the hell did we get a car without a damn radio?!" Doc challenged.

"Older model. It's all they had in the motor pool on short notice."

Doc sat back and stared at Harden who was intently focused on avoiding an accident as they raced north along the river attempting to keep the boat in sight off to their left.

"You gonna tell me where he's going or do I get three guesses?" Doc finally pushed.

"He's heading for Tunlaw Road!"

"What's on Tunlaw Road?"

"The Russian Embassy." Harden answered. "He gets inside he knows we can't touch him."

"How far to the embassy from here?"

"About four and a half miles north by car. By water, shave a mile off that!"

Harden cut west to pick up Wisconsin Avenue north and sped up to the Calvert Street exit where he knew there was an access road coming out behind the embassy.

"After he gets off the boat, he's still gotta go west across a klick of real estate to get to the embassy. If we're lucky we can still catch him!"

Minutes later they turned onto Tunlaw and approached the embassy drive in time to see Sabrinsky on the back of a motorcycle being let in through the gate by the military guard.

Sabrinsky dismounted the motorcycle, smiled and waved from behind the ten-foot-high wrought iron fence as the gate slowly slid shut and Doc and Harden slowly drove past and headed down Tunlaw Road.

"SHIT! Can't believe we let him get away!" Doc slapped the dashboard.

"Not to worry Doc. We'll know what he's up to by this afternoon!"

"How?!"

"Back in Sixty-nine and again in the late Seventies when the new building was put up we bugged the walls. Same as they did with our embassy in Moscow."

"Then . . . then surely they must know they've been bugged?"

"They do. They find a bug every other month or so, but what they may or may not know is there were

238

over 265 different bugs planted throughout the place and every time they call out for routine maintenance the owner of the building company over in Rockwood, who's a Belarussian, is on our payroll. For every repair bill he sends them he gets 100% bonus from us!"

"How do we know he won't turn and go to the Russians?"

"We have something he needs!"

"Which is?"

"His and his family's visas and passports."

"Pretty good insurance!" Doc commended.

Harden turned the car around and headed back to O Street.

By that time Natasha was safely tucked away in a Company safe house.

*** *** ***

Back in what was now the TFR team room Harden, Doc, MacDonald, Danno Byrd and Ricky Matson were gathered for the first time since the RYAN Operation. They all sat around the large round restaurant table Doc and Mac had procured from salvage.

"Gentlemen, listen up. You too Doc."

"Fuck you very much. Sir."

"Wow, this is just like Old Home Week!" Ricky Matson quietly declared.

"Here's the deal. There're some bad guys on the loose and they want to do something bad. We are tasked with finding them and stopping them. This one comes down straight from Casey! Questions, comments, snide remarks?"

"Way too much detail sir!" Danno quipped.

"Yeah, could you give that to us one more time? Maybe a little slower sir?" Ricky added mockingly poised with pad and pen.

"It's good to see you assholes again!" Harden fought back a smirk. A few weeks ago Bill Casey approached me about digging up some info on an unknown entity."

"You two have gotten quite chummy in the last year sir!" Danno quipped. "Last year you get us a high speed mission to rescue some important spy type. Another mission comes down the pipe. We get our own team room, you get bumped up a grade! Something we should know about sir?"

"Yeah, the **mission** I'm about to brief you on and am seriously reconsidering the line-up for!" Everyone got the message and tuned in. "The yokels I found out about call themselves the Hezbollah."

"Who exactly are they when they're home?" Danno asked.

"They believe themselves to be the specially appointed army of God because they believe an illiterate peasant sheep herder fought some battles and then wielded a flaming sword as he rode a white, winged steed to heaven where he is now plotting the end of the known universe when all men like us infidel assholes are gonna fry like bacon."

"What about women sir?" Matson asked.

"They'll fry like eggs!" Mac added.

"So basically they're just the next gang of anti-civilization terrorists to come down the line?" Doc summarized.

"Pretty much, yeah." Harden confirmed.

"What do we know about them sir?"

"Not enough Danno which is why everybody is getting an additional homework assignment." He announced as he passed out some typewritten sheets. "I had a very productive interview with a professor the Agency uses as a resident expert on Lebanon but for obvious reasons I couldn't go too deep into the military aspects. That's where you losers come in. Here's a list of some questions we need answered before we dive any deeper. The reference notes at the bottom of the page list some suggested material as a launch point to dig up what we need."

"What'a we do after we get our info sir?"

"We meet back here on Monday, concoct a plan. Questions, comments, snide remarks?"

****

With Bill Casey's intervention it was only a matter of a week before Natasha was debriefed, cleared and officially granted political asylum.

Initially it was with close supervision that she was assigned to help the Agency with declassified material such as intercepted communiques from Russian cut-outs especially related to the PLO & the Hezbollah.

It was during a casual dinner conversation in a quiet restaurant just a couple of weeks after her grant of asylum that the entire hunt for TFR's mystery man, code named Akbar, was inadvertently cracked open.

"I am wanting to thank you for all you have done for me!" Natasha humbly thanked.

"Twarn't nuthin' little lady!"

"Sorry? I don't understand." She explained.

Doc could do a lot of things but one of them was not an acceptable John Wayne impression.

"Nothing, it was a bad joke. As long as we're sharing, I have to tell you everyone's pretty impressed with your work, even if was for the bad guys."

"First off is not much difference between your White House Congress and Kremlin!"

"How so?!" Doc pushed.

"Bureaucratic politicians lying to the people while they trying to fill own pockets!" She began.

"Hard to argue when you put it that way!" He nodded. "How can you tell when a politician is lying? He asked.

"Mouth is moving!" Natasha shot back. "We have same joke in Russia."

"Huh! Maybe there isn't that much difference!" Doc conceded.

"Major difference is in management of industry." She continued.

"Really? Please, continue." Doc said with genuine interest. With no objection to her theory about politicians he was interested in knowing more about her personal ideology. "So you know about these things?" He teased.

"In university I finish with 5's across board!"

"FIVES?! That's terrible! Here I finished with ones in all my medical subjects!"

"ONES?! Horrible! In Soviet Union ones is failure!"

"Well that's because in Soviet Union you do everything backwards!"

"What?!"

"Sure! Look at how you write the first person singular! A backwards R! What's that all about? That's not letter, much less a whole word!" He teased.

Natasha sat back, crossed her arms and launched a stern look across to Doc as she caught on that he was winding her up.

"We will talk serious now or you want to play like schoolboy all night?!"

"I'm sorry! I'll be serious. Please tell me more about industrial theory." He acquiesced.

"In Soviet Union because of lack of infrastructure is very difficult to distribute goods."

"Even with infrastructure, NINE TIME ZONES?! That's more than twice as many as we have here!"

"Eleven time zones! Even my professors admit communist system cannot win industrial race with U.S. This is in secret of course."

"Of course."

"Your country was essentially untouched by Second World war. Your economic system allow for factories to operate on incentive system for profit, so manufacturers have good reason to find most efficient system."

"How is it different in Soviet Russia?"

"In Soviet Union government sends 'experts' to tell factory how to better produce goods."

"And?"

"Always fails. So called experts are nephew of someone or cousin of important politician or just stupid."

"We saw the same dynamic here with Carter the peanut farmer."

"Is not practical to have autocratic central planning of all social systems, especially in country with eleven time zones and hundreds of cultures."

Continually frustrated at how little Americans knew about Russia and its culture, she emphasized 'eleven' time zones before continuing. "This is same reason ancient Babylon failed. This aggravated by overspending on military while neglecting consumer goods is very stupid path to follow."

"But it appears to be changing somewhat now, no?" Doc probed.

"In reality no. Entire system will collapse in next decade if not sooner."

"Wow! Pretty bold prediction!"

"It will happen! You can be putting money on this." She casually added.

Doc continued to gaze at her and smile.

"Why you look on me this way?" Natasha challenged.

"I'm even more impressed then when we first met."

"Why so?"

"Smart and beautiful." He complimented to her embarrassment.

"Okay I spill my stomach on you. Now you spill your stomach on me."

"'Guts' Sweetheart! It's 'spill your guts'. Not stomach. Guts." He fought back his laughter.

"What is guts?"

"The things below your stomach. Here." He gestured.

"Ahh! Kishki! The kishki!" She nodded.

"Yeah, kishki. Okay, I'll spill my kishki." He conceded. "I lucked into a sports scholarship, was aiming for medical school but wound up here."

"Here?"

"In the navy. They have a very good medical program and if I chose they will send me to medical school. Providing I stay in the navy."

"This is good system! We have same in Soviet military, but don't pay for medical school. Only engineering."

"A slot, a position, came open for an instructor at the combat swimmer's course in Coronado and I got it."

"You like water?"

"Sweetheart, between you and I if I could have gills, you know like the fish, I would be a happy camper!"

"You don't swim here now, is much too cold!"

"No, no. Now I'm same as you working in Intel."

"Perhaps we one day work together?" She smiled.

"I suppose anything's possible but the group I'm with is a special team, men only."

"We have special teams also. Called Spetnaz teams, men only. Many special missions but now are mainly for fighting terrorists."

"The Lieutenant Commander tells me you're starting in a new department on Monday?"

"Yes, I request transfer to place where I can use my engineering and statistical degree."

"Statistics huh?"

"I will now work under Office of the Directorate of Analysis, Russian and European Division as Analytic Methodologist."

"Sounds . . . analytical." Having no idea what that was he cluelessly joked.

"I have strong interest in numbers mostly statistical analysis. When I was little girl I always trick my uncle to play . . . how you say, game with three cups and one coin?"

"The shell game."

"Yes, shell game. I always find penny. Make him very angry!" She giggled.

"Interesting." Doc's mathematical cortex was kicking into overdrive. Which didn't take much as he scored a C+ in Statistics. "How did you beat your uncle when you played the shell game?"

"Why? You wish to play?" She teasingly challenged.

"No, but help me out here. What was your method, your reasoning for always finding the coin?"

"Well, I don't find coin one hundred percent of time!"

"How often? Roughly?" He pushed and for the first time she sensed his seriousness.

"Perhaps eighty, eighty-five percent of time."

"But do you remember how you did it?"

"Yes, I count number of strokes my uncle use to move cups then calculate odds divided by three. If comes even number is probably center cup if comes odd number is probably left or right cup which mean my chances increase from 33% to 50%. 50/50 is best odds you can get without knowing anything. So then I guess."

"And you were right 80 to 85% of the time?"

"Yes. Doc why your interest?"

"If I gave you a list of say potential locations and then a shorter list of time frames and targets previously attacked could you analyze the probability of the secondary target?"

"Is not impossible. Naturally the more data you can provide the more accurate will be possible answer. There are many variables, would be only guess."

"But a best guess? Theoretically we could assign it a numerical quotient, a percentage, no?"

"I suppose yes. Why?"

"I can't share details with you right now but Monday evening come around to my place for dinner and I'll go over what I've found and you can give me your opinion."

**

Doc's Apartment
Monday Evening
October 3rd

Following a light dinner of Chinese fast food with Natasha that night Doc quickly cleaned up then left the table and retrieved a briefcase from the bedroom. Three folders appeared on the table in front of Natasha as he took the chair opposite.

"What is all this?" She innocently asked.

"The commander assigned us some homework. He gave us each a short list of questions to research."

"And what was your research topic? How to make bad jokes?"

"That's good, that's good! You're definitely on your way to becoming a real American!"

"Why is that?"

"Proficiency in sarcasm and insults is imperative if you're to travel abroad meet people from other cultures and want them to think you're American!"

"What is all this?" She reiterated.

"Okay, this folder contains all the research reference material. This one, potential secondary research stuff and this one the two lists."

"Lists of . . .?"

"List #1, targets and types hit in the last year since our discovery of Hezbollah. It's a terrorist group."

"I know them." She said.

"Of course you do." He passed her the folder which she began to leaf through.

"Some of these maybe not hits by Hezbollah." She observed.

"Maybe not but it's almost certain they were still financed and coordinated by Hezbollah through the Iranian mullahs."

"I see."

"List #2 is sixteen potential targets divided into three classes of impact, small impact, moderate impact and serious or large impact. All calculated by potential casualty rate, L.O.C. disruption and lasting or strategic value"

"Sorry what means L.O.C.?" She asked.

"Lines of Communication. rail lines, roads, waterways, electronic or telephone communications, supply lines. Anything that could disrupt flow."

"Da! Linii svyazi we say!"

"Linii svyazi, Wow, it's like you people have a different word for everything!"

"No time for bad jokes! Focus on work!" She snapped.

"Yes ma'am!" Doc saluted as he answered.

With an analytic methodologist primarily concerned with developing ways to strengthen Intel analysis and collection through statistical, econometric and mathematical assessments, geospatial modeling or operations research, Kavolchuck was in her element.

"What is this?" She asked.

"The check mark followed by the number cross references the list of targets already hit. They're coordinated as closely as possible with the potential list. Roads to roads, vehicles to vehicles, buildings or structures to buildings and so forth."

"They are always using explosives?" She queried.

"It appears yes, exclusively. The FBI have developed a pretty efficient residual analysis ability following each attack and the chemical composition and quantitative analysis seem to match up pretty good."

"So is possible to assume a bomb attack which will mean personal access required?"

"Yes."

"You have three bridges on list here. Are they having ability to destroy a large bridge?"

"Nothing like the Brooklyn Bridge or the George Washington, but a smaller one yes, if well supplied and planned." Doc opined.

"To destroy bridges is maybe important in war during battle but I am thinking Muslim terrorists will waste no time and money on something we can rebuild quickly and easily. Also, even at busiest time casualty rate would be low."

"Good point. Okay let's rule out bridges for now. My overall guess, from this list, is one of the three regular air flights between major metropolitan areas, probably one traveling over water. Especially given they've hit so many passenger flights in the last year and a half."

"We were thinking same thing at Lubyanka. But now that many countries are having stronger security at airports is more difficult for such attacks."

"True, makes them more difficult but does not eliminate them."

"Why do you believe over water? Because you are liking water?"

"No, we came across some intel a few weeks back, some commo with the quote, 'going to make a big splash'. The Israelis gave it to us. Even the best English speaking Arabs don't usually use colloquial metaphors like 'big splash'."

"So you think perhaps bomb on plane over water?" She offered.

"Perhaps not over water but only near water?" He added.

"Like maybe on boat or dock area?" She extrapolated.

"Could be."

"Which structure would be near large body of water to blow up?" She mused. He stared off for a moment.

Suddenly McKeowen jumped from his chair and ran to the bookshelf where he pulled one of his many dictionaries from the shelf.

"What you are looking for?" She walked over and read the book's cover aloud. "English to Arabic? What you look for?"

"It's NOT missiles! It's one MISSILE! One rocket!"

"Okay crazy man, explain!"

"According to this dictionary there's no plural in Arabic only in Persian!"

"So?"

"In Arabic the word for Missile and the word for rocket are the same thing! Räkət! Both words translate to Räkət!"

"What is significance?" She called over to him as he dialed the phone.

"I know the target!" He declared. She scurried to the table and perused the list.

"Which number?" She excitedly asked as she perused their list.

"It's not on the list!" Someone picked up on the other end. "Lieutenant Commander, its Doc. I think Natasha and I figured out the next target!"

He smiled over at Kavolchuck.

****

CHAPTER FIFTEEN

West Foster Street
Chicago, Ill.

Dad, here do you want these flats of herbs, in the fridge or downstairs?" Byblos called into through the rear door.

"Oregano in the kitchen, the rest in the fridge. Then fill and light up the Bain Marie when you finish!" His father called back.

It was during the First World War when Abdel Khalil's father escaped the genocide of the last of the crumbling Ottoman Empire and re-established his family on the shores of Lake Michigan by opening a small kebab stand in the expanding city of Chicago.

That was back in 1914.

Now *A Taste of Lebanon*, moving into its third generation, was a family oriented, BYOB, ninety-eight seat eatery serving traditional Lebanese fare on West Foster Avenue in the North Park district.

It was just after ten that morning when Farez Khalil looked up from behind the reception counter near the front door where he was stacking menus under the counter to see a pair of Adidas track-suited individuals stroll in through the front door.

"Sorry guys, we are closed. We will open at eleven." He politely informed without interrupting his work.

"We don't come for your food, though we are sure it is delicious . . . Mr. Khalil."

Shocked that they knew his name he halted his chores and stood upright.

"Do I know you?" They came closer. "Have we met?"

"As of yet, no." The shorter one responded. "Allow me to introduce myself. I am Doctor Abib. Now you are thinking, 'I didn't call for a doctor! No one I know is sick!' But you would be wrong Monsieur Khalil. Your mother land is sick, and she needs your help. Brother Abdel." He smiled.

The taller one moved to stand on the opposite side of Farez who had stepped around from behind the counter.

"What do you want?!" Khalil became slightly more astute. The short one didn't immediately answer but slowly perused the premises before answering. "If you are from a charity looking for donations I give to the Children's Hospital every year." Khalil defended.

"We do not represent a charity Monsieur Khalil, but we **are** here for a donation."

"I don't understand."

"I cannot help but notice you have built a fine establishment here." The one calling himself Abib commented as he perused the gaily decorated main room.

Khalil slowly moved towards the end of the waist-high counter as the stranger continued his speech. "Here it is **truly** the land of opportunity. Many have worked hard to make it so. However, the motherland does not have the ability to offer such opportunities.

The opportunities they deserve." He stopped and stood with hands behind his back. "The people I represent are currently fighting to afford our citizens these opportunities by driving out the Zionist invaders."

Suddenly the hairs on the back of Khalil's neck stood on end.

Carrying the last of the herbs Byblos wandered in and closed the back door over behind him.

"Byblos, go to the office!" Khalil called to the back of the restaurant.

"I thought you said-"

"GO TO THE OFFICE! NOW! I call you when I am finished here."

"Nice looking boy." The tall stranger complimented as he watched the teen ascend the stairs up to the office.

"I ask you one last time. What do you want?!" Farez challenged.

"Simply a small contribution to the struggle." The short one resumed.

"What struggle?" Farez Khalil stood silent.

"Surely you remember your homeland Farez! Lebanon?"

Khalil's face slowly transformed as the fear and anger slowly rose to the surface.

"Surly you know that even here in the Land of the Free that there are those who object to our presence here? Just another group of dark skinned invaders. Some of these people may seek to do you, or worse yet your family, harm. Physical harm! We can guarantee such things won't happen."

"Or a fire perhaps?" For the only the second time the bigger one spoke. "Would be pity to lose all this fine Lebanese fret work on walls."

Unbeknownst to Lt. Cmdr. Harden or any of the numerous D.C. alphabet Intel agencies Hezbollah had already realized the potential profitability of taking advantage of the lax U.S. banking and charity codes. Nearly a full year had passed since they had 'collection agents' working the urban neighborhoods of the U.S., mainly in the east. Now they were attempting to blaze new trails westward.

Murder, assassination and blackmail worked well back in the Med but in America the most low profile tactic and therefore most profitable, at the time was extortion. In the Lebanese enclaves across the Mid-East extortion had become a favorite pastime of the Local Hezbollah agents and supporters.

The Fifty-six year old Farez had cleverly worked his way to a baseball bat stashed underneath the counter, grabbed for it and quickly brandished it overhead.

"GET OUT YOU BASTARDS! GET THE HELL OUT OF MY RESTAURANT!"

Unfortunately for the middle-aged man he never was an athlete and the few second's pause it took him to react were a few seconds too late.

Upstairs in the office his son Byblos heard the commotion and appeared from the office just in time to see his father sprawled out on the floor bleeding from the face and head as the two thugs disappeared out the front door.

The cash register had been knocked over onto the floor, coins strewn about and the day's opening cash, a messily $125 in small bills, was gone.

Byblos quickly tended to his father's wounds, then called an ambulance.

A half hour earlier, from down the block and across the street four burly men, two well-dressed, two in work clothes, had watched the two track suited individuals enter the restaurant and now, from inside a car, watched them dash out.

The engine of the 1984, fire engine red Cadillac was heard to kick over and the expensive land yacht drifted away from the curb and leisurely coasted at a reasonable distance from the thieves as they slowed their run to a jog and finally down to a quick walk.

The two thugs headed down the block turning right onto Clark Street where they ducked into an alley.

The red Cady slowly drove down West Carmen perpendicular to Clark but parallel to the alley where it discharged the two men in work clothes then pulled around into Clark Street and headed back north and blocking off the alleyway from the east end.

The two thugs were now boxed in.

When the two husky guys in work clothes slowly walked up on the two Arabs counting the money one asked the taller one if he had the time then quickly cracked him over the scull with a black jack several times more than was necessary. Simultaneously, as he watched his friend collapse the shorter Arab threw his hands up in surrender, but to no avail. The pugnacious Italian, a semi-pro boxer used him as a punching bag until his legs collapsed.

The two Italians fished through the two unconscious Arabs' pockets and confiscated everything they had, including the hundred and twenty-five dollars.

"Youse ain't in Arabia no more Dorothy!" The big one mumbled. "So get on your fuckin' magic carpets and fly the fuck back to your cave!" He administered one last kick to the stomach before they headed away up the alley.

"So Gino what'a ya wanna do?"

"Jeet yet?"

"Yeah, I ate, but I could eat again." Big Gino answered.

"You could always eat again! Your folks must'a been glad when you finally moved out!"

It was just before lunchtime so they walked back around the corner to enjoy a kebab.

As the Washington D.C. gurus had failed to fully understand the cultures of the tribes which currently occupied Lebanon and the Levant, the ex-pat Lebanese, Syrian and Arab supporters of the groups who had immigrated to America often also failed to allow for the indigenous American tribes. Failed to understand that in America there was only room for one organized crime syndicate.

And the Italians had beaten the Hezzis to it by eighty years.

****

Colonel Sharin, an IDF tech type, had only been appointed Assistant Director of R&D for the Israeli Defense Force for less than eight months when he made the deliberate decision to disregard a government regulation and violate Knesset Directive #1109.

Laws concerning the use or even engaging in the consultation of private contractors is strictly regulated by Israeli law with stiff penalties able to be levied against offenders. #1109 expressly forbids unauthorized communications with private contractors, military or otherwise.

Kitty's Kitchen is a twenty seat luncheonette across the Potomac ten miles west of the Capitol building in a small suburb called Falls Church.

It was mid-morning when Sharin grabbed his briefcase, paid the taxi driver and entered the near empty eatery.

Ordering a black tea as he passed the register on his way to the back he slid into the last booth on the left to sit across from a middle-aged man who, though dressed casually allowed his black leather Tom Ford Gianni's and Ralph Lauren polo shirt, the one where you have to wear with the collar flipped up, announce who he was.

Sharin was careful to sit so as to keep the front door in full view.

"Mr. Crew I assume?" The IDF officer, also in civilian clothes though much less fashionable, inquired.

"Yes, and you must be Mr. Baum? Nice to meet you sir."

"Nice to meet you as well. Glad you got my classified telex."

"Read and destroyed as per your request." Mr. Crew assured.

"Thank you. I'll explain as we go." The officer set his case on the seat next to him, opened it via the combination lock then produced a palm-sized device. He activated it and began scanning under the table and along the seat back as inconspicuously as possible. When he was satisfied with the results he quickly slipped the magnetic detector back into the bespoke holster in the briefcase lid just as his tea arrived.

"Will there be anything else?" The waitress asked. Mr. Crew signaled for a coffee refill as he contemplated the fact that this guy Baum was either a certified nutter or the real thing. Time would tell.

Baum gently pushed the condiments, napkins and silverware aside and laid out a 12" x 24" drawing.

"Would you have a look at this drawing, please?" Crew leaned in to peruse the rough sketch. He immediately noted that all dimensions had been redacted.

"I've had under-the-table talks behind closed doors with several Pentagon officials." Baum informed. "They have all told me such a system wasn't possible, that it would be doomed to failure or that I wouldn't be able to produce such a system."

After a moment Crew sat back and smiled.

"Firstly, I know why you have come to me, word travels fast in this town especially when money is involved. And secondly Colonel, you are no fool. You know exactly why they peddled you this fairy tale!"

"Because they wanted me to offer them the contract." The tech officer admitted.

"Precisely. Well, I've heard nothing of your proposal and have no idea what you're after but I'm here to tell you that, if this drawing is accurate, it can be done." The officer authoritatively stated.

"It's an anti-missile defense system."

"So I gathered. But . . . I understood the IAF had the PLO rocket attacks more or less under control?" Crew probed.

"Arafat and his monkeys have graduated from hanging munitions from balloons and sending them over Israel to sewer pipe rocket launchers with sugar based propellants! The Iranian engineers have been directed by the Imams to teach the PLO how to build better rockets. And now our Mossad people in Beijing and in Gaza tell us that the PLO, using Arafat's diplomatic immunity have been negotiating for Katyushas from the Red Chinese."

"I thought they were using that U.N. humanitarian and NGO charity money to buy arms from the Russians?"

"Not after the PLO-backed kidnap of those Russian diplomats, especially after executing one."

"Not very smart business practice is it?!" Crew opined.

"It's difficult for people to think straight when their heads and hearts are full of hatred."

Crew returned to studying the drawing before he spoke again.

"I'll need more detailed info about the concept in order to pin down the specifications of the system." Crew insisted.

They stopped talking as the waitress brought Crew's refill then resumed when she left.

"The system should be able to counter short range and 155mm artillery shells" Baum informed.

"It will likely have to be deigned in several component parts."

"Yes, of course." Baum agreed.

"From this sketch I see it as having separate detection and tracking components with separate light vehicle transport capability."

"It will have to be mobile and quick to assemble."

Mr. Crew pulled a paper napkin from the chrome dispenser on the table and began to sketch. "We could design it so several launch units could be serviced by a single detection and launch activation system." He suggested.

"What about the danger of the detection unit getting knocked out? Then we would lose that entire sector of coverage?!"

"Simple! We make the detection unit to operate remotely from the launch system or systems. This way the enemy can't reverse track on the projectile's azimuth and fire on those coordinates."

"We'll need to minimize the number of troops required to operate the system as well." Mr. Baum added.

"I should think we can manage with a squad or less."

"That's acceptable. What about ammo loads?"

"I will have to give it some thought but, ultimately it will depend on the launch requirements which will dictate the tube size et cetera."

"Do you see it being able to reach a ten kilometer intercept range?"

"Perhaps. The prototype performance will tell us what to do to make the necessary modifications I think."

Approximately forty-five minutes after their meeting Colonel Sharin a.k.a. Mr. Baum and the contractor from Rathmeyer Systems, Mr. Crew also an alias, parted company.

Outside the restaurant neither had noticed the young Arab man with the 1200 mm, telephoto Canon lens who walked back around the corner, climbed into his converted van with the tinted out windows, developed the dozen frames he had shot and by noon the photos, sealed in a manila envelope, had been handed off to a bike messenger who in turn had peddled the ten kilometers back across the Potomac.

****

By one thirty that afternoon the photos had found their way into the hands of a light-skinned, African-American female, a senator, who met the bike messenger just outside, behind the Capitol, passed him some cash in exchange for them and then scurried up the steps and into a Capitol building restroom.

From inside a toilet stall, after quickly checking their authenticity, she emerged, donned a headscarf, checked her make-up and went back out and down the hall where she handed over the envelope to a well-dressed gentleman.

Known as one of the hundreds of lobbyists constantly haunting the halls of Congress, he immediately made his way to the exit and took a taxi the three miles to the Saudi embassy over by the river.

Unknown to the public, or most of D.C., operatives inside the embassy were secretly acting as one of the intermediaries for Arafat's PLO in turn working with Hamas & Hezbollah through cutouts.

Meanwhile, back at the Capitol the African-American senator, Ayaan Noon Omar adjusted her head scarf, checked her lipstick in her compact mirror then made her way out onto the floor of the House of Representatives where she nodded across the aisle to her fellow Muslim representative who nodded in return just as the session was called to order.

The two were about to vote to block funding to Israel to repair the damage caused by the latest PLO rocket attacks.

*** * ***

CHAPTER SIXTEEN

Boris Solomatin's Office?
Lubyanka Building
KGB Headquarters, Moscow

Presently Viktor Mikhailovich Chebrikov, newly ascended head of the KGB, adjusted his glasses as he read to himself, cigarette in hand, from a copy of a recently intercepted Top Secret CIA report which only two days ago was sent to the U.S. Senate Oversight Committee via, what the Americans believed was a secure line.

We believe strongly that Soviet actions are not inspired by, and Soviet leaders do not perceive, a genuine danger of imminent conflict or confrontation with the United States.

Ten years younger than William Casey, the sixty year old Chebrikov didn't share Casey's background in intel work. While Casey had been working with the office of Strategic Services the forerunner of the CIA, during WWII Viktor Chebrikov was working as a battalion commander in the Red Army fighting Germans. To this day the five foot nine Viktor wore the corrective lenses that compensated for his deficient eyesight, the physical anomaly which terminated his military service after the war.

A loyal party member since the days in his homeland of the Ukraine, after the war Chebrikov slid easily into administration and was quickly posted to Moscow first as a manager for the Central Committee and then as Deputy Director of the KGB under Yuri Andropov then Director.

Sharing Andropov's hatred of internal corruption he joined, along with others, to vigorously seek out and prosecute the wide spread political corruption of the Brezhnev hold-over's with such vehemence that several of them blew their own brains out or gassed themselves before they were discovered or betrayed.

The two gelled well and now along with Dmitriy Ustinov, Minister for Defense, the three formed the backbone of the Politburo.

Despite the fact that the HVA and KGB working in tandem had revolutionized 20th Century military intelligence data collection methods and amassed the largest collection of Intel data in the world to date, unlike the NATO Pact powers, the Soviets were mysteriously unable to analyze the data and apply the information to real world, strategic thinking.

Like American investigators working for a prosecutor it was as if they were collecting data to be taken at face value to prove an established point rather than gathering evidence to reveal the truth of a situation.

The day Yuri Andropov moved office into the Kremlin's Presidium to assume the duties of Premier just over a year ago, Viktor Mikhailovich Chebrikov, now Chairman Chebrikov, moved into Yuri's old desk in the Lubyanka building as Head of the KGB.

Presently he sat reading a thin file as he smoked.

There was a knock at the door.

"Enter." It was an agent, Rosavitch, recently returned from Bucharest and a meeting with the head of Nicolae Ceauçescu's Securitate of secret police.

"Rosavitchin! Come in, have a seat. Drink? Cigarette?"

"No thank you Chairman."

"Your trip was productive?"

"Yes Comrade Chairman. The Romanian natives are restless but Nicolae's people have them under control."

"Good to hear. You were assigned to the Arafat operation were you not?"

"From early '68 until late '69, yes."

"Tell me about this fat little fellow we made president of the PLO. Is he really a Jerusalem Arab?"

"No, Equiptian bourgeoisie. Western liberal education. We identified him early on as a potential Marxist when he was leader of al-Fatah before they were declared a terrorist group. KGB recruited and trained him at Balashikha. We destroyed his birth records in Cairo and gave him new ones saying his was born in Jerusalem. It adds legitimacy to the Arab's claims to the territory." He casually shrugged.

"How did he come to lead the PLO? He doesn't seem to be particularly ferocious or motivated."

"In '67 Nasser suggested we make him Chairman of the PLO so we did. Then In '78 when Carter called his peace conference we assigned a Romanian Intel agent to take him to Bucharest for instructions on how to talk and to what to say at the conference."

"Which was?"

"To keep telling Carter you'll renounce terrorism and recognize Israel if Arabs are allowed more land in Gaza."

"Which the world bought."

"Yes, but more importantly Carter bought it."

"Of course! Anything to keep the peace, even if it means an increased chance of war." Chebrikov lit another cigarette. "What's your current assessment of him?"

"He has been a faithful dog since the Sixties but the wolves are increasingly testing his limits."

"How do you mean?"

"Mossad has made three or four attempts on his life, there have been at least three by insiders and now there are four splinter groups. It's to the point now that he never sleeps in the same bed twice."

"That might explain why he is making public overtures at renouncing' violence!" Chebrikov groaned.

"Since last year's actions by the Israelis he's retreated from Lebanon to Tunisia to lick his wounds and, with the promise of some Western funding, appears to be shifting from backing open conflict to negotiations."

"You think we have lost him?"

"The Anti-Semitism and anti-Imperialism strategies have become limited in use, particularly as an anti-American tool. However I think he may yet have use on the diplomatic front. That is if he's not assassinated in between time."

"You think that's a possibility?"

"As I said, there have been several attempts and he's not cementing old friendships or making new friends by his constant political flip flopping."

"The Americans appear to have their hands full in Lebanon." Chebrikov threw out.

"Has Hezbollah made any contact with Washington about their abducted CIA Chief of Station?"

"None they are telling us about. The latest CIA intercept we have says his whereabouts are still unknown."

"I'll tell you his whereabouts. About two steps from death by torture! That is if he's still alive. The Americans have no idea who they are dealing with. Hezbollah are animals! But at the moment they are necessary animals to use."

"Which is why we must continue to keep them at arm's length!"

"Reagan was advised not to send in the Marines by his head of the JCS. But you and I know as well as anyone, politics are only good for starting war. Once the first shot is fired the politicians need to get the hell out of the way."

"Also, the kidnaped American agent."

"Yes?"

"One of our contacts in Washington was in the Pentagon last week and overheard some discussion about a reference to 'TFR'. With all this new space mumbo jumbo and acronyms I can't keep up!"

"TFR? What is it?"

"No idea. That's what you're going to find out for us! Get somebody on that. Keep me posted."

"I have just the person in mind!" He boasted.

Rosavitch, having just returned to Moscow, having spent the last week in Budapest, was yet to hear of Kavolchuck's defection. With the CIA sending daily falsified reports back to Lubyanka in her codename he additionally had no way to know of Arnt Sabrinsky's recent capture.

Now outside The Presidium Chebrikov's car pulled up and as soon as he got in, the driver turned and handed him a sealed message. The Director opened it.

Three diplomats freed. In route to Moscow. Body of fourth returned to family. Is follow-up required?

"The Presidium." He ordered.

"Yes sir!" He glanced at the message again and nodded in approval as the car pulled away.

*

CHAPTER SEVENTEEN

Palma de Mallorca Airport
Majorca, Spain
October 11th, 11:00

The final boarding call had sounded ten minutes ago as the couple stumbled out of the taxi and burst through the front doors of the terminal. Holding hands, shoulder bags dangling, the young newly-weds ran past the long line of kiosks and down the concourse as fast as their hang-overs allowed.

The flight attendant at the ticket counter spotted them just as the workers moved to retract the boarding ramp.

"We're soooo sorry!" The young, out of breath, brunette blurted as they reached the check-in counter.

"No need." The middle-aged attendant politely shot back. "At least you made it!" She added as she collected their boarding passes.

The Boeing 737 which was Lufthansa flight 837 left Palma de Mallorca to Frankfurt, Germany on time with seventy-six passengers and five crew on board. Captain Heinrich Köhl and Hans Kessler as co-pilot mentally prepared to finish off their post take-off routine and were looking forward to a couple of hours of autopilot induced relaxation.

Thirty minutes later, with everyone else settled in for the afternoon flight, as the Head Stewardess was attending to the passengers in first class, a tall, male passenger seated in the first row casually stood, rummaged through the overhead bins and removed his gym bag. He then made his way back to the toilets.

It was ten minutes after that, as the plane entered Marseilles airspace, he returned to his seat next to the dark-haired woman he had boarded with.

It was then that the man and woman seated just behind the cockpit, smiled, kissed each other then stood and brandished their weapons, he a fully assembled Uzi and she a 9mm Glock.

"EVERYONE STOP WHAT YOU ARE DOING AND PUT YOUR HANDS ON YOUR HEAD! DO IT! DO IT NOW!"

At the same time two more appeared at the back of the plane also brandishing automatics.

The terrorists had placed themselves well, strategically speaking, with two rising from the seats next to the last row next to the service prep area.

The four now had visual and physical control of the entire passenger compartment.

Patiently waiting for the loud chatter and screams to subside the tall, cleanly shaven man up front spoke again.

"We are confiscating this plane in the name of Allah and the jihadi movement!" He declared as he brandished the Uzi which had been smuggled on board. "We are the Children of the Islamic Jihad. You will follow our orders and no one will get hurt!" The fact that none of the four made any attempt to hide their faces began to sow panic amongst some of

272

the passengers. "Everyone hands in the air and keep them there until told to lower them." He ordered then spoke again to the woman this time in Farsi.

The two men in the rear of the plane, also armed with an Uzi and 9mm's, had been busy corralling the flight crew into the small kitchen prep area.

The woman with the leader stepped out from behind her seat and aimed her Glock 9mm down the center of the aisle. Her well-dressed compatriot then forced his way into the cockpit.

In the rear of the plane one of the flight crew had already slipped into the kitchen area and dialed up the cockpit in the plane's intercom to alert Captain Kőhl.

He already knew.

"Put it down!" The hijacker quietly demanded as he leveled the Uzi at the Captain. "Pay attention! This plane is going to Cyprus!" He demanded.

"That' not possible!" Was all the captain was able to get out before he was butt stroked across the side of the head. The Hijacker then manhandled the dazed pilot out of the cockpit and instructed the woman to get him to the back of the plane.

"Cyprus!" He again demanded of the copilot.

Switching off the auto-pilot Kessler ordered the flight engineer to reset course for Cypress. It was less than a minute after that the engineer informed Kessler that fuel was an issue.

"We're currently exiting Parisian airspace. At this altitude and speed we'll fall into the Med somewhere near Sicily!" He calmly but firmly announced.

Kessler looked up at the hijacker. "This is a short hop flight!" He said. "We've a total of three and a half hours of fuel and have already burned through forty-five minutes of that!"

"Then you have precisely two hours and forty-five minutes to figure it out." He calmly pronounced. Kessler and the flight engineer exchanged glances.

"Give me the nearest international!" Kessler instructed the navigator.

*

Leonardo di Vinci-Fumicino, International, Rome

It was 45 degrees, humid and sticky throughout the fuselage as flight 837 sat on the runway while the fuel truck disconnected its hose and pulled away from Lufthansa flight 837.

"What now?" Kessler demanded from the hijacker.

"How long to Cyprus?" He barked back.

"As long as there's no weather and with no strong headwinds approximately three hours." The flight engineer answered.

"Then get the plane airborne and let's get moving!"

"It's customary protocol to contact the destination first and inform them you are coming."

His ploy of clandestinely extracting information from the thug failed.

"No!"

"If we don't contact them first when we do show up they'll get suspicious and who knows what they'll do!"

The terrorist thought it over for a brief time before responding.

"Do it once we are in the air! And choose your words carefully when you contact them!" He ordered,

Meanwhile the other two male terrorists were taking turns patrolling up and down the aisle. The short one noticed a woman occupying an aisle seat mid-fuselage and who was in apparent pain.

"Was ist los?" He asked her in heavily accented German.

"I don't . . . understand . . . you." She eked out.

"Was ist los bei dir?!" He demanded. The head stewardess over heard the commotion and moved up the aisle past the other terrorist to investigate.

"What's wrong dear? Can I get you some water or an aspirin?"

"I'm . . . pregnant."

"Was gibt?!" He demanded.

"Sie ist swanger." The stew informed the thug whose face immediately turned white.

"SWANGER?!" He yelped.

Finally entering Greek airspace Kessler radioed Cypriote air control.

"Cypress control this is Lufthansa flight 837 on emergency waylay from Palma de Mallorca. We are requesting permission to land."

There was a pause without answer. "Cypress control this is Lufthansa flight 837 on emergency waylay from Palma de Mallorca. We are requesting permission to land."

Lufthansa 837, this is Nicosia control. We have you on radar. We have been informed that following take-off from Leonardo di Vinci-Fumicino in Rome it is reported that you set your transponder to 7-7-0-0. What is your emergency?

"We are requesting permission to land. We are reporting a 7-5-0-0 situation. I say again, we have a seven-five-zero-zero situation and are requesting permission to land."

There was a longer pause.

Lufthansa 837, do you have any life threatening injuries to passengers at his time on board?

"Negative Nicosia. But we have seventy-six passengers and five crew. One pregnant, three children and several elderly."

Lufthansa 837, stand-by.

There was no contact for the next ten minutes before, without warning, a pair of F-14Tomcats slowly drifted into view off the left wing of the jetliner.

Unidentified Lufthansa fight, this is Mikos One Alpha, please identify yourself. I say again identify yourself.

The hijacker pressed the muzzle of his Uzi against the co-pilot's shoulder.

"I have to answer him!" Kessler insisted. The thug nodded. Before the co-pilot could respond the fighter escort again came up on the net.

Unidentified Lufthansa flight, this is Mikos One Alpha -

"This is Lufthansa 837 requesting permission to land! We are reporting a seven five zero zero situation!"

Lufthansa 837, we regret to inform you that we are not able to grant you permission to land at his time.

At the unexpected news Kessler's heart sank as an expression of total shock registered on the terrorist's face.

"Tower, Mikos One Alpha, 837 is repeating our request to land on humanitarian grounds!" Kessler tried again.

Again there was no response from the tower.

The hijacker signaled for the mike which Kessler passed to him.

"Nicosia tower, this a soldier of the Hezbollah! I demand you allow us to land or we will be forced to begin to execute passengers. To include your women and children!"

There was a pause followed by an unwelcome response.

837 this is Nicosia tower control. We are requesting that you vacate Cypriote air space at once or we will be compelled to give the Alphas the order to fire. Please comply at once!

Kessler and the terrorist traded glances.

"We are declaring an emergency! Do you read?" Again there was no response. "This is Lufthansa flight 837 –"

The port side fighter jet waved his wings then pointed from his cockpit to the other side of the jetliner where his wing man did a partial roll to starboard to display the AIM-9 missiles under his wings. The message was clear.

What the Jihadists had failed to account for was the fact that although they thought they could find safe haven on the Turkish side of the island the Greeks currently controlled the airspace and having dealt with Turkish terrorism since the First World War, especially in the case of an airliner with no Greek or Cypriote citizens on board, the Greeks saw no good reason to assist the terrorists in whatever destructive crimes they planned.

"They're denying us permission to land!" Kessler reiterated. "I can't just fly over and announce, 'here we are!'"

"Try again!"

"It's no use! They're not going to reverse their decision! There are too many terrorists hijacking too many planes! Nobody wants a repeat of Munich!"

"TRY AGAIN!"

Now nearly eight hours in the plane without a break both men's patience was wearing thin.

Kessler repeated his plea but this time with no response from the tower.

The terrorist grabbed the mic and yelled into it. "TOWER! WE NEED TO LAND!"

"You want to die for your god?! Then shoot me and die now!" Kessler defiantly declared.

Visibly angered the terrorist threw down the mike and stormed out of the cockpit to gather the others at the rear of the plane and quietly inform them of their newly developed situation.

In line with the international situation at the time Kessler was by no means shocked at the tower's refusal. Considering the recent long spate of hijackings compounded by the long feuding Greek-Turkish situation Kessler's mind had already begun scrolling through alternative destinations.

Kessler immediately took the opportunity to man the radio. He tuned it to the international emergency channel. 121.5 MHz VHF, the International Air Distress frequency or IAD.

"ATTENTION, ATTENTION ALL STATIONS! This IS LUFTHANSA FLIGHT 837. WE HAVE BEEN COMMANDEERED BY FOUR, I SAY AGAIN FOUR HIJACKERS! THREE MALES AND ONE FEMALE. KNOWN ARMAMENT INCLUDES THREE PISTOLS AND ONE UZI POSSIBLY TWO UZI MACHINE GUNS! WE ARE CURRENTLY –"

Just then the terrorist stepped back through the hatchway.

"WHO WERE YOU TALKING TO!" He demanded leveling his weapon at Kessler. The engineer quickly stood between them and spoke.

"We were trying to find a place to land before fuel again becomes critical." He urged.

"You must have had some kind of alternative plan?" Kessler meekly ventured.

"OF COURSE WE HAD ALTERNATIVE PLAN! YOU THINK WE ARE IDIOTS?!"

"Look, we are a German aircraft with much of the passenger list being German and Austrian, we were suggesting to divert back to Germany. It would look very bad if the German government denied us to land in our own country! At least from there you can buy time to calculate your next move." Kessler reasoned.

"Besides, Germany has a strict no shooting around civilians policy." The engineer added.

"YOU LIE!"

"No! He is telling the truth! Ever since the airport fiasco in Munich in 1972, 'no shooting' is a standing order!" The pilot affirmed.

Although neatly dressed, groomed and shaved the signs of stress were now beginning to show on the hijacker as the gang's international adventure hit one more unexpected hurdle.

Meanwhile a Sicilian fishing vessel which had just finished laying her nets picked up the plane's IAD call. The vessel's captain immediately ordered Palermo be notified who in turn notified Rome.

Thirty-five minutes later the Auswärtige Amt, the Department of State, in the Reichstag, Berlin was notified and a well-rehearsed bureaucratic routine was put into motion.

GSG9 were unleashed.

****

Rhein-Mein International
Frankfurt am Mein

It was around half past seven, the sun had dipped below the horizon forty minutes ago and further negotiations were underway as the hijacking was now an international news event.

At that exact moment a white Step-In van marked 'Knobloch Electrical Contractors' with a small box trailer hitched from behind raced across the rear access road of an abandoned hanger just inside the airport's perimeter fence.

The vehicle slowed, turned left and drove along the building then stopped short of the front entrance where a black clad man jumped out and entered the six digit code for the electronic lock to the personnel door to the left of the hanger door. Once inside he knew exactly how to activate the electric mechanism to raise the hanger's front door.

The large van entered the near empty hanger and pulled off to the side as the over-sized door reversed direction and rumbled closed.

Dressed in matching black utilities, black watch caps and combat boots around twenty men poured from the front and rear of the van and, without a word quickly formed up into a platoon formation.

One who appeared to be in charge stepped to the front.

"Alpha Squad, layout duty." He called out. "Bravo Squad, fuselage interior set-up and Charlie

Squad gear inventory and weapons issue. Sit-rep update in thirty minutes! LOS!"

As the men disbursed around the hanger and went to work the leader changed into a white dress shirt, dark blue blazer, dark tie and Lufthansa pilot's cap then grabbed a brief case from inside the van and headed off to the main tower.

Unbeknownst to the terrorists the pilots were not lying about German political policy concerning live fire around civilians, it was forbidden. Except in the case of one group. A secret group considered the most efficient anti-terrorist unit in Europe. Word had eventually gone out to Sankt Augustin, Rein-Seig, headquarters of the GSG9.

Grenzschutzgruppe 9 or the GSG-9, are the Federal Border Patrol Unit 9.

Commissioned after the Munich Olympic massacre perpetrated by Yasser Arafat's PLO, who were later to spawn the Hezbollah, it was by 1984 that the unit had achieved a world class level of proficiency.

In September of 1972 the GSG-9 were the Federal Border Patrol Unit '9' because they were christened the ninth border patrol unit to be formed.

At the time the GSG-9 were the only dedicated anti-terrorist unit on the Continent, had been trained by the British SAS and, in an ironic twist of historical fate also trained by the Sayeret Met'kal of Israel, at the time the only two dedicated anti-terrorist forces in the world.

As a branch of the German Federal Border Patrol the GSG9 fall under the jurisdiction of the Federal Ministry of the Interior.

By now Flight 837 was on runway 6 at Rhein Mein Flughafen in Frankfurt-on-Mein and the pregnant lady along with several of the younger children had been allowed to disembark in exchange for more fuel, a cursory maintenance check along with some food and fresh water.

By eight that evening patience of all on board was wearing extremely thin, a medic on board the plane had diagnosed the pilot as having a severe concussion from the blow he took at the start of the ordeal and, although a trained negotiator had been sent by the Federal Ministry of the Interior, things were not going well.

"Where do we stand?" The GSG9 commander, Oberleutnant Dee asked of the air base supervisor as he stepped off the control tower's lift onto the main operational space.

"They demanded we let them leave immediately or they will start killing passengers!"

"We are under strict orders from the minister to not allow them to take off!" Dee informed.

"But-"

"They have the same amount of hostages as they did at Entebbe! The Chancellor is adamant that we show the world Germany will not submit to terrorists. Otherwise, he reasons that we are vulnerable to further attacks."

The airport supervisor appeared far from convinced however offered no objection. Commander Dee continued.

"You have an open com line to the Bundeswehr commander?"

"Yes."

"Good. Has he checked in yet?"

"He reports the entire perimeter is secure and awaits your orders."

"Are your medics standing by?"

"As are the fire crews, commander."

"Well done. My call sign is Alpha Actual. Here's our plan . . ."

It was Commander Uwe Dee's Team Einsatzeinheiten Nummer Ein of the GSG9 who got the call so by practical protocol it was he who would make the calls as regarded tactical planning.

As with any other Western military commando unit, dispatched to resolve a land or sea-borne terrorist takeover of a vessel or land base, the final say so as to the 'when' was the responsibility of the politicians and so it was they who would give the green light of 'when' to go. However it always fell to the commander of the assaulting unit to determine the 'how' the assault would be executed.

Dee had been a policeman, a corporal, back in 1972 and could never divest himself of the fear, anger and frustration he felt that week in September as he, like the rest of the civilized world, watched on TV as a gang of racist murderers attacked the three thousand year old sanctity of the Olympic games.

Paddy Kelly

Worse yet was his life-long hatred of bullies. Bullies of any kind from school yard thugs to defective teachers to political adversaries who willingly employed strong arm tactics as a means to an end. A hatred he would channel into becoming an avowed enemy of terrorists for the remainder of his professional life.

"Upon successful completion of the assault I will radio the code word 'Frühlingszeit!' three times. Got it?" He clarified.

"Yes. The Chancellor has asked we set up a direct line to his office and we notify him when you go and it is finished." The supervisor informed.

Dee turned to the negotiator sitting at the coms console.

"What's your opinion?"

"I think that unless something happens to change-" He was cut off by a radio transmission coming over the frequency they had dedicated to the plane.

Gentlemen! Look to the left side of your airplane! Came the command which was followed by a transmission of people screaming.

In the left forward exit hatch stood the plane's pilot, a gun to his head. The terrorist pulled the trigger. Blood spattered as the pilot went limp and was allowed to tumble from the plane smacking down onto the tarmac. The murder was followed by another transmission of people screaming from behind the terrorist leader's next demand.

Unless our demands are met in the next fifteen minutes you shall witness a repeat of that demonstration!

"I think you are going to get your green light sooner than you think!" The negotiator informed Commander Dee.

Leaving a pre-set walkie-talkie with the supervisor Dee promptly returned to his operational center over in the hanger.

Alpha Squad, assigned layout duty, had set to work with chalk, mason's snap lines and tape measures. Working from a set of scale drawings provided by the manufacturer, reproduced an exact outline of the Boeing's fuselage to include pilot's and passenger's cabins, wing locations and most critical, locations of the aircraft's eight emergency exits. Two fore, two aft and four amid-ship.

Overhead clearances were annotated where needed.

Bravo Squad, in charge of the fuselage interior, had set up 80 folding chairs the exact distance apart as on the plane, forming the aisle, including the crew's cockpit seating, kitchen prep area and toilet cubicles on the rear right,

Meanwhile Charlie Squad, containing the chief armorer, had been assigned gear inventory and weapons, was occupied doing basic functions checks, loading extra magazines and recording serial numbers to be issued to which commandos. Weapons issued included one HK 9mm machine gun and three thirty round mags, one 9mm Glock with two mags and, compliments of their SAS counter parts, two purpose designed stun grenades.

Back in the tower another transmission came through.

They . . . they just killed Captain Kőhl. It was the voice of a shaken Kessler.

The eerie green glow of the radar tracking screen highlighted the ATC's face as he spoke into his headset.

"Roger 837. We saw it from the tower. Tell them we are in contact with Berlin seeking permission to proceed."

"Wilco."

****

"We are going to use *Operation Isotope* as a base plan." Commander Dee informed his men. Back in the hanger with the crews gathered around a folding table, Dee laid out his plan.

"Isotope?" One of the troops asked.

"It was an operation by the Israelis back in the early Seventies . . . seventy three or four I think."

"1972! I remember because it was the same year as Munich." His number two man added. "It was one of the first hijackings."

"So under strict orders to be careful to keep out of sight, the Bundeswehr has surrounded and secured our perimeter." He continued.

"Commander are we going to post a sniper over watch?"

"Unfortunately no. there are no suitable vantage points anywhere round the airfield. Anyway I don't expect any action outside the aircraft." He shifted to the open floor and stood just outside the center of the life-sized mock-up of the Boeing and pointed as he spoke.

"These aircraft have eight emergency exits. Two just behind the cockpit, four amidships and two either side in the aft section. Each emergency exit will be breeched simultaneously by two man shooter teams with the primary and back-up shooter.

"These tools the guys from Einsatzeinheiten Nummer Vier are passing out are on loan from aircraft maintenance." As he spoke two members of Einsatzeinheiten Vier, the supply, repair and maintenance unit of GSG9 wheeled out a door from a Boeing 737 mounted on a dolly. The commander approached, inserted the modified Allen wrench into a hole midway down on the right hand side and twisted left. There was a relatively loud click.

"Not very clandestine sir!" Someone called out.

"Pay attention. The doors open to the right. Five seconds prior to breech there will be a distraction provided by our friends from the Bundeswehr. I'm banking on the terrorists running towards the front of the aircraft to investigate. The sound of them running stimulating the passengers nervously murmuring should cover our opening of the exit doors. On my signal, once all the doors are unlocked, we breech."

"Standard assault entry commander?"

"Yes and mind the flash grenades, the Brits tell me they're made so they can't be thrown back or kicked away, so they have a short fuse."

"How short sir?"

"About three seconds."

"Assignment stations sir?" Dee walked to the front of the floor diagram. "Alpha Team! Two men each door!" He pointed. A he spoke four men, weapons at the low ready, scrambled forward and took up stations just outside each marked exit. He walked to center aircraft. "Bravo Team, two men port side two starboard!" The men repeated his instructions.

"How do we handle prisoners sir?" One of them asked prompting dead silence.

"It's his first non-training op commander." One of the senior troops volunteered.

"What's your name troop?" Dee asked.

"Shank sir," He snapped to attention. "Corporal Shank sir."

"Prisoners won't be a consideration Corporal."

"Yes sir." He understood.

"The remainder of the teams will be assigned ladder duty and passenger direction and rescue. Ambulances and medics will be standing by and drive out as soon as the all clear is sounded. Code word for completion is 'Frühlingszeit' repeated three times. Questions, comments snide remarks?"

Dee then raised the Bundeswehr commander on his radio.

"Lieutenant colonel, this is Alpha Actual. One of my men will be standing by at the north end of the tarmac, directly in line with the target, out near the perimeter fence line. We need a large fire to erupt on my signal. Can you comply?"

Wilco commander. Need ten minutes to arrange. Send signal when ready.

"Tower this is Alpha Actual. We are moving into place. In three minutes. Go ahead and tell them they have clearance to taxi. Do not tell them there will be a malfunction. It will be one serious enough to need repair and prevent take off. Tell them you have maintenance standing by and pretend to dispatch them."

Understood Alpha Actual. Tower out.

*****

Meanwhile inside the aircraft cabin, despite the mounting chill outside, the rising temperature inside combined with the encroaching stench to raise the tension to just short of breaking point. Save for the occasional change of positions, the four fanatics remained standing and slowly patrolling the limited space in the aircraft the entire time.

The fear and uncertainty of their future maintained its vice-like grip to hold the passengers frozen in place.

Carrying six padded aluminum ladders the teams hustled out single file to the left of the hanger and under cover of the encroaching dark approached the aircraft straight-on from the nose bifurcating to either side once underneath.

Once below the plane a ladder was raised then steadied upright by two others while a fourth climbed up and accessed the rear hydraulic lines.

In the cockpit Kessler had received the clearance to take off. He assumed the pilot's seat and with the engineer acting as his second, completed the preflight procedures and started the engines. Almost immediately a panel light began flashing and a low level alarm sounded.

"What now!" The head thug standing in the doorway demanded.

"There's a leak in a hydraulic line. It looks like . . . like the line to the stabilizer."

"FIX IT!"

Kessler, despite the last hours of stress and tension remained alert to what was happening around him and so was suspicious. Hydraulic lines don't just leak.

"Tower, we've an indicator light flashing. There appears to be a hydraulic line leak somewhere."

837 are you requesting we send maintenance out to you?

"Stand by tower." Kessler turned to the terrorist. Like a pair of school boys having to play chicken they stared at each other.

837 are you requesting maintenance?

"Yes or no?" Kessler pressed the terrorist.

"How long?"

"If it's only a simple leak fifteen maybe twenty minutes." Kessler didn't know why he lied but his instincts told him to.

"Yes. One man only. If he's armed he dies as do two other passengers with him!" He dictated,

"Tower this is 837, that's a yes on the repair. One man only."

Affirmative 837. I'll have a man enroute immediately.

Suddenly, through the front windshield they saw a fire erupt about 300 meters away, out by the perimeter fence.

Kessler quickly grabbed for the mike.

"Tower what was that?! There appears to be a petrol fire a couple of hundred meters in front of the aircraft beyond the tarmac."

The female terrorist and one of her male cohorts scurried forward and squeezed into the cockpit. The other remained in the rear opposite the toilets.

As they traded radio messages Commander Dee stood below the aircraft with all six commando teams in assault position. They were tuned into a common frequency monitoring the conversations.

"Wrenches!" Dee quietly ordered and Allen wrenches carefully slid into the access holes of the doors.

"Don't be nervous!" Kessler suggested attempting to calm the terrorists. "This is not uncommon on these older aircraft. "Yesterday we-"

Suddenly six of the exit doors simultaneously sprang open, stun grenades rolled up the aisle and deafening blasts accompanied by blinding flashes of light filled the cabin as a thin film of grey smoke seeped from the canisters to permeate the air.

"GET DOWN, DOWN, GET DOWN!" Shouting punctuated by coughing and screams and sporadic gunshots rang out.

"TWO TANGOS DOWN!" Someone called from the front of the cabin.

"ONE TANGO DOWN HERE!" Another called out. Three terrorists were accounted for. One missing. Suddenly, as the smoke began to clear more orders were issued.

"EVERYONE STAY DOWN! REMAIN WHERE YOU-"

Shots registered from back near the kitchen area and flew forward to chew at the forward partitions up front. The Alpha team men dodged them as the two commandos in the rear exit nodded to each and immediately two lines of bullet holes, one high one low, drilled through the flimsy walls of the kitchen. A loud thud was heard. A small pool of blood seeped out into the aisle.

"Alpha Actual this is Assault Leader. Aircraft secure."

Assault Leader, confirm all Tangos dead! Dee radioed back."Four dead confirmed Alpha."

Good. Evac all passengers and crew. Screen as they exit. Search all bodies for intel and beware of explosives!

"Roger Alpha."

Up in the control tower the supervisor, with his ear to the walkie-talkie heard the message: *Frühlingszeit! Frühlingszeit! Frühlingszeit!* A broad smile crept across his face.

Brief details followed.

When Two Tribes Go To War

Three dead one severely wounded. One passenger and one GSG-9 commando wounded. 'Four opponents down. All hostages free.' Commencing evac of aircraft.

****

At the Chancellery in Berlin a messenger interrupted a meeting with the Chancellor and some dignitaries.

"Herr Chancellor, this just arrived for you." He passed the folded over message across the desk.

"Call a press conference. Make the announcement." The Chancellor Helmut Kohl responded. "I'll say a word to the cameras after the Chief of Police speaks."

"Yes Chancellor."

****

Perhaps not so coincidentally, in the following months a rash of over half a dozen, supposedly unrelated suicides of convicted terrorists in German high security prisons was reported in the press.

Coincidentally all the deceased were members of associated terrorist groups of the PLO or their support group Der Rote Fraktion Armee, the Red Army Faction.

Memories of WWII evils die hard in Germany.

****

CHAPTER EIGHTEEN

By now the terminally ill Andropov and the majority of the Kremlin clearly imagined a developing world wide plot against them led by the U.S.

President Reagan's continued push for a world-wide embargo against the Soviets following their inadvertent shoot down of the KAL 007 passenger liner began to generate quiet but justified speculations of igniting WW III.

No one will ever know exactly what Andropov really believed about responsibility for the KAL shoot down, but whatever it was Reagan's snub of diplomacy and pursuit of extremely aggressive political tactics clearly had their intended effect. They backed the Russians into a corner leaving them no choice, in their minds, but to defend themselves.

Reagan's decision to use the KAL 007 shoot down to persuade Congress to support his requests for increased defense spending, the MX missile project and now his proposal of the SDI, Strategic Defense Initiative a.k.a. Star Wars system, no doubt added fuel to the fire.

A campaign of this magnitude and scope, which just happened to coincide with the Pentagon's ongoing PSYOPS incursion operations, where there just happened to be an RC-135 in the vicinity of the KAL aircraft was too much for Andropov to accept as a mere 'chance' coincidence.

When Two Tribes Go To War

Taken together with the fact that the men of the Politburo were exclusively made up of WWII era politicians who clearly remembered the 25 million Russians lost in the war, in no small part due to Hitler's treachery, one wonders how a war scenario hadn't developed sooner.

The Russians, no less than the Americans, were prone to developing complexes of paranoia and, like the joined continents of Pangaea, their world-wide, future image fit their respective imagined scenarios.

This series of events could only have the same effect it has always had and will always have: the development and propagation of unfounded aggression.

The U.S.'s continued unprovoked incursions into Soviet airspace had finally reached their inevitable conclusion – last September's escalation to a DEF CON 2 status in the U.S. which brought the world, (considering the Mutually Assured Destruction or MAD protocol of the time), closer to nuclear war then even the October 1962 Cuban Missile.

Fortunately what would become known as 'The 1983 Nuclear War Scare' was kept away from the press and so deterred the world-wide panic seen in 1962.

****

It was approaching half past seven when Doc and Mac came in off their morning run back at the team house. Harden had arrived early and Danno and Ricky Matson had yet to return from the gym.

Mrs. Gaffney worked office hours but usually showed up a half hour early to get her assignments for the day, have some coffee and get settled in.

Doc and Harden were over in McKeowen's space going over a medical resupply list . . .

"Lt. Commander Harden!" Mrs Gaffney called out from her office.

"Be right back." He told Doc. "Mrs. G, please call me Dave." He requested for the third time that week.

"And Lieutenant Commander, please don't call me 'Mrs. G'!"

"Message received Mrs. Janean Gaffney. What is it?"

"You just got a request to report over to the main desk at admin. There's an overseas classified message for you."

"Classification?"

"Eyes Only."

"Does that mean I only have to send my eyes?!" He joked. Gaffney didn't laugh. "Sounds important!" He added. "Doc, I'm off to admin. Tell the others to hang around until I get back." He called into Doc's office.

"Will do sir!" Doc yelled back.

Fifteen minutes later Harden had signed for his message and had slipped into the empty men's room and ducked into a stall. He ripped open the message to see it was from Colonel Kristina Naheem. His heightened attention was dashed as he read the few words on the telex paper.

Your FBI working on lead.
Believe it is your man they are hunting.

"Clever girl!" Dave said to himself as he realized that not only were the FBI monitoring the Mossad who were not only monitoring the FBI by reading their inter-departmental traffic, but the Israeli agency appeared to be two steps ahead of the American agency. Added to these facts Naheem showed she was fully aware of the lack of interdepartmental cooperation in the U.S. agencies, a detrimental habit carried over from the Second War.

Briefly considering his next move Harden returned to the team house.

"Mrs. Gaffney, ring the motor pool please. Tell them we need a car."

"Where to sir?"

"The Hoover Building, Penn Avenue." As they spoke Doc appeared from his area.

"What's up sir?"

"You wanna take a ride downtown?"

"Last time I heard that was from a cop when I was in high school! Sure why not?" He shrugged. "What's the mission?"

"Motor pool officer says five minutes Mr. Harden." Mrs. Gaffney called out from her desk.

"Thank you Janean . . . eh Mrs. Gaffney."

Twenty minutes later Doc and Harden arrived at the J. Edgar Hoover Building where Harden instructed the driver to wait down in the parking garage.

"What's up here sir?"

"Old friend from the LDO course, Phil Murphy. Got out, joined the Bureau and graduated Quantico, did four, five years field work then transferred here. Always was an office man."

The Limited Duty Officer course was a program whereby an enlisted sailor, if he qualified, could cross over into the officer's corps and eventually gain a limited command.

They signed in and made their way up to the fourth floor to Murphy's office.

"DAVE! Long time no see!" The tall, lanky brown-haired man behind the desk rose to shake hands as he eyed Doc who wasn't in uniform. "Who's your running mate?"

"Doc meet Phil Murphy. Phil this Doc McKeowen, he's helping me out over on O Street." They shook hands.

Harden was careful to skimp on any details concerning Task Force Romeo.

"What can I do for you Dave?"

"Phil I've been pulled for a job for some Pentagon boys and I thought it best to approach someone I knew and trusted."

"I appreciate that Dave. How can I help?"

"I'm told on the Q.T. by higher up that your guys in Anti-Terror are tracking down an individual that might himself be a higher up in this new terror group we've uncovered operating in and around Lebanon."

"I'm **on** the Anti-Terror squad and I'm not sure what you're getting at Dave?" Murphy appeared slightly defensive.

Murphy became visibly uncomfortable as he answered and Harden realized why his former class mate from the Limited Duty Officer's course didn't last as a field man.

"Doc step outside for a moment would ya?" He requested.

"Sure thing sir." Doc complied.

"The terrorists you're dealing with call themselves Hezbollah." Harden definitively informed.

"How do you know that?! That's not due cleared for release until next week sometime!"

Dave leaned forward and set his arms on Murphy's desk.

"Hezbollah, it means the Army of God. Additionally you're guys are pretty sure they're the assholes that snatched Bill Buckley off the street in Beirut. They're probably right."

Murphy shot forward in his seat.

"How in the hell do you know all this?!"

"Phil, we're on the same team! If we work together, even if it has to be under the table, we can fight these bastards a lot more effectively! This inter-agency rivalry bullshit is totally political!" Harden opined.

Murphy sat back in his chair and pondered.

"Jesus Dave you think I don't know that?! You think I don't cringe every time I think about what happened last year with the *Able Archer* operation.

How close we came to ending it all?!" Murphy stared dead out into space. "Hell I was right there when Casey told Reagan our sat photos showed the Russians had their missile silos around Moscow open and activated! Hell, Reagan's face turned three shades of white before he fell back into his chair!" Murphy shook his head. "I have no Idea what field team went in there and rescued Gordievsky but that took some brass balls, I tell ya!"

Harden maintained his poker face.

"I need a name Phil. How do I get that name?" Dave again asked. Murphy didn't respond. "You know I can submit a 549 then they'll be all kinds of inquiries as to why we're not sharing intel." Harden gently reminded.

Murphy shifted his gaze to glare at Harden with a mixture of distain and empathy. Finally he sat forward, unlocked his middle desk drawer and copied a name from a document onto a Post-it before passing it over the desk to Harden.

"The name they're tracking down is Nabal Saleh Mubarak." Murphy said.

"Nabal Saleh Mubarak!" Harden repeated as he read.

"As far as I know all they have is the one name." Murphy added. "You didn't get that from this office, you read me?!"

"Mubarak! Of course not!" Harden stood to leave. "How solid is this?"

"Straight from the head of The Bureau!"

"Are they still active on it?" Dave probed.

"I've not been briefed on the current status." Murphy again shifted in his seat.

As Dave made it to the door Murphy called after him.

"What's your source Harden? How do you know about the Hezbollah?"

"Just good field work, Phil. Just good field work." As he reached for the door handle he added. "By the way, I can also confirm for you that the Islamic Jihad Organization a.k.a.the IJO is fronting for Hezbollah who in turn is being funded primarily by the Iranians. They're essentially the same gang." Murphy stared in disbelief at Harden's level of knowledge of a group the Agency was only just investigating.

****

**Century House,
Westminster Bridge Road,
Lambeth, Central London**

FLASH MESSAGE: EYES ONLY!

LOCAL: Tel Aviv, Israel

TIME: 07:44:16 AUG 84

SUBJECT: *Addendum to Dafqat Jabira intercept.*

Sources confirm subject Romeo Tango has travelled to U.S. and is believed to be in same at this time.

Exact whereabouts unknown.

---- END MESSAGE ----

In his Century House office in London John Scarlett, Senior Intel Analyst at MI6 read the message as it came across the secure teletype from Tel Aviv.

Mossad had been decoding traffic all morning and passing relevant bits to MI6. This one originated from an intercept from Hezbollah to the head Imam in Tehran.

The message intercepted and passed to MI6 was sent from the Iranian Intel Service MOIS. MOIS, founded in 1983 and now under the leadership of Mohammad Reyshahri, a known terrorist, replaced the dreaded SAVAK which operated under the Shah.

MOIS are responsible for intel, counter-intel and supervision of the Iranian secret police.

Scarlett reached over and depressed his desk intercom.

"Saxon, can you come in here please?" He directed more than requested.

"Yes sir?" The middle-aged man inquired as he entered and approached his desk.

"Drop what you're doing, go downstairs and send this to Langley now!"

"Cover letter sir?"

"Not necessary. They'll know what it is."

"Very good sir." He turned to leave.

"Saxon!" Saxon stopped at the door.

"Sir?"

"Sorry I snapped at you yesterday."

"Not at all sir. Comes with the territory I suppose." He shrugged and left. Scarlett sat back in his chair and smiled.

However the amusement melted from his face as he again realized the meaning of the message; There would be some kind of an attack in next few days somewhere in the States perpetrated by subject Romeo Tango. AKA: Ali Akbar Aminpur.

****

Senator Omar, now dressed in jeans, casual shirt and jacket but minus a head scarf, made her way to the American Fazi Mosque on Leroy Place in the city center of D.C.

The oldest mosque in the city rather than an elaborately decorated, towering stone structure the Fazi was little more than a converted three story, red brick Georgian-styled residence.

However she chose the place as her next meet specifically for its low profile, out-of-the-way local as well as the fact that she had connections there. A private room had been arranged.

As she passed by several parked vehicles in the residential neighborhood a tall, well-dressed man of obvious middle-eastern ethnicity in his thirties exited a parked car up the block and followed her into the mosque.

Once in a sound proofed room in the basement, behind locked door their meeting commenced.

"We have new orders." She curtly delivered.

"I was told the mission was cancelled."

"Then perhaps you also got word that the Russians have cancelled the rocket shipment to Tehran!" She informed.

"No I don't hear this. Why, cancelled? We have no money?"

"No! Because your out-of-control idiots in Beirut decided to go off on their own and stage a kidnaping! Of some Russian diplomats no less!"

"Yes I read in papers."

"Fortunately we were able to strike a deal with the Chinese."

"Okay, so we are back on?"

"Do you know what an MK 153 is?"

"Of course! It's a SMAW. A Shoulder Launched Multipurpose Weapon. Intended for anti-tank operation." He shot back.

"Very good, now pay attention! Five hundred of them were shipped from Beijing to Beirut and landed last Thursday."

"What good they are to us there? We need them in Florida!"

"If you stop interrupting me you will find out!" She stared him down. "Before heading to the Med the tanker sailing under a Thai flag, diverted south in the Atlantic and met a fishing vessel where a half dozen of them with rockets were off loaded at sea 100 miles off the coast of Freeport in the Bahamas. They were put onto a boat posing as a deep sea fishing tour vessel. This boat, the *Lucky Lady*, is due to return and dock at Port Saint John just west of the target area in the morning."

"I go to Florida?" He queried with a tinge of hope.

"No, you are going to get a message to your team there and inform them of the arrangements to collect the weapons, *Lucky Lady* slip number 17, Understand? Think you can remember that?" She sarcastically quipped.

"Why you always talk down on me?"

"Because every time I think that the success of the struggle against these western infidels comes down to dinks like you I get depressed that's why!"

"What is 'dink'?"

"It means great warrior! Now go! And tell your Muppets to cease going on independent adventures of their own! We have limited funds from the U.N. to work with! Those imbeciles cause any more international embarrassments and the Security Council in Tehran is likely to shut us down for good!"

A short while later they made staggered exits from the house.

****

CHAPTER NINETEEN

O Street Team Room

Since moving in some weeks ago Lt. Commander Harden had put together a to-do list for Mrs. Gaffney to upgrade the warehouse space into a suitable team room. In addition to gear lockers for each of the TFR team, some chairs, a work bench for equipment repair and a used round conference table they now had a half-finished shower area adjacent to the existing toilet.

In addition Doc McKeowen finagled, traded and appropriated some Spec Ops gear for a pair of medicine cabinets, an exam table, a kick bucket, a doctor's medical stool and an autoclave that needed some repair.

Harden had gathered his four man team at the old, round conference table for the first official gathering in their new home.

"We need a brainstorm session lads! I'll need all the brain power I can get for this one too! Mac, just contribute what you can."

"Sir?" Mac raised his hand as he interrupted. "What do can-trib-butte mean?" He asked in a mock brain-damaged voice.

"It means be a good boy and I'll get you something good to eat when we're done with this meeting." Harden retorted.

"Oh goodie! What's her name?" Mac asked.

"You're a pervert!" Danno laughed.

"I don't know, he doesn't come to the meetings!" Ricky jumped in.

"Sure he does, I seen him there!" Doc defended. "What's up sir?" Doc finally broke in.

"Thank you Doc! We have a lead on one of the Hezzies. We think he is here, in country. It's a bit of a thin lead but it's hot off the FBI teletype."

"What is it sir?"

"A name."

"That's it, one name?!" Matson challenged.

"No, there's more. We have both his names." The Skipper tossed the Post-it note with the name on it into the middle of the table. Danno picked it up and read aloud.

"Nabal Saleh Mubarak!"

"So, if you were a bad guy-" Harden began.

"You mean a disgruntled, raghead who's hatred and jealousy extended to all western cultures because they were better educated, more well-off financially and who had more opportunities, didn't dress their women like bee keepers and didn't look like Big Foot wrapped in a black table cloth? Those guys?"

"Yeah Ray, those guys." Harden sat back and smiled. "You ever considered a career with the U.N.?" Harden asked. "You'd make a helluva diplomat."

Since last year's mission, compounded by MacDonald's experiences on the SEAL Team, he had lost all respect for his Arab adversaries.

"As I was saying, if you were a bad guy and wanted to get yourself noticed, you know make a 'big splash' in the media. How would you go about it?" Dave proposed.

"Well in keeping with their underhanded, cowardly ways I'd pick a very public event." Doc contributed.

"One with a crowd!" Danno added.

"Of civilians!" Ricky chimed in.

"Yeah, it's gotta be civilians they can't fight back." Doc concurred.

"Maybe a school or a hospital?" Danno offered. "Those assholes in Beirut and Gaza are always firing off rockets from schools, hospitals and mosques to bait the Israelis to fire back!"

"Yeah, then they parade the useful idiots in the corporate media through the wreckage and cry foul!" Mac added.

"Best case scenario to me seems to be a bomb during a public event like a holiday or festival or something." McKeowen deduced for the group.

"Okay we're making progress." Harden encouraged.

"Now all we need to do is figure out where these assholes might strike next, where they are now, who this Mubarak clown is and where they might plant the bomb!" MacDonald sarcastically added.

"Or bombs!" Ricky threw in.

"That's encouraging!" Danno grunted.

After a moment of silence Doc slid his chair out from the table, dashed into his clinic and returned. He tossed a copy of a glossy periodical on the table face-up and opened to a half page story on the seventh page of the tabloid.

"What the hell is that?" Mac asked.

"The July issue of *Dos Yiddishe Licht*. It's a Yiddish monthly on international events, cultural affairs and so forth. I brought it back from Tel Aviv as a souvenir. You know, a curiosity."

Mac picked it up and perused the cover.

"Doc, you can read this gibberish?" MacDonald asked.

"It's called Yiddish, you heathen!"

"Yiddish?"

"Yes. It's evolved from medieval German with some Polish and Russian mixed in. But basically it's a Germanic language."

"Still gibberish to me." He quipped. Doc snatched the magazine from Mac's hands.

"Give a guy a library card, teach him to read, send him to school and he eats the pages out of the books!" Doc quipped. "The man who does not read has nothing on the man who can't read!" McKeowen scolded.

"That's pretty good Doc! You make that up?" Ricky asked.

"No it's from Twain."

"It's still gibberish." Mac whispered.

"Yes, 'gibberish' from the Yiddish word 'gib-rish' for nonsensical, rubbish, balderdash." McKeowen sarcastically informed.

"Fucking guy thinks he knows everything!" Mac mumbled as he sat back, turned and shrugged to Harden.

"Not true!" Doc protested. "There are a great number of things I don't know Mac."

"At least he's modest!" Harden defended.

"Just nothing of any significance." Doc added. Mac flipped him off.

"Where you going with this Doc?" Harden asked.

"The article is about a big launch . . . . set to . . ."

"To . . . ?"

"A launch next month out in L.A.!" He finished. Danno Byrd's face lit up.

"You're talking about the fucking Olympics!" Danno Byrd realized.

"No, no! The fucking Olympics were last week, at the twin's house!" Mac quipped.

Harden sat forward in his chair and smiled. "Doc, I think you're on to something!"

"Thank you sir! At least someone recognizes talent when they see it."

"If this guy's target really **is** the Olympics we've got some homework to do!" Harden declared.

"Talk to us Skipper!" A fired up Matson said.

"Here's the deal; Ricky and Danno, I want a complete report on The Games coming up next month, opening ceremonies to closing. Events, times dates and above all venues. Run us five copies of the entire daily schedule. I need that by the morning. And make sure to find rosters accompanying the events."

"Why rosters sir?" Danno asked.

"Couple'a reasons. We know this guy's a Muslim. It's against the Quran for a Muslim to kill another Muslim, if a given heat in any certain event has a significant number of Muslims competing he's less likely to do something that might kill one of them. Additionally he might have accomplices posing as coaches, trainers or even fellow competitors."

"Jesus sir! You should'a been a cop!"

"What'a you need from me sir?"

"Doc, you get with Mrs. Gaffney and get us a list of POC's to include all the local authorities up to and including the local chapter of the L.A.P.D. and the FBI. Whatever you do don't contact any of them! This one is under the wire. And see if you can't scare up a couple of maps of the L.A. Olympic area too."

"Will do sir!"

"Then coordinate with Ricky and Danno and together start trying to pinpoint events he's likely to hit."

"Skipper?" MacDonald shrugged.

"Mac, you're with me."

"Aye sir!"

"We need to plan a gear and weapons list."

"I'm on it sir."

"Everyone back here by 1800 ready to brief the others!"

*

LAX
Thursday, August 7th

In civilian attire Harden, Doc, MacDonald, Danno Byrd and Ricky Matson touched down at the Mayor Tom Bradley Terminal in LAX.

Still under construction, flooded with the usual tourist traffic and now compounded by a plethora of Olympic visitors, finding the Courtesy Information Booth was no easy task. When they did they were faced with a reality none of them had banked on.

Their hotel reservation had been mistakenly cancelled and rented to another party and by that late date there was not even a folding bed to be rented within 100 miles of the Memorial Coliseum in Central L.A.

At the Courtesy Information desk in the noisy, chaotic terminal they were further informed that ten days ago the International Olympic Committee moved several venues to larger locations and relocated others miles away from the city center thus significantly affecting their proposed operational area.

After a short discussion of what their next move should be Danno turned, grounded his bag and started to walk away.

"Leave it to me!" He confidently declared.

"Where you going?" Harden asked him.

"To find a phone."

"Sir, is your call a local one?" The pretty Latina behind the courtesy desk asked.

"Huntington Park?" Danno said.

"If that's the case you're welcome to use our courtesy phone." She smiled. Danno moved to the phone at the end of the desk.

He found his friend's number and called but the line was engaged. He tried again and again. And yet again.

"It's still busy." After nearly a full hour Dave Harden decided that time was now a factor.

"Danno, we appreciate the effort but we can't hang around here all day. We've got to get settled in and set up somewhere!" Harden pushed. Danno thought for a bit then announced.

"Skipper he owns his own house, he's got to be home soon. Let's just shift ourselves and wait around out there. It's only a fifteen minute taxi ride. I mean better than just sitting here." He argued.

Harden considered the suggestion and ten minutes later they were in a taxi van heading west.

Nearly an hour into their fifteen mile trip, they were in a palm festooned, working class neighborhood and pulling up to a grey two story on a palm lined street adjacent to a sprawling, palm packed park.

"Guess these people like palm trees!" Ricky observed as they piled out of the van and unloaded their gear.

"You sure this is gonna fly with your mate, what's his name?" Doc asked.

"Jimbo Kearney we did the basic radiomen's course at Fort Knox together. Then we were both assigned to Bragg." He explained in all sincerity. "You guys are gonna love him! He's the original party animal! Don't be surprised if he offers to break out the beer and weed as soon as we get inside!" Danno rang the bell again.

"Alcohol at 1300 in the afternoon?!" Mac exclaimed. "I like this guy already!"

The door opened and there stood a five foot five slightly balding, pot-bellied late thirty-something in a tee shirt and blue cargo shorts holding a six month old teething infant. Another scurried up to the open door and latched on to the man's bare leg and stared up at Danno.

"Yes?" The man asked as he wiped the infant's perpetually leaking mouth.

"Jimbo! It's me Danno! Danno Byrd!" A smile crept across Jimbo's face.

"Danno! How the hell are ya?! How ya been Dude?!"

"I been good, been good, thanks. Hey Jimbo, we got a little problem with this Olympic thing going on and all-"

"Yeah, the whole city's a mess, man!" He concurred.

"Here's the deal, our hotel rooms got fucked up-"

"You said a bad word!" The two year old attached to Jimbo's leg giggled and pointed at Danno.

"He always says bad words Honey, He's a bad man!" Doc said to the kid as he peeked over Danno's shoulder into the house.

"Our hotel rooms got . . . screwed up and we're really pressed for some digs." Danno finished.

"Wow man that's a drag dude! But -"

"WHO'S THERE?!" A women's voice yelled from inside the house.

"NO ONE! JUST SOME OLD FRIENDS." Jimbo yelled back. "I'd really like to help you guys out Bro but we got no room at the inn man, you dig?" He nodded to his kids.

"Come on Jimbo, it's only for one night, two at most. Besides, we'll be out seeing the sights and looking around most of the time."

"Danno, seriously it's not a good time man! My old lady, Mary just got back to work, we got this new kid!"

Just then a well built, woman in an L.A.P.D. patrolman's uniform appeared from the hallway and stood assessing the human pile-up at the front door.

"These your friends?" She asked.

"Yeah, but ahhh-"

"Well what the hell you doin' keepin' ya friends outside?! Bring 'em in ya inhospitable oaf! Ya want them to fry in the sun?!" She nudged Jimbo aside and gestured them in. "You'll have to excuse him." She sarcastically confided. "He was in the Army!"

"I know what you mean ma'am. No manners!" Mac concurred.

That night the TFR team slept on the most comfortable basement floor on Zoe Avenue in L.A.

****

Next morning, armed with their reassessed location intel and now on the clock so-to-speak, Harden decided the team needed a locale they could have a modicum of privacy to solidify a plan.

Jimbo's wife Mary directed them to a small place, a restaurant away from the beaten path and the hub bub of the city that hosted no crowds at least until

316

around the lunch hour. The name she recommended, *The Happy Cow* should have been a dead give-away.

It wasn't.

They found a large booth in the back corner where there was no one within earshot and waited for a waiter.

"I'll have a roast beef sandwich with-" Mac was the first to order.

"I'm sorry sir this is a meat free zone." The chartreuse adorned waiter with the prominent man bun informed.

"'Meat free zone?' What the hell does that mean?" Mac challenged.

The visibly annoyed server batted his heavily purple shadowed, eyes and sighed.

"It means sir that we don't serve any dead animal flesh."

"Well bring me a live one, I'll kill it!" Mac chuckled. The Elton John wanna be wasn't amused.

"I think he's trying to tell you it's a vegetarian restaurant, Mac." Ricky informed.

Mac raised and read from the menu.

"*Foot Long* hot dog. *Quarter Pounder* hamburger?" Mac read out loud. "What's that? I thought this was a vegetarian restaurant?"

"Those are all vegetarian options, made without helplessly slaughtered, animal flesh."

"Vegetarian huh?"

"We not only cater to vegetarian's sir but lacto vegetarians, ovo-vegetarians, lacto-ovo vegetarians, vegans, pescatarians and Fletchertarians as well."

The five of them exchanged stares. Danno fought back a smile threatening to erupt into laughter.

"Ball's in your court Mac!" Doc declared.

"What in the hell is a Fletchertarian?'!" Ray MacDonald inquired.

"I'm glad you asked! You see, back before the Civil War a man named Horace Fletcher-"

"Forget it! Sorry I asked. Gimme a salad, oil and vinegar." Mac snapped as he handed the menu back to the waiter. "And bring some vegetarian bread too, please. With vegetarian butter. And a large vegetarian Coke!"

The others gave their orders and as the waiter left they set to work.

They had been given a preliminary briefing back in D.C. at the O Street team house but now on the ground with eyes on the operational area was the time to sort out the details.

"First off remember, this is an internal mission with no external agency awareness." The Skipper started.

"Or permission!" Mac added.

"Meaning?" Ricky asked.

"Meaning one of us goes down we all bite the dust." Doc informed.

"Doc lived out here for a year or so after he trained at Coronado. He has some useful input on our situ. Especially the heat. Doc?" Harden relinquished the floor to McKeowen.

"95 to 100 degrees every day. Muggy nights, no rain. Avoid the local cops! These guys are some sharp troopers but because they see so much weird shit they're conditioned to shoot first and ask questions later. And they don't piss around with back-up. If they call for a 10-999 you will be knee-deep in blue in a matter of minutes! All with itchy trigger fingers!" Doc added. "Finally the city is sprawling! We're not in D.C.! As you can see the scheduled Olympic events are spread out over one hundred miles apart. Lastly this place is known for traffic and derelicts!"

"So what you're saying is basically we're not in Kansas anymore Dorothy?"

"Yes. If one of us gets in the shit with the local constabulary out-running them is highly unlikely. Since they have race riots out here every couple of years they have the largest helicopter fleet of any police department in the country. As we are on our own out here I suggest we consider ourselves behind enemy lines."

"I've laid out a plan for after we've located this guy." Harden announced as he passed out some thin packets.

"What'a we do with this guy after we have him sir?" Ricky asked.

"I'll get to that in a minute. As we learned back in D.C. our man according to the FBI is a Mr. Nabal Salah Mubarak. The bureau guy I spoke to over at the Hoover Building had no other details to pass on.

"We think we know he is likely to be found somewhere in the vicinity of the Memorial Stadium at a time yet to be determined." Harden said as he distributed the standard manila envelopes to each member of the team.

"The ragheads in Munich attacked on the tenth day." Ricky pointed out.

"Yes, but just as we learned a lot about security since then, we have also learned to bank on the idea that they too have learned to up their game."

"Like how sir?" Matson asked.

"Like how to cause not only maximum deaths but also maximum disruption to our routines and life styles." They all opened the packets. "Inside each packet is a map of the Greater L.A. area, a list of all our call signs, a surveillance photo of who we think is our man and since we don't know if he speaks English very well a brief list of commands in French and Arabic."

"Sir this surveillance photo is useless!" Mac complained as he examined the photo he found in the packet. "The lighting is terrible, it's out of focus and from this three quarter profile I could be looking for Harry Belafonte, Bill Cosby or Idi Amin Dada!"

"Cosby is out here somewhere working on his new TV show, Belafonte is appearing at *The Sands* in Vegas and according to the CIA Idi Amin is dead. Do the best you can." Harden snapped.

"Impressive sir! Never knew you were so culturally aware and socially well-informed!" Mac shot back.

"Which is why I'm The Intel Officer and you're the enlisted puke. I mean that in the nicest way possible, Petty Officer MacDonald."

"I complexly understand sir." Mac humbly replied.

"I remind you all, for Intel purposes this guy has to be taken alive!" Harden added.

"Does that mean unharmed sir?" Ricky pushed.

"Breathing." Harden reiterated.

"Any skinny on possible body guards, secondaries or back-up he might have?" Danno asked.

"No intel Danno."

"Nothing like launching off on a mission with a full and complete intel picture, hey?" Mac quipped.

"Danno, you wanna give them the good news?" Harden offered.

"My pleasure sir." Danno reached into his bag and produced copies of the roster for the Men's Marathon and passed them out. "Gentlemen may I call your attention to runner number 291 please?"

"IT'S MUBARAK!" Ricky declared.

"A little louder Matson! I don't think the cashier up front heard you!" Danno chastised as he looked around.

"He's actually competing?! That can't be right!" Ricky mumbled.

"I guess you can't get any more undercover than to not be undercover!" Danno commented.

"He's listed as a late entry!" Doc observed.

"Sounds like he's been activated just for this mission. But we still don't have a photo or description." MacDonald added.

"He's African, Moroccan. I'm guessing average height, black curly hair, brown eyes–" Danno added.

"Dark complected!" Mac chimed in.

"You're a raciest!" Ricky quipped.

"I don't know, he doesn't come to the meetings." Doc added.

"Okay listen up. You'll notice that Danno has traced out the route of the marathon. What I want is two teams. Team A comprised of Doc and Mac and Team B Danno and Ricky." They nodded in acknowledgement. "The route is forty three klicks long, from Santa Monica college east to the Memorial Coliseum downtown. I divided it into four legs. Each rendezvous point is marked by a red dot on your map. Team A take R-1. Team B R-2. Team A as soon as our man's heat passes call it in then shift to R-3. Likewise Team B. Team B as soon as you confirm he's still in the race bail from R-4 and join the rest of us here on the corner of South Hoover in front of this car dealership which will be closed on the day. I checked." Each man took notes as needed. "They start at the college and finish in the stadium so it stands to reason that if he suddenly disappears during the race, he's likely headed for his target."

"And if he does slip away during the race?" Ricky asked.

"We scramble and look for him. Shouldn't be too hard to find a sweaty African guy in running shorts." Danno argued.

"Keep in mind he may not necessarily be looking to set off an explosive device. He may have been sent in on a hit mission or to aid on a snatch of some description."

"Have we checked to see if there are any potential targets along the route?" Mac probed.

"Yes, there are two." Harden replied. "One here, the B'nai Shalom Jewish Rec center and another a block away, Temple Beth-el. Since the race is on a Friday it's more likely there'll be more people in the rec center but we need to watch both." Harden explained.

"And if it's neither?"

"Then we keep tailing him until he makes his move." Harden explained.

"Afterwards, if he goes to the end, he'll likely be heading back to the Olympic Village to clean up and rest."

"The program says the runners are staying at the Olympic Village, Westwood at UCLA between Hollywood & Santa Monica." Danno added before Harden picked it up again.

"And that brings us to the primary and secondary ambush sites. I have two pre-paid rental cars and a van on stand-by at AVIS Rentals. We pick them up the morning of. The Olympic Village is likely to be too heavily guarded and the athletes' entrance and exit at the Coliseum, which is into Lot 4 on the south side of the Coliseum, will also be too high profile."

"That leaves us taking him in route." Doc observed. Harden continued pointing out the locales as he spoke.

"Exactly. There are multiple overpasses across the Harbor Freeway but here just after the seventh overpass is a short tunnel with a shoulder lane. Once we pick him up we tail him until the tunnel, Team B you will have to maneuver in front of him by the sixth over pass. Halfway through the tunnel you'll let him creep up on you then hit the brakes."

"Ahhh! The old Avis rental car-fake-fender-bender-in-the-tunnel trick! An oldie but goldie!" MacDonald interjected.

"Mac, focus!"

"Yes sir. Sorry sir."

"And what do we do once we collar this prick?" Ricky asked.

"We notify D.C. at which point I suspect they'll tell us to turn him over to the local FBI so they can interrogate him."

As Harden and the TFR planned their mission Akbar and company were on a mission of their own. . .

*** **** ***

The Marathon Route
08:00 Friday, August 8th

Having discovered that their target's cover was as a marathon runner and that he actually made it through U.S. customs by having entered the XXIII Olympics and having no idea what his plan might be, Harden had little choice but to locate and keep an eye on him.

Several of the team advised the Skipper to at least alert and coordinate with the L.A.P.D. and although Harden considered it he declined the idea based on the fact that if it leaked it could start a panic. Besides, he reasoned that no one, the FBI, the L.A.P.D. or even the TFR could do much else without a more solid lead or until their suspect definitively revealed himself.

Guessing there was a reasonable chance that whatever kind of attack he had planned there was a good bet it would be in front of the TV cameras for maximum effect.

By dividing the well-publicized marathon route into four sectors Harden arranged for the team to report when they spotted Nabal Salah Mubarak and so could know that he was still in the race. In essence tacking him.

To avoid as much heat as possible it was just after eight in the morning that the race kicked off from the sports field of the Santa Monica college track field. Harden, with the other four TFR members at their respective stations standing by, I.D.'d runner #297 at the start as best fitting the vague description they had after the runners exited the school stadium. Harden even managed to snap a few photos with a disposable camera he had picked up at a tourist kiosk.

On station six miles away, from inside the vestibule of a near-by bar Doc and Mac stared up at the TV set as the stadium's P.A. blared announcements and updates.

Ladies and gentlemen may I remind you that when the runners return to enter the Coliseum they must go to the finish line then make one full lap to complete the race.

325

As the peloton of runners headed south towards Culver City Doc and Mac moved back out into the street to watch for the racers to pass by.

Led by a motorcycle, piggy backed with a cameraman being kept at a distance by the city cops the front runners were led through the streets of L.A. neighborhoods while L.A.P.D. motorcycle cops intermittently placed, controlled the crowd as the main body progressed.

"Hats off to these guys!" Mac commented to Doc as the lead group ran by.

"Who?"

"The runners!"

"Why?"

"A lot of them ran a marathon only weeks ago up in Albany, New York."

A by-stander next to Mac was overheard to comment. "Looks like Jerry Kiernan's in fourth." Mac quickly checked his program.

"Hey Doc, there's one'a your people in fourth and fifth!" He nudged McKeowen.

"Yeah, who's that?"

"John Treacy. He's Irish!"

"Never heard of the bum!"

"Except for a free drink, a free meal or from the cops I never knew Irish could run so fast!" Mac quipped.

"You're a barrel of laughs. Ask Danno, he's from Bean Town!" Doc suggested. Mac manned his hand held.

"Hey Danno, you ever of-"

No! Fuck off! Came the terse reply from the grey Ford Tempo parked a few miles down the route at the R-2.

"Fuckin' Irish! Always so cordial!" Mac mumbled. Doc manned his radio.

"Skipper?"

Go Doc.

"I see him, he's still in the race."

Roger target sighted.

"A Team shifting to R-3. Out.". Doc informed.

Over an hour later Team A of Task Force Romeo, consisting of Doc McKeowen and Ray MacDonald, had just rotated to the R-3 local and again spotted runner #297 as he was rounding the corner well to the rear of the lead heat of runners. Harden, having picked up the surveillance at the marathon's start point on the Santa Monica College campus was now making his way crosstown to the Coliseum and was becoming concerned.

With the runners well passed the B'nai Shalom Jewish Rec center and the Temple Beth-El the entire TFR unit was wondering where Mubarak was planning his attack.

By the time the terrorist essentially finished the marathon in 44th place the TFR unit had assembled in the area of the car dealership opposite Lot 4 of the L.A. Coliseum it had become clear that Mubarak's mission or his target wasn't along the race route.

A new guessing game began.

With A and B Team's two door sedans parked a block apart but at forty-five degree angles, essentially at the four and eleven o'clock positions relative to the south gate of the stadium, the teams had a commanding view of the entirety of Gate #4 to include the whole south side of the Coliseum.

Nearby Lt. Commander Harden sat on one of the few small hills in the whole of L.A. standing by to play quarterback as well as a back-up chase vehicle if needed.

It was then that their oversight hit them. An IOC bus pulled up to the gate not only blocking their view but reminding them of something they hadn't planned for. Transport other than Mubarak's own car.

Banking on the fact that Mubarak would have to drive west across town to reach the Olympic Village back in Santa Monica, Harden decided that failure to spot him now would mean they would have to wait until that evening when their mark would be out and about in public. A much more dicey scenario Harden immediately realized.

Just as the bus was preparing to load up MacDonald grabbed the walkie-talkie off the dashboard, jumped out of the black Ford Taurus and dashed across Bill Robertson Lane to Martin Luther King Boulevard and innocuously strolled to within close sight of the bus.

Noting there were only three black track and field competitors there, all wearing Nigerian colors, all took seats together and one of them with a bronze medal around his neck by the time the bus had loaded, closed its doors and pulled out, MacDonald had correctly deduced that Mubarak was not among those aboard.

"Dry hole fellas! No terrorists in deese here parts." He called in via the radio.

"Roger that Mac." Harden called back.

"Sorry sir. No idea where he is."

"Bring it in. Form up on my vehicle, time for Plan B!" Harden radioed back.

"Roger that sir."

From the driver's seat in the Taurus Doc maintained surveillance.

"You guys are not gonna believe this!" Doc radioed.

As the bus was pulling out of the opposite end of the parking lot he watched as a chauffeur-driven, black limo pulled up into the bus loading area. The over-weight driver climbed out and opened the trunk. A man carrying a gym bag with track shoes draped over the outside and fitting Mubarak's rough description came through the athlete's exit, tossed an over-sized gym bag into the trunk and climbed into the back of the limo.

"I think I found him lads!" Doc announced.

"Where!?" Danno and Harden called simultaneously causing transmission interference. "Where?!" Harden repeated.

"Black Lincoln limo, two o'clock, my position!" Doc sent as he watched. "Gentlemen start your engines!" McKeowen mumbled to himself.

MacDonald was already in motion running back to Doc while Danno, Ricky and Harden were buckling in.

"Please explain to me how some dirt farmer from Bumfuck, Lebanon can afford a fucking limo?!" Doc said to no one in particular.

"All that bomb money must pay pretty good!"

"Okay, Danno, you have the lead. On my signal switch with Doc. Right before the tunnel I'll pull ahead and make the hit, everybody Green?"

"Roger that L.T."

"Green sir." Mac radioed. "And by the way B Team, it's not L.T. anymore." Mac added.

"Sorry sir, force of habit." Ricky transmitted.

Knock off the chatter! Harden's voice broke in.

Danno drifted down to the next intersection and put his blinker on as the limo drove to Exposition Park Drive to South Figueroa and then over to the on ramp of the Harbor Freeway.

Doc in the black Taurus kept Danno's grey Ford Tempo in sight as both cars followed suit.

"Grab the map and navigate." Doc instructed Mac as they came up onto the freeway.

"Why? I thought you lived here before?!" Mac protested.

"I didn't live in the middle of downtown! Have you never seen a movie set in L.A.?! This ain't Manhattan with perfectly planned streets! I've seen better organized riots then the road system in this town! Map, please!" Doc reiterated. Mac dug through the glove box and found the map provided with the rental.

"Okay, we're heading north on Harbor Freeway getting ready to pass the exit for U.C. Cal." He reported.

McKeowen may have been irritated by the lack of urban planning in the greater L.A. area but the whole team was grateful for the seemingly endless bumper-to-bumper traffic they were currently engaged in that afternoon allowing them to more easily track their prey.

Of course this worked both ways.

As the limo crossed into the left hand lane just before the Interstate 10 interchange so did the grey Tempo three cars behind.

In his rear view mirror, as he watched the cars behind him shift ever so slightly in and out of alignment, the chauffeur casually noticed the same grey Ford he had seen get on the motorway back near the Coliseum but then quickly dismissed it as coincidence.

Okay Danno, Doc switch here at the interchange. Harden radioed as they came off the cloverleaf and exited left heading west.

Doc went to move the Taurus up leaving Harden's white van four cars behind in second and Danno's grey Tempo bringing up the rear but three tractor trailers in a row passed on the left and blocked Doc from moving over and up into place.

"We're approaching the Western Ave exit." Doc relayed.

"Got it!" Mac shot back. "Next check point . . . the exit for Le Brea."

With the Lt. Commander's white van now three cars behind the black Taurus which was now several car lengths behind the limo, they followed west on the freeway for a short time more until the limo's blinker came on and drifted into the right hand lane.

"Orders sir?" Ricky, sitting next to Danno radioed with his walkie-talkie well below the dash board out of sight.

At that point the two cars in front of the Tempo both switched lanes to exit leaving Danno directly behind the limo and Doc's Taurus to within two car lengths of the mark.

Doc instinctively dropped back and let the mini-van full of Asian tourists signaling to merge over and fill in the space.

Danno, get in the far left lane! Take the next exit and then get back on behind us.

"Roger that sir." Danno signaled, then drove into the left lane and sped up.

The limo driver noticed Danno's car as he made his way up the outside lane and exited ahead.

Suddenly the limo's right blinker came on and he drifted into the right hand lane.

"Where the hell is he going?" Mac asked referring to the limo. "We're a good ten klicks from Santa Monica."

"Obviously not going to Santa Monica!" Doc commented.

"Maybe he just wants a burrito." Keeping a discreet distance Doc followed as did Harden.

They followed the Lincoln as a quarter of a mile later the limo led them off the I-10 down into the Northeast district and up 26th Street.

"Where the hell are you guys?" Danno's voice suddenly broke in as he was now separated from the group.

"We're approaching the corner of 26th and Wilshire. Where are you?" Doc reported.

"North of the I-10 coming . . . there's no god damn street signs in this - I see Wilshire!"

"Head east on it, I'll meet you on the corner of 26th." Harden ordered.

"Be right there!"

"Doc, stay on the Lincoln."

"We've got him."

The limo pulled into a large corner parking lot of a stripmall with a supermarket and several other businesses. Doc continued up the street, pulled into a driveway and turned around.

"He just ran a marathon now he's going food shopping?" Doc questioned.

"Read the other sign!" Mac instructed. Doc looked up to the front of the building.

ABE'S Jewish Restaurant & Delicatessen

"Stand by lads, this may be the pay off!" Mac's voice filled Doc's vehicle just as Danno's grey Tempo suddenly appeared on the side street next to the supermarket.

333

The limo drove past the deli a little further but not before the limo driver glanced up onto his rear view mirror and spotted Danno's car rounding the corner.

An instant later with the TFR's vehicles spread out across the intersection, the limo continued across the spacious parking lot and out the opposite end without stopping.

"Looks like he might be on to us." Doc radioed to no one in particular.

"Maybe, let's see what he does." Harden suggested. "He hasn't made me yet. Danno, park and feign like you're going into the store. Doc drive left around the block I'll keep him in sight and radio you where we are."

What the limo did was to drive a little faster back over to Wilshire and head east up the boulevard. Harden, still unnoticed, followed from a distance and radioed the others his location and direction.

Doc and Mac caught up to him as the moderate traffic on Wilshire again afforded a measure of cover.

As they found themselves cruising the boulevard at 25 miles per hour Mac took in the sights.

"So, this is how the other half lives!" Mac quipped as they drove past the elaborate clothing and jewelry shops. "HOLY SHIT!" Ray suddenly declared as he spotted a couple holding hands window shopping.

"What?" Doc asked as he turned to look.

"Is that . . . two boys trying to be girls or two girls trying to be boys?"

If the object of the pair being watched was to be noticed they succeeded admirably. The muscle bound one was short while the other was taller but barley over one hundred pounds. Both sported shoulder-length, bleached blond, razor cut hair while both wore matching skimpy, skin tight shorts and thigh-high, multi-colored leg warmers which nicely set off their stiletto heels.

"I read the researchers have made great strides in genetic engineering at Berkley!" Doc commented. "That's what they say we're fighting for Bro!"

"Only in La La Land!" Mac shook his head as several other 'interesting' characters were seen sprinkled across the next few blocks as they drove down the boulevard.

They continued east on Wilshire for the better part of twenty minutes and on into the residential areas where they took a left onto Crescent Heights Boulevard and headed north through a middle class but more densely packed neighborhood.

"Danno where are you?" Harden radioed.

"Heading north on . . . I just turned onto La Jolla."

"Okay, we're heading north on Crescent Heights. Stay to the west of us in case he made you. I'll contact you when he changes direction or stops."

"Roger that sir."

They drove on and made a right heading east on Beverly Boulevard south of Hollywood through Central L.A. to head north.

A right on Fountain Avenue over the 101 brought them through Thai Town to Western Ave then north on Los Feliz where the limo turned into Griffith Park.

By the time the black limo turned left into the park and started snaking its way up the hill, they lost

Danno and Ricky but Harden in the van had taken the lead with Doc and Mac about a quarter mile behind.

As the two TFR units passed an L.A.P.D. squad car parked off to the side of the road just inside the entrance of the park, one of the two uniforms glanced up as they drove past. The cops' suspicions were aroused.

"Hey Paco, you see that?" He asked his partner. Paco looked up from his beef burrito.

"See what?"

"A seemingly empty limo being followed by two vehicles with three guys in military styled haircuts heading up the hill towards the observatory."

"Maybe they're a couple of gay Cholos who just want to spoon under the stars!"

"Well, it's a free country, but the observatory's closed for the marathon." He manned his radio.

"Dispatch this is Three Charlie 12. Our 20 is the main gate of Griffith Park. We spotted a suspicious vehicle heading into park. We're going 10-37."

Roger Three Charlie 12, investigating suspicious vehicle. Use caution.

The two cops hurriedly finished off their tacos, stuffed all the refuse into the food bags and started up the long, winding hill of Canyon Road to track the vehicles.

About halfway up the hill on Fern Dell the Lincoln slowed, pulled over and the overweight driver got out.

Skipper, what's happening? Doc's voice filled Harden's passenger cabin.

336

"They stopped and the pudgy driver is waddling back to my Victor." Harden replied.

"Keep his hands in sight sir!"

Doc wasted no time but quickly pulled out into the road, sped up around the van and pulled in front of it to block the limo, slammed the car into park and both he and Mac jumped out, 9mm's drawn.

"RIGHT THERE FELLA! HANDS WHERE WE CAN SEE THEM!" Mac yelled.

The startled driver threw both hands in the air and froze in place halfway to Harden's vehicle.

Just then an unmarked black sedan coming down from up the hill suddenly swerved right, slammed on the brakes blocking both lanes and expelling four armed men in plain clothes who surrounded the entire scene,

"EVERYONE FREEZE! FBI! LAY YOUR WEAPONS ON THE GROUND, HANDS BEHIND YOUR HEADS AND BACK AWAY FROM THE VEHICLES!"

As the driver and the TFR guys were complying the L.A.P.D. squad car came up the hill, stopped in the middle of the road and the two uniforms jumped out service revolvers drawn and yelling.

"EVERYONE FREEZE! LAY YOUR WEAPONS ON THE GROUND, HANDS BEHIND YOUR HEADS AND BACK AWAY FROM THE VEHICLES!"

Just then Danno and Ricky slowly meandered up the road and pulled over on the perimeter of the scene about a hundred yards back.

"This is gonna make a great war story!" Danno quietly declared to Ricky who hung his head and softly chuckled.

Following a brief stare down one of the FBI carefully produced his bi-fold I.D. and approached the senior cop.

"Special Agent Johnson, Anti-terrorism Unit." He explained. "Downtown got a call there was a suspicious van prowling around down by the Coliseum We picked these guys up just off of Wilshire."

At the same time Johnson was briefing the cops and requesting they station themselves at each end if the road to control any traffic, the other agents were identifying Mubarak and questioning Harden and company.

"Lieutenant Commander Harden, these are my men, petty Officers McKeowen and MacDonald."

"Just who in the hell are you guys?" He asked Harden as he returned their I.D.'s.

"We're federal agents, Office of Naval Intelligence. Commendations on your security." Dave congratulated. "Secondarily, where'd **we** fuck up?" Harden asked.

"We got a repot several rough looking men with walkie-talkies were spotted mingling with spectators during the race so, we set up an observation tail. Followed you here."

"Agent I need a word with the guy in the limo." Harden explained. The agent nodded.

They walked over to the limo's passenger being detained by the other two agents.

"You are Mr. Salah Nabal Mubarak, no?" Harden challenged.

"I am Doctor **Nabal Salah** Mubarak, yes!" He nodded over to the agent who still had his passport and I.D.

"**Nabal Salah** Mubarak?!" Harden repeated.

"YES! And who are you?!"

"Looks like your friend in D.C. got the names screwed up, sir." Doc pointed out.

"Obviously." He conceded. "Why were you obviously avoiding us Dr. Mubarak?" Harden pushed. "This is not some police state like in the Middle East!"

They all glanced around at the black FBI sedan, the white unmarked van, the grey Ford and the L.A.P.D. squad car, lights flashing all surrounded by six cops and three feds.

Doc concealed his involuntary smirk.

"Okay, maybe for now with the Games and all. But, it's L. A." Harden defended.

"Yes, Los Angeles U.S.A.!" Mubarak shot back. "The city with some of the highest gang and racial violence in the world! Including car jackings!" Mubarak complained.

"Do we look like car jackers?!" Harden asked.

"No! But you do look like the White Police!" Mubarak rebuffed.

"Who the hell are the White Police?!" Dave pushed.

"Special secret police paid by the Emir to eliminate his enemies."

"The Emir?"

"Yes! The Emir, that is what I said! Emir Isa bin Salman Al Khalifa." They looked puzzled. "Of Bahrain!" He added.

Harden glanced down again at Mubarak's Bahrainian passport.

"I had to finish the race first before turning myself in." The exasperated doctor explained.

"Why did you have to finish the race? And 'turn yourself in' for what?"

"I had to appear legitimate for as long as possible. Until I was absolutely sure of my chances."

"And where were you going?"

"There is no embassy here so I was heading to The Office of Foreign Missions."

"The Office of Foreign Missions on –"

"Yes! Wilshire Boulevard! Which is when my driver spotted your grey car. For the third time!"

"Wait here." Harden said then headed back over to Agent Johnson.

"Looks like this guy is some kind of diplomat or something. Apparently he wants to declare political asylum."

"Closest place'd be at the Office of Foreign Missions over on –."

"Yeah, yeah, Wilshire." Dave blurted out with anger and exasperation.

Harden excused himself and walked back over to Doc and Mac by the van to inform them.

"So this guy's not our terrorist?" Doc asked.

"No. He's come here under cover of The Games to defect. He just requested political asylum."

"Sir, ask the agents to take him and escort him to —"

"You say Wilshire and I'm gonna wrap you upside the head!"

"I was gonna say the Federal Building downtown." Mac sheepishly explained.

Watching Harden's reaction when Special Agent Johnson offered to take custody of Mubarak Doc was compelled to add. "Pretty serious fuck-up, huh?!"

"Yeah, but an honest mistake!" Harden replied.

"At least no one was hurt!" McKeowen added as Johnson walked back over to them.

"Ya know I could hook you guys up with a week at our tailing course in Virginia." Johnson quipped.

"Thanks!" Harden puffed.

Johnson squinted as he perused Harden and McKeowen more carefully.

"Do I know you two from somewhere?!"

"Don't think we've ever met agent." Harden replied.

"Weren't you two with that Marine Corps Ball party down in Long Beach we raided about a year or so ago?"

"No idea what you're talking about Special Agent Johnson. We're in the Navy not the Marines." Doc replied.

"Get the hell outta here!" He turned and called over to another agent sitting against the car. "Jenkins, get these guys their weapons and I.D.'s back!"

"Yes sir. Follow me guys." He led them over to the FBI vehicle and complied by returning their weapons and I.D.'s.

****

Taberna Saloon
Wisconsin Place
Los Angeles, CA

In a small joint called la Taberna in a back alley off Wisconsin Place just west of the L.A. Memorial Stadium the guys indulged in a struggle not to slip too far down into a pity party.

"Well we know one god-damn thing for sure! All this shit they're pulling off isn't being done on a Diners Club card!"

"Jesus Danno! I think that's the longest sentence I've ever heard you string together!" Mac commented.

"Danno's right" Ricky re-enforced. "Whoever's holding the purse strings is the key to who exactly these assholes are and that's who we need to find and tag!"

Doc looked up from his drink.

"L.T., you think these two yahoos are on to something?" He asked.

"Yeah but they're about a day late and a dollar short." Harden responded. "But well done anyway."

"How do you mean sir, 'late'?" Ricky challenged.

"Last week, using the U.S.'s account with the International Monetary Fund, accessing the World Bank and the U.N.'s 'peace keeping' accounts, all twenty-seven of them, I asked the guys at Langley to run a trace on all the significant financial threads leading into and coming out of the Lebanese territory in the last five years."

"To what end sir?"

"I have a strong suspicion all roads lead to –"

"Rome?" Ricky guessed.

"No Tehran. Not just Tehran but the same gang . . . the Imams of Iran."

"So our holier than thou holy men are basically just like the greedy Bozos in D.C.?" Ricky postulated.

"All about the cash?!" Doc added.

"Yes, only difference is in D.C. the cash goes . . . most of the cash goes to . . . okay **some** of the cash goes to helping people it's supposed to be helping, not burning shit down, blowing shit up and causin' death and destruction." Mac contributed.

Doc tossed a twenty on the bar and signaled for another round.

"I don't know guys, you seen the footage of those Democrat-backed riots last week?" Ricky asked.

"Pick a team Matson! Pick a team." Harden chastised.

"I'm just sayin' sir." Ricky shrugged as he glanced up at the T.V. "Sir, look at the TV I think our little playmates have come out of their holes again." Ricky interrupted.

When Two Tribes Go To War

The team grabbed their drinks and relocated closer to the wide screen TV in the back section of the lounge where NBC was broadcasting news of the Lufthansa 837 highjack situation.

Ricky asked the barmaid to turn up the volume slightly, she handed him the remote and they all looked up towards the wide screen TV.

". . . all passengers are reported safe while all of the terrorists are believed to have been killed by the German police. As of this time, although no known terrorist group has been definitively associated with the highjacking, several groups are suspected."

The NBC news anchor Tom Brokaw reported.

"Sir, you think those were some of the guys we're chasing? That this was the 'big s[lash; they'd been talking about?"

"No Danno. This was a couple of fringe radicals not some well-organized, well-financed group like Hezbollah. We'll know more once we're back in D.C. I'll check back in with the Bureau guys and see what they know."

"You think they'll share what they got on this with us, some of those Bureau guys can be pretty cantankerous?" Doc challenged.

"I figure after screwing up Mubarak's name they owe us one plus I asked the International Finance guys at Langley to keep track of Tehran's cash flow. Either way I'm confident we'll find something to go on." Dave answered.

They sat through the short remainder of the broadcast, checked the ABC and CBS channels, found no new information and finished their drinks.

"Alright here's the plan." Harden offered. "Just as soon as I can confirm a suspected cash flow between the Med area and the U.S. region we're on the move again. Questions, comments snide remarks?" There were none. "Danno, back at the hotel room I need you to get us an antecedent, off schedule commo link. We need to advise D.C. of our movements. I'll get you the encoded details by 1500."

"Roger that L.T."

****

CHAPTER TWENTY

JFK International
Queens, NYC
Monday, November 5th

Flight 307 from Paris touched down at 10:26 New York time.

The well-dressed, late thirty-something man strode purposely through the arrivals gate and after collecting his luggage headed straight for the exit. As he did he carried little more than a small suitcase and a brown leather gym bag with a black murse, or man purse, draped over his shoulder.

After weaving through the crowd it was outside that he flagged a yellow cab from the cue and climbed in the back. The cabbie slid the bullet proof window between the seats open and barked.

"Where to Mack?"

"Hotel Empire, Manhattan." He said in his best English.

"Ninth Avenue or Uptown?" The man momentarily became flustered, fished his jacket pockets for a scrap of paper and read the Arabic scribbles.

"The one on Ninth Avenue."

The cabbie knew the neighborhood well and smiled as they pulled away and headed south.

Flooded with drug dealers and prostitutes the Ninth Avenue district on the Lower West Side is where many of the dregs ended up when Mayor Ed Koch instituted his aggressive clean-up of the Times Square district transforming it back into the tourist friendly area it was intended to be.

"In for business or pleasure?" The taxi driver asked.

"I am businessman, sometimes. Now tourist."

'*Pleasure*' the cabbie thought to himself.

"Well you'll see some interesting things in that part of town!"

It was his first time in the U.S. and as they cruised into Lower Manhattan looking out from the back seat the man was in awe if the magnitude of what he was observing.

The sky was blocked out for the buildings, the immense amount of everything including new cars, people and above all the abundance of food. Fruit stands, shops and food carts on nearly every corner. Restaurants as far as the eye could see and although no two pedestrians were dressed the same they were all draped in what appeared to be new, high quality clothing.

It was just after ten in the morning so having missed most of the rush hour traffic it was just over thirty minutes later that they pulled up in front of a run-down 19th Century, six story tenement in the middle if the block on 41st Street.

The dilapidated neon sign with half the glass tubes busted out hadn't seen a coat of paint since it was first installed back in the late Fifties, the glass windows were dirty enough to be translucent and there was the requisite panhandler sitting on the ground to the right of the entrance.

The Empire Hotel on 9th Avenue and 41st Street, a former luxury establishment had over the years descended into what was little more than a dive masquerading as a legitimate business enterprise. Stepping into it was like stepping back into the 1960's when they were trying to emulate the 1940's but never really succeeded.

The man paid the driver and headed inside. He entered the lobby and approached the desk casually perusing for CCTV cameras. There were none.

The generously tattooed young girl with the nose ring slid the bullet-resistant window open and greeted the man.

A lot had changed since the Sixties.

"I am Mr. Omari, I am to meet a Mr. Abib here at eleven thirty?" The girl without a dragon tattoo scanned through a near-by rolodex before answering.

"Dr. Abib'll be back in soon." She read from a piece of note paper. "You're welcome to wait in our lobby." She invited.

"Thank you." He moved to take a seat on the only available chair, an old, upholstered piece in the far corner of the abandoned lobby but he no sooner turned to sit when he perused the claustrophobic lobby to see a pair of Adidas track-suited individuals enter through the vestibule. One tall and husky the other short and light-of-frame.

348

Paddy Kelly

Despite the early hour both sported ladies of the night under their arms, one bleached blond the other a flaming red head.

The short one, the one who referred to himself as 'Dr. Abib' a self-bestowed title meant to enhance his personal prestige, spotted the man and crossed over to greet him.

"You must be Mr. Ameri!" He greeted with an extended hand. The well-dressed man ignored the mispronunciation and made no attempt to reciprocate.

The short one returned to his mates, passed the girls some cash then told them he would see them later before he and the husky one signaled Omari over to the lift.

They spoke in a familiar dialect of Farsi however Omari waited until the three were in the elevator to unleash.

"What the hell kind of place did you pick to bring me to?! This place is a shithole! I've been in cleaner toilets in the slums of Calcutta!"

"Apologies if the décor is not to your liking Akbar! But we are on something of a budget."

"Your budget does not include taking the ways of the infidels with common prostitutes!"

"Ohhh! These prostitutes are not very common!"

Akbar's face turned red, he dropped his bags and moved to attack.

"IF YOU CAN'T DO YOUR PART IN THIS STRUGGLE . . ."

The big guy moved in to forcefully separate them before it became more serious.

349

"IT'S A SPECIAL KIND OF HOTEL!" Abib yelled back cowering in the corner while rubbing his neck. "They were just for cover!" He moved to escape the elevator as soon as they reached the fifth floor and the doors opened.

Abib took them down the hall to room 507. Stepping aside he allowed Akbar in first before he carefully revealed the Smith and Wesson tucked into his belt under his coat and nodded down at the brown bag. The big guy nodded back and went in next.

Once inside Akbar carefully perused the set up and proceeded straight to the kitchenette area to the right claiming the seat furthest from the door and sat with his back to the wall of the narrow kitchenette. He set the gym on the floor beside him. Abib sat at the opposite end of the table while the big guy stood arms folded leaning against the kitchen door jamb.

"So you're a doctor now are you?" Akbar challenged.

"It is helpful for the dealings!" Abib shrugged.

"What is our status?!" Akbar pushed. Abib produced a small note book from his side pocket and began his report.

"Starting with the SMAW rockets there will be only two. Not four."

"Why not?"

"I don't know, I wasn't told."

"Carry on."

"I was told you have made arrangements for the money yourself?" Abib responded.

"I have."

350

"Next, papers - Here are the back-up passports and the travel documents you might need to leave America and return to Paris next week." He passed a thick envelope across the table. "Itinerary and flight tickets also."

"How were rental arrangements for the cars made?"

"Fake phone set up. A Motorola mobile phone was purchased and used for all the arrangements and rentals."

"ALL ON THE SAME PHONE?!"

"Yes all on the same phone!" He snapped back."Those bloody phones cost $4,000 U.S. each! Again there is a budget!" He argued. "Anything else?" Akbar calmed as he asked while he stood to leave.

"Yes one more thing Monsieur." Abib replied as he reached to draw the wheel gun from his belt. Akbar smiled at him.

The old saying goes there are two kinds of people in war; the quick and the dead. Abib had never been in war and so was not quick enough.

The small kitchen table hit him so hard in his pelvis as he started to stand that it drove him back into the refrigerator behind him forcing him to fumble his weapon as it slid across the table towards Akbar.

The big guy in the doorway was alert enough but as he moved to confront Akbar Abib's crumpled body blocked the way. By that time Akbar had not only ventilated the left side and front of Abib's head he also had the pistol levelled at the thug who immediately raised both hands and stepped back.

Akbar stepped over what used to be Abib and backed the thug into the living room area holding the pistol on him as he signaled for him to turn around,

"Tell me big one . . ." He said as he carefully lifted a throw pillow from the couch and rapped it around the weapon unseen by the thug. "Have you prepared your soul for Allah?"

"Brother Akbar, please don-" Were the final words of the big young man as the last thing that crossed his mind was a .38 caliber slug.

He crumpled into a pile in the middle of the floor.

Akbar looked down at the body.

"Don't worry brother. It's only for cover!"

Akbar returned to the kitchen, searched Abib's corpse then also emptied the last three bullets from the gun's cylinder, pocketed them and the gun then retrieved the brown leather bag and stuffed the thick envelope into it.

"And the name is Omari you idiot! Not Amari!"

Unfortunately for the two flunkies muffled gun shots were not a cause for alarm in that particular neighborhood. Especially in the Empire Hotel.

He grabbed his bags and careful to leave no prints on the front door left.

Once back out on the streets, amid mid-morning traffic, he located the first sewer grate he came to and surreptitiously dropped the three cartridges between the grate.

Two blocks away he bent to tie his shoe and slid the pistol down into the warren of New York sewers.

Then he went to eat a slice of pizza.

****

O Street Team House
Tuesday, November 6th

That morning around nine, as the team impatiently waited for their delinquent commander to arrive, Mrs. Gaffney emerged from her office to inform them the commander had sent word for them to stand-by in the team room until he returned.

What she didn't say was that earlier that morning Lt, Commander Harden was unexpectedly summoned to William Casey's office. Not by phone but by jeep courier which took Dave to the airfield for a chopper flight down to Langley.

When he arrived and was brought down to a place he had seen only once before he realized the seriousness of the situation.

On the way his mind frantically searched for the proper words to defend what happened out in L.A.

Escorted by a pair of burly M.P.'s and accompanied by the most important intel man in the Free World, Bill Casey, the C.O. of Task Force Romeo was, for the second time in a year led down the long narrow corridor at the end of which was an elevator.

On the way in Harden was told that Rear Admiral John L. Butts, Director of ONI would also be in attendance.

Last year, Harden recalled as they proceeded down the hall, when the members of the Russian salvage fleet in the Sea of Japan were becoming increasingly belligerent towards the Allied fleet searching for the black box of KAL flight 007, George Schultz advised The President, who was in agreement with him, that the Admiral should remain behind at naval ops to monitor the situation in the event there was an unforeseen escalation.

However today it would be Lt. Commander Harden alone in Room X-Ray with Bill Casey and Butts of the ONI. William Webster, Director of the FBI, perhaps the law enforcement professional most invested in the neutralization of Ali Akbar Aminpur's most recent killing spree.

Already rumors were being floated about the possibility of Webster ascending to the throne of the CIA as early as next year.

Waiting for the elevator in the brightly lit, grey hall no one spoke and when the lift arrived the four men got into the car. Casey didn't need to tell the M.P. which floor, he knew. The B-2 button was pressed,

Seconds later the small contingent disembarked into the lower basement of the Langley Building and with a definite, shared sense of purpose turned left, followed the hall to a cross corridor and turned left again. At a pair of sliding glass doors the lead M.P.

swiped a card which hung around his neck and they entered an all metallic vestibule, moved to the next door and stopped.

"Thank you Lieutenant!" Director Casey said and the officer along with his sergeant broke off from the politician and exited out the same sliding doors they had entered through.

Casey stepped forward to the right of the polished steel door and placing his right palm on a clear glass, wall pad while simultaneously setting his eye against a protruding lens. He spoke into a voice recognition microphone.

"Casey, William J. Fourteen-four-fourteen." Hidden servos were activated, a light beam scanned the hand and the door was heard to unlock.

"Thank you Director Casey." The electronic recording of the female voice said in a neutral tone as the double thick door slid into the wall.

Harden allowed Casey to lead as they turned right down yet another short corridor with only one door and followed The Director as he entered that room. The door to this room was simply labeled:

"X-RAY"

The room was smaller than you would expect a high level conference room to be but there was the usual rectangular table albeit with only six chairs. A white board hung on the wall parallel with the long axis of the room and in one corner what appeared to be a mini-fridge, like the sort you'd find in a cheap hotel room, was mounted on a table. Save for the white board, the walls were bare.

"Director Webster, good to see you again."

"Like wise Lt. Commander. I hear good things about your task force." He complimented.

"Thank you sir."

Casey opened the briefing.

"Commander Harden today I'm taking the highly unusual step of calling in an outside party for assistance."

Harden understood immediately.

"With all due respect Directors, why the TFR?" Harden probed.

"Because of the sensitive political nature of who we are dealing with. Israelis, thanks to the recent Hezbollah connected attack the Canadians and to an extent the Jordanians." Casey explained. "Not to mention most of the NATO nations."

"More importantly, outside of the men in this room, no one else knows you exist." Webster added then nodded across the table to Admiral Butts who picked up the narrative.

"I take it the latest peace talks over Lebanon are not going so well sir?" Harden ventured.

"Secretary Weinberger along with National Security Adviser Clark and Bush are against helping Israel at all." Casey informed him.

"As you may have read Philip Habib was appointed special emissary to the Syrians after Bud McFarland failed with al Asad & Bagin. So that was a dead end."

"Habib was next at bat but he failed and the guy we were most counting on to be able to talk some sense into was a guy named Gernayel."

"What happened to him?" Harden enquired.

"Assassinated, blown up!" Butts added.

"Along with 26 others when somebody put a bomb in his sister's apartment next door." Weber tacked on.

"Sounds like they didn't get enough hugs when they were kids." Harden remarked.

Casey resumed his brief.

"Three days ago perimeter security at a NASA facility observed a male Caucasian, blond hair taking photos of a launch pad."

"Which one sir?"

"40B I think. Why?"

"Have you ruled out a tourist? I mean those of us growing up in the Sixties have spawned quite a significant crop of space enthusiasts. After all we were promised we'd have a colony on the moon by the Eighties and-"

"Moon colonies, flying cars, ray guns, and Trekies aside. . . " Butts angrily growled. "we have additional information that Hezbollah have had a falling out with the Russians after they were supposed to sell the Arabs some hand launched missiles but cancelled the order after a rogue group-"

"A supposedly rogue group!" Casey corrected.

"Okay 'supposedly rogue' group in all likelihood financed by the Hezzies, kidnaped three Russian diplomats in Lebanon."

"The Russians rescued two of them the other was murdered by the group. Needless to say the missile deal was cancelled." Webster finished.

"Well, that's a good thing no?" Harden sought to confirm.

"No. Because we now have word that the Red Chinese have been negotiating with the Hezzies and we have no one on the inside with the Chinese." Butts added.

"So we have no way to know if a deal has been made or if the so called 'party of God' has missiles?" Dave extrapolated.

"Precisely." Casey concluded.

"To add to our headaches the Israelis have intercepted a cryptic reference to a mission they believe refers to an impending attack and decoded a message about 'making a 'dafqat kabira' meaning 'Big Spalsh' which they passed on to MI6 who passed it on to us and-" Webster started but was cut off by Harden.

"**Make** a big splash! I believe was the exact wording, sir." Harden corrected.

"Yes, how do you know that?" Butts asked.

"Apologies for interrupting you earlier sir but one of my men theorized what exactly 'Big Splash' could mean."

"And how exactly did he do that? Is he a methodological analyst? A cryptographer of some sort?" Butts questioned.

"No sir. He's a corpsman."

"A CORPSMAN! Like a medic?!"

"No sir, better. A navy corpsman. But a very good one."

"Well just how in hell did a navy corpsman come to theorize–"

"If I may sir," Harden again interrupted. "The Doc, our corpsman, has a girlfriend,"

"This girlfriend, she an intel analyst?"

"Not exactly sir. She's a Russian."

"A RUSSIAN! You gotta be shittin' me son!"

"A Russian spy actually, KGB." Harden nonchalantly explained.

Butts turned and glanced across the table to Casey.

"Bill do we gotta call an M.P. in here God damn it!"

"Give the young mam a chance John, hear him out."

Butts begrudgingly turned back to Harden.

"As I was saying sir, our Doc has been with us on this chase from the beginning, Roughly around January. His friend-"

"The Russian?!"

"Yes Admiral, she has degrees in mathematics, statistical analysis to be exact. Together they've assembled a list of likely domestic targets cross referenced by criticality to our L.O.C.'s and then using statistical formulae calculated a probability of attack, expressed as a percentage, on each location."

"And how exactly did your two Einsteins come up with the appropriate Lines of Communication they think might be targeted?"

"They based it on a pattern. The pattern of international attacks these gangsters, Hezbollah, have been following since they kidnaped Bill Buckley. It's roughly the same pattern the gangsters of the Thirties and Forties followed fighting each other. Kidnappings graduating to bombings, stepping it up to car bombs except now they have the ability to launch rocket attacks. After all, they've had plenty of time to test them out along the Gaza strip. Now that we know they have access to shoulder fired rockets it's highly likely they'll want to play with their new toys outside of The Levant."

"Don't sound very logical to me." Butts grumbled.

"Admiral when have terrorists ever followed conventional logic?" Harden challenged. "Besides, one of the major tenants of war is to keep your enemy off balance whenever possible. How better to disrupt our balance then to initiate a new form of attack? One we're theoretically not prepared for? At some point they'll want to get them into the U.S. to field test them so-to-speak." Harden explained.

"How do you see them gettin' rockets into this country?"

"Same way hundreds of Cartel members get drugs, guns and counterfeit money in here, across the southern border or by sea."

"Son-of-a-gun! Maybe he was right!" Webster quietly declared.

"Maybe who was right?" Casey asked.

360

"Some crazy New York business man in a TV interview last week was asked what he'd do if he were president. He said we need to build a wall across the southern border. If he were in charge first thing he'd do would be build one. Maybe he was on to something."

"Huh! A New York businessman instead of a career politician in the White House. That'd be something to see!" Butts commented.

"Why not? We got a Hollywood actor running things now." Webster opined.

"Director, Admiral, with no objections?" Bill Casey announced. Both understood and nodded their approval. Casey turned and addressed Harden.

"We suspect that there's a good chance they may try something down at Canaveral at the launch this week. I'm authorizing you and your team to get on down to Florida and have a snoop around."

"Aye aye sir!" Harden replied as he stood to leave.

"And Harden, you're on your own down there. Clandestine is the watch word of the day!"

"Understood Director." He replied. "And about the L.A. thing sir-"

"What L.A. thing?" Casey shot back.

******

CHAPTER TWENTY-ONE

West Foster Street
Chicago's North Side

Only two days ago on Saturday he was scurrying through Heathrow airport trying to shake off the wet and cold of the London streets while rushing to be on time for his overseas flight to JFK.

Just over nine hours after New York he was trying to shake off the bitter cold of the Chicago streets as he waited inside an Arab themed café near West Foster Street on the city's north side.

Now, following his third cup of Volcanica Ethiopian Yirgacheffe as his patience was wearing thin, a pair of Adidas track-suited men, one tall one noticeably below average height, approached his table.

"Salaam alaikim." The hoodie covered one greeted.

"Alaikim salam!" He answered looking up, "Rajul Mudarib?"

"Yes, I am the Rajul. You are Mr. Aminpur?" Akbar nodded yes.

The Rajul drew up a seat while, oblivious to the spectacle he presented, his strong man remained prominently standing beside the table facing the front door, hands crossed in front.

"You have something for me?" Akbar pushed.

362

"Yes of course, forgive me brother." He said reaching into his overcoat pocket. "Apologies for being late. The weather here is horrible. I don't know how people can live in this climate," He complained sliding the thick envelope across the table.

Akbar retrieved it, held it below the table and flipped through the modest stack of greenbacks.

"Don't you trust me brother?" There was no answer. "It's all there. Five thousand four hundred."

"Word in Tehran was that there would be nearly twice that!" Akbar quietly barked. The young Boss Man was visibly embarrassed.

"Not everyone is as cooperative once they get here and start to think that they are Americans." He shrugged his excuse attempting to dispel Akbar's suspicion that perhaps this 'Rajul' was skimming his pay off.

"LOOK HERE MR. BOSS MAN. . ." Akbar paused to regain control and moderate his voice as the two or three other patrons turned to notice. "If we are to win this war we must be stronger, braver and show more effort than the infidel! The non-believers must be left to their fate and pay for their atrocities." Akbar's eyes appeared to turn black as a cobra's as they seemed to hypnotize the younger gang boss making direct eye contact with their prey. "Do you truly desire to win this war? Are you able to show more effort?"

"Y. . . ye . . . yes Monsieur Aminpur. Yes I am. I will."

"Good." He smiled, pocketed the envelope, stood and headed for the door.

"Peace be with you." The local gang boss called after him.

"And with you." Akbar mumbled as he left with his surreptitiously gained pay-off money from his 'side' operation which was unknown to his PLO or the Hezbollah henchmen overseers.

****

If it is one thing Akbar Aminpur could never be accused of it was lack of planning. To that end one of his first moves before leaving for America was to assemble a skeleton crew of four men. Two would set up and prepare to receive him in New York. They had now been forcibly retired, permanently. The other two, both of which who were already state-side, would take separate routes and rendezvous with him in Florida.

Akbar, might have been most conveniently described as a wild-eyed fanatic who claimed to not be afraid of death, but his defining characteristic was that he, under no circumstances did he trust anyone ever. That included the straight travel arrangements the Hezbollah leadership in Tehran had planned out for him; Tehran, London, New York, Miami.

As a consequence, using a portion of the $225,000 operational fund he was given, and figuring he had plenty of time to reach his destination and be ready before Thursday the eighth of the month, he discarded the ticket for the Chicago's O'Hare to Orlando leg of his journey, took the train a short way

Paddy Kelly

to a small town in western Illinois and rented a car to convolute his trail.

Akbar then drove from the Chicago suburb south to Houston, where he again rented a car from a rival agency outside the city and drove the over 900 miles to Orlando where he again rented yet another car under a third alias this one a dark blue mini-van, to later cruise past Canaveral and actually visualize his target area for the first time.

That afternoon he made his way out to the A1A thoroughfare, a.k.a. the Martin Anderson Expressway, across the two kilometers of the Banana River and through Merritt Island Past Kelly Park and out onto the cape proper.

Once there, consulting the map he purchased at a Chevron Food Mart, he saw that he was in the commercial center of the Cape and that the south A1A led down to Cocoa Beach and the recreation and tourist areas, so he turned north towards the space complex.

He travelled with false I.D. and a back-up story that he was an Egyptian engineer on holiday to see the space center. Keeping within the designated tour zones he was never questioned save for when he reached the main gate of the military side of the base.

The sharply uniformed Air Policeman stepped out of the guard shack and waved Akbar's van down.

"Sorry sir, no civilians allowed beyond this point."

"Sorry officer! I was looking for museum."

"You passed it up. Just back it up into that space behind you and head back down the same way you came. You'll see the sign on your right."

"Yes, of course. Thanking you very much officer."

Complying he backed up but as he did he was careful to observe the two sentries in the guard shack. When he determined they were not looking he quickly lifted the instamatic camera on the seat next to him and snapped off a quick half-dozen photos of the gate area. Then as he headed back south he stopped on the gentile left hand turn a hundred meters down the road and snapped a few more across the water to the west side of the base.

When he felt comfortable about his over-all bearings he backed tracked out across the Banana River to the mainland and to a road-side motel he had found in the phonebook, the U-Need-A-Rest Inn at the intersection of U.S. Route 1 and State Route 528. The cloverleaf at that particular intersection provided no less than four separate possibilities of escape routes should things go south.

By that time it was nearing 1600 so he set out on his last mission of the day, to scout potential escape routes.

U.S. Route One ran north and south along the coast but would surely be blocked off almost immediately after the attack. State route 528 he noted ran almost directly east-west but also afforded several cut offs.

That section of the State, west from Canaveral all the way to the Gulf of Mexico, spanned barely 400 miles wide and knowing that the American police had helicopters the route he chose would have to be definitive and as safe as possible. Akbar calculated that he would have less than fifteen minutes to affect his escape from the Cape or spend the rest of his life in a U.S. dungeon eating the hog slop the Americans called food.

After satisfying himself that he had the lay of the land he decided to call it a day. He had yet to say his evening prayers, eat and prepare for tomorrow when he was due to meet the third of his stateside accomplices who were due to land tomorrow afternoon at 1400.

*

Following morning prayers and breakfast, Akbar scratched out a wanted ad on a yellow piece of legal pad and headed over to the mainland to the Western Union Telegraph office where he sent a message,

'Dear Unkel I am having here a great time here. STOP All going well. STOP'

At the window he was greeted by an elderly clerk.

"Hey mister, you spelt uncle wrong. Ya'll want I should fix it and make it into proper English like fer ya?" The grey-haired clerk offered.

"Oh sorry! My English not so good. Thank you sir."

His next stop was the office of the local newspaper with the
largest distribution in central Florida, the *Orlando Sentinel*. However it was not the *Sentinel* that he was interested in but the editor's direct pipeline to the *New York Times* and its international distribution. For a small fee he could pay that office to not only run the ad but wire it to New York where it would make the morning edition of the *New York Times* as well.

Since just after the turn of the century the *Times* had been used to pass cryptic Intel between operatives of all nations, friends and enemies alike.

Some things never change.

SAVAK, the Shah's and now the imam's secret police under a different name, as well as Hezbollah had learned their lessons well from MI6 and the CIA before the fall of the Shah and the 1979 Islamic Revolution.

The telegram was sent to Akbar's Hezbollah brothers while the fake wanted ad in the *Times* was intended to assure their financiers in Tehran that all was going according to plan.

With his chores done by noon Akbar made his way to Orlando International to collect his first accomplice, a Mr. Abdul Mamoud LeMiel.

Obtaining a temporary student visa was relatively straight forward for LeMiel, he was a good looking, slender, twenty-two year old with two years of university engineering and no criminal record, according to INTERPOL. His English was a solid B2 level and he had distant relatives in New Jersey.

Lebanese by birth LeMiel was recruited last year after the success of the U.S, embassy bombing, was radical Muslim by persuasion and was a relatively new inductee to Hezbollah.

Young Abdul had shunned his Christian name Arthur for the Arab handle 'Abdul' meaning 'Servant of God'.

In the van ride on the way back from the airport to the out-of-the-way, second rate motel the delayed conversation was only interrupted when an exuberant Abdul, tinged with just enough anger to be acceptable as a terrorist, asked an obvious question.

"When do we strike?"

"Soon enough my brother. Thursday morning, early."

"Why do we wait?" Abdul pushed.

Akbar stifled his annoyance at what he saw as a question of his leadership but calmed himself before replying.

"All must be in alignment for this holy mission to succeed."

"There are others?"

"Yes."

"Who are they?"

"A complete brief will be given you when the last member of our team arrives."

"When is that?"

"He is due to land tomorrow at two o'clock. You'll meet him then."

Akbar was careful not to reveal any more information about this third party.

When Two Tribes Go To War

****

Instead of landing by plane Jack Crenshaw, Akbar's accomplice number two, met them the next afternoon at a Denny's restaurant off route 528. He saw no reason to disclose that he had landed in Athens Georgia and booked a private flight to the East Coast Regional airfield just south of the 405 then bused down to the meeting point.

Crenshaw was a twelve year, former 18Bravo Special Forces weapons sergeant with training as a demolitions engineer as well as a former NYPD cop who spoke fluent Spanish. Amongst all of his qualifications he was also currently a wanted felon.

He was at present wanted for two separate bank jobs one of which he had nothing to do with and the last of which didn't go as planned. One of the trigger happy yahoos he'd hooked up with for the job shot and killed a security guard and who was later taken out by the police during his attempted getaway. Crenshaw escaped but not before he was I.D.'d.

It was then that Crenshaw decided he should earn the money he needed some other way. The phone call from his underground connection offering the job with Akbar two weeks ago was his ticket out of the Bronx where he was hold up under an alias.

Problem was that, as of yet Jack Crenshaw had no details of the job he had accepted. He was in for a rude awakening.

Akbar believed he brought Crenshaw, an American, in on the gig for deep cover. With his dirty blond hair and hazel eyes Akbar felt Crenshaw would help to dissipate any reservations or suspicions Americans might have about dealing with a dark, short, hairy Arab stranger. Once again Akbar misjudged the American attitude and mentality towards race and their life's priorities.

As far as Crenshaw was concerned, he was along for one reason and one reason only - the money.

For an extra $5,000 Crenshaw had also agreed to arrange for a getaway driver.

Akbar was due to pick Crenshaw up at Orlando International the next afternoon but was shocked when the motel's front desk sent a runner with a message to meet his 'friend' at a restaurant a half hour west of the Cape at a Denny's restaurant in lieu of the airport.

Crenshaw was advised to look for a lightly bearded Middle Eastern man in a New York Yankees T-shirt driving a blue van.

From his window seat in a back booth table Crenshaw watched as Akbar, bearing a passenger pulled the van into a parking space adjacent to the large restaurant window.

Crenshaw nodded to Akbar as he climbed out of the vehicle and Akbar instructed Abdul to wait in the van.

Approaching Crenshaw's table the Arab made no effort to hide his annoyance.

"Who's the kid?" Crenshaw enquired as he continued to eat.

"His name is Abdul."

"You want a coffee?" Jack offered.

"No I don't want coffee!" He loudly whispered then checked himself. "I want the soldiers working for me to obey orders!"

Crenshaw momentarily hesitated then scooped up his last forkful of scrambled eggs and hash then wiped his mouth with his napkin as a bus boy appeared and picked up his empty plate.

He folded his arms on the table and leaned forward.

"Let's tune our PRC 77's to the same freq, shall we? You're not in Kansas anymore Dorothy! I don't work for you. More importantly I don't give two shits about your 'cause', your 'struggle' or how many infidels you have to smite to earn your 72 virgins. I'm muscle for hire, no more no less. I help you with this job, you pay me the rest of my money and we say adios amigo! Are we green Aladdin?" Crenshaw locked eyes with Akbar initiating a stare-down which silently spoke volumes.

Akbar sat speechless. Although he understood only half of what Crenshaw just said, the tone relayed the message loud and clear. In Akbar's world others obeyed without question. But as the American just pointed out, Akbar wasn't in his own world anymore.

The Arab cleared his throat and spoke in a respectful, subdued tone.

"I have set us up in a place a little east of Orlando International, south from State Road 528 off of the Interstate Number Four."

Thirty-five minutes later the three saboteurs turned into the gravel drive of the Uneed-A-Rest Inn.

In reality the 'inn' was a motel which featured fresh linen and a continental breakfast of morning coffee, fruit juice and Danish.

The coffee came in a ten ounce Styrofoam cup, the fruit juice was in reality watered down Kool-Aid and the Danish came sealed in cello wrap and was usually a week or so old. All these amenities were available 24/7. Providing you had enough change for the three vending machines.

There was also daily clean linen.

Most of the time.

For a small sir charge.

Due to a shortage of help there were never enough employees and the four or five who worked alternating shifts spoke only sketchy Spanglish at best. However, there was an ice machine on the ground floor.

Oh yeah and a pool.

The first thing Jack Crenshaw noticed as he climbed out of the van was the wall sign near the moss-covered pool:

Truckers must shower before entering pool!

He quickly glanced over at the thin film of yellowish-green moss coating the top of the water.

"Huh, classy! No expense spared!" He quipped as he made his way to the office.

Crenshaw registered up front, received his room key, agreed to meet Akbar later and retired to his room to clean up and rest before their big strategy meet later.

**

Akbar's Meeting
Tuesday, 6 November

After hearing the details of Akbar's plan for the first time that morning Crenshaw was shocked. He had been made aware of Akbar's background but believed this to be a simple sabotage operation. Destruction of some government property or supplies. But there would be astronauts on board this rocket, actual human beings. Murder of noncombatants was not what he signed up for. He didn't know everything about the guy but he knew enough about this emotionally unstable Arab that if he tried to bail out he probably wouldn't make it past the front door.

However he was too far into it to try and bail now.

At that moment, when Akbar got to the part in his brief about blowing up the Space Shuttle, maintaining his calm, it was then that Crenshaw made a quiet decision.

"Now the MK-153's are still to be collected." Akbar's gruff voice broke into Crenshaw's mental meanderings. "Abdul and Jack you will take van and drive to McDonald's restaurant in Port St. John. There is small marina behind restaurant. There you will meet with a grey-haired fishing boat captain."

"What is his name?" Abdul asked.

Paddy Kelly

"Not important. He will wear blue short sleeved Izod shirt."

"What is Izod?"

"I'll tell ya later." Jack, sensing Akbar's irritation, volunteered.

"On board he will deliver to you one Styrofoam container holding our rocket launchers."

"How many? How do we know we're getting the right number?" Crenshaw pushed.

"This man is trusted, we have worked with him before and the launchers were counted before being loaded. We have very secure communications through Washington."

Fucking figures! Jack thought to himself.

"Container will be marked as some sort of fish. You will bring rockets here where we will keep them until Thursday morning. Launch is scheduled from Launch Complex 40B at 0820 Thursday morning, weather allowing and we will be waiting!" He made eye contact with both and they nodded. "Mr. Crenshaw, have you arranged for driver?"

"Yeah, yeah, He will meet us at this point east of the north beach on the 402 where we'll head west and catch transport north via train." Jack pointed to the map spread out on the kitchenette table in front of the three. "He'll be in a white Ford van labelled, 'Central Florida Electrical'. The boat can drop us here when he takes us back to the mainland. The beach is shallow enough to walk ashore and there are no sandbars to get hung up on."

"Good! You and Abdul will fire one rocket each, drop the tubes into the sea and calmly make your way

375

back to land. Have you calculated ranges and blast area of the explosion?" Akbar asked.

"Yes, the blast area will be 500 to 800 meters but the fuel spray is unpredictable. If we fire from three or four hundred meters out, are underway immediately after firing and **IF** we hit the EFT while they are still on the pad we should be clear enough." He reported as he again used the map to indicate his reference points. He then directed his remarks to Abdul. "Remember, the rocket must travel 250 meters to arm and has a maximum effective range of 1800 meters. The strand with the Max Brewer Parkway is about 500 meters from Launch Complex 40B. It should be a clear shot for both of us." He affirmed.

"This is good news! Allah akbar!" Akbar declared while raising his outstretched arm, a gesture Jack felt eerily resembled a Nazi salute.

"Allah akbar!" Abdul parroted.

"Fuckin' hey Bubba!" Crenshaw added before he threw back his shot of Jack Daniels.

*

McDonald's parking lot
Port Saint John
Wednesday, 7 November

Jack Crenshaw and Abdul LeMiel pulled into the McDonald's beach side parking lot north of Canaveral and drove around through the drive-thru window. Then with their breakfast orders of coffee and pastry pulled into a spot in the back of the restaurant and shut the engine down. They sat and nibbled at their pastries and sipped their coffee as they waited for their contact to arrive.

"Akbar says you do not believe in our cause?" LeMiel challenged.

"Any causes I had faith in long ago abandoned me son!" He drained his coffee and sat without making eye contact.

"You know what I mean!" His rejoinder was heavily tinged with anger. Crenshaw drew back and stared at him as he crumpled up his coffee cup.

"You're awfully young to be so mad all the time. That hatred's gonna burn you up some day!"

The younger man settled into a sulky pout. "It keeps me warm." He shrugged before returning to gazing out the passenger side window before he finally answered. "It will be worth the fight when we have won!"

"No, no it won't, because you'll be dead!"

"What are you talking about?! Only Allah knows when I will die!"

"Don't bet your last Piaster on that Kid! You have exactly two chances of coming out of this so called 'struggle' alive and in one piece. Slim and none and Slim just left town."

Abdul pulled back and stared.

"If you are so bitter about our cause why do you take part?" The young man challenged.

"Simple! Cash!"

"Why is money so important to all you Americans?"

"I can't speak for all Americans, only myself. I need the money, that's why."

"What good will money be if we are all to die?"

"I got something I gotta make right. Besides I didn't say 'we were going to die', I said 'you'!" He quietly answered.

"You think I am unable to handle myself?!"

"Don't matter if you can or you can't."

"What do you mean?" Abdul demanded.

Crenshaw turned and adjusted in his seat to face the kid.

"The people who recommended me for this job gave me the low down on this guy. This Akbar character is what we call in English a 'fanatic'. He is a complete loon. Certifiable! He'll get anyone who follows him when he goes too far killed."

"Then why do you follow him?!"

"I ain't followin' nobody Kid! Just doing a job, like your local neighborhood plumber. I'm being paid for my expertise, contract work that's all. I do my part, get my dosh and vanish." He emphasized. "What I'm trying to tell you is, you seem like a nice kid. Just watch your ass around this guy, you savvy?"

For the first time in his young life Arthur LeMiel, alias Abdul, was being counselled by an infidel, a non-believer, a member of the enemy.

"Well what'a ya know?" Crenshaw suddenly blurted out as he peered through the windshield and spotted a grey-haired husky guy in shorts, deck shoes and dark blue, short sleeved Izod. "Looks like Santa's here with the goodies!" He said.

They climbed out of the van, approached the old sailor, engaged in a short exchange then proceeded down to the dock.

With the loan of a trolley from the dock master they loaded a two meter by one meter grey Styrofoam container marked 'Fresh Redfish' from his fishing boat and wheeled it up to the van.

An hour and a half after arrival they were driving south down Route #1 and back to the hotel where Jack instructed Abdul to remove the Fresh Redfish label on the container before they man-handled the long box into the room where Akbar was impatiently waiting.

By the time Jack and Abdul had reached the motel Akbar had already prepared the floor of his room to hide the rocket launchers until the morning.

He had pushed the bed aside, pulled back the rug from the wall and then prided several floorboards loose in order to access the two foot deep ventilation space under the floor. Carefully replacing the boards and pulling the carpet back he was ready to stash the munitions once they had arrived.

He heard the van backing in outside the front door and thirty minutes later the SMAW's were safely hidden in the floor, floorboards, carpet and bed replaced.

****

Unknown to anyone including the young flunky or Crenshaw the 153's were only there as back-up.

Akbar and his comrades, commensurate with their complete inability to trust anyone, had secretly laid out a much more audacious and clandestine plan for their attack on the people they had been conditioned to bitterly despise since childhood.

Already in place attached to the giant, orange fuel tank, a.k.a. the External Fuel Tank, or EFT, was a tiny explosive device.

Designed by Iranian engineers to be command detonated, the three inch square, radio controlled mechanism, painted the same bright orange as the EFT and stashed underneath an aft strut attachment, was easily lost in the 154 foot long, 28 foot diameter, 1.6 million pound fuel tank.

Its effectiveness lie in the fact that all that was required of it was to penetrate the external thermal protection system and puncture the smallest of holes any time just before or just after liftoff. The ensuing puncture would leak fuel eventually igniting and causing a catastrophic failure of the EFT, the two booster rockets and the shuttle itself.

In essence, the entire mission.

Attaching the three inch square explosive device to the EFT was troublesome but simple enough.

For a Hezbollah operator with Al Jazeera credentials it was a small matter posing as a journalist to show up on the dock with a dozen other reporters and journalists when the EFT was landed in Florida by barge from Louisiana only a few days ago, there was ample opportunity to get close enough to the giant tank to do the dirty deed.

Successful completion of that leg of the mission was signaled to Tehran in a wanted ad in the *New York Times* which in turn was signaled to Akbar by the same method the next day, the day he passed through New York.

The cedar tree has been planted
and should blossom on time.

****

CHAPTER TWENTY-TWO

Cape Canaveral
Brevard County, Florida

On Florida's central east coast, 867 miles south of D.C., two hours and thirty minutes by plane, lies 'The Cape'.

It is officially the third oldest settlement in the U.S and was first identified by the Spanish in the late 16th Century and given the name Cabo Cañaveral meaning 'bed of reeds'.

In 1605 they successfully negotiated a treaty with the local indigenous people offering a reward for returned ship wrecked sailors, of which there were apparently many.

The now iconic lighthouse, built in 1848 to alert ships during storms 37 years later in 1885 had to be relocated when it was nearly toppled and wrecked.

By a storm.

By 1920 settlements had begun to develop in the area and as early as 1878 the U.S. Navy petitioned Congress for funds to build a deep water port. Over fifty years later funds were finally approved in 1929.

It wasn't until the late 1940's that the military began to give serious interest to the Cape.

With the advent of the post WWII interest in rockets and the U.S. recruitment of Werner von Braun and his team President Truman approved it as a test site in 1949 and the Cape became a proving ground under the auspices of the newly formed U.S.A.F.

On July24th 1950 *Bumper 8* a refurbished V2 rocket was launched becoming the first missile launch of the site, giving rise to the Redstone, the Atlas and finally the rocket most are familiar with, the NASA work horse, the Saturn V.

Cape Canaveral including the Kennedy Space Center occupies the northern portion of the island while the U.S Air Force occupies the small out cropping island to the east of the Cape.

During his tenure LBJ wrote an executive order renaming Canaveral, much to the displeasure of the locals, Cape Kennedy. A decade later the locals successfully petitioned the state to rename the area back to its original four century old handle.

As perhaps a compromise the Space Center proper still bears the Kennedy name.

Scientifically speaking Canaveral is a near ideal locale from which to launch rockets. The closer to the equator the more engineers can take full of advantage of an eastwards launch and get the full effect of the earth's 1,000 mile per hour anti-clockwise rotation at the equator.

In addition, as early test launches had shown, it makes sense to launch over a non-populated area in case of an accident. Rockets don't usually crash. They explode.

It would be in less than 48 hours that on Launch Complex 40B on the extreme north end of the cape that Mission STS 51-A featuring the space shuttle

Discovery on NASA's 13th shuttle mission and her crew would head into space.

To record and share the journey an IMAX movie camera was on board and would document the first feature film shot in space.

They would call it "The Dream is Alive"

****

Because of the Presidential summit no military flights out of Washington were available so the team was to fly commercial. Due to a shortage of available civilian flights the TFR were compelled to fly space-A on the commercial carrier. As it was the middle of the week and they were flying out of D.C. Mrs. Gaffney had booked five seats by the time Harden returned to O Street.

Two hours after take-off the captain flashed the 'Fasten Seatbelt' sign and announced they were on final approach.

"Hope this is not another wild goose chase!" Ricky Matson quietly grunted to no one in particular.

"You get to shoot and blow shit up?" Mac sitting next to him asked.

"Yeah."

"You get to shoot shit?"

"All the time!"

"You get to go on fun, adventurous camping trips all over the world at taxpayer's expense?"

"I guess so."

"And you get paid even when you're not working?"

"So?"

"So quit bitchin'!"

Rather than travel civilian air while armed, loaner weapons were arranged with the chief armorer of the Canaveral Air Force base to be issued them upon arrival at the base. Paper work was sent via secure Telex and an array of .45's and 9mm's, magazines and holsters were set aside for the TFR as requested.

Following touch down at Orlando International Lt. Commander Harden Doc, Mac, Danno and Ricky landed and made their way to an out-of-the-way apron where they were met by a UH-60 Blackhawk which ferried them and their few bags of gear east to the Air Force base.

During the twenty minute ride at 5.000 feet straight to Canaveral they were able to see a brief over view of the Cape layout as they passed overhead.

"Skipper, we going to Cape Canaveral or the Kennedy Space Center?" Danno asked once they were airborne again.

"Cape Canaveral refers to the entire cape while the Cape proper contains the Kennedy Space Center and the U.S. Air Force who run the collection of launch sites known as LC's or Launch Complexes which are numbered." Harden replied,

As they flew over the Banana River to the west of the Cape each of them took detailed mental notes of the landscape, potential approach and evasion routes etc . . .

"It all started right down there with the launch of Bumper 8 back in the Nineteen Fifties!" Doc McKeowen expounded loudly as the chopper drifted over the area containing the launch platforms, banked south and drifted in.

"What the hell is Bumper 8?" MacDonald called back.

"A V2 rocket." Doc informed.

"That's the Nazi's you're thinkin' of Doc. The world-wide tour of that freak show was cancelled in 1945!"

"And what did the Nazi's produce for rockets, my historically challenged, uninformed friend?"

"I'm a demo man, not a fuckin' historian! How the hell should I know?!" Mac defended.

"The correct answer Mr. Fleming would be; 'What are V2 rockets?'" Doc mocked the game show answer. "And where, after capture, did said rockets get shipped to?"

"Seriously Doc, you need to go on Jeopardy." Danno called over.

"He needs to go somewhere. Somewhere else!" MacDonald snipped. Doc blew Mac a kiss.

Harden, watching the two smiled and shook his head.

Once they touched down just outside the HQ building they were greeted south of the CCAF Skid Strip by the Skid Strip boss, an Air Force Captain who escorted them into the building.

They were taken to a small briefing room where they were introduced to the base commander, a general Bigby and the lead FBI agent who had been sent down the day before.

Harden was taken off guard when he was introduced to the special agent. He had not been informed that the agency was on the case but he was not nearly half as surprised as the Special Agent who stepped forward with an extended hand.

"Dwayne Skidmore, Special Agent FBI. I'll be in charge of this case." He tersely informed in an effort at self-reassurance. He made no attempt to introduce the second agent with him.

"Lieutenant Commander Harden, I'm with the GAO." Dave introduced himself.

"The GAO? What does the Government Accounting Office care about a potential sabotage mission?"

"In essence it doesn't. I'm here on a separate task. I just happened to be here when the general called me in and asked me to assess whether or not they may need extra surveillance equipment." Harden bluffed. He briefly glanced over at Bigby who stood poker-faced and offered no comment.

The long history of rivalry between intelligence agencies inside the D.C. beltway was no secret.

Skidmore was a bit full of himself but as a government investigator he wasn't stupid. Five military types suddenly show up without explanation, in civilian attire wasn't going to fool him.

"What'a you fellows know about the situation?"

"Not much. All we've been told is there was some guy taking some pictures." Harden summarized.

"In a restricted area." Skidmore insisted.

"Outside the perimeter. But anything I, we can do to help just let us know." Dave, as authorized by Director Casey, offered assistance if required. Skidmore felt the situation called for some clarification.

"Well, I think we can handle a couple of misguided religious fanatics." Dwayne Skidmore, Special Agent-in-Charge quickly rebuffed.

Harden casually smiled, nodded and made direct eye contact.

"Gentlemen, shall we start?" Bigby indicated and they all took a seat in what essentially was a small classroom. "When we finish here you will be issued I.D. badges to allow you access to most areas of the base." Bigby began. "Tomorrow at zero eight twenty STS51-A Discovery will lift off. It will not only be the 13th SST mission but will also be her maiden voyage. The reason you all are here is as a precaution. A prophylaxis if you will."

"Great!" Mac whispered over to Doc in the back of the room. "Guy asks for our help then calls us all condoms!"

"Mac stow it!" Harden softly barked.

"During a routine preparatory pre-launch procedure a man was sighted outside the perimeter taking photographs through the fence. Security was notified, the man was chased away and per our routine S.O.P. the GCM submitted a 1424."

"GCM, EFT, STS! These jamokes have abbreviations for everything! I feel like I'm watching

The Count on Sesame Street!" Mac whispered to his note pad.

"You sound more like Oscar the Grouch!" Doc whispered.

"Problem gentleman?" Bigby asked.

"No General. We were just wondering, we had a question about GCM?" Doc asked.

"Sorry lads, I forget you're not part of the program. GCM that's Ground Crew Manager."

"Thank you sir!"

"The standard launch procedure will commence as such; the astronauts will be awakened at 04:30, they will eat and be prepared with assistance from the ground crew, escorted and transported out to Discovery approximately one hour prior to lift-off, be secured in, and once system checks are complete CAPCOM will receive the go for launch from their respective consoles and countdown will begin."

"Sir what have you currently got in place in terms of security?" Harden asked.

"Commander, as I informed Special Agent Skidmore when he first arrived, we employ a three tiered system. As we are a government facility the primary responsibility for security lies with the Air Force police who control all movement of personnel in and out of the perimeter. Backing up the AP's are a cadre of civilian security who are primarily restricted to the outer perimeter and they are in turn reinforced by our electronic facilities, mainly CCTV and in select areas, ground motion sensors."

"Any ground motion detectors outside the circumference of perimeter sir?" Harden asked.

"None, too impractical. Too much civilian traffic, animals etc. When they were first installed we were being alerted every ten minutes. Stray dogs, gators and so forth. Finally we had to have them removed."

"Inside the perimeter, along the fence line, sir?"

"Same story, especially the God damned pelicans!"

"We assume you have a central location to monitor security general?" Doc asked.

"Yes we do, downstairs adjacent to the front desk. When we finish here I'll introduce you all to the head of security. He's on patrol just now."

There were a few more questions before Bigby called down to security alerting them 'that a couple of guys from the GAO' would be down for a brief orientation.

After they were dismissed Harden approached Skidmore.

"Agent Skidmore-"

"It's **Special** Agent Skidmore." He corrected. Harden was reminded who he was dealing with.

"Well . . . we're all special aren't we? I mean each in our own special little way, no?" Harden proposed.

Taken off guard the agent wasn't sure how to take Dave's remark.

"Ya know, I got a call from the guys in the bureau in D.C. yesterday afternoon." Skidmore warned. "They warned me about some 'mystery boys' that might show up from The Agency. I got a news flash for you 'Agency Boy!'"

"Do tell, Dwayne." Dave affected a mock attentive smile.

"20,000 personnel, a 1.5 billion dollar annual budget, the most advanced forensics in the world, and access to nearly every recognized expert in the United States and the free world. I think we're pretty good at solving crime!"

"Oh really? The Lindberg baby, your work with the Pinkertons, Inga Arvad and JFK, the Viola Liuzzo murder, the Media Pennsylvania records heist back in ''71, the Walker family spy ring, the Hansen spy case, Whitey Bulger and let's not forget COINTELPRO, the ChiCom contributions to the DNC with PRISM and all your work in Latin America. Shall I continue?" Harden politely asked.

"PRISM was the NSA God damn it!" He defended,

"Sorry, it's easy to confuse all you alphabet agencies." Harden quipped in return.

Skidmore gave no retort but made for the door.

"Gonna be a real day at the beach working with those two!" Doc standing just within earshot remarked to MacDonald.

The general's aid, a major, approached Harden and the men to escort them down to security to obtain security badges and asked if there was anything else Harden needed.

"Yes, transport. What's the motor pool situation here?"

"I'll be happy to arrange some vehicles for you how many do you need?"

"Three will do." Harden answered perusing his men.

"You're billeted at the Dignitaries' Bungalow or what we unofficially refer to as the Astronaut's Beach House a short drive from here. It's on the north side of the spaceport between pads 40 and 41."

"Sir, Discovery is due to launch from LC 40 isn't it?" Doc asked the major.

"Yes 40B. that's correct. The motorpool officer will have your vehicles brought over. I'll escort you down to security Lieutenant Commander then you and your men can go to lunch well I arrange your transport over at the motorpool. The dining facility is just outside to the left."

"Spaceport?" Ricky silently mouthed to Mac behind everyone's back as they headed for the door.

"Let's go Spock!" Mac mocked.

After getting their security badges and having a look around to assess the station's security capabilities Harden called the team aside.

"Alright, grab a quick lunch, we'll get the vehicles then meet out at the Bungalow in half an hour. Questions, comments snide remarks? No, good, Dismissed." Harden snapped then walked away.

Mac turned to the others until the C.O. was out of ear shot.

"Is it me or did any of you others notice how the L.T. has become that much more strack since we've landed?"

"He's just heavily focused on the mission that's all." Doc offered. "This one's pretty big. We fuck this up and it'll not only be the end of our careers but the end of the TFR."

"Good point." Byrd said. "I can just see a gaggle of pansy-assed congressmen tripping over themselves to roast us and the Skipper, especially given the fact they don't even know we exist! No pressure mind you." Danno added.

"Damn Danno, that's the second time you've spoken in compound sentences instead of two word phrases!" Mac remarked. "Well done!"

"Fuck you!" Danno answered.

"That's better!" Doc said.

**

Following lunch the team was met outside the chow hall with a white sedan and two Kawasaki F9 350cc motorcycles.

The Tech Sergeant delivering the vehicles approached with a clipboard and offered a pen to Harden.

"What's this?" Dave asked.

"You ordered three vehicles sir. We were ordered to bring them over to the dining hall. I need you to sign here please." He presented a clipboard with a form attached.

"We requested three cars." Harden objected.

"Sorry sir with the big launch tomorrow we have a boat load of dignitaries coming in. Plus the two FBI agents took the last car. This is all we have left until next Monday."

Harden suddenly heard the revving of motorcycles. He turned to see Doc and Mac speeding around the parking lot both pulling wheelies.

"How old are those bikes?" He challenged.

"Wouldn't know for sure sir. I suppose about ten years old. We used to use them for patrolling the rough areas where cars couldn't go, but they've been completely refurbished. Sign here please sir." He again offered the clipboard.

The skipper shook his head and reluctantly signed for the vehicles as Doc and Mac pulled up alongside him.

"Sir, I take back everything I said about you! Brilliant piece of strategy, bikes and cars. Your normal everyday officer would never have thought that strategically!" Mac congratulated.

"Beach, road or brush we can chase the bad guys anywhere!" Doc added before he looked over at Mac and the two simultaneously broke into their rendition of *No Where to Run To, Nowhere to Hide* by Martha Reeves and the Vandellas.

"Ricky, Danno, get in the damn car!" Harden ordered. "You two, Peter Fonda, Dennis Hopper meet us up at the Beach House. And try not to break a leg!" He said. "Or do." He added as he took the driver's seat. "Bunch of adolescents I got here." He bitched.

Harden reconvened the team in the beach-side bungalow about half a mile into the space station on the Eastern shore where they would be billeted for the next few days.

"Nice digs!" Danno declared as they entered the three bedroom, two bath, one story structure.

"Looks like a refurbished 1960's beach bungalow." Doc commented.

"'Dignitary', 'Bungalow', 'Dining Hall', vehicles delivered! Anybody else get the feeling we signed up with the wrong branch?" Mac asked to no one in particular.

"Okay, ground your gear and form up over here." Harden instructed. "Danno bring the radios."

"Roger that sir."

Only slightly distracted by the FBI agent's rebuff of help, Dave thought it prudent to immediately get to work on a proactive plan intended to be flexible yet ready for an unconventional attack from any angle.

"The bad news is we have no idea who these guys are, what they look like, or how many there are."

"Other than that, what's the downside sir?"

"All joking aside Mac, we have to assume there are more than one, it's not in their nature to launch a one-man, commando-styled attack. There's no potential here for a suicide bomber which means they only have two avenues of approach, sea or land either outside the perimeter or inside the perimeter to launch their attack. Given the overwhelming amount of security inside the station I'm betting they'll try something from outside the perimeter."

"Sir you think we're looking at shoulder launched weapons or drones maybe?" Ricky Matson asked.

"I'm not sure but I don't think they have drones at that technical level. Yet."

"So you're thinking some form of SMAW or something?" Doc pushed.

"There's no way to be sure just now but, the point is they're most likely to attack just before or just after lift-off. Meaning-"

"Meaning that we will have a very narrow window to locate these bastards!" Ricky pitched in.

"Exactly! Which is why we have to find them **before** the launch!" Harden emphasized. "Which gives us roughly nineteen to twenty hours."

Having little or no information regarding a description of Akbar, his men or anyone who might be working with him, Harden split them up into teams consisting of Doc and Mac as Team Alpha and Bravo Team formed by Danno and Ricky.

Haden then gave each man a radio, a call sign and with a map provided by the base Head of Security, assigned each team a sector to scout then patrol reporting back to him by 1700.

Putting his confidence in the air force units to maintain security inside the perimeter Harden focused on the exterior.

Alpha Team was assigned to scout the western landward sector while Bravo Team was assigned to scout the eastern seaward sector.

"Its 12:40 now, head out to your sectors for a familiarization patrol. Danno, Ricky take the car and patrol the Cape Road, Doc and Mac the Titan III Road on the west side is a bit rougher so take your bikes north to the end of the road then back south. Take note of what you can see. Same for you guys

Danno. Those are the only two roads this far north so pay particular attention to other routes you think they might use."

"Base security sir?" Doc questioned.

"If you run into the Air Police just flash your base I.D. Bigby gave orders not to question anyone with I.D. who used the secret password of the day."

"Which is?"

"Gulf Alpha Oscar!"

They all laughed.

"What about you Skipper?" Mac asked.

"I'll set us up a temporary base here. Call sign TFR Actual. Doc you're TFR Delta, Mac TFR Mike, Danno TFR Byrdo and Ricky TFR Mike-Mike. Questions, comments, snide remarks? No? Good now move out and draw fire assholes!"

"Now that's the L.T. I remember!" Danno remarked as he and Ricky climbed into the car.

*

Having been alerted by Agent Skidmore to the fact that a possible sabotage effort might take place, that afternoon Bigby ordered extra ground crew to be called out to Launch Complex 40B and they be instructed to scour the platform, the shuttle, the boosters and the EFT with a visual inspection.

By this time the Space Shuttle Discovery had been raised and attached to the gantry along with the two white booster rockets which would lift the load to and just past the Max Q point that is the point of maximum stress on the shuttle, along with the

External Fuel Tank while ascending into low earth orbit. At that point the two boosters would be jettisoned and fall back to earth.

With the final attachments completed and the extra ground crew well into their last minute head-to-toe inspection of the shuttle, the boosters and the EFT, Skidmore was mounted on a cherry picker overseeing the effort when he looked down and noticed a commotion had erupted on the south side of the Launch Complex just below the EFT.

He quickly manned the controls lowering the basket to the ground and scurried over to the small crowd which had gathered at the base of the gantry.

The topic of discussion when he arrived was a small three inch square, orange device which one of the workers had found under one of the rear struts of the External Fuel Tank.

Special Agent Skidmore was smiling broadly as he carefully removed the magnetized item then held the 3-inch square, orange device in his hand.

"GOD DAMN! We got the bastards!" He confidently declared to his second in charge.

"What do you suppose it is?" His junior agent asked.

"I don't know maybe something to disrupt the trajectory, a magnetic device or something." Skidmore speculated. "The rest of you back to it! The people we are dealing with are fanatical, not stupid. There might be a second device."

The ground crew dispersed and returned to their searches.

"Looks more like a miniature explosive device to me. Kind'a like a mini bomb." The junior agent commented.

"A mini bomb?! Did your mother drop you? What kind of an idiot would plant a three inch bomb on a 200 foot rocket? Besides where's the wires? The blasting cap? Hell a blasting cap alone is nearly three inches!" Skidmore chastised. "Here!"

"What do you want me to do with it?" The agent asked.

"We'll send it to Washington for analysis. Put it in my briefcase, it's in the backseat of the car. And be careful with it."

"So you **do** think it's a bomb?!" The agent quickly held it at arm's length.

"No! I mean my briefcase! It's brand new, an anniversary gift from my wife."

Skidmore and the workers were not the only ones taking note of events. From just over a kilometer away across the bay, outside the perimeter fence, a pair of binoculars was also observing the commotion.

Not sure exactly what went wrong the observer knew something was not right.

"GOD DAMN IT!" He cursed before crawling backwards from between the bushes, climbing into the stolen Honda motorcycle and heading south back towards the town.

**

U-Need-A-Rest Motel
Wednesday Night, 21:30

Crenshaw had made his decision. Knowing that Akbar and Abdul were at dinner at the cape's only Indian restaurant and would be gone for the better part of an hour, he decided to make his move.

Picking the lock on Akbar's door, he went to work quickly. Sliding the single bed to one side he moved several items which were stashed underneath including a brown leather, gym bag.

He peeled back the flimsy carpet then using a Leatherman he prided up the first floor board and then lifted the others out and set the two rocket launchers on the bed.

The MK-153's had several weak points. One was that the trigger was extremely vulnerable to cold, wet and dirt. Knowing this Crenshaw produced a Bobby pin, cut it in half and jammed a piece up behind each of the triggers and their trigger guards. As extra insurance he removed the two projectiles from their packing tubes, disassembled the warheads and removed the striking pins on each before replacing them in the shipping tubes.

He just as quickly replaced everything pulling back the carpet and sliding the bed in place. However, as he lifted the brown, leather gym bag to set it back under the bed where he found it he noted the weight. Despite being under a time constraint his curiosity won out.

Hefting the case onto the bed he unzipped and opened it. What greeted his eyes was a shock. Three different FBI wanted posters we're neatly rolled up and held with a rubber band.

Removing the rubber band and unfurling them revealed his picture, description and the offering of a reward of $50,000.

It became immediately apparent that Akbar, once the job was finished, intended to turn Crenshaw in. But there was also good news - remnants of the bulk of the $225,000 in 20s and 50s was also in the bag.

Thinking quickly, he scurried to the small linen closet in the bathroom, grabbed a pillowcase and emptied the cash and posters in to it. Sliding the two phone books next to the television off the chest of drawers he set them into the brown leather bag and replaced it under the bed exactly the way it was.

Crenshaw then went to his room, packed a small bag, walked out to the main road on 528 and flagged a passing taxi.

*** * ***

After returning to their rooms that evening neither Akbar nor Abdul bothered to seek out Crenshaw. They merely assumed he was sleeping off an early drunk and they too retired to their beds.

That night, tossing and turning in his bed, young Abdul's mind was slowly succumbing to what Crenshaw had said to him yesterday about not trusting Akbar.

It was just past two a.m., believing Crenshaw in his room sleeping off a mild drunk and Akbar in his room snoring away, Abdul also made a decision.

He quietly rose from his bed and carefully snuck through the interior door separating the two rooms and headed into the other room with Akbar snoring away.

Abdul had earlier seen him stash a gym-like, brown leather bag under the bed on several occasions. The same bag Akbar had refused to let leave his person the entire time since they had arrived in Florida. Abdul found it curious that he guarded the bag so closely.

Once in the room he found the bag easily enough, instead of under the bed it was in the bed with Akbar. His arm threaded through the handles with him cradling it close to him.

Abdul immediately aborted his mission and crept back and scurried back to his bed.

As he prepared to slip back into bed a thin wire was quickly slipped over his head and around his neck, there was a sharp yank and suddenly the young man couldn't take in a breath. His last breath.

Straining to see over his shoulder he saw a dark figure bent over him looking down watching, as the young man whose mother wanted him to build schools and bridges now writhed on his knees as he grasped at his neck quietly emitting gurgling noises while trying to beg for help. Blood began to seep from around the wire.

It was merely a matter of forty-five seconds or so before Arthur Mamoud LeMiel was a corpse.

Unbeknownst to himself Akbar was not alone on this mission. The 'Wahid Wulf' was being paid separately by the imams of Iran as a secret back-up. The Wolf was the same man who had been using Senator Omar as a cut out. Enduring her verbal abuses for the sake of the mission.

In keeping with their inability to trust anyone, particularly with their biggest most spectacular attack to date, the imams had commissioned a back-up. Only their additional contractor wasn't just a trouble shooter. He was credited with thirty-seven personal kills to date.

Now thirty-eight.

Wahid Wulf a.k.a. the Lone Wolf, was a man without a history. No one knew exactly where he came from originally, who his family were or, other than money, what his motivation was.

The Wolf seemed to materialize out of the shadows during the second year of the Lebanon conflict and appeared to have no real ideology, political or religious and had only one semi-reliable connection – the imams of Tehran.

However, even they were unable to contact him at will, they merely had to wait until he 'checked in' with them to be alerted about any contracts that may or may not be floating around out there.

Taking time to quickly wrap Abdul's neck in a hand towel to stem what little hemorrhage there was, the assassin retrieved one of the sheets from the linen closet, rolled the still warm body into it and propped the corpse sitting up in the hall closet. He then commenced his primary task – locate the MK-153's to complete his mission.

Perusing the room with a powerful compact flashlight he scanned the ceiling but could detect no anomalies that might indicate the plaster board had been disturbed recently.

Glancing down at his watch he begun to become concerned, time was ticking. He must be in position by half past five at least to avoid the daylight. His escape vehicle, a speed boat and driver moored on the eastern shore of the Banana River adjacent to the launch site, had orders to wait only fifteen minutes after the explosion then leave with or without his passenger so as not to risk being captured.

Finally realising the rocket launchers were not in Abdul's room he deduced they must be in Akbar's.

Thinking quickly he made his way around back of the motel where he found a collection of propane canisters. Carefully cutting a length if nearby garden hose and prying open the small toilet window to Akbar's room, he opened the valve and via the hose leaked some propane into the bathroom.

Quickly sprinting back around to the front, he produced a 9mm with silencer, knocked on the front door.

Akbar awoke quickly, kicked the bag under the bed, drew his pistol from beneath his pillow and stumbled to the door as he detected the faint odor of gas.

"Who is there?"

"It's housekeeping, please open we think there is a gas leak!" The Wolf announced feigning an Hispanic accent.

The Arab fell for it and opened the door where he was greeted with a 9mm muzzle to his face.

Closing the door behind him the Wolf slipped inside and motioned for Akbar to turn around as he relieved him of his Beretta.

"Who are you?" The Arab demanded.

"A guardian angel." He whispered before whacking Akbar hard across the back if the head with a police issue blackjack.

The Arab crumbled to the floor holding his head and moaning in pain. The Wolf wasted no time. From his pocket he removed a syringe and injected the Arab through his boxers with thirty cc's of chloral hydrate to keep him under for the time required.

He quickly set to work scanning the perimeter of the room where the wall and the floor met.

In less than a minute he spotted the disrupted line of dirt accumulated under the bed where the flimsy rug had been peeled back. He moved the bed exposed the floorboards and pried one up.

"Hello pretty!" He quietly mumbled as he spied the launchers. Minutes later he had the launchers and the detonator for the explosive device he believed to be still planted on the EFT, replaced the boards and slid the rug back in place. A minute later he had found the keys and had them all loaded into to the back of Akbar's blue rental van.

It would have been much simpler to merely kill Akbar however the Wolf had no such orders besides, he was loath to unnecessarily invoke the wrath of Hezbollah.

****

It was early dawn Thursday when Akbar, still lying on the floor rolled over and held his head. Memories slowly flooded into his brain regarding recent events. Glancing out the window he saw daylight encroaching and checked his watch. Twenty after five!

In a panic he quickly dressed, shoved his bed aside and pulled back the carpet. The color drained from his face when he pulled the first floorboard, then the second and finally the third.

The rockets and launchers were gone as was the detonator.

"ALCQIRAFU! Crenshaw!" He cursed.

Scrambling to his feet Akbar dashed to the door between the rooms and banged on it calling Abdul's name. He discovered the door unlocked and entered.

After calling around the room without response and seeing that Abdul's clothes and personal things were still in place Akbar finally went to the closet.

When he pulled open the door the color drained from his face. Abdul was unrecognizable. The pale blue, bloated features, wide opened eyes and swollen tongue were beyond grotesque.

Being accustomed to killing people from a distance with demolitions Akbar and people like him where not accustomed to seeing death up close, face-to-face.

A thousand thoughts flooded his mind. Was the CIA so far ahead of those pretending to fight this, yet another, holy war? Certainly the FBI could not have engineered such acts!

MI6? Or perhaps or those bastards Mossad?!

Regardless, Akbar realized that he was on his own and the mission was now impossible. His only alternative- escape!

Quickly gathering a few personal items along with the brown leather gym bag he stepped out to the main road and flagged down a taxi.

"How much to go to airport?" He asked the large black driver as they turned onto the parkway to cross the river.

"About nine, ten bucks." The driver called back over his shoulder.

Staring out the window as they crossed the river and hit the parkway Akbar's mind raced to digest events.

He mentally scrambled through excuses of how he would explain his colossal failure to all those who had invested so much in his 'mission'.

As the taxi pulled to up to the curb outside the terminal Akbar lifted the brown leather gym bag to the side and unzipped it to retrieve some cash.

Feeling the bile rise in his stomach he retched trying to keep it down.

He couldn't and vomited all over the phone books.

****

It was just past 05:30 when Lt. Commander Harden radioed out to his team members for a sitrep.

"TFR Teams TFR Actual here, report your 20's and status, over." Harden having set up an impromptu base of operations in the Beach House initiated a status check.

"Alpha Team here. We're currently about three klicks south of the Beach House. Nothing much here, save for the occasional AF patrol there's negative traffic on the river. Alpha over." Doc informed as he and Mac guided their bikes off to the side of the road.

"TFR Actual, Bravo here. We are approximately two and a half klicks north of the Beach House just at the LC 41 turn off road. No activity here." Ricky reported from inside their car. We see a few small pleasure craft just outside the surf zone. It appears they have dropped anchor for the night not much else. Bravo over."

"TFR Actual, Alpha Team here. Any word from base security?"

"Negative Alpha, nothing."

"Actual, we're rolling back north and are now observing about half a dozen civilians setting up small tents, lawn chairs and a couple of barbecues across the river. Apparently they don't know its breakfast time."

"Barbeque for breakfast sounds pretty good to me!" Harden transmitted back."

"Apparently they bought early tickets to the front row seats for this morning's big show, over." Doc reported as he and Mac pulled back out onto the dirt road.

"Bravo, the local CG will screen the small boat traffic and keep them outside the red zone, Just keep your eye on any suspicious activity especially along the river banks as we get closer to launch time, over."

"Bravo copies Actual. Out," Ricky signed off.

"TFR Actual here, Alpha Team did you copy my last? Over."

"Roger Actual. Copied all. Over."

"Both teams be aware, NASA has Morning Nautical Twilight at 06:37 with sunrise listed at 07:01. So we can count on daylight for at least an hour and a half before launch. How copy?"

"Roger sir, ninety minutes of daylight, copy."

"TFR Actual, Alpha Team here, interrogative. Sir, what time did security tell you they normally close these two service roads prior to launch?"

"One hour prior but I convinced them to allow us to patrol until fifteen minutes prior, I promised them we'd radio them on their common freq as we fall back to the Beach House by 0805, over."

"Okay so Beach House in about fifteen? Over" McKeowen confirmed.

"Affirmative Alpha. Bravo you copy?" Harden asked.

"Bravo copies Actual. Have the steak and eggs ready sir. See you then. Bravo out."

A short time earlier as Doc and Mac were heading south on their run they passed a blue van driving north. The windows were tinted and it was still dark so they only got a glimpse of the guy driving but the platinum blond in the passenger seat next to him looked pretty good to both of them.

****

Meanwhile oblivious to the espionage drama taking place outside at ground level a mile away, the five person shuttle crew were in their suits and prepared for transport out to their ship.

After being suited up the astronauts were led out of their locker room in the prep building and escorted to the shuttle bus waiting outside. The small bus took the crew to the base of the gantry on the Launch Complex.

Once there the crew took the elevator to Level 195 adjacent to Discovery's cockpit.

The crew, in good spirits as usual, prompted Fredrick Hauck, the space flight commander, to joke in the elevator on the way up.

"Shoot! We have to go back!" Which alarmed everyone.

"What for?" Dave Walker the mission's pilot asked.

"I forgot the ignition keys!" Hauck joked.

Reaching Level 195 they were turned over to the Closeout Crew a specially trained team whose responsibility was to double check all of the astronauts' equipment, get them strapped into the shuttle, review their emergency gear and seal the cockpit.

Once the Close Out crew exited the platform and contacted Mission Control and cleared the pad count down would commence.

******

Meanwhile, the Wolf after driving since 0300 that morning taking the long way around to the north in order to access the location he wanted while still dark, had made his way to just north of the Launch Complex and set up at about the eleven o'clock position.

With ample foliage between the north-south running Titan III hard top road and Launch Complex 40B pad there was ample foliage to camouflage the van, remove what he needed and set up a firing position unseen about 1,000 meters away from the shuttle array.

He calculated that the Palmetto plants although providing no cover afforded good concealment and still put him inside the 1800 meter firing range limit of the MK-153's. He arrived and was settled in long before the countdown was to begin.

It was 08:05 when the loudspeakers around the base again blared to life.

Attention, attention, all personnel on or in the vicinity of Launch Complex 40B this is your final warning to clear the area I say again clear the area. Countdown will commence in 15 minutes. Countdown will commence in 15 minutes.

Not knowing for sure what the earlier hub bub on the pad was about and following the start of the countdown the Wolf manned and set the remote device to trigger the mini-explosive he still believed was planted on the EFT.

Attention, attention, all personnel on or in the vicinity of Launch Complex 40B, countdown will commence in five minutes. Countdown will commence in five minutes.

Over in the Beach House the TFR teams were glued to the in-house monitor.

As the engines began to spit their ferocious flames and the over-sized countdown clock reached the count of twenty seconds, The Wolf smiled as he pointed then pressed the red button on the radio detonator and ducted down to shield himself from the explosion.

Nothing happened.

He again pressed the red detonate button and ducked down. Again nothing happened. He pressed it repeatedly several more times without results. When the EFT didn't explode he cursed and flung the detonator across the field into the water.

The explosion that occurred inside special agent Skidmore's briefcase caused him and his Number Two sitting in the front seat of their car back down by the Headquarters building to jump and draw their service pistols frantically scanning around.

After they realized no one was shooting at them, they both turned and looked into the back seat at what was left of Skidmore's tattered briefcase.

"Shit! My wife's gonna kill me!" Dwayne mumbled.

****

"ALCQIRAFU! Akbar!" Back in the bushes the Wolf again cursed as the launch pad's P.A. system continued to blare.

Ten, nine, eight, seven, six . . .

He hurriedly grabbed one of the MK-153's and took aim, braced himself and squeezed the trigger. He heard a low 'click' then nothing.

"Fucking made in fucking China piece of shit!" The Wolf cursed as he slammed the launcher to the ground.

Closely monitoring the station's loudspeakers as the countdown progressed, he prepared and loaded the other launcher.

As the engines began to spit their ferocious flames and the countdown reached,

Three, two, one . . .

Everyone watched the gargantuan rocket slowly rose and lifted to leave the LC pad on its way to space.

The Lone Wolf came face-to-face with the reality of his failure.

However his melancholy musings were shocked back to reality as the loudspeakers again came to life.

When Two Tribes Go To War

All stations all units, all stations all units be advised we have a report of a potentially hostile, unauthorized suspicious vehicle on the station. Florida State PD has reported a missing vehicle. Ford Econo-line, late model, dark blue in color. No description of driver available at this time. However if cited detain and report to headquarters.

Realizing his mission was terminated the Wolf quickly sprang from his nest and sloshed across the soggy ground making his way back to the van to drive back north the same way he had snuck in.

Just as he was about to climb into the van he spotted a pair of motor cycles bearing down on him from the north.

As he had previously arranged, Harden had set the extra hand radio to the base security freq allowing him to monitor base communications and dispatching both his teams after Doc and Mac informed him that they had passed a blue Ford van earlier on the Titan Road.

Without hesitation The Wolf quickly jumped in started the engine and turned the vehicle back south.

When Doc and Mac spotted the van turning around they shifted into high gear and initiated a pursuit.

"TFR Actual, we've located the blue van. Heading south on the Titan III two klicks south of The Beach House."

"Roger Doc. I'll notify the AF Police to alert the civilian cops." Harden returned.

"Make sure you tell them the guys on the motorcycles are good guys!" Mac followed on.

Racing south the van passed the storage facility and sped into the ITL warehouse area and was fast approaching the *Morrel Operations Center* where, in response to Harden's call, there were two AF Police cars parked across the road as a blockade.

The AFP's drew their weapons and took cover behind the cars.

When it crested the rise the van's speed combined with the fact that it maintained a path in the middle of the road clearly indicated he had no intention of stopping.

The four Air Police now stationed around the cars were only able to fire off a couple of rounds each before they themselves became targets.

The compact, light patrol cars were no match for the heavy late model van which literally blasted through the blockade however, not without sustaining some damage to the rack and pinion steering.

As the van with the two motorcycles in tow continued south down the 401 to the major civilian Canaveral Port still partially crowded with rocket watchers clogging the road, the van was able to zoom past the undulating gaggle of cars before the foot traffic spilled over into the street.

Doc and Mac however got caught in the middle of the controlled melee of the crowd as men, moms and kids in Mickey Mouse ears brandishing balloons shuffled in front, around and between Doc and Mac as they slowly guided their bikes through the crowd.

When Two Tribes Go To War

As the seemingly endless mob disembarking the Disney Cruise liner filled the quay-side and streamed across the road and the distance between pursuers and pursuee widened, Mac made a decision.

He nodded at Doc and guided his Kawasaki up onto the sidewalk with Doc following suite. Cutting through the expansive parking lot they rode for about another one hundred meters before Mac steered to the right through the drainage ditch and hit the throttle. He cleared the three foot high, chain link fence landing well past the crowd. Doc was right behind him. They sighted the van about a quarter mile ahead.

Now fifteen minutes into the chase the road suddenly curved 90 degrees to the left into the *West Turning Basin* area as the 401 led into State Route A1A heading east towards the *Exploration Tower*.

Unfortunately for the panicked terrorist due to the play in the van's damaged steering he didn't quite make the turn and the damp road caused the van to slide sideways then topple left onto its side and skid across the road coming to rest up against a telephone pole.

By the time several civilians pulled over and ran to the site of the wreck the Wolf had made his way out of the passenger side window and was dodging traffic heading across the street for the busy restaurant, *Rusty's Oyster House*, on the boardwalk across the road.

As he approached, out of breath he caught sight of the valet who had just pulled a 1967, red Chevrolet

Impala around from the back to a waiting family of four.

Without hesitation, as the car owner was tipping the young valet, the terrorist hopped in through the open door and left the poor driver in the Hawaiian shirt and shorts hopelessly chasing after him hurling abuse.

Doc cut across the corner and over the sidewalk while Mac nearly laid his bike down as he too skidded across the intersection but quickly recovered. Having to cut into a parking lot as the red Chevy turned a 180 and headed west to cross the Banana River, Doc and Mac had fallen four or five hundred meters behind but quickly closed the distance.

They chased the Chevy around to the A1A turn off to cross the mile long *Martin Anderson Beachline Expressway*, which they were quickly approaching.

"Hey Mac, those old Chevys got front wheel drive?" Doc yelled over as they gained on him before the bridge.

"No, rear wheel. Why?"

"Fall back before that rise in the bridge up ahead and slow the traffic."

Mac complied and rode the middle of the road, slowed and signaled the few cars to his rear to stay behind him.

One tough guy cowboy in a pick-up truck flipped Mac off and started to drive around him.

Being sure that there were no civilians in the line of fire Doc pulled up to within four or five meters of the car and loosed three rounds at the front right tire.

One round found its mark and the tire exploded throwing the car into an uncontrolled 'S' pattern while the Wolf wrestled to regain control.

Spotting the gun the tough guy in the pickup couldn't drop back fast enough as he screeched on the brakes and fish-tailed off to the left hand shoulder.

As the perfectly restored, red Chevy swerved out of control they watched wide-eyed as the car pin-balled off the concrete crash barriers on either side of the two lane blacktop, jumped the curb then crashed over the three foot high barrier and guard rail on the right plummeting the fifteen foot to the river below splashing and sticking nearly straight up dart-like into the mud.

Doc was nearly right on top of him but pulled off onto the narrow shoulder just in time, laid his bike down and rolled forward as he scrambled to get to his feet and peer over the low railing.

Mac pulled up beside Doc as traffic on the bridge slowed and rubber-neckers began to accumulate.

"That's gonna leave a mark." Doc remarked as Mac stepped up beside him.

"Too bad huh?!" MacDonald remarked.

"No, he's alive. I can see him moving around inside."

"No I mean about the car! Beautiful ride ruined!" MacDonald added.

Unaware of the shallow depth they both watched over the railing fascinated by the terrorist's reaction as he painfully kicked out what was left of the rear windshield then climbed out onto the trunk of the vehicle then jumped, splashing into the chest-deep, muddy water while he fought to climb out of the marsh.

Doc and Mac both drew their weapons and put a bead on the Wolf but it was blatantly obvious he had lost his weapon in the crash, had a gash across his forehead and was in no condition to continue resistance.

By now several bystanders had gathered at the guardrail as well and were looking on either side of Doc and Mac.

Several of the Good Samaritan bystanders rushed to their vehicles and raced the 500m to the west end of the bridge to attempt to render assistance. They were too late. The Lone Wolf was not alone.

Two large congregations of alligators, partially submerged just offshore on either bank of the river were alerted by the crash and interpreted the tumultuous splashing as a dinner bell.

Trapped helplessly in the mud the man the imams of Tehran paid to murder five American astronauts, now struggled and splashed to free himself and wade through the thick muck to safety ashore.

Somewhere in the crowd a woman screamed from above they all watched on in horror, disgust and fascination as the short but bloody and brutal feeding frenzy ensued accompanied by a few blood-curdling shrieks as several death rolls unceremoniously dismembered the former terrorist in a matter of minutes and sent him to claim his seventy-two virgins.

"Well, scratch one terrorist!" MacDonald sighed.

"Hey Mac, you suppose he only gets 36 virgins because he fucked up his mission?" Doc commented as they all stared down at the slowly widening red-tinged water and floating shards of clothing.

"Not sure Doc. I count one arm, both legs and a torso. So maybe he gets all seventy-two but eighteen at a time!"

"Makes sense!"

"Garden variety gators one, terrorists zero!" Mac added.

"They ain't no regular gators!" The middle-aged, overweight guy in the Harley Davidson T-shirt and grey cargo shorts next to him commented.

"What are they some special Florida species?" Doc asked.

"Yes sir. We call them babies American gators!" The big man responded,

****

CHAPTER TWENTY-THREE

Dirty Nellie's Irish Pub
Mass Avenue, D.C.
November 10th, 1984

By a quarter past seven that evening the full moon was threatening to dip below the Potomac as it hung in the matte black sky to peer down on the neat little rows of white and pale amber colored street lights which seemed to radiate from the city center.

The Italians are known for their multiple pasta dishes, the French are known for their wines. The Chinese for their savory dishes and the Russians for their vodka which they can apparently distill from any garden vegetable, leaves or even tree bark. But if it's a night out of drinking and rowdy music you want . . .

Dirty Nellie's was the classic American fantasy of what an Irish pub should look like. The fact that no one has ever seen a pub in Ireland that actually looks like a *Bennigan's* an *O'Reilly's* or a *Dirty Nellie's* is a mere technicality.

Nellie's contained all the faux Irish paraphernalia including beat-up old instruments in the front window, reproductions of Dublin street signs and framed pictures of Maureen O'Hara in *The Quiet Man* with John Wayne and Victor McLaglen duking it out.

The pub was packed to capacity but having arrived early enough Harden, Doc Natasha and Mac were able to stake out a claim to one of only two snugs in the place and so were afforded a modicum of peace allowing conversation.

Harden and MacDonald were entangled in a discussion regarding the first Women's Marathon out in L.A. last month and expressed they were both impressed with the runner from the U.S. Joan Benoit the world record holder. Harden added that Greta Weiss of Norway, the silver medalist and winner of seven marathons as well as the 1983 world champion was not to be ignored either.

Both additionally agreed that it was too bad the Russians boycotted the games in retaliation to the U.S doing the same thing to the 1980 games.

"Gotta give it to the Ruskies! They don't be playin' n' shit!" Mac added in his best 'hood' dialect.

"Imagine the damage we could do if we joined forces?!" A half lit Harden added.

"We'd own the world!" Mac slid across the bench over to Natasha.

"Hey Natasha, how's tricks?"

"Hello Petty Officer MacDonald."

"You okay? You look a little down."

"No, not really. Actually I am not down, I am completely up."

"What's ya doin'? Ya seem pretty intense."

"Actually, I am missing my family a little,"

"Don't let it get ya down!" He hugged her. "Goes with the territory! Besides now you have a new family, doesn't she guys?!"

Doc and Harden raised their glasses to her as they finished off their drinks.

"Which territory do you speak of Petty Officer?" She asked.

"Never mind. Say Natasha did I ever tell you about all the beautiful Jewish girls where I used to go to school out in Long Island?"

Doc and Dave sat back and watched Mac launch into his performance.

"Long Island? Is in New York yes?" Natasha confirmed.

"Yes, New York. Long Island is an upper class area so there's lots'a Jews out there. I made lots'a friends when I lived there, see?"

"No."

"No as in you don't understand?"

"No. No as in I have never seen Long Island."

"Oh."

"But I am certain it is beautiful!" She reassured not wanting to dampen his story.

"It is. So back there we have all these jokes called 'JAP' jokes. Because –"

"Because there are also many girls from Japan living there!"

"Ah . . . no. Because we have many rich Jewish American Princesses living there. J-A-P, Jewish American Princesses. Get it?"

"But . . . Israel is an internationally, trade-based, free enterprise democracy. There is no royalty in this country."

"Natasha! Ya gotta work with me here sweetheart!" He desperately coaxed.

"And now it gets interesting!" Doc quietly commented to Dave.

"Sorry Petty Officer MacDonald. Please continue." She apologized.

"Thank you. J.A.P.'s are girls who have never had to work for anything in their lives. Everything they have has been handed to them by their rich parents. They're spoiled."

"AHHH! These we have in Russia also. Mostly in Petersburg! But sometimes Moscow as well yes, yes. I know these womans."

"Okay, great! So . . . how can you tell when a J.A.P. has an orgasm?"

"I don't know, I have never known one such woman."

"She drops the nail file!" Mac delivered laughingly. Natasha stared. "Get it? Nail file!" He coaxed.

"Why will she be having nail file in the bed?" The awkward silence tipped her off. "OHH! I understand it is joke! Okay, okay." She enthusiastically prepared and adjusted in her seat before she reciprocated.

"Okay . . . One very frightened man goes to Lubyanka and reports, 'My talking parrot has disappeared'." She related in a comically deep voice. "The desk sergeant tell him, 'That's not the kind of case we handle. Go to Moscow police. 'Of course I know that I must go to Moscow police!' he say. 'I only want to tell you I officially disagree with my parrot!'"

Doc and Harden both cracked up laughing.

"You see Mac? That's how you tell a joke!" Doc badgered. Mac declined response.

"What is the difference between Constitutions of US and that of the USSR?" Natasha pushed.

"Both of them guarantee freedom of speech." Dave bit.

"True, but Constitution of U.S. also guarantees freedom after the speech." Doc quipped.

"Ahhhh! But Russia also guarantees such freedom!" Natasha argued. "In USA, you can stand in front of White House in Washington and yell, 'Down with Ronald Reagan!' and you will not be punished. Equally, you can also stand in front of Kremlin in Moscow and yell, 'Down with Ronald Reagan!' and you will not be punished!"

Doc, deciding to join the fun nudged the Commander as he addressed Natasha.

"Natasha, is it true that the in the Soviet Union there is no freedom of the press?" Doc asked.

"Not sure. My brother is investigative journalist. He went to Kremlin five years ago to investigate. "

"What did he find?"

"Don't know. He has not come back yet." She said straight-faced.

"You takin' notes Mac?" Harden teased.

"So what's everybody doing for Thanksgiving?" Mac asked seeking refuge from his failed comedy attack.

"I'll be heading back to Iowa to celebrate with the family." Harden answered. "What about you Natasha? What are your plans for the holiday?" Harden asked. Before she could answer Doc jumped in.

"Natasha's coming home with me to New York so we can get away from all this D.C. elitism and she can see what a real Yankee Thanksgiving is all about."

"I am told by some people that real America starts at Mississippi and ends at Rocky Mountains. Is this factual?"

Her comment set off a flurry of debate through two more rounds until the discussion inevitably came around to Akbar's clever escape.

Everyone had a theory as to where exactly TFR and or the intel services dropped the ball on capturing Akbar but there evolved an unspoken consensus that Harden would have the most accurate opinion on the question.

"What'a you think sir?" Doc pushed.

"What do I think Doc?" He looked down and twirled his drink as he considered his answer. As if on cue the juke box went silent awaiting its next feed.

"When I was about four or five I was running and fell. Skinned both palms of my hands. I cried but my grandmother told me, 'you'll be okay, things have a way of working out.' Then in high school I wanted to run track but couldn't make the team. Didn't have the wind for distances and not enough speed for sprints. Nana baked me some cookies and told me, 'don't worry, things have a way of working out'. She was right I found I could do pretty good at middle distances. Then when I signed on in the Navy I was elated to be assigned here. But then this toilet scum gave us the slip. So now all I can tell myself is-"

"Don't tell us! Things have a way of working out!" Mac interceded.

Harden threw back the last of his drink and made eye contact around the table.

"Hell no! I'm gonna use every God-damned resource we have including a Lamont Cranston secret decoder ring to hunt that son-of-a-bitch until I find that bastard, bottom feeder and he gets what he deserves!" He stood grabbed his pint glass and calmly asked: "Anyone else want a drink?" He made his way up to the bar.

There was momentary silence until Doc spoke.

"I think the price of Iranian oil just went up by $200 a barrel!" Doc commented.

"Why?" Natasha asked.

"Because the ragheads in Tehran are gonna have to cough up enough cash to pay all of Hezbollah, the PLO and most of ISIS to hide old Akbar the Bomber from that Iowa farm boy!" Mac explained.

✱

North West District
Washington DC
January 17th, 1985, 15:10

That Thursday it was windy and cold with the light whisp of snow which had fallen the night before having melted almost completely.

The blond-haired forty-something detective in the heavy overcoat smiled as he quickly flashed his badge and I.D. to the pudgy doorman standing watch at 431 Watson Street Towers in the upscale district of the city.

"Evening sir. My name's Detective Sergeant Dawson."

"Evening Detective! Chilly one tonight, ain't she?" He jovially replied.

"You bet." He agreed as he tugged at his heavy wool coat. "There was a robbery down the block about a week back. I'm here to question a witness lives up on seven."

"No problem officer. You want I should ring up, let 'em know you're coming up?"

"Not necessary I just talked to her on the phone not ten minutes ago. She knows I'm coming by. But thanks."

"Sure thing officer." He held the door open as he nodded him through then watched as the cop approached the elevators. "Take the one on the left, the other one takes forever."

"Thanks!"

Out of boredom the door man stood and watched the arrow of the ornate dial on the wall above the lift as it slowly climbed to '7' and stopped.

Once upstairs out of the elevator the detective headed to the fire stairs donning rubber gloves as he

428

descended back down to the fifth floor and sought apartment 513.

Within half a minute he had picked the lock, slipped in and carefully did a visual search of the premises. Finding the place empty as he knew he would at this hour, he set to work in the back bathroom.

From beneath his heavy overcoat he produced a curious collection of items. First he assembled and set up a Bunsen burner and screwed together a small ring stand over it before setting a small retort flask on the ring stand.

Next he attached a tubed, rubber cork running to the bent glass tube to a shallow Pyrex dish. And set aside a small can of butane he'd bought from a camping store.

When he was finished he had produced a rudimentary distillation apparatus. Filling a 300cc Earl-Meyer flask with a yellowish liquid he poured from a plastic Coke bottle.

As a finishing touch he set a small crack pipe with residual crack in it, some used matches, a pack of single edged razor blades, one open, and several pairs of disposable rubber gloves and paraphernalia along with a quarter pound of sodium bicarbonate, six ounces of phencyclidine and just under half a kilo of uncut cocaine.

As a finishing touch he left a small pair of used surgical gloves in the waste basket and about 25 grams of finished crack on the counter. The whole operation was completed and he was back up on the seventh floor ringing for the elevator in under fifteen minutes.

"You get what you came for officer?" The friendly doorman asked as the cop stepped off the elevator and whizzed by him on the way out.

"Nah, she wasn't home. But I left her a message." He said in passing.

"Have a good evening!" The doorman said.

"You too!"

Twenty minutes later, from a public phone a few blocks away, as an anonymous, 'concerned' neighbor, he then called the D.C. Capitol Police.

Senator Omar received an unwelcome surprise that afternoon when leaving the capitol building following a session. She was taken into custody, booked and eventually brought to trial where she received six months' probation.

Jack Crenshaw was never heard from again.

Crenshaw's motivation? The oldest of all motives – revenge.

Years back Omar was strongly suspected of substantial campaign finance misappropriation. Crenshaw, originally from Minneapolis, was a cop after leaving the Army. After making detective he and his partner were getting close to nailing Omar and had uncovered evidence of her guilt when they were ambushed one night by a gaggle of thugs.

His partner was killed and Crenshaw wounded. Two of the thugs, one dead the other captured, were found through police files to be active members in the radical racist group the BLA or Black Liberation

Army a major supporter, donator and sometimes body guards of Omar and her cronies. Crenshaw swore revenge.

He finally got it.

Omar was eventually censored then impeached and forced to step down from her seat in the House.

Eventually her political donations dried up and she was reduced to teaching Marxist theory at a suburban community college.

In a predominantly conservative, white neighborhood.

*

3 months later . . .

CHAPTER TWENTY-FOUR

Residential Area
District 22 Tehran, Iran
April 1st, 1985

The streets of Tehran that Sunday increasingly swelled with traffic heading out of the central district as the population were preparing to wind down from the work day's activities.

Shops and traders were leisurely taking in their wares at the various small bazars along Haraz Street.

Women adjusted their head scarves least they show too much hair and be issued a summons by the Morality Wardens randomly patrolling the streets.

After leaving his neighborhood traditional tea house that afternoon Akbar Aminpur stopped by the neighborhood produce market and selected a few tomatoes for his dinner.

Biting into one once outside the market he bent forward to avoid the juice which dripped from his chin to prevent staining his shalvar.

He was two blocks from his friend's apartment on Hirmand Street where he had been keeping a low profile while he planned his next attack.

On a small side street just north of the tower the dark grey 1979 Citroen with the 'For Sale' sign in the back window, save the occasional glancing notice, attracted little attention.

He turned the corner onto Hirmand and noticed the neglected Citroen and started past it.

Like the flash from a giant instamatic camera a massive burst of light momentarily filled the immediate area followed by a deafening roar which blew out shop windows, sent glass fragments flying in all directions, knocked over several pedestrians fifty yards away and tossed the grey Citroen twenty feet into the air before the charred chassis slammed back down onto the glazed over street.

Minor shrapnel wounds to the extremities were sustained by three passers-by but the only discernable casualty was what was left of Mr. Akbar Aminpur's fragments pasted to the wall of the corner chemist's shop.

Two blocks away, just off Haraz Street, replacing the binoculars into the glove box the man in the Iowa Hawkeye's baseball cap sitting in the black coupe, slowly backed up into the side street and quietly drove off.

"Says in the Bible, 'Those that live by the sword . . .'" Lt. Commander Dave Harden said to himself as he headed off towards the motorway. "Asshole!"

THE END